TO
KILL A
KINGDOM

Books by Alexandra Christo

To Kill a Kingdom
Princess of Souls

Into the Crooked Place
City of Spells

Coming in October 2023
The Night Hunt

TO KILL A KINGDOM

ALEXANDRA CHRISTO

HOT
KEY
BOOKS

First published in Great Britain in 2018 by
HOT KEY BOOKS
4th Floor, Victoria House
Bloomsbury Square
London WC1B 4DA
Owned by Bonnier Books
Sveavägen 56, Stockholm, Sweden
bonnierbooks.co.uk/HotKeyBooks

A CIP catalogue record for this book is available from the British Library.

ISBN: 978-1-4714-0739-0
Also available as an ebook and in audio

18

Designed by Perfect Bound Ltd
Printed and bound in Great Britain by Clays Ltd, Elcograf S.p.A.

Hot Key Books is an imprint of Bonnier Books UK
bonnierbooks.co.uk

For those I love, who never got the chance to see this happen

I

Lira

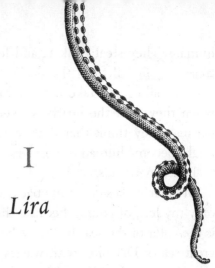

I HAVE A HEART for every year I've been alive.

There are seventeen hidden in the sand of my bedroom. Every so often, I claw through the shingle, just to check they're still there. Buried deep and bloody. I count each of them, so I can be sure none were stolen in the night. It's not such an odd fear to have. Hearts are power, and if there's one thing my kind craves more than the ocean, it's power.

I've heard things: tales of lost hearts and harpooned women stapled to the ocean bed as punishment for their treachery. Left to suffer until their blood becomes salt and they dissolve to sea foam. These are the women who take the human bounty of their kin. Mermaids more fish than flesh, with an upper body to match the decadent scales of their fins.

Unlike sirens, mermaids have stretched blue husks and limbs in place of hair, with a jawlessness that lets their mouths stretch to the size of small boats and swallow sharks whole. Their deep-blue flesh is dotted with fins that spread up their arms and spines. Fish and human both, with the beauty of neither.

They have the capacity to be deadly, like all monsters, but where sirens seduce and kill, mermaids remain fascinated by humans. They steal trinkets and follow ships in hopes that treasure will fall from the decks. Sometimes they save the lives of sailors and take nothing but charms in return. And when they steal the hearts we keep, it isn't for power. It's because they think that if they eat enough of them, they might become human themselves.

I hate mermaids.

My hair snakes down my back, as red as my left eye – and only my left, of course, because the right eye of every siren is the color of the sea they were born into. For me, that's the great sea of Diávolos, with waters of apple and sapphire. A selection of each so it manages to be neither. In that ocean lies the sea kingdom of Keto.

It's a well-known fact that sirens are beautiful, but the bloodline of Keto is royal and with that comes its own beauty. A magnificence forged in salt water and regality. We have eyelashes born from iceberg shavings and lips painted with the blood of sailors. It's a wonder we even need our song to steal hearts.

"Which will you take, cousin?" Kahlia asks in *Psáriin*.

She sits beside me on the rock and stares at the ship in the distance. Her scales are deep auburn and her blond hair barely reaches her breasts, which are covered by a braid of orange seaweed.

"You're ridiculous," I tell her. "You know which."

The ship ploughs idly along the calm waters of Adékaros, one of the many human kingdoms I've vowed to rid of a prince. It's smaller than most and made from scarlet wood that represents the colors of their country.

Humans enjoy flaunting their treasures for the world, but it only makes them targets for creatures like Kahlia and me, who can easily spot a royal ship. After all, it's the only one in the fleet with the painted wood and tiger flag. The only vessel on which the Adékarosin prince ever sails.

Easy prey for those in the mood to hunt.

The sun weighs on my back. Its heat presses against my neck and causes my hair to stick to my wet skin. I ache for the ice of the sea, so sharp with cold that it feels like glorious knives in the slits between my bones.

"It's a shame," says Kahlia. "When I was spying on him, it was like looking at an angel. He has such a pretty face."

"His heart will be prettier."

Kahlia breaks into a wild smile. "It's been an age since your last kill, Lira," she teases. "Are you sure you're not out of practice?"

"A year is hardly an age."

"It depends who's counting."

I sigh. "Then tell me who that is so I can kill them and be done with this conversation."

Kahlia's grin is ungodly. The kind reserved for moments when I am at my most dreadful, because that's the trait sirens are supposed to value most. Our awfulness is treasured. Friendship and kinship taught to be as foreign as land. Loyalty reserved only for the Sea Queen.

"You are a little heartless today, aren't you?"

"Never," I say. "There are seventeen under my bed."

Kahlia shakes the water from her hair. "So many princes you've tasted."

She says it as though it's something to be proud of, but that's because Kahlia is young and has taken only two hearts of her own. None of them royalty. That's my specialty, my territory. Some of Kahlia's reverence is for that. The wonder of whether the lips of a prince taste different from those of any other human. I can't say, for princes are all I've ever tasted.

Ever since our goddess, Keto, was killed by the humans, it's become custom to steal a heart each year, in the month of our birth. It's a celebration of the life Keto gave to us and a tribute of revenge for the life the humans took from her. When I was too young to hunt, my mother did it for me, as is tradition. And she always gave me princes. Some as young as I was. Others old and furrowed, or middle children who never had a chance at ruling. The king of Armonía, for instance, once had six sons, and for my first few birthdays, my mother brought me one each year.

When I was eventually old enough to venture out on my own, it hadn't occurred to me to forgo royalty and target sailors like the rest of my kind did, or even hunt the princes who would one day assume their thrones. I'm nothing if not a loyal follower of my mother's traditions.

"Did you bring your shell?" I ask.

Kahlia scoops her hair out of the way to show the orange seashell looped around her neck. A similar one just a few shades bloodier dangles from my own throat. It doesn't look like much, but it's the easiest way for us to communicate. If we hold them to our ears, we can hear the sound of the ocean and the song of the Keto underwater palace we call home. For Kahlia, it can act as a map to the sea of Diávolos if we're separated. We're a long way from our kingdom, and it took nearly a week to swim here. Since Kahlia is fourteen, she tends to stay close to the palace, but I was the one to decide that should change, and as the princess, my whims are as good as law.

"We won't get separated," Kahlia says.

Normally, I wouldn't mind if one of my cousins were stranded in a foreign ocean. As a whole, they're a tedious and predictable bunch, with little ambition or imagination.

Ever since my aunt died, they've become nothing more than adoring lackeys for my mother. Which is ridiculous, because the Sea Queen is not there to be adored. She's there to be feared.

"Remember to pick just one," I instruct. "Don't lose your focus."

Kahlia nods. "Which one?" she asks. "Or will it sing to me when I'm there?"

"We'll be the only ones singing," I say. "It'll enchant them all, but if you lay your focus on one, they'll fall in love with you so resolutely that even as they drown, they'll scream of nothing but your beauty."

"Normally the enchantment is broken when they start to die," Kahlia says.

"Because you focus on them all, and so, deep down, they know that none of them are your heart's desire. The trick is to want them as much as they want you."

"But they're disgusting," says Kahlia, though it doesn't sound like she believes it so much as she wants me to think that she does. "How can we be expected to desire them?"

"Because you're not just dealing with sailors now. You're dealing with royalty, and with royalty comes power. Power is *always* desirable."

"Royalty?" Kahlia gapes. "I thought . . ."

She trails off. What she thought was that princes were mine and I didn't share. That's not untrue, but where there are princes, there are kings and queens, and I've never had much use for either of those. Rulers are easily deposed. It's the princes who hold the allure. In their youth. In the allegiance of their people. In the promise of the leader they could one day become. They are the next generation of rulers, and by killing them, I kill the future. Just as my mother taught me.

I take Kahlia's hand. "You can have the queen. I've no interest in the past."

Kahlia's eyes are alight. The right holds the same sapphire of the Diávolos Sea I know well, but the left, a creamy yellow that barely stands out from the white, sparkles with a rare glee. If she steals a royal heart for her fifteenth, it'll be sure to earn her clemency from my mother's perpetual rage.

"And you'll take the prince," says Kahlia. "The one with the pretty face."

"His face makes no difference." I drop her hand. "It's his heart I'm after."

"So many hearts." Her voice is angelic. "You'll soon run out of room to bury them all."

I lick my lips. "Maybe," I say. "But a princess must have her prince."

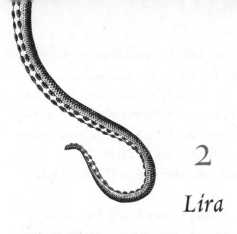

2

Lira

THE SHIP FEELS ROUGH under the spines of my fingers. The
wood is splintered, paint cracking and peeling over the body.
It cuts the water in a way that is too jagged. Like a blunt
knife, pressing and tearing until it slices through. There is rot
in places and the stench makes my nose wrinkle.

It is a poor prince's ship.

Not all royals are alike. Some are furnished in fine clothes,
unbearably heavy jewels so large that they drown twice as
fast. Others are sparsely dressed, with only one or two rings
and bronze crowns painted gold. Not that it matters to me. A
prince is a prince, after all.

Kahlia keeps to my side, and we swim with the ship while
it tears through the sea. It's a steady speed and one we easily
match. This is the agonizing wait, as humans become prey.
Some time passes before the prince finally steps onto the deck
and casts his eye at the ocean. He can't see us. We're far too
close and swim far too fast. Through the ship's wake, Kahlia
looks to me and her eyes beg the question. With a smile as
good as any nod, I return my cousin's stare.

We emerge from the froth and part our lips.

We sing in perfect unison in the language of Midas, the

most common human tongue and one each siren knows well. Not that the words matter. It's the music that seduces them. Our voices echo into the sky and roll back through the wind. We sing as though there is an entire chorus of us, and as the haunting melody ricochets and climbs, it swirls into the hearts of the crew until finally the ship slows to a stop.

"Do you hear it, Mother?" asks the prince. His voice is high and dreamlike.

The queen stands next to him on the deck. "I don't think . . ."

Her voice falters as the melody strokes her into submission. It's a command, and every human has come to a stop, bodies frozen as their eyes search the seas. I set my focus on the prince and sing more softly. Within moments his eyes fall to mine.

"Gods," he says. "It's you."

He smiles and from his left eye slips a single tear.

I stop singing and my voice turns to a gentle hum.

"My love," the prince says, "I've found you at last."

He grips the ratlines and peers far over the edge, his chest flat against the wood, one hand reaching out to touch me. He's dressed in a beige shirt, the strings loose at his chest, sleeves torn and slightly moth-bitten. His crown is thin gold leaf that looks as though it could break if he moves too quickly. He looks desolate and poor.

But then there is his face.

Soft and round, with skin like varnished wood and eyes a penetrating shade darker. His hair swings and coils tightly on his head, a beautiful mess of loops and spirals. Kahlia was right; he's angelic. Magnificent, even. His heart will make a fine trophy.

"You are so beautiful," says the queen, staring down at Kahlia with reverence. "I'm unsure how I've ever considered another."

Kahlia's smile is primordial as she reaches out to the queen, beckoning her to the ocean.

I turn back to the prince, who is frantically stretching out his hand to me. "My love," he pleads. "Come aboard."

I shake my head and continue to hum. The wind groans with the lullaby of my voice.

"I'll come to you then!" he shouts, as though it was ever a choice.

With a gleeful smile, he flings himself into the ocean, and with the splash of his body comes a second, which I know to be the queen, throwing herself to my cousin's mercy. The sounds of their falls awaken something in the crew, and in an instant they are screaming.

They lean over the ship's edge, fifty of them clinging to ropes and wood, watching the spectacle below with horror. But none dare throw themselves overboard to save their sovereigns. I can smell their fear, mixed with the confusion that comes from the sudden absence of our song.

I meet the eyes of my prince and stroke his soft, angelic skin. Gently, with one hand on his cheek and another resting on the thin bones of his shoulder, I kiss him. And as my lips taste his, I pull him under.

The kiss breaks once we are far enough down. My song has long since ended, but the prince stays enamored. Even as the water fills his lungs and his mouth opens in a gasp, he keeps his eyes on me with a glorious look of infatuation.

As he drowns, he touches his fingers to his lips.

Beside me, Kahlia's queen thrashes. She clutches at her throat and bats my cousin away. Angrily, Kahlia clings to her ankle and keeps her deep below the surface, the queen's face a sneer as she tries to escape. It's futile. A siren's hold is a vice.

I stroke my dying prince. My birthday is not for two weeks.

This trip was a gift for Kahlia: to hold the heart of royalty in her hands and name it her fifteenth. It's not supposed to be for me to steal a heart a fortnight early, breaking our most sacred rule. Yet there's a prince dying slowly in front of me. Brown skin and lips blue with ocean. Hair flowing behind him like black seaweed. Something about his purity reminds me of my very first kill. The young boy who helped my mother turn me into the beast I am now.

Such a pretty face, I think.

I run a thumb over the poor prince's lip, savoring his peaceful expression. And then I let out a shriek like no other. The kind of noise that butchers bones and claws through skin. A noise to make my mother proud.

In one move, I plunge my fist into the prince's chest and pull out his heart.

3

Elian

TECHNICALLY, I'M A MURDERER, but I like to think that's one of my better qualities.

I hold up my knife to the moon, admiring the polish of blood before it seeps into the steel and disappears. It was made for me when I turned seventeen and it became clear killing was no longer just a hobby. It was unseemly, the king said, for the Midasan prince to carry around rusted blades. And so now I carry around a magic blade that drinks the blood of its kill so quickly that I barely have time to admire it. Which is far more seemly, apparently. If not a little theatrical.

I regard the dead thing on my deck.

The *Saad* is a mighty vessel that stretches to the size of two full ships, with a crew that could've been over four hundred, but is exactly half that because I value loyalty above all else. Old black lanterns adorn the stern, and the bowsprit stretches forward in a piercing dagger. The *Saad* is so much more than a ship: It's a weapon. Painted in midnight navy, with sails the same cream as the queen's skin and a deck the same polish as the king's.

A deck that is currently home to the bloody corpse of a siren.

"Ain't it supposed to melt now?"

This is from Kolton Torik, my first mate. Torik is in his early forties, with a pure white mustache and a good four inches of height on me. Each of his arms is the size of each of my legs, and he's nothing short of burly. In summer months like these, he wears cutoff shorts, the fabric fraying by his kneecaps, and a white shirt with a black waistcoat tied by red ribbon. Which tells me that of all the things he takes seriously – which, really, is most things – his role as an almost pirate is probably not one of them. It is a contradiction to crewmen like Kye, who takes absolutely nothing seriously and yet dresses like he's an honorary member of the infamous Xaprár thieves.

"I feel weird just lookin' at it," Torik says. "All human up top."

"Enjoy looking up top, do you?"

Torik reddens a shade and turns his attention away from the siren's exposed breasts.

Of course I understand what he meant, but somewhere along the seas I've forgotten how to be horrified. There's no looking past the fins and blood-red lips, or the eyes that shine with two different colors. Men like Torik – good men – see what these creatures could be: women and girls, mothers and daughters. But I can only see them as they are: monsters and beasts, creatures and devils.

I'm not a good man. I don't think I've been one for a long time.

In front of us, the siren's skin begins to dissolve. Her hair melts to sea green and her scales froth. Even her blood, just a moment before threatening to stain the deck of the *Saad*, begins to lather until all that is left is sea foam. And a minute later that, too, is gone.

I'm grateful for that part. When a siren dies, she turns

back into the ocean, which means that there's no unseemly burning of bodies. No dumping their rotting corpses into the sea. I may not be a good man, but I'm good enough to find that preferable.

"What now, Cap?"

Kye slides his sword back into place and positions himself alongside Madrid, my second mate. As usual, Kye is dressed all in black, with patchwork leather and gloves that end at the fingertips. His light brown hair is shaved on both sides, like most men who are from Omorfiá, where aesthetics are valued above all else. Which, in Kye's case, also includes morals. Luckily for him – and, perhaps, for us all – Madrid is an expert at compelling decency in people. For a trained killer, she's oddly ethical, and their relationship has managed to keep Kye from sliding down even the slipperiest of slopes.

I shoot Kye a smile. I like being called Cap. Captain. Anything other than My Liege, My Prince, *Your Royal Highness Sir Elian Midas*. Whatever it is the devouts like to spit out in between the constant bowing. Cap suits me in a way my title never has. I'm far more pirate than prince, anyway.

It started when I was fifteen, and for the last four years I've known nothing like I know the ocean. When I'm in Midas, my body aches for sleep. There's a constant fatigue that comes with acting like a prince, where even conversations with those at court who fancy me one of them become too exhausting to stay awake for. When I'm on board the *Saad*, I barely sleep. I never seem to be tired enough. There's a constant thrumming and pulsing. Zaps like lightning that shoot through my veins. I'm alert, always, and so filled with anxious excitement that while the rest of my crew sleeps, I lie on the deck and count stars.

I make shapes of them, and from those shapes I make

stories. Of all the places I have been and will be. Of all the seas and oceans I've yet to visit and the men I've yet to recruit and the devils I've yet to slay. The thrill of it never stops, even when the seas become deadly. Even as I hear the familiar song that strikes my soul and makes me believe in love like it's the first time. The danger only makes me thirstier.

As Elian Midas, crown prince and heir to the Midasan throne, I'm more than a little dull. My conversations are about state and riches and which ball to attend and which lady has the finer dress and if there are any I think are worth a tumble. Each time I dock at Midas and am forced to play the part feels like time lost. A month, a week, a day I can't get back. An opportunity missed, or a life not saved. One more royal I may as well have fed to the Princes' Bane.

But when I'm just Elian, captain of the *Saad*, I transform. When the boat docks on whatever isle I've chosen for the day, as long as I have my crew, I can be myself. Drink until I'm dizzy and joke with women whose skin feels warm with exploits. Women who smell of rose and barley and, on hearing I'm a prince, cackle and tell me it won't earn me a free drink.

"Cap?" asks Kye. "State the play."

I jog up the steps to the forecastle deck, pull the golden telescope from my belt loop and press it to my kohl-rimmed eyes. At the edge of the bowsprit, I see ocean. For miles and miles. Eons, even. Nothing but clear water. I lick my lips, hungry for the thrill of more.

There's royalty in me, but stronger than that there is adventure. Unseemly, my father had said, for the Midasan heir to have a rusted knife, or set sail into open waters and disappear for months at a time, or be nineteen and still not have a suitable wife, or wear hats shaped like triangles and rags with loose string in place of gold thread.

Unseemly, to be a pirate and a siren hunter in place of a prince.

I sigh and turn to face the bow. So much ocean, but in the distance, too far to make out, there is land. There is the isle of Midas. There is home.

I look down to my crew. Two hundred sailors and warriors who see my quest as honorable and brave. They don't think of me like those at court, who hear my name and imagine a young prince who needs to get exploration out of his system. These men and women heard my name and pledged their undying allegiance.

"Okay, you ragtag group of siren gizzards," I call down to them, "turn the lady left."

My crew roars their approval. In Midas, I make sure they're pampered with as much drink and food as they like. Full bellies and beds with silken sheets. Far more luxury than they're used to sleeping on in the *Saad*, or on the hay-filled beds of inns we find on passing lands.

"My family will want to see how we've fared," I tell them. "We're going home."

A thunder of stamping feet. They applaud in triumph at the announcement. I grin and decide to keep the cheer on my face. I will not falter. It's a key part of my image: never upset or angry or deterred. Always in charge of my own life and destiny.

The ship turns hard starboard, swinging in a broad circle as my crew scurries around the deck, anxious for the return to Midas. They're not all natives; some are from neighboring kingdoms like Armonía or Adékaros. Countries they grew bored of, or those that were thrown into mayhem after the death of their princes. They're from everywhere and their homes are nowhere, but they call Midas so because I do. Even if it is a lie for them and for me. My crew is my family and though I could never say it – perhaps, don't need to say it – the *Saad* is my true home.

Where we're going now is just another pit stop.

4

Elian

IN MIDAS, THE OCEAN glitters gold. At least, that's the illusion. Really it's as blue as any sea, but the light does things. Unexplainable things. The light can lie.

The castle towers above the land, built into the largest pyramid. It's crafted from pure gold, so that each stone and brick is a gleaming expanse of sunlight. The statues scatter on the horizon, and the houses in the lower towns are all painted the same. Streets and cobbles glow yellow, so that when the sun hits the ocean, it glitters in an unmistakable reflection. It's only ever during the darkest parts of night that the true blue of the Midasan Sea can be seen.

As the Midasan prince, my blood is supposed to be made of that same gold. Every land in the hundred kingdoms has its own myths and fables for their royals: The gods carved the Págos family from snow and ice. Each generation gifted with hair like milk and lips as blue as skies. The Eidýllion royals are the descendants of the Love God, and so any they touch will find their soul mate. And the Midasan monarchs are crafted from gold itself.

Legend says my entire family bleeds nothing but treasure. Of course, I've bled a lot in my time. Sirens lose all serenity when they turn from hunter to prey and pieces of their nails become embedded in my arms. My blood has been spilled more often than any prince's, and I can attest to the fact that it has never been gold.

This, my crew knows. They've been the ones to clean my wounds and stitch my skin back together. Yet they entertain the legend, laughing and nodding dubiously whenever people speak of golden blood. They would never betray the secret of my ordinariness.

"Of course," Madrid will say to any who ask. "The cap's made from the purest parts of the sun. Seeing him bleed is like looking into the eyes of the gods."

Kye will always lean in then and lower his voice in the way only someone who knows all of my secrets could. "After a woman is with him, she cries tears of nothing but liquid metal for a week. Half for missing his touch so terrible, and the other half to buy back her pride."

"Yeah," Torik always adds. "And he shits rainbows too."

I linger on the forecastle of the *Saad*, anchored in the Midasan docks. I'm unsettled at the idea of having my feet on solid ground after so many weeks. It's always the way. Stranger still is the thought that I'll need to leave the truest parts of myself on the *Saad* before I head to the pyramid and my family. It's been nearly a year since I've been back, and though I've missed them, it doesn't seem like long enough.

Kye stands beside me. The rest of the crew has begun the walk, like an army marching for the palace, but he rarely leaves my side unless asked. Boatswain, best friend, and bodyguard. He would never admit that last part, though my father offered him enough money for the position. Of course, at the time, Kye had already been on my crew for long enough to know better than to try to save me, and my friend long enough to be willing to try anyway.

Still, he took the gold. He took most things just because he could. It came with the territory of being a diplomat's son. If Kye was going to disappoint his father by joining me on a siren scavenger hunt rather than spending a life in politics and cross-kingdom negotiations, then he wasn't going to do it by halves. He was going to throw everything he had into it. After all, the threat of disinheritance had already been carried out.

Around me, everything shimmers. Buildings and pavements and even the docks. In the sky, hundreds of tiny gold lanterns float to the heavens, celebrating my homecoming. My father's adviser is from the land of fortune-tellers and prophets, and so he always knows when I'm due to return. Each time the skies dance with flaming lanterns, bejeweled beside stars.

I inhale the familiar smell of my homeland. Midas always seems to smell of fruit. So many different kinds all at once. Butter pears and clingstone peaches, their honey-stuck flesh mingling with the sweet brandy of apricots. And under it all is the fading smell of licorice, which is coming from the *Saad* and, most likely, me.

"Elian." Kye slings an arm over my shoulder. "We should get going if we want anything to eat tonight. You know that lot won't leave any chow for us if we give them half a chance."

I laugh, but it sounds more like a sigh.

I take off my hat. I've already changed out of my sea attire and into the one respectable outfit I keep aboard my ship. A cream shirt, with buttons rather than string, and midnight-blue trousers held up by a golden belt. Not quite fit for a prince, but nothing of the pirate in it either. I've even removed my family crest from the thin chain around my neck and placed it on my thumb.

"Right." I hook my hat over the ship wheel. "Best get it over with."

"It won't be so bad." Kye hitches his collar. "You might find yourself enjoying the bowing. Might even abandon ship and leave us all stranded in the land of gold." He reaches over and messes up my hair. "Wouldn't be such a bad thing," he says. "I quite like gold."

"A true pirate." I shove him halfheartedly. "But you can get that idea out of your head. We'll go to the palace, attend the ball they'll no doubt throw in my honor, and be gone before the week is out."

"A ball?" Kye's eyebrows rise. "What an honor, My Liege." He bends over in a swooping bow, one hand to his stomach.

I shove him again. Harder. "Gods." I wince. "Please don't."

Again he bows, though this time he can hardly keep from laughing. "As you desire, Your Highness."

MY FAMILY IS IN the throne room. The chamber is decorated in floating balls of gold, flags printed with the Midasan crest, and a large table filled with jewels and gifts. Presents from the people to celebrate their prince's return.

Having abandoned Kye to the dining hall, I watch my family from the doorway, not quite ready to announce my presence.

"It's not that I don't think he deserves it," my sister says.

Amara is sixteen, with eyes like molokhia and hair as black as mine, and almost always sprinkled with gold and gemstones.

"It's just that I hardly think he'll want it." Amara holds up a gold bracelet in the shape of a leaf and presents it to the king and queen. "Really," she argues. "Can you see Elian wearing this? I'm doing him a favor."

"Stealing is a favor now?" asks the queen. The braids on

either side of her fringe swing as she turns to her husband. "Shall we send her to Kléftes to live with the rest of the thieves?"

"I wouldn't dream of it," says the king. "Send my little demon there and they'll see it as an act of war when she steals the crest ring."

"Nonsense." I finally stride into the room. "She'd be smart enough to go for the crown first."

"Elian!"

Amara runs to me and flings her arms around my neck. I return the hug and lift her off the floor, as excited to see her as she is to see me.

"You're home!" she says, once I set her back on the ground.

I look at her with mock injury. "For five minutes and you're already planning to rob me."

Amara pokes me in the stomach. "Only a little."

My father rises from his throne and his teeth gleam against his dark skin. "My son."

He envelops me in a hug and claps me on each shoulder. My mother descends the steps to join us. She's petite, barely reaching my father's shoulder, and has delicate, graceful features. Her hair is cut bluntly at her chin, and her eyes are green and catlike, lined in wisps of black that lick her temples.

The king is her opposite in every way. Large and muscular, with a goatee tied with beads. His eyes are a brown that match his skin, and his jaw is sharp and square. With Midas hieratic decorating his face, he looks every bit the warrior.

My mother smiles. "We were beginning to worry you had forgotten us."

"Only for a little while." I kiss her cheek. "I remembered as soon as we docked. I saw the pyramid and thought, *Oh, my family lives there. I remember their faces. I hope they bought a bracelet to celebrate my return."* I shoot Amara a grin and she pokes me again.

"Have you eaten?" my mother asks. "There's quite the feast in the banquet hall. I think your friends are in there now."

My father grunts. "No doubt eating everything but our utensils."

"If you want them to eat the cutlery, you should have it carved from cheese."

"Really, Elian." My mother smacks my shoulder and then brings her hand up to brush my hair from my forehead. "You look so tired," she says.

I take her hand and kiss it. "I'm fine. That's just what sleeping on a ship does to a man."

Really, I don't think I looked tired until the moment I walked off the *Saad* and onto the gold-painted cement of Midas. Just one step and the life drained out of me.

"You should try sleeping in your own bed longer than a few days a year," says my father.

"Radames," my mother scolds. "Don't start."

"I'm just speaking to the boy! There's nothing out there but ocean."

"And sirens," I remind him.

"Ha!" His laugh is a bellow. "And it's your job to seek them out, is it? If you're not careful, you'll leave us like Adékaros."

I frown. "What does that mean?"

"It means that your sister may have to take the throne."

"We won't have to worry, then." I sling my arm around Amara. "She'd definitely make a better queen than me."

Amara stifles a laugh.

"She's sixteen," my father chides. "A child should be allowed to live her life and not worry about an entire kingdom."

"Oh." I fold my arms. "She should, but not me."

"You're the eldest."

"Really?" I pretend to ponder this. "But I have such a youthful glow."

My father opens his mouth to respond, but my mother places a gentle hand on his shoulder. "Radames," she says, "I think it's best Elian gets some sleep. Tomorrow's ball will make for a long day, and he really does look tired."

I press my lips to a tight smile and bow. "Of course," I say, and excuse myself.

My father has never understood the importance of what I'm doing, but each time I return home, I lull myself into thinking that maybe, just once, he'll be able to put his love for me above the love for his kingdom. But he fears for my safety because it would affect the crown. He has already spent too many years grooming the people into accepting me as their future sovereign to change things now.

"Elian!" Amara calls after me.

I ignore her, walking in long and quick strides, feeling the anger bubble under my skin. Knowing that the only way to make my father proud is to give up everything that I am.

"Elian," she says, more firmly. "It's not princess-like to run. Or if it is, then I'll make a decree for it not to be if I'm ever queen."

Reluctantly, I stop and face her. She sighs in relief and leans against the glyph-carved wall. She has taken her shoes off, and without them she's even shorter than I remember. I smile, and when she sees this, she scowls and smacks my arm. I wince and hold out my hand for hers.

"You antagonize him," she says, taking my arm.

"He antagonizes me first."

"You'll make a fine diplomat with those debate skills."

I shake my head. "Not if you take the throne."

"At least then I'd get the bracelet." She nudges me with her elbow. "How was your trip? How many sirens did you slaughter like the great pirate that you are?"

She says this with a smirk, knowing full well that I'll never tell her about my time on the *Saad*. I share many things with my sister, but never how it feels to be a killer. I like the idea of Amara seeing me as a hero, and killers are so very often villains.

"Barely any," I say. "I was too full of rum to think about it."

"You're quite the liar," says Amara. "And by quite, I mean quite awful."

We come to a stop outside her room. "And you're quite nosy," I tell her. "That's new."

Amara ignores this. "Are you going to the banquet hall to see your friends?" she asks.

I shake my head. The guards will make sure my crew finds good beds for the night, and I'm far too tired to plaster on another round of smiles.

"I'm going to bed," I tell her. "Like the queen ordered."

Amara nods, perches on her tiptoes, and kisses my cheek. "I'll see you tomorrow then," she says. "And I can ask Kye about your exploits. I don't imagine a diplomat would lie to a princess." With a playful grin, she turns to her room and shuts the door behind her.

I pause for a moment.

I don't much like the thought of my sister swapping stories with my crew, but at least I can trust Kye to tell his tales with less death and gore. He's fanciful, but not stupid. He knows that I don't behave the way a prince should any more than he behaves as a diplomat's son should. It's my biggest secret. People know me as the siren hunter, and those at court utter those words with amusement and fondness: *Oh, Prince Elian, trying to save us all.* If they understood what it took, the awful and sickening screams sirens made. If they saw the corpses of the women on my deck before they dissolved to sea foam, then my people wouldn't look upon me so fondly. I would no longer be a prince to them, and as much as I might desire such things, I know better.

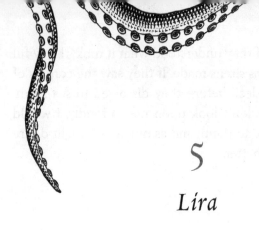

5

Lira

THE KETO PALACE LIES within the center of the Diávolos Sea and has always been home to royalty. Though humans have kings and queens in every crevice of the earth, the ocean has only one ruler. One queen. This is my mother, and one day it will be me.

One day being soon. It's not that my mother is too old to rule. Though sirens live for a hundred years, we never age past a few decades, and soon daughters look like mothers and mothers look like sisters, and it becomes hard to tell how old anybody truly is. It's another reason why we have the tradition of hearts: so a siren's age is never determined by her face, but always by how many lives she has stolen.

This is the first time I've broken that tradition, and my mother is furious. Looking down at me, the Sea Queen is every bit the tyrannical sovereign. To an outsider, she may even seem infinite, as though her reign could never end. It doesn't look like she'll lose her throne in just a few years.

As is customary, the Sea Queen retires her crown once she has sixty hearts. I know the exact number my mother has hidden in the safe beneath the palace gardens. Once, she had announced them each year, proud of her growing collection.

But she stopped making such proclamations when she reached fifty. She stopped counting, or at least, stopped telling people that she did. But I never stopped. Each year I counted my mother's hearts just as rigorously as I counted my own. So I know that she has three years before the crown is mine.

"How many is that now, Lira?" asks the Sea Queen, looming down at me.

Reluctantly, I bow my head. Kahlia lingers behind me, and though I can't see her, I know she's shadowing the gesture.

"Eighteen," I reply.

"Eighteen," the Sea Queen muses. "How funny you should have eighteen hearts, when your birthday is not for two weeks."

"I know, but—"

"Let me tell you what I know." The queen settles on her carcass throne. "I know that you were supposed to take your cousin to get her fifteenth, and somehow that proved too difficult."

"Not especially," I say. "I did take her."

"And you took a little something for yourself, too."

Her tentacles stretch around my waist and pull me forward. In an instant, I feel the crack of my ribs beneath her grip.

Every queen begins as a siren, and when the crown passes to her, its magic steals her fins and leaves in their place mighty tentacles that hold the strength of armies. She becomes more squid than fish, and with that transformation comes the magic, unyielding and grand. Enough to shape the seas to her whim. Sea Queen and Sea Witch both.

I've never known my mother as a siren, but I can't imagine her ever looking so mundane. She has ancient symbols and runes tattooed over her stomach in red, stretching even to her gloriously carved cheekbones. Her tentacles are black and scarlet, fading into one another like blood spilled into ink, and her eyes have long since turned to rubies. Even her crown is a magnificent headdress that peaks in horns atop her head and flows out like limbs down her back.

"I won't hunt on my birthday as recompense," I concede breathlessly.

"Oh, but you will." The queen strokes her black trident. A single ruby, like her eyes, shines on the middle spear. "Because today never happened. Because you would never disobey me or undermine me in any way. Would you, Lira?"

She squeezes my ribs tighter.

"Of course not, Mother."

"And you?" The queen turns her fixation to Kahlia, and I try to hide any signs of unease. If my mother were to see concern in my eyes, it would only be another weakness for her to exploit.

Kahlia swims forward. Her hair is pulled back from her face by a tie of seaweed, and her fingernails are still crusted with pieces of the Adékarosin queen. She bows her head in what some might interpret as a show of respect. But I know better. Kahlia can never look the Sea Queen in the eye, because if she did, then my mother might know exactly what my cousin thinks of her.

"I only thought she would kill him," says Kahlia. "I didn't know she'd take his heart, too."

It's a lie and I'm glad of it.

"Well, how perfectly stupid you are not to know your own cousin." My mother eyes her greedily. "I'm not sure I can think of a punishment unpleasant enough for complete idiocy."

I clench a hand against the tentacle that grips my waist. "Whatever the punishment is," I say, "I'll take it."

My mother's smile twitches, and I know that she's thinking of all the ways this makes me unworthy to be her daughter.

Still, I can't help it. In an ocean of sirens who watch out only for themselves, protecting Kahlia has become somewhat of a reflex. Ever since that day when we were both forced to watch her mother die. And throughout the years, as the Sea Queen tried to mold both Kahlia and I into the perfect descendants of Keto. Carving our edges into the right shape for her to admire. It's a mirror to a childhood I'd sooner forget.

Kahlia is like me. Too much like me, perhaps. And though it's what makes the Sea Queen hate her, it's also the reason I choose to care. I've stuck by her side, shielding her from the parts of my mother that are the most brutal. Now protecting my cousin isn't a decision I make. It's instinct.

"How caring of you," the Sea Queen says with a scornful smile. "Is it all those hearts you've stolen? Did you take some of their humanity, too?"

"Mother—"

"Such fealty to a creature other than your queen." She sighs. "I wonder if this is the way you behave with the humans, too. Tell me, Lira, do you cry for their broken hearts?"

She drops her grip on me, disgusted. I hate what I become in her presence: trite and undeserving of the crown I'm to inherit. Through her eyes, I see my failure. It doesn't matter how many princes I hunt, because I'll never be the kind of killer that she is.

I'm still not quite cold enough for the ocean that birthed me.

"Give it to me so we can get on with it," the Sea Queen says impatiently.

I frown. "Give it to you," I repeat.

The queen holds out her hand. "I don't have all day."

It takes me a moment to realize that she means the heart of the prince I killed.

"But . . ." I shake my head. "But it's *mine*."

What an incredible child I've become.

The Sea Queen's lips curl. "You will give it to me," she says. "Right now."

Seeing the look on her face, I turn and swim for my bedroom without another word. There the prince's heart lies buried alongside seventeen others. Carefully, I dig through the freshly placed shingle and pull the heart out of the floor. It's crusted in sand and blood and still feels warm in my hands. I don't stop to think about the pain the loss will bring before I swim back to my mother and present it to her.

The Sea Queen strikes out a tentacle and snatches the heart from my open palm. For a while she stares into my eyes, gauging my every reaction. Savoring the moment. And then she squeezes.

The heart explodes into a gruesome mass of blood and flesh. Tiny particles float like ocean lint. Some dissolve. Others fall like feathers to the ocean bed. Shots plunge through my chest, slamming into me like whirlpools as the heart's magic is taken from me. The jolts are so strong that my fins catch on a nearby seashell and rip. My blood gushes alongside the prince's.

Siren blood is nothing like human blood. Firstly, because it is cold. Secondly, because it burns. Human blood flows and drips and pools, but siren blood blisters and bubbles and melts through skin.

I fall to the floor and claw the sand so deeply that my finger stabs a rock and it cleaves my nail clean off. I am breathless, heaving in great gasps of water and then choking it back up moments later. I think I might be drowning, and I almost laugh at the thought.

Once a siren steals a human heart, we become bonded to

it. It's an ancient kind of magic that cannot be easily broken. By taking the heart, we absorb its power, stealing whatever youth and life the human had left and binding it to us. The Adékarosin prince's heart is being ripped from me, and any power it held leaks into the ocean before my eyes. Into nothingness.

Shaking, I rise. My limbs feel as heavy as iron and my fins throb. The glorious red seaweed that covers my breasts is still coiled around me, but the strands have loosened and hang limply over my stomach. Kahlia turns away, to keep my mother from seeing the anguish on her face.

"Wonderful," says the queen. "Time for the punishment."

Now I do laugh. My throat feels scratchy, and even that action, the sound of my voice so wrought with magic, takes energy from me. I feel weaker than I ever have.

"That wasn't punishment?" I spit. "Ripping the power from me like that?"

"It was the perfect punishment," says the Sea Queen. "I don't think I could have thought of a better lesson to teach you."

"Then what else is there?"

She smiles with ivory fangs. "Kahlia's punishment," she says. "Per your request."

I feel the heaviness in my chest again. I recognize the dreadful gleam in my mother's eyes, as it's a look I've inherited. One I hate seeing on anyone else, because I know exactly what it means.

"I'm sure I can think of something fitting." The queen runs a tongue across her fangs. "Something to teach you a valuable lesson about the power of patience."

I fight the urge to sneer, knowing no good will come of it. "Don't keep me in suspense."

The Sea Queen leers down at me. "You always did enjoy pain," she says.

This is as much of a compliment as I'm going to get, so I smile in a way that is sickeningly pleasant and say, "Pain doesn't always hurt."

The Sea Queen shoots me a contemptuous look. "Is that so?" Her eyebrows twitch upward and my arrogance falters somewhat. "If that's how you feel, then I have no choice but to decree that for your birthday, you will have the chance to inflict all of the pain you like when you steal your next heart."

I eye her warily. "I don't understand."

"Only," the queen continues, "instead of the princes you are so adept at trapping, you will add a new kind of trophy to your collection." Her voice is as wicked as mine has ever been. "Your eighteenth heart will belong to a sailor. And at the ceremony of your birth, with our entire kingdom present, you will present this to them, as you have done with all of your trophies."

I stare at my mother, biting my tongue so hard that my teeth almost meet.

She doesn't want to punish me. She wants to humiliate me. Show a kingdom whose fear and loyalty I've earned that I'm no different from them. That I don't stand out. That I'm not worthy to take her crown.

I've spent my life trying to be just what my mother wanted – the worst of us all – in an effort to show that I'm worthy of the trident. I became the Princes' Bane, a title that defines me throughout the world. For the kingdom – for my mother – I am ruthless. And that ruthlessness makes each and every sea creature certain I can reign. Now my mother wants to take that from me. Not just my name, but the faith of the ocean. If I'm not the Princes' Bane, then I'm nothing. Just a princess inheriting a crown instead of earning it.

6

Elian

"I DON'T REMEMBER THE last time I saw you like that."

"Like what?"

"Put together."

"Put together," I repeat, adjusting my collar.

"Handsome," says Madrid.

I arch an eyebrow. "Am I not normally handsome?"

"You're not normally clean," she says. "And your hair isn't normally so—"

"Put together?"

Madrid rolls up her shirtsleeves. "Princely."

I smirk and look in the mirror. My hair is neatly slicked back from my face, every speck of dirt scrubbed away so that there isn't an ounce of the ocean left on me. I'm wearing a white dress shirt with a high-button collar and a dark gold jacket that feels like silk against my skin. Probably because it is silk. My family crest sits uncomfortably on my thumb, and of every piece of gold on me, that seems to shine the brightest.

"You look the same," I tell Madrid. "Only without the mud smears."

She punches me in the shoulder and ties her midnight hair away from her face with a bandana, revealing the Kléftesis tattoo on her cheek. It's a brand for children taken by the slave ships and forced to be murderers for hire. When I found her, Madrid had just bought her freedom with the barrel of a gun.

By the doorway, Kye and Torik wait. Just as Madrid, they look no different. Torik with his shorts unraveling at the shin, and Kye with sharp cheeks and a smile made for trickery. Their faces are cleaner, but nothing else has changed. They're incapable of being anything other than what they are. I envy that.

"Come with us," says Kye, threading his fingers through Madrid's. She glares at the uncharacteristic display of affection – the two of them are far better fighters than they are lovers – and breaks away to run a hand through her hair.

"You like the tavern so much more than this place," Madrid says.

It's true. A horde of my crew has already made their way to the Golden Goose, with enough gold to drink until the sun comes up. All that remains are my three most trusted.

"It's a ball thrown in my honor," I tell them. "It wouldn't be very honorable for me not to show up."

"Maybe they won't notice." Madrid's hair swings wildly behind her as she speaks.

"That's not comforting."

Kye nudges her and she pushes him back twice as hard. "Quit it," she says.

"Quit making him nervous, then," he tells her. "Let's leave the prince to be a prince for once. Besides, I need a drink, and I feel like I'm messing up this pristine room just by standing here."

I nod. "I do feel poorer just looking at you."

Kye reaches over to the nearby sofa and throws one of

the gold-threaded cushions at me with such poor aim that it lands by my feet. I kick it away and try to look chastising.

"I hope you throw your knife better than that."

"Never had a siren complain yet," he says. "Are you sure you're okay for us to go?"

I stare back into the mirror at the prince before me. Immaculate and cold, barely a glint in my eyes. As though I'm untouchable and I know it. Madrid was right; I do look princely. Which is to say, that I look like a complete bastard.

I adjust my collar again. "I'm sure."

THE BALLROOM SHINES LIKE its own sun. Everywhere glitters and sparkles, so much so that if I concentrate too much on any specific thing, my head begins to pound.

"How much longer do you plan to have your feet on land?"

Nadir Pasha, one of our highest dignitaries, swirls a gold glass of brandy. Unlike the other Pashas I've spent the evening in idle conversation with – either political or military ranking – he's not nearly as trite. It's why I always save him for last when I consult with court. Matters of state are the furthest thing from his mind, especially on occasions when the brandy glasses are so large.

"Only a few more days," I say.

"Such an adventurer!" Nadir takes a swig of his drink. "What a joy to be young, isn't it?"

His wife, Halina, smooths down the front of her emerald dress. "Quite."

"Not that you or I would remember," remarks the Pasha.

"Not that you would notice." I lift Halina's hand to my lips. "You shine brighter than any tapestry we have."

The transparency of my compliment is easy to recognize, but Halina curtsies all the same. "Thank you, My Lord."

"It's an astonishment how far you go to do your duties," Nadir says. "I've even heard rumors of all the languages you're said to speak. No doubt that'll be of help with future negotiations among neighboring kingdoms. How many is it now?"

"Fifteen," I recite. "When I was younger, I had it in my mind that I could learn each language of the hundred kingdoms. I think I've failed quite splendidly."

"What's the point of such things anyway?" asks Halina. "There's barely a person alive who doesn't speak Midasan. We're at the center of the world, Your Highness. Anyone who can't be bothered to learn the language simply isn't worth knowing."

"Quite right." Nadir nods gruffly. "But what I actually meant, Your Highness, was the language of *them*. The forbidden language." He lowers his voice a little and leans in close, so that his mustache tickles my ear. "*Psáriin.*"

The language of the sea.

"Nadir!" Halina smacks her husband's shoulder, horrified. "You shouldn't speak of such things!" She turns to me. "We're sorry to offend you, My Liege," she says. "My husband didn't mean to imply that you'd sully your tongue with such a language. He's had far too much brandy. The glasses are deeper than they look."

I nod, unoffended. It's just a language after all, and though no human can speak it, no human has ever devoted their lives to hunting sirens, either. It isn't a leap to imagine I've decided to add the dialect of my prey to my collection. Even if it's forbidden in Midas. But in order to do so, I'd need to keep a siren alive long enough to teach me, and that isn't something I ever plan on doing. Of course, I've picked up a few words here and there. *Arith*, I quickly learned to mean *no*, but there are so many others. *Dolofónos. Choíron.* I can only ever guess at what they mean. Insults, curses, pleas. In some ways, it's best I don't know.

"Don't worry," I tell Halina. "It's not the worst thing someone has accused me of."

She looks a little flustered. "Well," she whispers delicately, "people do talk."

"Not just about you," Nadir clarifies with a loud exhale. "More about your work. It's most definitely appreciated, considering recent events. I would think our king would be proud to have you defending our land and those of our allies."

My brow creases at the idea of my father being anywhere close to proud at having a siren hunter for a son. "Recent events?" I ask.

Halina gasps, though she doesn't seem at all shocked. "Have you not heard the stories about Adékaros?"

There's something dreadful in the air. Just yesterday my father spoke of Adékaros and how, if I wasn't careful, Midas would end up the same.

I swallow and try to feign indifference. "It's hard to keep track of all the stories I hear."

"It's Prince Cristian," Halina says conspiratorially. "He's dead. The queen, too."

"Murdered," clarifies Nadir. "Sirens set upon their ship and there was nothing the crew could do. It was the song, you understand. The kingdom is in turmoil."

The room dulls. From the gold, to the music, to the faces of Nadir Pasha and Halina. It all becomes out of focus and stifled. For a moment I hesitate to breathe, let alone speak. I never had much dealing with the queen, but whenever the *Saad* was close to Adékaros, we docked without hesitation and Prince Cristian welcomed us with open arms. He made sure the crew was fed, and joined us in the tavern so that he could listen to our stories. When we left, he would gift us something. A lot of countries did it – small tokens that we never had much use for – but it was different for Cristian. He relied solely on scarce crops and loans from other kingdoms just to survive. Every gift he gave was a sacrifice.

"I heard it was the Princes' Bane." Halina shakes her head in pity.

I clench my fists. "Says who?"

"The crew said her hair was as red as hellfire," Nadir explains. "Could it have been any other?"

I want to argue the possibility, but I'd be fooling myself. The Princes' Bane is the greatest monster I've ever known, and the only one who's escaped death once I've set my sights on her. I've hunted the seas tirelessly, searching for the flaming hair I've heard of in so many stories.

I've never even seen her.

I had begun to think that she was just a myth. Nothing more than a legend to scare royals from leaving their lands. But every time I entertain the thought, another prince turns up dead. It's yet another reason why I can't return to Midas and be the king my father wants me to be. I can never stop. Not until I've killed her.

"Of course, how could they know?" asks Halina. "It isn't the right month for it."

I realize that she's speaking the truth. The Princes' Bane only attacks in the same month each year. And if she murdered Cristian, then she was over a fortnight early. Does that mean she's changed her habits? That no prince is safe on any day?

My lips twitch. "Evil doesn't follow a calendar," I say, even though this particular evil has always seemed to do just that.

Beside me, someone clears their throat. I turn and see my

sister. I'm not sure how long she's been standing there, but the amicable smile on her face leads me to assume that she's heard most of the conversation.

"Brother." She takes my arm. "Dance with me, won't you?"

I nod, welcoming the break from the sort of polite conversation the Pasha and his wife seem to enjoy. Which makes me want to be anything other than polite.

"No suitors vying for your attention?" I ask Amara.

"None worth my time," she says. "And none our charming father would approve of."

"Those are the best kind."

"You try explaining that when the boy's head is on a chopping block."

I snort. "Then it would be my pleasure," I tell her. "If only to save some poor boy's life."

I turn to Nadir and Halina and give a swift bow, then let my sister lead me onto the floor.

7

Elian

DESPITE ITS NAME, THE Golden Goose is one of the only things in Midas that is not painted to match the pyramid. The walls are crusted brown and the drinks follow in the same hue. The clientele is nothing short of brutish, and most nights, glass crunches underfoot, with blood patching the beer-soaked tables.

It's one of my favorite places.

The owner is Sakura and she has always just been Sakura. No last name that anyone knows of. She's pretty and plump, with white-blond hair cut above her ears and thin, angled eyes that are the same brown as the walls. She wears red lipstick dark enough to cover her secrets, and her skin is paler than anything I've ever seen. Most people have guessed that she's from Págos, which sees constant snow and little sun. A land so cold that only natives are able to survive it. It's rumored, even, that the Págese rarely migrate to other kingdoms because they find the heat to be suffocating. Yet I can't remember a time when Sakura didn't own the Golden Goose. She seemed to always be there, or at least, she has been there since I started visiting. And though she's beautiful, she's also cruel enough that not even the thieves and felons try to get past her.

Luckily, Sakura likes me. Whenever I'm in Midas, it's common knowledge that I'll visit the Golden Goose, and even criminals can't resist a chance to meet the famous pirate prince, whether it's to shake my hand or try to con me at cards. And so when I visit, Sakura gives me a smile that shows her straight, milky teeth and lets me drink for free. A thanks for bringing in more customers. It also means that my crew is allowed to stay long after closing to discuss sensitive matters in the dead of night with people I don't dare bring to the palace.

I suspect half of this is because Sakura enjoys being privy to my secrets. But that doesn't bother me. As many secrets as Sakura knows about me, I know far more about her. Far worse. And while she may choose to sell the best of mine to the highest bidder, I've kept her most valuable mysteries close. Waiting for just the right price.

Tonight my inner circle sits around the crooked table in the center of the Golden Goose and watches as the strange man in front of us fiddles with his cufflinks.

"The stories don't lie," he says.

"That's what a story is," Madrid says. "A bunch of lies by no-good gossips with too much time on their hands. Right, Captain?"

I shrug and pull the pocket watch from my jacket to check the time. It's the one present from my father that isn't gold or new or even *princely*. It's plain and black, with no ornate swirls or sparkling stones, and on the inside of the lid, opposite the clock face, is a compass.

I knew it wasn't an heirloom when my father gifted it to me – all Midasan heirlooms are gold that never lose their shine – but when I asked my father where the watch came from, he simply said that it would help me find my way. And it does just that. Because the compass doesn't have four points, but two, and neither represents the cardinal points. North is for truth and South is for lies, with a resting place between that indicates either may be possible.

It's a compass to split the liars from the loyal.

"My information is solid," the man says.

He's one of the many who approached me near closing, guaranteeing information to hunt down the mighty Princes' Bane. I put the word out after the ball that I won't stop until I've found her, and any clues leading to that will be met with a heavy reward. Most of the information was useless. Descriptions of the siren's burning hair, talk of her eyes or seas she apparently frequents. Some even claim to know the location of the underwater kingdom of Keto, which my compass was quick to see through. Besides, I already know where the kingdom is: the Diávolos Sea. The only problem is that I don't know where the Diávolos Sea is. And neither does anyone else, apparently.

But this man piqued my interest. Enough so that come midnight, when Sakura announced she was closing and motioned for everyone to leave, I gave her a nod and she proceeded to lock the doors with me and my crew – and this strange man – inside, before heading to the back room, for whatever it was she did when princes commandeered her bar.

The man turns to me. "I'm telling you, Lord Prince," he says. "The crystal is as real as I am."

I stare at him. He's different from the usual caliber I see in the Golden Goose, refined in a way that is forcibly precise. His coat is made of black velvet and his hair is combed into a tidy ponytail, with his shoes polished to gleam against the crusty floorboards. But he's also uncommonly thin – the lavish coat swallows his pinched shoulders – and his dark skin is quilted red by the sun, like my crew when they've spent too long on the deck after a hard day's sail.

When the man taps his fingers on the table impatiently, the ends of his bitten-down nails catch in the cracks of the wood.

"Tell me more."

Torik throws his hands up. "You want more rubbish to line your ears with?"

Kye produces a small knife from his belt. "If it's really rubbish," he says, thumbing the blade, "then he'll get what's coming to him."

I turn to Kye. "Put it away."

"We want to be safe."

"Which is why I'm telling you to put it away and not throw it away."

Kye smirks and places the knife back into his belt.

I tip my glass toward the man. "Tell me more."

"The Crystal of Keto will bring peace and justice to our world."

A smile tugs at my lips. "Will it now?"

"It'll save us all from the fire."

I lick the liquor from my lips. "How does that work?" I ask. "Do we clutch it tight and wish upon a star? Or perhaps tuck it under our pillows and exchange it to the fairies for good luck."

Kye pours some liquor into a shot glass. "Dip it in wax and light it up to burn away the flames of war," he says, sliding the glass over to Madrid.

She laughs and brings the glass to her lips. "Kiss it and maybe it'll turn into a prince who doesn't speak such drivel," she says.

"Or throw it into the pile of shit that it was made from."

This is from Torik, whose perfectly neutral face only makes me laugh harder, until the only sounds that can be heard are our snickers and the sharp bangs as my crew slaps their hands against the tables.

Then, amid it all, a deathly quiet voice: "By killing the Sea Queen."

I stop laughing.

My gaze snaps back to the man, and I pull my knife from my belt loop, feeling its thirst for a kill. Slowly, I bring it to the man's throat. "Say that again."

He swallows as the tip of my blade presses against his jugular. He should be scared. He *looks* scared; his eyes squint the right way and his hands even quake as he picks up his glass. But it seems rehearsed, because when he speaks, his voice is smooth. No sign of fear. It's as though he's used to having a knife at his throat.

"The crystal was crafted to bring justice to our world by destroying the Sea Queen," he explains.

"Crafted by who?" I ask.

"By the original families," he says. "They were the greatest magicians of the age, and together they agreed the territories of the world, each taking a corner for themselves so that they could have peace and never be victims of the old border wars."

"Yes," I say, impatient. "We're all aware of the original families. It's a fairy tale every child in the hundred kingdoms knows." I pocket my knife with a sigh. "Even these racketeers."

"It is not a fairy tale!" The man slams his fists on the table. "What those stories never told you is that the original families created peace on land, but below a battle waged on. A goddess ruled the ocean, spreading her evil throughout the waters. Soon she bore children who became devils. Monstrous creatures whose voices brought the death of men."

"Sirens."

The man nods. "They could transform, existing on land and under it. Under the goddess Keto's rule they terrorized humanity, and so the one hundred magicians combined their power and declared war on the ocean. After a decade of death they were finally able to destroy Keto and weaken the monsters she'd created. From her remains, they conjured a keepsake that could destroy the sirens forever."

"If that's true," I say, "then why didn't they use it?"

"Because the sirens fashioned a stone from her remains too. It gave their new queen the power to control her kind, and she promised to keep them at bay. She even took away the sirens' ability to walk on land as a show of good faith. Without that, they weren't a large enough threat to warrant the original families committing genocide. So they took mercy and formed a treaty. The land belonged to the humans, and the seas belonged to the devils. If either of them crossed into each other's territories, then they were fair game. The crystal was hidden for a day when the hundred kingdoms could no longer honor the bargain."

Around me, my crew breaks into mocking laughter, but I can barely hear them over the sound of my own pulse as I look down at the compass face.

North.

Resolutely, the arrow neither moving nor swaying. I shake it in disbelief and when it doesn't tremble, I tap it against the table. The arrow stays where it is.

North.

Truth.

By now my crew has resumed their jeering, poking holes at the myth and chastising the stranger for daring to bring fairy tales to their captain. Something in me, right there on the surface, thinks they're right. That it's nothing but children's tales and a waste of my time. It tells me to listen to my crew and ignore the madness. But the compass has never been wrong, and beneath the surface, right down in my gut, I know it can't be. This is my chance to finally slay the beast.

"Where is it?" I ask.

My voice cuts through the laughter of my crew, and they stare at me as though I've finally lost my mind.

The man gulps down a drink and meets my eyes with a smile. "You mentioned a reward."

I arch an eyebrow at Kye. Without the need for any convincing, he plunges his knife into the table. The man flinches, staring in horror at the blade nestled neatly in the space between his thumb and forefinger. The look of fear on his face isn't so practiced now.

"You'll get your reward," Kye tells him. "One way or the other."

"It's in the only place they were sure the Sea Queen could never reach it," the man says quickly. "As far from the ocean as possible. The highest point in the world."

My heart sinks. The highest point in the world. Too cold for any to venture and live to tell the tale.

"The Cloud Mountain of Págos," the man says.

And with that, hope slips away.

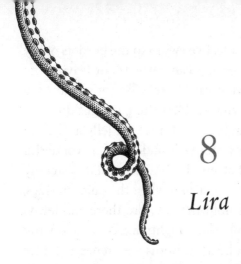

8

Lira

ONE WEEK IS ALL I have. In seven days I'll turn eighteen and my mother will force me to steal the heart of a sailor. A better creature would take the punishment and be glad that it's all the Sea Queen has decreed.

I'm not a better creature.

It's foolish to think about disobeying the queen again, but the thought of being told who I should and shouldn't kill rattles me. It makes me feel every bit the rabid dog for my mother to release on whoever she decrees. Of course, since killing humans itself is an order given by her, I suppose it's always been that way. I've become so used to being brutal, that I almost forget it didn't begin as a choice, but a requirement. Kill the humans. Help finish the war they started when they killed Keto. *Be a true siren.*

I think for a moment about whether I would still be such a monster if my mother and those before her decreed peace in place of war. Let Keto's death be the death of our battle and turn hatred to bygones. We're taught never to question or to think of ourselves as anything other than what we are, and it's smart, perhaps, to ignore the idea. After all, the punishment for refusing to kill would be beyond imagination.

I braid my hair to one side. I've swum to the borders of my sea, as far from my mother as I can get without leaving the kingdom. I don't know what my anger will turn into if I see her now. I can't think of what reckless thing I might do.

I lie down on the ocean bed and nudge the jellyfish beside me. Its tentacles graze my stomach and I feel a wonderful burst of pain. The kind that numbs and calms and clears my mind. It's a release like no other, and when the pain subsides, I do it again. This time, I hold the creature there and let its tentacles dance across my skin. Lightning courses up my stomach and into my still heart. It burns and itches, and I let my mind go foggy with agony.

There's nothing in the world but pain and the rare moments that exist in between.

"Pretty princess, so alone," comes a whisper of *Psáriin*. "Wanting pain, wanting bone."

"Not bone, but heart," says another. "See inside, see the spark."

I push the jellyfish away and sit up to look at the two creatures hovering nearby. They are both dark navy with slick fins and the bodies of eels. Their arms are covered in black gills like razors up to their elbows, and their stomachs form large, rigid muscles that press against skeletal breasts. As they speak, their loose jaws go as slack as fishes'.

Mermaids.

"Pretty princess," says the first of the two. Her body is covered in rusted metal, no doubt scavenged from pirate ships or given as tribute when she saved a wounded human. She has stabbed them through her flesh. Brooches and daggers and coins with threaded wire, all piercing through her like jewelry.

"Wants to be free," her companion says.

"Free from the queen."

"Free her heart."

"Take a heart."

"Take the queen's."

I wrinkle my nose at them. "Go and follow a human ship to the end of the earth until you all fall off it."

The one with the rusted metal swishes her tentacle hair, and a glob of slime trails down to her eel tail. "Fall from the earth," she tells me.

"Fall from grace."

"Can't fall from it if you never had it."

They laugh in hisses. "Go now then," they chorus. "Go find the heart."

"What are you talking about?" I ask impatiently. "What heart?"

"Win the queen's heart."

"A heart to win the queen's."

"For your birthday."

"A heart worthy for eighteen."

Their tediousness grates. Mermaids are ghastly things with minds that work in mysteries and lips made from riddles. Wearily, I say, "The Sea Queen has decreed I steal a sailor's heart for my eighteenth. Which I'm sure you know."

They tilt their heads in what I imagine is their way of nodding. Mermaids are spies, through and through, their ears pressed to every corner of the ocean. It's what makes them dangerous. They devour secrets as easily as they could loosen their jaws and devour ships.

"Go," I tell them. "You don't belong here."

"This is the edge."

"The edge is where we belong."

"You should think less of the edge and more of your heart."

"A heart of gold is worth its weight to the queen."

The one with the metal rips a brooch from the base of her fin and throws it to me. It's the one thing from the mermaid that hasn't rusted.

"The queen," I say slowly, twisting the brooch in my hands, "does not care for gold."

"She would care for the heart of its land."

"The heart of a prince."

"A prince of gold."

"Bright as the sun."

"Though not as fun."

"Not for our kind."

"Not for anyone."

I'm about to lose all patience when I grasp the weight of their words. My lips part in realization and I sink back to the sand. The brooch is from Midas, the land of gold ruled by a king whose blood flows with it. A king to be succeeded by a pirate prince. A wanderer. A siren killer.

I stare at the mermaids, with their lidless black eyes like endless orbs. I know they can't be trusted, but I can't ignore the brutal brilliance of their words. Whatever ulterior motives they have won't matter if I succeed.

"The Midasan prince is our murderer," I say. "If I bring the queen his heart as my eighteenth, then I could win back her favor."

"A heart worthy for the princess."

"A heart worthy for the queen's forgiveness."

I look back at the brooch. It gleams with a light like I've never seen. My mother wants to deny me the heart of a prince, but the heart of this prince would be enough to erase any bad feelings between us. I could continue with my legacy, and the queen would no longer have to worry about our kind being hunted. If I do this, we would both get what we want. We would be at peace.

I toss the brooch back to the mermaid. "I won't forget this," I tell her, "when I'm queen."

I give them one last glance, watching as their lips coil to smiles, and then swim for gold.

9

Elian

FOUR DAYS SPENT SCOURING the castle library and I've found exactly nothing. Numerous texts detail the deathly ice of the Cloud Mountain and illustrate – rather graphically – those who have died during their climb. Which isn't a great start. The only saving grace seems to be that the royal family is made of colder ice than the rest of their natives. There's even a tradition in Págos where the royals are required to climb the mountain once they come of age, to prove their lineage. There isn't a record of a single member of the royal family having ever failed. But since I'm not a Págese prince, this isn't particularly encouraging.

There must be something I'm missing. Legends be damned. I find it hard to believe that something in the Págese lineage allows them to withstand cold. I know better than anyone not to believe in the fairy tales of our families. If they were true, I'd be able to sell my blood to buy some real information.

The Págese must be made more of flesh and bone than frost and ice and, if that's the case, then there must be an explanation for how they survive the climb. If I have any hope of getting revenge for Cristian's death, then I need to know the answers. With that knowledge, I could find a way to kill the Princes' Bane and the Sea Queen. If I do that, the sirens left behind won't have magic to guard them. Perhaps they'll even lose some of their abilities. After all, if the Sea Queen has a crystal like the one hidden in the Cloud Mountain, then taking that should take away some of the gifts it bestowed on their kind. They'd be weakened at the very least and exposed to an attack. And after a time – however long – we could push the devils that remain to the far ends of the world, where they can't do harm.

I close the book and shiver a little at the breeze. The library is always cold, open windows or not. There seems to be something in the very structure of it that's designed to make me shiver. The library stretches to fifty feet, with white shelves that spread from the floor to the high arches of the ceiling. The ground is white marble and the ceiling is pure crystal that blankets the room. It's one of the only places in Midas untouched by gold. Nothing but vast white, from the painted chairs to the thick cushions, to the ladders that climb to the volumes at the very top. The only color is in the books – the leather and the fabric and the parchment – and in the knowledge they hold. It's what I like to call the Metaphor Room, because that's the only explanation for the expanse of white. Everyone is a blank canvas, waiting to be filled with the color of discovery.

My father really is theatrical.

I hoped there would be something in the volumes to help me. The man in the Golden Goose was so sure of his story, and my compass was so sure of its truth. There's no doubt in me that the Crystal of Keto is out there, but the world doesn't seem to know a thing about it. Books and books of ancient texts and not one of them tells me a thing. How can something exist if there isn't a record of it?

Fairy tales. I'm chasing damn fairy tales.

"I thought I'd find you here."

I look up at the king. "It's no wonder I don't come home more often," I say. "If you have your adviser keeping track of me whenever I'm inside the castle."

My father places a gentle hand on the back of my head. "You forget that you're my son," he says, as though I ever could. "I don't need a seer to tell me what you're up to."

He pulls up the chair beside me and examines the various texts on the table. If I look out of place in the castle, then my father definitely looks out of place in the stark white of the library, dressed in shimmering gold, his eyes dark and heavy.

With a sigh, the king leans back into his chair as I did. "You're always looking for something," he says.

"There's always something to find."

"If you're not careful, the only thing you'll find is danger."

"Maybe that's exactly what I'm looking for."

My father reaches over and grabs one of the books from the table. It's carefully bound in blue leather with the title etched in light gray script. There are fingerprints in the dust from where I pulled it from the shelf.

"*The Legends of Págos and Other Tales from the Ice City*," he reads. He taps the cover. "So you've set your sights on freezing to death?"

"I was researching something."

He places the book back down on the table a little too harshly. "Researching what?"

I shrug, unwilling to give my father any more reason to keep me in Midas. If I told him that I wanted to hunt for a mythical crystal in mountains that could steal my breath in seconds, there's no way he'd let me leave. He'd find any way to keep his heir in Midas.

"It's nothing," I lie. "Don't worry."

My father considers this, his maroon lips forming a tight line. "It's a king's job to worry when his heir is so reckless."

I roll my eyes. "Good thing you have two, then."

"It's also a father's job to worry when his son never wants to come home."

I hesitate. I may not always see eye to eye with my father, but I hate the idea of him blaming my absence on himself. If the kingdom wasn't an issue, I would take him with me. I'd take all of them. My father, mother, sister, and even the royal adviser if he promised to keep his divinations to himself. I'd pack them onto the deck like luggage and show them the world until adventure caught in their eyes. But I can't, so I deal with the ache of missing them, which is far better than the ache of missing the ocean.

"Is this about Cristian?" my father asks.

"No."

"Lies aren't answers."

"But they sound so much better than the truth."

My father places a large hand on my shoulder. "I want you to stay this time," he says. "You've spent so long at sea that you've forgotten what it's like to be yourself."

I know I should tell him that it's the land that steals away who I am and the sea that brings me back. But to say that to my father would do nothing but hurt us both.

"I have a job to do," I say. "When it's done, I'll come home."

The lie tastes awful in my mouth. My father, King of Midas and so King of Lies, seems to know this and smiles with such sadness that I'd buckle over if I weren't already sitting.

"A prince may be the subject of myth and legend," he explains, "but he can't live in them. He should live in the real world, where he can create them." He looks solemn. "You should pay less mind to fairy tales, Elian, or that's all you'll become."

When he leaves, I think about whether that would be awful, or beautiful. Could it really be such a bad thing, to become a story whispered to children in the dead of night? A song they sing to one another while they play. Another part of the Midasan legends: golden blood and a prince who once upon a time sailed the world in search of the beast who threatened to destroy it.

And then it comes to me.

I sit up a little straighter. My father told me to stop living inside fairy tales, but maybe that's exactly what I need to do. Because what that man told me in the Golden Goose isn't a fact that can be pressed between the pages of textbooks and biographies. It's a story.

Quickly, I pull myself from the chair and head for the children's section.

IO

Lira

THERE'S GLITTER AND TREASURE on every speck of every street. Houses with roofs thatched by gold thread and fanciful lanterns with casings brighter than their light. Even the surface of the water has turned milky yellow, and the air is balmy with the afternoon sun.

It is all too much. Too bright. Too hot. Too opulent.

I clutch the seashell around my neck to steady myself. It reminds me of home. My kind aren't afraid of their murderous prince; they just can't bear the light. The heat that cuts through the ocean's chill and makes everything warmer.

This is not a place for sirens. It's a place for mermaids.

I wait beside the prince's ship. I wasn't certain it would be here – killing took the prince to as many kingdoms as it did me – and if it was, I wasn't certain I would know it. I only have the frightful echoes of stories to go from. Things I've heard in passing from the rare few who have seen the prince's ship and managed to escape. But as soon as I saw it in the Midasan docks, I knew.

It's not quite like the stories, but it has the same dark ambiance that each of the tales had. The other ships on the dock are like spheres instead of boats, but this one is headed by a long stabbing point and is larger by far than any other, with a body like the night sky and a deck as dark as my soul. It's a vessel worthy of murder.

I'm still admiring it from the depths of the water when a shadow appears. The man steps onto the ledge of the ship and looks out at the sea. I should have been able to hear his footsteps, even from deep beneath the water. Yet he's suddenly here, one hand clutching the ropes for support, breathing slow and deep. I squint, but under the sheen of gold it's hard to see much. I know it's dangerous to come out from the water when the sun is still so high, but I have to get a closer look. Slowly, I rise to the surface and rest my back against the damp body of the ship.

I spot the shine of the Midasan royal insignia on his thumb and lick my lips.

The Prince of Midas wears the clothes of royalty in a way that seems neglectful. His shirtsleeves are rolled up to the elbows and the buttons of his collar are undone so the wind can reach his heart. He doesn't look much older than I do, yet his eyes are hard and weathered. They're eyes of lost innocence, greener than seaweed and constantly searching. Even the empty ocean is prey to him, and he regards it with a mix of suspicion and wonder.

"I've missed you," he says to his ship. "I bet you missed me too. We'll find it together, won't we? And when we do, we'll kill every damn monster in this ocean."

I scrape my fangs across my lips. What does he think could possibly have the power to destroy me? It's a fanciful notion of slaughter, and I find myself smiling. How wicked this one is, stripped of the innocence I've seen in all the others. This is not a prince of inexperience and anxious potential, but one of war and savagery. His heart will be a wonder to behold. I lick my lips and part them to give way to my song, but I barely have the chance to suck in a breath before I'm wrenched beneath the water.

A mermaid hovers in front of me. She is a splash of color, pinks and greens and yellows, like paint splatters on her skin. Her fin snakes and curls, the bony armor of seahorse scales protruding from her stomach and arms.

"Mine!" she says in *Psáriin*.

Her jaw stretches out like a snout, and when she snarls, it bends at a painful angle. She points to the prince above the water and thumps her chest.

"You have no claim here," I tell her.

The mermaid shakes her head. She has no hair, but the skin on her scalp is a kaleidoscope, and when she moves, the colors ripple from her like light. "Treasure," she says.

If I ever had patience, it just dissipated. "What are you talking about?"

"Midas is ours," the mermaid screeches. "We watch and collect and take treasure when it falls, and he is treasure and gold and *not yours*."

"What's mine," I say, "is for me to decide."

The mermaid shakes her head. "Not yours!" she screams, and dives toward me.

She snatches my hair and pulls, bearing her nails into my shoulders and shaking me. She screams and bites. Sinks her teeth into my arm and tries to tear away chunks of flesh.

Unimpressed by the attack, I clasp the mermaid's head and smash it against my own. She falls back, her lidless eyes wide. She floats for a moment, dazed, and then lets out a high shriek and comes for me again.

As we collide, I use the force to pull the mermaid to the surface. She gasps for breath, air a toxic poison for her gills. I laugh when the mermaid clutches at her throat with one hand and tries to claw at me with the other. It's a pitiful attempt.

"It's you."

My eyes shoot upward. The Prince of Midas stares down at us, horrified and awestricken. His lips tilt a little to the left.

"Look at you," he whispers. "My monster, come to find me."

I regard him with as much curiosity as he regards me. The way his black hair sweeps messily by his shadowed jaw, falling across his forehead as he leans to get a better look. The deep dimple in his left cheek and the look of wonder in his eyes. But in the moments I choose to tear my gaze from the mermaid, the creature seizes the opportunity and propels us both forward. We smash against the ship with such force that the entire vessel groans with our shared power. I have little time to register the attack before the prince stumbles and crashes into the water beside us.

The mermaid pulls me under again, but once she sees the prince in the water, she backs away in awe. He sinks like a stone to the bottom of the shallow sea and then makes to propel his body back toward the surface.

"My treasure," says the mermaid. She reaches out and clutches the prince's hand, holding him beneath the surface. "Is your heart gold? Treasure and treasure and gold."

I hiss a monstrous laugh. "He can't speak *Psáriin*, you fool."

The mermaid spins her head to me, a full 180 degrees. She lets out an ungodly squeal and then finishes the circle to turn back to the prince. "I collect treasure," she continues. "Treasure and hearts and I only eat one. Now I eat both and become what you are."

The prince struggles as the mermaid keeps him trapped beneath the water. He kicks and thrashes, but she's transfixed. She strokes his shirt, and her nails rip through the fabric, drawing his blood. Then her jaw loosens to an unimaginable size.

The prince's movements go slack and his eyes begin to drift closed. He's drowning, and the mermaid plans to take his heart for herself. Take it and eat it in hopes that it might turn her into what he is. Fins to legs. Fish to something more. She'll steal the thing I need to win back my mother's favor.

I'm so furious that I don't even think before I reach out and sink my nails into the mermaid's skull. In shock, the creature releases the prince and he floats back to the surface. I tighten my grip. The mermaid thrashes and scratches at my hands, but her strength is nothing compared to that of a siren's. Especially mine. Especially when I have my sights on a kill.

My fingers press deeper into the mermaid's skull and disappear inside her rainbow flesh. I can feel the sharp bone of her skeleton. The mermaid stills, but I don't stop. I dig my fingers deeper and pull.

Her head falls to the ocean floor.

I think about bringing it to my mother as a trophy. Sticking it on a pike outside of the Keto palace as a warning to all mermaids who would dare challenge a siren. But the Sea Queen wouldn't approve. Mermaids are her subjects, lesser beings or not. I take one last disdainful look at the creature and then swim to the surface in search of my prince.

I spot him quickly, on the edge of a small patch of sand by the docks. He's coughing so violently that the act shakes his entire body. He spits out great gasps of water and then collapses onto his stomach. I swim as close to shore as I can and then pull myself the rest of the way, until only the tip of my fin is left in the shallows of the water.

I reach out and grab the prince's ankle, dragging him down so his body is level with mine.

I nudge his shoulder and when he doesn't move, I roll him onto his back. Sand sticks to the gold of his cheeks and his lips part ever so slightly, wet with ocean. He looks half-dead already.

His shirt clings to his skin, blood seeping through the slashes the mermaid tore. His chest barely moves with his breath and if I couldn't hear the faint sound of his heart, then I would think for certain he was nothing more than a beautiful corpse.

I press a hand to his face and draw a fingernail from the corner of his eye to his cheek. A thin red line bubbles above his skin, but he doesn't stir. His jaw is so sharp, it could cut through me.

Slowly, I reach under his shirt and press a hand against his chest. His heart thumps desperately beneath my palm. I lean my head against it and listen to the drumming with a smile. I can smell the ocean on him, an unmistakable salt, but mingled beneath it all is the faint aroma of aniseed. He smells like the black sweets of the anglers. The saccharine oil they use to lure their catch.

I find myself wishing him awake so I can catch a glimpse of those seaweed eyes before I take his heart and give it to my mother. I lift my head from his chest and hover my hand over his heart. My nails clutch his skin, and I prepare to plunge my fist deeper.

"Your Highness!"

I snap my head up. A legion of royal guards runs across the docks and toward us. I look back to the prince and his eyes begin to open. His head lolls in the sand and then his gaze focuses. On me. His eyes narrow as he takes in the color of my hair and the single eye that matches. He doesn't look worried that my nails are dug into his chest, or scared by his impending death. Instead he looks resolute. And oddly satisfied.

I don't have time to think about what that means. The guards are fast approaching, screaming for their prince, guns and swords at the ready. All of them pointed at me. I glance down at the prince's chest once more, and the heart I came so close to winning. Then quicker than light, I dart back to the ocean and away from him.

II

Elian

MY DREAMS ARE THICK with blood that is not mine. It's never mine, because I'm as immortal in my dreams as I seem to be in real life. I'm made of scars and memories, neither of which have any real bearing.

It's been two days since the attack, and the siren's face haunts my nights. Or what little I remember of her. Whenever I try to recall a single moment, all I see are her eyes. One like sunset and the other like the ocean I love so much.

The Princes' Bane.

I was half-groggy when I woke on the shore, but I could have done something. Reached for the knife tucked in my belt and let it drink her blood. Smashed my fist across her cheek and held her down while a guard fetched my father. I could have killed her, but I didn't, because she's a wonder. A creature that has eluded me for so long and then, finally, appeared. Let me be privy to a face few men live to speak about.

My monster found me and I'm going to find her right back.

"It's an outrage!"

The king bursts into my room, red-faced. My mother floats in after him, wearing a green kalasiris and an exasperated expression. When she sees me, her brow knits.

"None of them can tell me a thing," my father says. "What use are sea wardens if they don't warden the damn sea?"

"Darling." My mother places a gentle hand on his shoulder. "They look for ships on the surface. I don't recall us telling them to swim underwater and search for sirens."

"It should go without saying!" My father is incensed. "Initiative is what those men need. Especially with their future king here. They should have known the sea bitch would come for him."

"Radames," my mother scolds. "Your son would prefer your concern to your rage."

My father turns to me, as if only just noticing I'm there, despite it being my room. I can see the moment he notices the line of sweat that coats my forehead and seeps from my body to the sheets.

His face softens. "Are you feeling better?" he asks. "I could fetch the physician."

"I'm fine." The hoarseness of my voice betrays the lie.

"You don't look it."

I wave him off, hating that I suddenly feel like a child again, needing my father to protect me from the monsters. "I don't imagine anyone looks their best before breakfast," I say. "I bet I could still woo any of the women at court, though."

My mother shoots me an admonishing look.

"I'm going to dismiss them all," my father says, continuing on as though my sickliness hadn't given him pause. "Every sorry excuse for a sea warden we have."

I lean against the headboard. "I think you're overreacting."

"Overreacting! You could have been killed on our own land in broad daylight."

I lift myself from bed. I sway a little, unsteady on my feet, but recover quickly enough for it to go unnoticed. "I hardly blame the wardens for failing to spot her," I say, lifting my shirt from the floor. "It takes a trained eye."

Which is true, incidentally, though I doubt my father cares. He doesn't even seem to remember that the sea wardens watch the surface for enemy ships and are not, in any way, required to search underneath for devils and demons. The *Saad* is home to the few men and women in the world mad enough to try.

"Eyes like yours?" My father scoffs. "Let's just hire some of those rapscallions you ramble around with, then."

My mother gleams. "What a wonderful idea."

"It was not!" argues my father. "I was being flippant, Isa."

"Yet it was the least foolish thing I've heard you say in days."

I grin at them and walk over to my father, placing a comforting hand on his shoulder. The anger disappears from his eyes and he wears a look similar to resignation. He knows as well as I do that there is only one thing to be done, and that's for me to leave. I suspect half of my father's anger comes from knowing that. After all, Midas is a sanctuary my father spouts as a safe haven from the devils I hunt. An escape for me to return to if I ever need it. Now the attack has made a liar of him.

"Don't worry," I say. "I'll make sure the siren suffers for it."

It isn't until I speak the words that I realize how much I mean them. My home is tainted with the same danger as the rest of my life, and it doesn't sit right with me. Sirens belong in the sea, and those two parts of me – the prince and the hunter – have remained separate. I hate that their merging wasn't because I was brave enough to stop pretending and tell my parents I never plan on becoming king and that whenever

I am home, I feel like a fraud. How I think carefully about every word and action before saying or doing anything, just to be sure it is the right thing. The done thing. My two selves were thrust together because the Princes' Bane forced my hand. She spurred into action something I should have been brave enough to do myself all along.

I hate her for it.

On the deck of the *Saad* later that day, my crew gathers around me. Two hundred men and women with fury on their faces as they regard the scratch below my eye. It's the only wound they can see, though there are plenty more hidden beneath my shirt. A circle of fingernails right where my heart is. Pieces of the siren still embedded in my chest.

"I've given you dangerous orders in the past," I say to my crew. "And you've done them without a single complaint. Well" – I shoot them a grin – "most of you."

A few of them smirk in Kye's direction and he salutes proudly.

"But this is different." I take in a breath, readying myself. "I need a crew of around a hundred volunteers. Really, I'll take any of you I can get, but I think you know that without some of you, the journey won't be possible at all." I look over to my chief engineer and he nods in silent understanding.

The rest of the crew stares up at me with equally strong looks of fidelity. People say you can't choose your family, but I've done just that with each and every member of the *Saad*. I've handpicked them all, and those who I didn't sought me out. We chose one another, every ragtag one of us.

"Whatever vows of loyalty you've sworn, I won't hold you to them. Your honor isn't in question, and anyone who doesn't volunteer won't be thought any less of. If we succeed, every single member of this crew will be welcomed back with open arms when we sail again. I want to make that clear."

"Enough speeches!" yells Kye. "Get to the point so I know whether to pack my long johns."

Beside him, Madrid rolls her eyes. "Don't forget your purse, too."

I feel laughter on my lips, but I swallow it and continue on. "A few days ago a man came to me with a story about a rare stone that has the power to kill the Sea Queen."

"How's it possible?" someone asks from the crowd.

"It's not possible!" another voice shouts.

"Someone once told me that taking a crew of felons and misfits across the seas to hunt for the world's most deadly monsters wasn't possible," I say. "That we'd all die within a week."

"I don't know about you lot," Kye says, "but my heart's still beating."

I shoot him a smile.

"The world has been led to believe the Sea Queen can't be killed by any man-made weapons," I say. "But this stone wasn't made by man; it was crafted by the original families from their purest magic. If we use it, then the Sea Queen could die before she's able to pass her trident on to the Princes' Bane. It'll rid their entire race of any true power once and for all."

Madrid steps to the front, elbowing men out of her way. Kye follows behind her, but she keeps her eyes on me with a hard stare. "That's all well and good, Cap," she says. "But isn't it the Princes' Bane who we should be worrying about?"

"The only reason we haven't turned her to foam is because we can't find her. If we kill her mother, then she should show her face. Not to mention that it's the queen's magic that gives the sirens their gifts. If we destroy the queen, they'll all be weak, including the Princes' Bane. The seas will be ours."

"And how do we find the Sea Queen?" Kye asks. "I'd follow you to the ends of the earth, but their kingdom is in the middle of a lost sea. Nobody knows where it is."

"We don't need to know where their kingdom is. We don't even need to know where the Diávolos Sea is. The only thing we need to know is how to sail to Págos."

"Págos." Madrid says the word with a frown. "You're not seriously considering *that*."

"It's where the crystal is," I tell her. "And once we have it, the Sea Queen will come to us."

"So we just head on down to the ice kingdom and ask the snow folk to hand it over?" someone asks.

I hesitate. "Not exactly. The crystal isn't *in* Págos. It's on top of it."

"The Cloud Mountain," Kye clarifies for the rest of the crew. "Our captain wants us to climb to the top of the coldest mountain in the world. One that's killed everybody who's tried."

Madrid scoffs as they start to murmur. "And," she adds, "all for a mythical crystal that may or may not lead the most fearsome creature in the world to our door."

I glare at them both, unamused by the double act, or the sudden doubt in their voices. This is the first time they've questioned me, and the feeling isn't something I plan to get used to.

"That's the gist of it," I say.

There's a pause, and I try my best not to move or do anything but look unyielding. Like I can be trusted. Like I have any kind of a damn clue what I'm doing. Like I probably won't get them all killed.

"Well." Madrid turns to Kye. "I think it sounds like fun."

"I guess you're right," he says, as though following me is an inconvenience he never considered before. He turns to me. "Count us in then."

"I suppose I can spare some time too, since you asked so nicely!" another voice shouts.

"Can hardly say no to such a temptin' offer, Cap!"

"Go on then, if everyone else is so keen."

So many of them yell and nod, pledging their lives to me with a smile. Like it's all just a game to them. With every new hand that shoots up comes a whooping holler from those who have already agreed. They howl at the possibility of death and how much company they're going to have in it. They're insane and wonderful.

I'm no stranger to devotion. When people at court look at me, I see the mindless loyalty that comes with not knowing any better. Something that is natural to those who have never questioned the bizarre order of things. But when my crew looks at me now, I see the kind of loyalty that I've earned. Like I deserve the right to lead them to whatever fate I see fit.

Now there's just one thing left for me to do before we set sail for the land of ice.

12

Elian

THE GOLDEN GOOSE IS the only constant in Midas. Every inch of land seems to grow and change when I'm gone, with small evolutions that never seem gradual to me, but the Golden Goose is as it has always been. It didn't plant the golden flowers outside its doors that all of the houses once did, as was fashion, with remnants of them still seen in the depths of the wildflowers that now swallow them. Nor did it erect sandy pillars or hang wind chimes or remodel its roof to point like the pyramids. It is in untouched timelessness, so whenever I return and something about my home is different, I can be sure it's never the Golden Goose. Never Sakura.

It's early and the sun is still a milky orange. I thought it best to visit the dregs of the Golden Goose when the rest of Midas was still sleeping. It didn't seem wise to ask a favor from its ice-born landlord, with swells of patrons drunkenly eavesdropping. I knock on the redwood door, and a splinter slides into my knuckle. I withdraw it just as the door swings open. Sakura looks unsurprised on the other side.

"I knew it would be you." She peers behind me. "Isn't the tattooed one with you?"

"Madrid is preparing the ship," I tell her. "We set sail today."

"Shame." Sakura slings a dishrag over her shoulder. "You're not nearly as pretty."

I don't argue. "Can I come in?"

"A prince can ask for favors on a doorstep, like everyone else."

"Your doorstep doesn't have whiskey."

Sakura smiles, her dark red lips curling to one side. She spreads her arms out, gesturing for me to come inside. "I hope you have full pockets."

I enter, keeping my eyes trained on her. It's not like I think she might try something untoward – kill me, perhaps, right here in the Golden Goose – not when our relationship is so profitable to her. But there is something about Sakura that has always unnerved me, and I'm not the only one. There aren't many who can manage a bar like the Golden Goose, with patrons who collect sin like precious jewels. Brawls and fights are constant, and most nights spill more blood than whiskey. Yet when Sakura tells them enough, the men and women cease. Adjust their respective collars, spit onto the grimy floor, and continue on with their drinks as though nothing happened at all. Arguably, she is the most fearsome woman in Midas. And I don't make a habit of turning my back on fearsome women.

Sakura steps behind the bar and pours a slosh of amber liquid into a glass. As I sit opposite, she brings the glass to her lips and takes a quick sip. A print of murky red lipstick stains the rim, and I note the fortuitous timing.

Sakura slides the glass over to me. "Satisfied?" she asks.

She means because it isn't poisoned. I may scan the seas looking for monsters that could literally rip my heart out, but that doesn't mean I'm careless. There isn't a single thing I eat or drink when we're docked that hasn't been tasted by someone else first. Usually, this duty falls to Torik, who volunteered the moment I took him aboard and insists that he's not putting his life at risk because even the greatest of poisons couldn't kill him. Taking into account his sheer size alone, I'm inclined to agree.

Kye, of course, declined the responsibility. *If I die saving your life*, he said, *then who's going to protect you?*

I eye Sakura's smudged lipstick and smirk, twisting the glass to avoid the mark before I take a sip of whiskey.

"No need for pretense," says Sakura. "You should just ask."

"You know why I'm here, then."

"The whole of Midas is talking about your siren." Sakura leans back against the liquor cabinet. "Don't think there is a single thing that goes on here that I'm not aware of."

Her eyes are sharper than ever and narrowed in a way that tells me there are very few of my secrets she doesn't know. A prince may have the luxury of discretion, but a pirate does not. I know that many of my conversations have been stolen by strangers and sold to the highest bidders. Sakura has been one of those sellers for a while, trading information for gold whenever the opportunity presents itself. So of course she was careful to overhear the man who came to me in the dead of night, speaking stories of her home and the treasure it holds.

"I want you to come with me."

Sakura laughs and the sound doesn't suit the grave look on her face. "Is that an order from the prince?"

"It's a request."

"Then I deny it."

"You know" – I wipe the stain from my glass – "your lipstick is smudged."

Sakura takes in the print of dark red on the rim of my glass and presses a finger to her lips. When it comes away clean, she glowers. I can see her plainly now, as the thing I have always known she is. The snow-faced woman with lips bluer than any siren's eye.

A blue reserved for royalty.

The natives of Págos are like no other race in the hundred kingdoms, but the royal family is a breed unto themselves. Carved from great blocks of ice, their skin is that much paler, their hair that much whiter, and their lips are the same blue as their seal.

"Have you known for a while?" Sakura asks.

"It's the reason I've let you get away with so much," I tell her. "I didn't want to reveal your secret until I found a way to put it to good use." I raise my glass in a toast. "Long live Princess Yukiko of Págos."

Sakura's face doesn't change at the mention of her real name. Instead she looks at me blankly, as though it's been so long that she doesn't even recognize her own name.

"Who else knows?" she asks.

"I haven't told anybody yet." I emphasize the *yet* more crudely than necessary. "Though I don't understand why you'd even care. Your brother took the crown over a decade ago. It's not like you have a claim to the throne. You can go where you like and do as you please. Nobody wants to assassinate a royal who can't rule."

Sakura looks at me candidly. "I'm aware of that."

"Then why the secrecy?" I ask. "I haven't heard anything about a missing princess, so I can only assume that your family knows where you are."

"I'm no runaway," says Sakura.

"Then what are you?"

"Something you will never be," she sneers. "Free."

I set my glass down harder than I intend. "How lucky for you, then."

It's easy for Sakura to be free. She has four older brothers with claims to the throne before her and so none of the responsibilities my father likes to remind me are still heavy on my shoulders.

"I left once Kazue took the crown," Sakura says. "With three brothers to counsel him, I knew I'd have no wisdom to offer that they couldn't. I was twenty-five and had no taste for the life of a royal who would never rule. I told my brothers this. I told them I wanted to see more than snow and ice. I wanted color." She looks at me. "I wanted to see gold."

I snort. "And now?"

"Now I hate the vile shade."

I laugh. "Sometimes I feel the same. But it's still the most beautiful city in all of the hundred kingdoms."

"You'd know better than me," Sakura says.

"Yet you stay."

"Homes are hard to find."

I think about the truth of that. I understand it better than anyone, because nowhere I've traveled ever really feels like home. Even Midas, which is so beautiful and filled with so many people I love. I feel safe here, but not like I belong. The only place I could ever call home and mean it is the *Saad*. And that's constantly moving and changing. Rarely in the same place twice. Maybe I love it because it belongs nowhere, not even in Midas, where it was built. And yet it also belongs everywhere.

I swirl the final remnants of my whiskey and look to Sakura. "So then it would be a shame if people discovered who you were. Being a Págese immigrant is one thing, but being a royal without a country is another. How would they treat you?"

"Little prince." Sakura licks her lips. "Are you trying to blackmail your favor?"

"Of course not," I say, though my voice says something else. "I'm simply saying that it would be inconvenient if people found out. Especially considering your patrons."

"For them," says Sakura. "They would try to use me and I would have to kill them. I would probably have to kill half of my customers."

"I think that's bad for business."

"But being a killer has worked out so well for you."

I don't react to this, but my lack of emotion seems to be the exact reaction Sakura wants. She smiles, so beautiful, even though it's so clearly mocking. I think about what a shame it is that she's twice my age, because she's striking when she's wicked, and wild underneath the pretense.

"Come to Págos with me," I say.

"No." Sakura turns away from me.

"No, you won't come?"

"No, that isn't what you want to ask."

I stand. "Help me find the Crystal of Keto."

Sakura turns back to me. "There it is." There is no sign of a smile on her face now. "You want a Págese to help you climb the Cloud Mountain and find your fairy tale."

"It's not like I can just stroll in and scale your most deadly mountain with no idea of what I'll be dealing with. Will your brother even give me entry? With you by my side, you can advise me on the best course of action. Tell me the route I should take. Help convince the king to give me safe passage."

"I am an expert at climbing mountains." Sakura's voice is wholly sarcastic.

"You were required to do it on your sixteenth birthday." I try to hide my impatience. "Every Págese royal is. You could help me."

"I am so warm of heart."

"I'm asking for—"

"You're *begging*," she says. "And for something impossible. Nobody but my family can survive the climb. It's in our blood."

I slam my fist on the table. "The storybooks may peddle that, but I know better. There must be another route. A hidden way. A secret kept in your family. If you won't come with me, then tell me what it is."

"It wouldn't matter either way."

"What does that mean?"

She runs a tongue across her blue lips. "If this crystal does exist in the mountain, then it's surely hidden in the locked dome of the ice palace."

"A locked dome," I say blankly. "Are you making this up as you go along?"

"We're perfectly aware of the legends written in all of those children's books," she says. "My family has been trying to find a way into that room for generations, but there's no other entry than the one that can be plainly seen and no way of forcing our way in. It's magically sealed, perhaps by the original families themselves. What's needed is a key. A necklace lost to our family. Without that, it doesn't matter how many mountains you bargain your way up. You'll never be able to find what you're looking for."

"Let me worry about that," I say. "Finding lost treasure is a specialty of mine."

"And the ritual needed to release the crystal from its prison?" Sakura asks. "I'm assuming you found out about that, too?"

"Not any specifics."

"That's because nobody knows them. How do you plan to conduct an ancient rite if you don't even know what it is?"

In truth, I thought Sakura might be able to fill in the blanks there.

"The secret is probably on your necklace," I tell her, hoping it's true. "It could be a simple inscription we need to read. And if it's not, then I'll figure something else out."

Sakura laughs. "Say you're right," she says. "Say legends are easy to come by. Say even lost necklaces and ancient rituals are too. Say maps and routes are the most elusive thing. Who's to say I'd ever share such a thing with you?"

"I could leak your identity to everyone." The words taste petty and childish on my lips.

"How beneath you," Sakura says. "Try again."

I pause. Sakura isn't refusing to help. She's simply giving me the opportunity to make it worth her while. Everyone has a price, even the forgotten Págese princess. I just have to find out what hers is. Money seems irrelevant, and the thought of offering her any makes me grimace. She could take it as an insult (she is royalty, after all), or see me more as a child than a captain, which I so clearly am in her presence. I have to give her something nobody else can. An opportunity she'll never get again and so won't dream of passing up.

I think about how similar Sakura and I are. Two royals trying to escape their countries. Only, Sakura hadn't wanted to leave Págos because she disliked being a princess, but because the job had become useless once her brother took the crown.

No taste for the life of a royal who would never rule.

I feel a sinking sensation in my stomach. At heart, Sakura is a queen. The only problem is that she doesn't have a country. I understand then what my quest will cost me if I want it enough.

"I can make you a queen."

Sakura arches a white brow. "I hope that you're not

threatening to kill my brothers," she says. "Because the Págese don't turn against one another for the sake of a crown."

"Not at all." I compose myself as best I can. "I'm offering you another country entirely."

A slow look of realization works its way onto Sakura's face. Coyly, she asks, "And what country would that be, Your Highness?"

It will mean the end of the life I love. The end of the *Saad* and the ocean and the world I have seen twice over and would see again a thousand times. I would live the life of a king, as my father has always wanted, with a snow-born wife to rule by my side. An alliance between ice and gold. It'd be more than my father imagined, and wouldn't it be worth it in the end? Why will I have to search the sea once all of its monsters have been destroyed? I'll be satisfied, maybe, ruling Midas, once I know the world is out of danger.

But even as I list the reasons it's a good plan, I know they're all lies. I'm a prince by name and nothing else. Even if I manage to conquer the sirens and bring peace to the ocean, I've always planned to stay on the *Saad* with my crew – if they'd still follow me – no longer searching, but always moving. Anything else will make me miserable. Staying still, in one place and one moment, will make me miserable. In my heart, I'm as wild as the ocean that raised me.

I take a breath. I'll be miserable, then, if that's what it takes.

"This country. If there's a map that shows a secret route up the mountain so my crew and I can avoid freezing to death during the climb, then it'll be a fair trade."

I hold out my hand to Sakura. To the princess of Págos.

"If you give me that map, I'll make you my queen."

13

Lira

I'VE MADE A MISTAKE. It started with a prince, as most stories do. Once I felt the thrum of his heart beneath my fingers, I couldn't forget it. And so I watched from the water, waiting for him to reappear. But it was days before he did and once he had, he never neared the ocean without a legion by his side.

Singing to him by the docks was risk enough, with the promise of royal guards and passersby coming to the young hunter's rescue. But with his crew there, it was something else. I could sense the difference in those men and women and the way they followed the prince, moved when he moved, stayed still in rapt attention whenever he spoke to them. A kind of loyalty that can't be bought. They would jump into the ocean after him and sacrifice their lives for his, as though I would take such a trade.

So rather than attack, I watched and listened as they spoke in stories, of stones with the power to destroy worlds. The Second Eye of Keto. A legend my mother has been hunting for her entire reign. The humans spoke of heading to the ice kingdom in search of it, and I knew it would be my best opportunity. If I followed them to the snow sea, then the waters would be too cold for any human to survive, and the prince's crew could do nothing but watch him die.

I had a plan. But my mistake was to think that my mother didn't.

As I watched the prince, the Sea Queen watched me. And when I ventured from the Midasan docks in search of food, my mother made herself known.

The smell of desecration is ripe. A line of bodies – sharks and octopi – scatter through the water as a trail for me to follow. I swim through the corpses of animals I would have feasted on any other day.

"I'm surprised you came," says the Sea Queen.

My mother looks majestic, hovering in a circle of carcasses. Remains drip from the symbols on her skin and her tentacles sway lethally beside her.

My jaw tightens. "I can explain."

"I imagine you have many explanations in that sweet little head of yours," says the queen. "Of course, I'm not interested in them."

"Mother." My hands curl to fists. "I left the kingdom for a reason."

An image of the golden prince weighs in my mind. If I hadn't hesitated on the beach and been so concerned with savoring the sweet smell of his skin, then I wouldn't need explanations. I would only need to present his heart, and the Sea Queen would show me mercy.

"You saved a human." Her voice is as dead as night.

I shake my head. "That's not true."

The queen's tentacles crash into the ocean bed, and a mighty wave of sand washes over me, knocking me to the floor. I bite back a cough as the shingle catches in my throat.

"You insult me with your lies," she seethes. "You saved a human, and not just any human, but the one who kills us. Is it because you live to disobey me?" she asks. And then, with a disgusted snarl: "Or perhaps you've grown weak. Silly little girl, bewitched by a prince. Tell me, was it his smile that did it? Did it bring your heart to life and make you love him like some common mermaid?"

My mind spins. I can barely be outraged through the confusion. *Love* is a word we scarcely hear in the ocean. It exists only in my song and on the lips of the princes I've killed. And I have never heard it from my mother's mouth. I'm not even sure what it really means. To me, it has always been just a word that humans treasure for reasons I can't comprehend. There isn't even a way to say it in *Psáriin*. Yet my mother is accusing me of feeling it. Is it the same fealty I have for Kahlia? That force that drives me to protect her without even thinking? If that's true, then it makes the accusation even more baffling, because all I want is to kill the prince, and though I may not know what love is, I'm sure it isn't that.

"You're mistaken," I tell my mother.

A corner of the queen's lips coils in revulsion. "You murdered a mermaid for him."

"She was trying to eat his heart!"

Her eyes narrow. "And why," she asks, "would that be a bad thing? Let the creature take his filthy heart and swallow it whole."

"He was mine," I argue. "A gift for you! A tribute for my eighteenth."

The queen stops to comprehend this. "You hunted a prince for your birthday," she says.

"Yes. But, Mother—"

The Sea Queen's gaze darkens and in an instant one of her tentacles reaches out and snatches me from the ocean floor. "You insolent thing!"

Her tentacles tighten around my throat, squeezing until the ocean blurs. I feel the shiver of danger. I'm deadly, but the Sea Queen is something more. Something less.

"Mother," I plead.

But the queen only squeezes tighter at the sound of my voice. If she wanted, she could snap my neck in two. Take my head like I took the mermaid's. Perhaps even my heart, too.

The queen throws me onto the ocean bed and I grab at my throat, touching the tender spot, only to snatch my hand away as the bones crack and throb with the contact. Above me the queen rises, towering like a dark shadow. Around us the water dulls in color, becoming gray and then seeping to black, as though the ocean is stained with her fury.

"You are not worthy to be my heir," the Sea Queen hisses.

When I part my lips to speak, all I taste is acid. The ocean salt is replaced by burning magic that sizzles down my throat. I can barely breathe through the pain.

"You are not worthy of the life you have been given."

"Don't," I beg.

Barely a whisper, barely a word. A crack in the air masquerading as a voice, just like my aunt Crestell's had before she was killed.

"You think you're the Princes' Bane." The Sea Queen roars with laughter. "But you are the prince's savior."

She raises her trident, carved from the bones of the goddess Keto. Bones like night. Bones of magic. In the center, the trident ruby awaits its orders.

"Let us see," sneers the queen, "if there is any hope for redemption left in you."

She taps the base of the trident onto the floor, and I feel pain like nothing I could have imagined. My bones snap and realign themselves. Blood pours from my mouth and ears, melting through my skin. My gills. My fin splits, tearing me straight down the middle. Breaking me in two. The scales that once shimmered like stars are severed in moments, and beneath my breast comes a beating I have never known. It feels like a thousand fists pounding from the inside.

I clutch at my chest, nails digging in, trying to claw whatever it is out of me. Set it free. The thing trapped inside and so desperately pounding to be released.

Then, through it all, my mother's voice calls, "If you are the mighty Princes' Bane, then you should be able to steal this prince's heart even without your voice. Without your song."

I try to cling to consciousness, but the ocean is choking me. Salt and blood scrape down my throat until I can only gasp and thrash. But I hold on. I don't know what will happen if I close my eyes. I don't know if I'll ever open them again.

"If you want to return," growls the Sea Queen, "then bring me his heart before the solstice."

I try to focus, but my mother's words turn to echoes. Sounds I can't make out. Can't understand or bear to focus on. I've been torn apart and it's not enough for her.

My eyes begin to shut. The black of the sea blurring in the backs of my eyes. The seawater swirls in my ears until nothing but numbness remains. With a last glance at the blurry shadow of my queen, I close my eyes and give in to the darkness.

14

Elian

THE PYRAMID DISAPPEARS BEHIND the horizon. The sun is climbing higher, gold against gold. We sail onward, leaving the shining city behind, until the ocean turns blue once more and my eyes adjust to the vast expanse of color. It always takes a while. At first, the blues are muted. The whites of the clouds dotted with bronze as leftover shimmers from Midas float across my eyes. But soon the world comes bursting back, vivid and unyielding. The coral of the fish and the bluebell sky.

Everything is behind me now. The pyramid and my family and the bargain I struck with Sakura. And in front of me: the world. Ready to be taken.

I clutch the parchment in my hand. The map of passageways hidden throughout the mighty Cloud Mountain, kept secret by the Págese royals. Ensuring safety when they make their way up the mountain to prove their worth to the people. I've bargained my future for it, and all I need now is the Págese necklace. Good thing I know just where to look.

I didn't tell my family about my engagement. I'm saving that for after I get myself killed. Telling my crew was more than enough hassle, and if their mortifying jibes hadn't been trouble enough, Madrid's outrage that I would bargain myself away had been. Spending half her life being sold from ship to ship left her with an inflexible focus on freedom in every aspect.

The only comfort I could offer – and it seemed strange to be the one offering comfort in this kind of situation – is that I have no intention of going through with it. Not that I'm planning to go back on my word. I'm not that sort of a man, and Sakura is not the sort of woman who would take betrayal lightly. But there's something that can be done. Some other deal to be struck that will give us both what we want. I just need to introduce another player to the game.

I stand on the quarterdeck and survey the *Saad*. The sun has disappeared, and the only light comes from the moon and the flickering lanterns aboard the ship. Belowdecks, most of my skeleton crew – an apt name for my volunteers – are asleep. Or swapping jokes and lewd stories in place of lullabies. The few that remain above deck are still and subdued in a way they rarely are.

We are sailing toward Eidýllio, one of the few stops we have to make before we reach Págos and the very key to my plan. Eidýllio holds the only replacement for my hand in marriage that Sakura will consider accepting.

On deck, Torik is playing cards with Madrid, who claims to be the best at any game my first mate can think of. The match is quiet and marked only by sharp intakes of breath whenever Torik takes another smoke of his cigar. By his feet is my assistant engineer, who disappears belowdecks every once in a while only to reappear, take a seat on the floor, and continue sewing the holes in his socks.

The night brings out something different in all of them. The *Saad* is home and they're safe here, finally able to let their guards down for a few rare moments. To them, the sea is never the true danger. Even crawling with sirens and sharks and beasts that can devour them whole in seconds. The true danger is people. They are the unpredictable. The betrayers and the liars. And on the *Saad*, they are a world away.

"So this map will lead us to the crystal?" asks Kye.

I shrug. "Maybe just to our deaths."

He places a hand on my shoulder. "Have some confidence," he tells me. "You haven't steered us wrong yet."

"That just means nobody will be prepared when I do."

Kye gives me a disparaging look. We're the same age, but he has a funny way of making me feel younger. More like the boy I am than the captain I try to be.

"That's the thing about risks," Kye says. "It's impossible to know which ones are worth it until it's too late."

"You're getting really poetic in your old age," I tell him. "Let's just hope you're right and the map is actually useful in helping us not freeze to death. I'm pretty attached to all my fingers and toes."

"I still can't believe you bargained away your future for a piece of parchment," Kye says. His hand is on his knife, as though just talking about Sakura makes him think of battle.

"Weren't you just telling me that risks can be worthwhile?"

"Not the kind that land you in unholy matrimony with a *princess*." He says the last word like it's dirty and the thought of my marrying another royal doesn't bear thinking about.

"You make a good point," I tell him. "But I'm going to offer Sakura a better prize than myself. As unlikely as that may sound. It's the reason we're going to Eidýllio in the first place, so don't act so resigned to my fate just yet. I have a plan; the least you can do is have faith."

"Except that your plans always end in scars."

"The ladies love them."

"Not when they're shaped like bite marks."

I grin. "I doubt the Queen of Eidýllio is going to cannibalize us."

"There's a lot of land between us and her," says Kye. "Plenty of time for me to be eaten somewhere along the way."

Despite his qualms, Kye doesn't seem put out by my evasiveness. He never seems to mind elusive retorts and vague, almost flippant, answers. It's like the thrill of the hunt might just be in the not knowing. Often, I've shared the sentiment. The less I knew, the more I had the chance to discover. But now I wish I knew more than what was written in a children's book, tucked away in the desk of my cabin.

The text speaks of the very top of the Cloud Mountain, the farthest point from the sea, and the palace that was made from the last frozen breath of the sea goddess Keto. A holy place that only Págese royals are allowed to enter on their sacred pilgrimages. It's there that they sit in prayer and worship the gods who carved them. It's there they stay for sixteen days. And it's there, in the center of this holy palace, that the crystal lies. Probably.

This whole quest is based on rumor and hearsay, and the only upside to any of it is that the missing necklace has prevented Sakura and her family from ever getting inside the locked dome. It's not likely I'd be able to use the crystal if it was already in their possession. Just imagining the conversation with the Págese king makes me flinch. *Would you kindly allow me and my pirate crew to borrow one of the world's most powerful sources of magic for a few days? After I kill my immortal enemy, I promise I'll bring it right back.*

At least if I'm the one to find the crystal, it gives me the upper hand. But despite the small comfort that brings, Sakura's talk of hidden domes and lost keys in the shape of necklaces makes things trickier. If I can't find that necklace, then I've bargained everything for nothing. Then again, the fact that her family has been searching for generations without any luck doesn't mean much. After all, none of them are me.

"You fancy a game?" Madrid looks up at me. "As it happens, Torik is a sore loser."

"And you're a mighty cheat," says Torik. "She's got cards up her sleeve."

"The only thing I have up my sleeve is tricks and talent."

"There!" Torik points. "You see. Tricks."

From the floor, the assistant engineer looks up at them. "I didn't see any cheating." He threads a needle through a pair of patchwork socks.

"Ha." Torik clips him around the ear halfheartedly. "You were too busy knittin'."

"I'm *sewing*," he disputes. "And if you don't want me to, I'll throw your lot overboard."

Torik grunts. "Attitude," he says. Then, to me, "All I get is attitude."

"It's all you give, too," I tell him.

"I give my heart and soul," Torik protests.

"My mistake," I say. "I wasn't aware you had either of those things."

Beside me, Kye sniggers. "It's why he always loses," he says. "No heart and so no imagination."

"You be careful I don't imagine throwin' you overboard," Torik calls up to him. "What do you think, Cap? Do we really need another siren hunter on this quest?"

"Kye cooks, too," Madrid says, sorting the deck back in order.

Torik shakes his head. "I reckon we can lay the nets and catch our own fish for supper. We'll grill 'em up nice enough without your pretty boy."

Madrid doesn't bother to reply, and just as I'm about to come back in her place, something catches my eye in the distance. A strange shadow in the middle of the ocean. A figure on the water. I squint and pull the golden telescope from my belt loop.

To Kye, I say, "Northwest," and my friend produces a small pair of binoculars from his own belt. "Do you see it?" I ask.

"It's a man."

I shake my head. "Just the opposite." I squint, black-rimmed eye pressed fiercely to the looking glass. "It's a girl."

"What's a girl doin' in the middle of the damn ocean?" Torik climbs the steps toward us.

On the main deck, Madrid slots the cards back into the packet. Dryly, she says, "Perhaps she's catching her own fish for supper."

Torik shoots her a look. "There are sharks out there."

"Perfect with rice."

I roll my eyes.

Thankfully, the girl is floating and not drowning. Strangely, she isn't doing much else. She's just there, in the ocean, with nothing and no one around her. I suck in a breath and, in the same instant, the girl turns toward the ship. It seems impossible, but in that moment I swear she looks straight at me. Through me.

"What's she doing?"

I turn to Kye. "She's isn't doing anything," I say. "She's just there."

But when I turn to look back, she isn't. And in her place, there's a deadly stillness.

"Kye!" I yell, rushing to the edge of the ship. "Full speed ahead. Circle around and prepare the buoy. Wake the rest of the crew and have them at the ready. It could be a trap."

"Captain, don't be reckless!" shouts Torik.

"It's probably a trick," Madrid agrees.

I ignore them and head forward, but Kye puts a gloved hand on my shoulder, holding me back. "Elian, stop. There could be sirens in the water."

My jaw tightens. "I'm not letting anyone else die because of a damned siren."

Kye squares his shoulders. "Then let me go instead."

Madrid pauses for a moment and then, slower than usual, hoists her gun over her shoulder.

I place my hand on top of Kye's. His gesture has nothing to do with heroism – because he wants to save the drowning girl – and everything to do with loyalty. Because what he really wants is to save me. But if there's one thing in the world that I don't need, it's saving. I've risked my life enough times to know it's charmed.

"Don't let me drown," I say.

And then I jump.

The water feels like nails. A terrific legion of stabbing iron pierces my flesh until my breath catches in my chest and gets stuck there. I can't imagine what the Págese waters will feel like in comparison. I can't imagine their country and their mountain and my fingers remaining on my hands as I climb it.

I swim deeper and let my head spin.

It's dark enough beneath the water that the farther I swim, the more I doubt I'll reach the surface again. But in the distance, even buried beneath the ocean, I can hear the rumble of the *Saad*. I can feel the water being pushed and sliced as my ship chases after me. And then I see her.

Sinking to the bottom of the ocean, her eyes closed and her arms spread out like wings. A naked girl with hair to her elbows.

I swim toward her for an eternity. Closer and deeper, until it seems like she might hit the shingle before I get to her. When my hands finally clamp around her waist, I find myself wincing at how cold she is. Colder than the ocean.

She's heavier than I expect. A sinking stone. Dead weight. And no matter how roughly I haul her up, how my hands dig into her stomach and my arms crush around her ribs, she doesn't stir. I worry that I'm too late, but I can't bear the thought of leaving her to the sharks and monsters.

With an explosion of breath, I burst through the water's surface.

The *Saad* is close and within seconds a buoy is tossed into the ocean beside me. I slide it over the girl, wrapping her limp wrist around the rope so the crew can pull her in first.

It's an odd sight to see a lifeless body heaved onto the ship. Her skin is so pale against the dark wood of the *Saad*, one wrist tied to the buoy and the other hanging helplessly below. When my crew finally hauls me up, I don't stop to catch my breath before rushing over. I spit salt water onto the deck and fall to my knees beside her, willing her to move. It's too soon. Too early in our journey to have a body on our hands. And as much as I like to think that I've grown accustomed to death, I've also never seen a dead woman before. At least, not one who wasn't half-monster.

I look at the unconscious girl and wonder where she came from. There are no ships in the distance and no land on the horizon. It's as though she appeared from nowhere. Born from the ocean itself.

I unbutton my dripping shirt and slide it over the girl's naked body like a blanket. The sudden movement seems to jolt her, and with a gasping breath, her eyes shoot open. They're as blue as Sakura's lips.

She rolls to her stomach and coughs up the ocean, heaving until there seems to be no more water left in her. When she turns to me, the first thing I notice are her freckles, shaped like stars. Constellations dotted across her face like the ones I name while the rest of my crew sleeps. Her hair sticks to her cheeks, a deep, dark red. Muted and so close to brown. She looks young – younger than me, maybe – and, inexplicably, when she reaches for me, I allow myself to be pulled into her.

She bites her lip, hard. It's cracked and furiously pale, just like her skin. There's something about the action and how wild it looks on her. Something about her ocean eyes and the way she strokes my collar softly. Something familiar and hypnotic. She whispers something, a single guttural word that sounds harsh against her lips. I can't make sense of it, but whatever it is, it makes me dizzy. I lean in closer and place a hand on her wrist.

"I don't understand."

She sits up, swaying, and grips my collar more tightly. Then, louder, she says it again. *Gouroúni*. She spits it like a weapon and her face twists. A sudden change from the innocent girl to something far crueler. Almost murderous. I recoil, but for once I'm not quick enough. The girl raises a shaking hand and brings it down across my cheek. Hard.

I fall back.

"Cap!" Torik reaches for me.

I dismiss his hand and stare at the girl. She's smirking. A ghost of satisfaction painted on her pale, pale lips before her eyes flutter closed and her head hits the deck.

I rub the edge of my jaw. "Kye." I don't take my eyes off the ocean girl. "Get the rope."

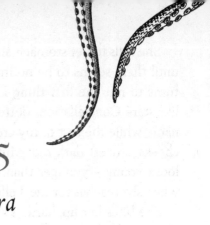

15

Lira

WHEN I WAKE, I'M bound to a railing.

Golden rope is looped around one of my wrists, lassoing it to the wooden barrier that overlooks the ship's deck. I taste bile that keeps on burning, and I'm cold, which is the most unnatural feeling in the world, because I've spent a lifetime marveling in ice. Now, the cold makes me numb and tinges my skin blue. I ache for warmth, and the faint glow of the sun on my face feels like ecstasy.

I bite my lip, feeling newly blunt teeth against my skin. With a shuddering breath, I look down and see legs. Sickly pale things that are crossed awkwardly beneath me, dotted by bruises. Some in big patches, others like tiny fingerprints. And feet, too, with toes pink from the cold.

My fins are gone. My mother has damned me. I want to die.

"Oh good, you're awake."

I drag my head from the railing to see a man staring down at me. A man who is also a prince, whose heart I once had within reach. He's watching me with curious eyes, black hair still wet on the ends, dripping onto perfectly dry clothes.

Beside him is a man larger than any I've seen, with skin

almost as black as the ship itself. He stands beside the prince, hand on the hilt of a long sword that hangs from a ribbon on his waistcoat. And two more: a brown-skinned girl with tattoos spread up her arms and on the sides of her cheeks, wearing large gold earrings and a suspicious glance. Standing defensively beside her is a sharp-jawed boy who taps his finger against a knife in his belt.

On the deck below, so many more glare up at me.

I saw their faces. Moments before the world went dark. Did the prince save me from drowning? The thought makes me furious. I open my mouth to tell him that he had no right to touch me, or that he should have let me drown in the ocean I call home just to spite my mother. Just because she deserved it. Let my death be a lesson to her.

Instead I say, "You're a good swimmer," in my best Midasan.

"You're not," he retorts.

He looks amused and not at all frightened by the deadly creature before him. Which means that he's either an idiot or he doesn't know who I am. Possibly both, though I don't think the prince would waste time binding me to a railing if he planned to kill me. I wonder how different my mother's spell has made me appear for him not to recognize me.

I look at the others. They watch the prince expectantly. Waiting for his orders and his verdict. They want to know what he plans to do with me, and I can sense how anxious they are as my identity remains a mystery. They like strangers even less than I do, and staring into each of their grimy faces, I know they'll toss me overboard if their prince commands it.

I look to the prince and try to find the right words in Midasan. What little I've spoken of the language tastes odd on my tongue, its vowels twisting together all too slowly. It tastes as it sounds, like warmth and gold. My voice isn't my own when I speak it. My accent is far too sharp to loop the words, and so my tongue hisses on the strange letters.

Carefully, I say, "Do you always tie women to your ship?"

"Only the pretty ones."

The tattooed girl rolls her eyes. "Prince Charming," she says.

The prince laughs, and the sound of it makes me lick my lips. My mother wants him dead, but she wants me to do it as a human to prove my worth as future ruler of the sea. If I can just get close enough.

"Untie me," I command.

"You should thank me before barking orders," says the prince. "After all, I saved you *and* clothed you."

I look down and realize that it's true. A large black shirt scratches my legs, the damp fabric sticking to my new body.

"Where did you come from?" the prince asks.

"Did someone throw you overboard while you were getting undressed?" asks the girl.

"Maybe they threw her overboard because she was getting undressed," says the boy with the knife.

This is met with laughter from the rest of them.

"Forgive us," says the prince. "But it's not every day we find a naked girl drowning in the middle of the ocean. Especially with no other ships in sight. Especially one who slaps me after I save her."

"You deserved it."

"I was helping you."

"Exactly."

The prince considers this and then pulls a small circular contraption from his pocket. It looks like a compass of some sort, and when he speaks again, his eyes stay pinned to it, voice deceptively casual.

"I can't quite place your accent," he says. "Where is it that you're from?"

An eerie sensation settles in my chest. I avert my eyes from the object, hating how it feels when I look at it. Like it's staring straight back.

"Untie me," I say.

"What's your name?" the prince asks.

"Untie me."

"I see you don't know much Midasan." He shakes his head. "Tell me your name first."

He switches his gaze from the compass to me, assessing, as I try to think of a lie. But it's hopeless because I don't know any human names to lie with. I've never lingered enough to hear them, and unlike the mermaids who spy on humans whenever they can, I've never cared to learn more about my prey.

With a fierce spit, I say, "Lira."

He glances down at the compass and smiles. "Lira," he repeats, pocketing the small object. My name sounds melodic on his lips. Less like the weapon it had been when I said it. "I'm Elian," he says, though I didn't ask. A prince is a prince and his name is as inconsequential as his life.

I lean my free hand against the top of the railing and pull myself to my feet. My legs shake violently and then buckle beneath me. I slam onto the deck and let out a hiss of pain. Elian watches, and it's only after a short pause that he holds out a wary hand. Unable to bear him standing over me, I take it. His grip is strong enough to lift me back onto my unsteady feet. When I nearly topple again, his hand shoots to my elbow and holds me firmly in place.

"It's shock." He reaches for his knife and cuts the thread that binds me to the railing. "You'll be steady again in no time. Just take a breath."

"I'd be steadier if I weren't on this ship."

Elian raises an eyebrow. "You were a lot more charming when you were unconscious."

I narrow my eyes and press a hand to his chest to balance myself. I can feel the slow drum of his heart beneath my hand, and in moments I'm taken back to Midas. When I had been so close to stealing it.

Elian stiffens and slowly prizes my hand from his chest, placing it back on the railing. He reaches into the pocket of his trousers and lifts out a small rope necklace. The string is a shimmer of blue, glistening like water under the sun. It's liquid made into something other, too smooth to be ice and too solid to be ocean. It sparkles against the gold of Elian's skin, and when he opens his hand, he reveals the pendant that hangs from the bottom. Sharply curved edges stained with crab red. My lips part and I touch a hand to my neck, where my seashell once hung. Nothing.

Furious, I leap toward Elian, my hands like claws. But my legs are too unsteady, and the attempt nearly sends me back to the floor.

"Steady on there, damsel." Elian grabs my elbow to hold me upright.

I rip my arm from him and bare my teeth monstrously. "Give it to me," I order.

He tilts his head. "Why would I do that?"

"Because it's mine!"

"Is it?" He runs a thumb over the ridges of the seashell. "As far as I know, this is a necklace for monsters, and you certainly don't *look* like one of those."

I clench my fists. "I want you to give it to me."

I feel maddened by the Midasan on my tongue. Its smooth sounds are too quaint to display my anger. I itch to spit the knives of my own language at him. Tear him down with the skewers of *Psáriin*, where each word can wound.

"What's it worth?" asks Elian.

I glare. "What do you mean?"

"Nothing's free in the ocean," he explains. "What's the necklace worth to you?"

"Your life."

He laughs, and beside him the large man lets out a good-natured chuckle. I'm unsure what's so funny, but before I can ask, Elian says, "I don't imagine my life is worth much to you at all."

He is so very wrong about that.

"Mine then," I say.

And I mean it, because that necklace is the key to finding my way home. Or at the very least, calling for help. If it can't lead me back to my kingdom as a human, then it can at least summon Kahlia. She can speak to the Sea Queen on my behalf and beg her to rescind the punishment so I won't have to.

"Your life," Elian repeats. He takes a few steps toward me. "Careful who you tell that to. A worse man might hold you to it."

I push him away. "And you're a better man?"

"I like to think so."

He holds the seashell up to the sunlight. Blood against sky. I can see the curiosity in his eyes as he wonders what a castaway is doing with such a trinket. I ponder if he knows what it's even for, or if it's just something he has seen on the necks of his murdered sirens.

"Please," I say, and Elian's eyes dart back to me.

I've never used that word in any language, and even though Elian can't possibly know that, he looks unsettled. There's a crack in the bravado. After all, I'm a half-naked girl being held prisoner and he's a human prince. Royal by birth and destined to lead an empire. Chivalry is in his veins, and all I need to do is remind him of it.

"Would you like me to beg you?" I ask, and Elian's jaw tightens.

"If you just tell me why you have it, then I'll give it back."

He sounds sincere, but I know better. Pirates are liars by trade and royals are liars by blood. I know that firsthand.

"My mother gave it to me," I say.

"A gift." Elian ponders this. "Passed through your family from how far back? Do you know what it does or how it works?"

I grind my teeth. I should have known his questions wouldn't end until he ripped the truth from me. I would give it to him gladly on any other day, but I'm defenseless on this ship without the music of my voice to sing him into submission. I can barely even stand on my own. The seashell is my last hope, and he's keeping it from me.

I lunge for it once more. I'm quick, even as a human, and my fingers close around his fist in an instant. But Elian is faster somehow, and as soon as my hand locks on to his, Elian's knife is on my neck.

"Really." He presses his blade firmly against my throat, and I feel a small slash of pain. "That wasn't so smart."

I tighten my hand around his fist, unwilling to let go. The cut on my neck stings, but I have felt and caused far worse. His face is roguish when I sneer up at him, nothing like the sweet and gentle princes I've taken before. The ones whose hearts are buried beneath my bed. Elian is as much a soldier as I am.

"Captain!" A man emerges from the lower deck, his eyes

wide. "The radars spotted one!"

Quickly, Elian looks to the knife-wielding boy. "Kye," he says. Just a name, just a word, and yet the boy nods abruptly and jumps the length of the stairs to the decks below.

In an instant Elian tears his blade from my throat and sheathes it. "Get in position!" he yells. He loops my seashell around his neck and runs for the edge of the ship.

"What are you doing?" I ask.

Elian turns to me, a glint of mischief in his eyes. "It's your lucky day, Lira," he says. "You're about to meet your first siren."

16

Lira

I WATCH THE HUMANS jumping from one end of the boat to another, pulling on ropes and yelling words and names I don't quite understand. At one point the boy with the knife – Kye – trips and slices his palm. Quickly, the tattooed girl rips the bandana from her head and throws it to him, before running to the wheel and lurching it left. The ship twists too quickly for me to stay steady, and I collapse to the floor again.

I screech in frustration and search the decks for my captor. Prince Elian leans over the edge, one arm tangled in rope, the other holding the mysterious object up to the light.

"Steady," he tells his crew. "Hold her steady."

He whispers something to himself. A slew of Midasan that I can't make out, much less understand, and then smiles at the compass and screams, "Torik, now!"

The large man leans his head into the lower decks and bellows at the crew. As soon as the boom of his voice shudders through my bones, a high-pitched whistle tears through the air. I bring my hands to my ears. It's not so much a noise as it is a blade carving through my skull. A sound so shrill, I feel like my eardrums could explode. Around me, the humans seem unaffected, and so with a grimace, I lower my hands and try to hide my discomfort.

"I'm going in," Elian calls over his shoulder. He throws the compass to the girl. "Madrid, lower the net on my signal."

She nods as he pulls a small tube from his belt and places it into his mouth. Then he's gone. He meets the water with barely a noise, so quiet that I stumble to the edge of the ship to make sure that he actually jumped. Sure enough, ripples pool on the surface and the prince is nowhere to be seen.

"What is he doing?" I ask.

"Playing the part," Madrid replies.

"What part?"

She pulls a small crossbow from her belt and fixes an arrow in the latch. "Bait."

"He's a prince," I observe. "He can't be bait."

"He's a prince," she says. "So he gets to decide who's bait."

Kye hands her a black quiver filled with arrows and cuts me a guarded glance. "If you're so concerned, we can always throw you over instead."

I ignore both the comment and the hostile look in his eyes. Human pettiness knows no bounds. "Surely he can't breathe for long," I say.

"Five minutes of air," Madrid tells me. "It's what the tube's for. Nifty little thing the captain picked up a while back in Efévresi."

Efévresi. The land of invention. It's one of the few kingdoms I've been careful to steer clear of, made cautious by the machinery that patrols their waters. Nets made from lightning and drones that swim faster than any mermaid. Ships more like beasts, with a knowledge and intelligence of their own.

"When the captain comes back up, you'll get to see

something wonderful," Kye tells me.

"Monsters," says Madrid, "are not wonderful."

"Watching them die is pretty wonderful." Kye looks pointedly in my direction. "That's what happens to our enemies, you see."

Madrid scoffs. "Keep watch for the captain's signal," she says.

"He told you to do that."

She smiles. "And technically, darling, I outrank you."

Kye scratches his face with his middle finger, which is apparently not a flattering gesture, because a moment later Madrid's jaw drops and she swipes to hit his shoulder. Kye weaves effortlessly out of the way and then grabs her hand midair, pulling her toward him. When Madrid opens her mouth to say something, he presses his lips to hers and snatches a kiss. Like a thief stealing a moment. I half-expect her to shoot him with the crossbow – I know I would – but when he breaks away, she only shoves him halfheartedly. Her smile is ruthless.

I turn from them and clutch the ship ledge for support. The sun boils down on my bare legs and the wind hums softly by my ear. The shrill ringing has mellowed to a faint echo around me, making everything seem too quiet. Too peaceful. Under the sea, it's never so serene. There's always screaming and crashing and tearing. There's always the ocean, constantly moving and evolving into something new. Never still and never the same. On land, on this ship, everything is far too steady.

"Ignore Kye," says Madrid. She stands beside me. "He's always like that."

"Like what?"

"Ridiculous," she says, then turns to him. "If the sonar cuts

~ 104 ~

again, go belowdecks and give that engineer a piece of your knife."

"The sonar?" I ask.

"It's that ringing," she explains. "Doesn't bother us much, but the sirens go mad on it. Hits their nerves and disables them."

Kye plucks the dirt from under his thumbnail with a knife. "It stops them from singing their little song and drowning us all."

I grit my teeth. Typical humans using their dirty tricks of technology to fight their wars for them. I've never heard of something that can take away a siren's power, but experiencing the awful tearing in my skull makes it easy to believe. I wonder how excruciating it would be to hear it in my siren form. If it would be akin to my mother's magic.

"I know we look pretty run-down," Madrid says. "The crew's normally a lot bigger, but we're on a bit of a special case. Captain cut us in half for his latest whim."

I eye her strangely. "I didn't ask you about your crew."

She laughs and pushes a curl from her face. Without the bandana, her hair is riotous. "I figured you'd have questions," she says. "Not everyone wakes up to find themselves on the infamous siren ship in the company of the golden prince. No doubt you've heard the best and worst about us. I just want you to know that only half the stories are true."

She grins at this last part, smiling as though we're old allies. As though she has reason to feel comfortable around me.

"You can't be aboard our ship and not know the ins and outs," Madrid says.

Kye makes a contemptuous noise. "I don't think Cap wants strangers knowing the ins of any of our outs."

"And what if she becomes part of the crew?"

"If wearing the captain's shirt made someone part of the crew, then half of the girls in Eidýllio would be sailing with us."

"Good," Madrid says. "We need some more female blood."

"We get enough of that spilled on the deck from sirens."

"Sea foam doesn't count," she snipes, and the disdainful look Kye had when talking about me disappears in place of an impish grin.

"You like making up the rules as you go along. Don't you, love?"

Madrid shrugs and turns back to me, inked arms spread open like wings. "Welcome to the *Saad*, Lira," she says.

And then Elian erupts from the ocean.

To my instant relief, the sonar dissipates, and though it leaves a ringing in my ears, the pain subsides instantaneously. Kye's lips draw a smile and, at the same time, Elian draws a breath, sending the ship into a frenzy. From the water, a net claws its way to the surface, turning the ocean to mighty waves. Inside, a creature thrashes and hisses, her tangled fin the only thing keeping her from the prince and his heart.

Elian sits on the other side, knife in hand, and watches the siren. She scratches at him, but the net is wide and they're separated by at least three feet. Still, Elian looks on guard, one hand gripped in the net to keep himself steady and the other clasping his knife.

"If you've got a minute," Elian calls up to the ship, "I wouldn't mind coming aboard."

"Get moving!" Torik bellows to the rest of the crew. "I want that damn net up here five minutes ago."

Kye rushes to his side and twists the rope that is hoisting the net up to them. He leans back so his entire body is balanced against it. He is breathless with the weight in moments.

Below, the siren screeches so venomously that I can barely make out the *Psáriin* on her tongue. She's bleeding, though I can't see from where. The red seems to cover so much of her, like paint against her skin. As the net is drawn back to the ship, she continues to thrash wildly and the whistle sounds again. I clench my hands by my sides to keep from bringing them to my ears. The siren is maddened. Her hands fly to her face and she tears her nails through her cheeks, trying to rip the noise out. Her screams are like death itself. A sound that makes my newly formed toes curl against the ship.

Kye pulls the rope harder, his arms dripping with sweat. When the net finally reaches the top, he hands the rope over to another crew member and then rushes to his prince's side. Within moments, the net is untangled and Elian is pulled free.

Kye and Madrid clasp his elbows and drag him out of harm's way. As they do, I see that his arms are cut. Slashes so similar to the day the mermaid tried to steal his heart from me. Quickly, Kye tears his sleeve and grabs Elian's hand. It's punctured with deep, dark holes. The blood is black red and nothing at all like the gold I've heard. The sight of it gives me pause.

"Are you mad?" Kye yells. He uses his shirt as a makeshift bandage. "I can't believe you got into that thing."

"It was the only way." Elian shakes his hand as though shaking off the injury. "She wouldn't be lured."

"You could've nicked an artery," Madrid says. "Don't think we'd waste good stitches on you if you were going to bleed to death anyhow."

Elian smirks at her insubordination. Everything is a game to him. Loyalty is mockery and devotion is kinship in place of fear. He is a riddle, disguised as a ruler, able to laugh at the idea of disloyalty as though it would never be an option. I can't fathom such a thing.

"If you're gonna keep this up," Kye says, "we should invest in some safer nets."

I look to the net in question and almost smile. It's a web of wire and glass. Shards weave into one another so that their twisted metal can make a nimble cage. It's monstrous and glorious.

Inside, the siren wails.

"She's clever," says Elian, coming to my side. "Normally the noise confuses them so much that I stand by the net and they fly in. She wouldn't have it though. Wouldn't go unless I did."

The crew gathers with their weapons at the ready.

"She was trying to outsmart you," I say, and Elian grins.

"She can try to be smarter, but she'll never be quicker."

I scoff at his arrogance and turn to the creature he has caught in his web. I'm almost eager to see the siren stupid enough to fall for such a trap, but at the sight of her face, an unfamiliar feeling settles into my stomach.

I know her.

A sleek charcoal fin that smudges across the deck. Cold black hair stringing over her cheeks and nails carved to shanks. She snarls, baring her fangs and slapping her fin violently against the wire. In the background the whistle hums, and whenever I think she might sing, she whimpers instead. I take a step closer and she narrows her eyes. One brown, the other a mix of blue and blood. Curdled by a scar that stretches to her lip.

Maeve.

"Be careful," Elian says, his hand hovering by my arm. "They're deadly."

I turn to him, but he's looking at the siren, seaweed eyes sharper than her nails.

"*Aidiastikó gouroúni*," Maeve growls.

Disgusting pig.

Her words are a mirror of the ones I spoke when Elian saved me from drowning.

"Be calm," I tell her, then grimace when I realize I'm still speaking Midasan.

When the siren's eyes meet mine, they're full of the same hatred we've always shared for each other. It almost makes me laugh to think that even as strangers, our animosity can be so ripe, stretching beyond the bounds of knowing.

Maeve spits on the deck. "Filthy human whore," she says in *Psáriin*.

Instinctively, I lurch forward, but Elian yanks me back by the waist. I kick violently against him, desperate to get at the defiant girl in front of me. Siren or not, I won't let the insult stand.

"Stop." Elian's voice is muffled by my hair. "If you want to get yourself killed, one of us can do the job a lot tidier."

"Let her go." Kye laughs. "I want to see how that ends."

I writhe against Elian, scratching at his arms like the animal I am. "After what she just called me," I say, "it's going to end with her heart on the floor."

Maeve cackles and uses her finger to draw a *Psáriin* circle on her palm. When my eyes widen at the insult, she only laughs more. It's a symbol reserved for the lowest beings. For mermaids that lie dying as their fins are stapled into the sand in punishment. For humans unworthy of a siren's presence. To make that gesture to the royal bloodline is punishable by death.

"Kill her," I seethe. "*Áschimi lígo skýla.*"

"Human scum!" Maeve screeches in return.

Elian's breath is hot on my neck as he struggles to keep

ahold of me. "What did you say?"

"Filthy little bitch," I translate in Midasan. "*Tha sas skotóso ton eaftó mou.*"

I'll kill you myself.

I'm about to break free, but the second Elian releases his grip on my waist, his hands clamp down on my shoulders. He twists me around and I'm thrown against the door of the lower deck. When he leans over me, the scent of black sweets is fragrant on his breath.

I dismiss him and make to move past, but he's too quick, even for me, and blocks my path, pushing me back against the varnished wood. Slowly, he brings a hand to the paneling beside my head, closing me in.

"You speak *Psáriin.*"

His voice is throaty, his eyes as dark as the blood that seeps from his hand. Behind him, the crew keeps a watchful eye on Maeve, but every moment or so they shoot surreptitious glances our way. In my madness, I forgot myself. Or perhaps I remembered myself. I spat my language like it was the most natural thing in the world. Which, to a human, it would never be.

Elian is close enough that if I listened, I'd be able to hear his heartbeat. If I stilled, I'd be able to feel the thumps pulsing through the air between us. I look down to his chest, where the strings of his shirt have loosened to reveal a circle of nails. My parting gift.

"Lira," he says. "You better have a damn good explanation."

I try to think of an answer, but out of the corner of my eye I see Maeve still at the mention of my name. Suddenly she's squinting at me, leaning forward so the net pierces through her arms.

I hiss and Maeve scrambles back.

"*Prinkípissa!*" she says.

Princess.

She shakes her head. She was ready to die at the hands of pirates, but now that she stares into the eyes of her princess, fear finally dawns on her face.

"You understand her," says Elian.

"I understand many things."

I push him away and he gestures for his crew to let me approach their prisoner.

"*Parakaló*," Maeve screams as I near. "*Parakaló!*"

"What's she saying?" asks Madrid.

She points her weapon at Maeve, as all of the crew does. Swords and bullets to hide behind, because humans don't possess the innate strength to defend themselves. Only unlike the others, Madrid's gun is not so much a gun at all. Somewhere along the way, she discarded the crossbow in place of something far more deadly. Gold-polished metal gleams in the shape of a rifle, but a long black spear rests below the site, the tip dipped in the purest silver. Yet despite having such an elaborate weapon, Madrid doesn't look eager to attack. She looks as though she would rather keep her hands clean of murder.

I turn back to Maeve and watch the fear settle into her eyes. There's never been anything close to tolerance between us, but it was only recently we began to consider ourselves enemies. Or rather, Maeve began to consider me an enemy and I enjoyed the compliment.

I take in her muddled eye, rippled by blood and shadowed by scars. I blinded her, not so long ago, with the blunt end of a coral piece. Now, whenever she blinks, her right eye stays open. Thinking back, I can't remember why I did it. Maeve said something, perhaps. Did something that I disliked enough to punish her. Really, she could have done anything and it wouldn't have mattered, because most of all I just wanted to hurt her. For whatever reason and no reason. I wanted to hear her scream.

It is like that in the sea. Brutal and unrelenting. Filled with endless cruelty that has no recompense. There was a time when I wanted nothing more than to kill Maeve but feared my mother's wrath too much to act. Now the opportunity is here. Perhaps not to do it myself, but to watch as someone else does. The enemy of my enemy.

"Tell us what she's saying," Kye demands.

"She's not saying anything." I stare at Maeve. "She's begging."

"Begging."

Elian is beside me, an unreadable expression on his face as he repeats my words. He clasps the knife in his wounded hand, and when his blood drips down the blade, it disappears. Metal drinking metal. I can feel the sorcery roll from it like thunder. The whispers of a weapon begging him to spill more blood so it can get its fill. It's soaked in enough magic to sing like one of my melodies, but Elian doesn't succumb to its refrain. His expression is hesitant and it's been a long time since I've seen such a thing in the eyes of a killer. Yet Elian stares down at Maeve as though the thought of her pleading makes the whole thing wrong. Dirty.

"She's begging," he says. "Are you sure?"

"*Parakaló*," I repeat. "It means 'please.' "

17

Elian

I'VE NEVER KILLED A begging thing.

As the siren cowers on my deck, I'm perfectly aware that she is a monster. She's whimpering, but even the sound is wicked. A mix of hisses and throaty laments. I'm not sure why she's so scared when moments ago a net made of glass and spikes barely made her wince. Part of me wants to feel proud that my reputation has finally preceded me. The other part, perhaps the smarter part, is sure that I have nothing to be proud of.

I gaze over at Lira. Her graveyard-dirt hair clings to her shoulders as she sways with the motion of my ship. There's something about her slight frame that makes her look menacing, as though every angle is a weapon. She barely blinks at the siren, who is now disfigured with gashes. As I stare at her, I see nothing of the wraith-like girl I pulled from the ocean. Whatever spell had threatened to transfix me when I saved her is broken now, and I can see quite clearly that she's no helpless damsel. She's something more, and it makes me too curious for my own good.

The *Psáriin* she spoke lingers in the air. A language forbidden in most kingdoms, including my own. I want to know how she learned it, when she got close enough, why she kept one of their necklaces noosed like a trophy around her neck. I want to know everything.

"Will you kill her?" Lira asks.

There's no more sweet pretense as she tries to speak my language. I'm not sure where she's from, but whatever kingdom it is clearly has no love for mine.

"Yes."

"Will it be quick?"

"Yes."

She scoffs. "Shame."

The siren whimpers again and repeats a slew of *Psáriin*. It's so quick and guttural that I barely make out the words. Still, one of them sticks in my mind, clearer than the others. *Prinkípissa*. Whatever it means, she says it with fear and reverence. A combination I'm rarely used to seeing. In my kingdom, those who revere me don't know me well enough to fear me. And those who fear me know me far too well to do something as unwise as adore me.

"Your knife," Lira says.

My hand forms a fist around the handle. My wound drips, and I feel the blade quickly soak it up. No blood gone to waste.

"It has a strange magic."

I look at her pointedly. "I don't think you're in a position to say what's strange."

Lira doesn't reply, and in her silence Kye steps forward. "Cap," he says. "Be careful. She can't be trusted."

At first I think he's talking about the monster on our deck, and I'm about to tell him that I'm not an idiot when I realize the siren isn't the one Kye's looking at. Lira is in his sights.

If there's one thing in the world Kye has never had, it's tact. But Lira doesn't pay attention to the accusation. She doesn't even glance in his direction, like the allegation is nothing more than ocean water dripping off her.

"I'll deal with her," I tell Kye. "When I'm ready."

"Maybe you should be ready now."

I tap the tip of my knife against my finger and step forward, but Kye grabs my arm. I look down at his hands, gripping the fabric of my shirt. Kye's greatest strength is that he's as suspicious as I am reckless. He doesn't like surprises and takes every possible threat as a threat on my life. Every warning as a promise. But with him to do it for me, there's no need for me to waste time worrying. Besides, spending my life on the ocean has taught me to see what others can't and to expect what they won't. I know better than to trust a stranger on a pirate ship, but relying on instinct is far better than relying on doubt.

"Didn't you hear what I just said?" he asks.

Carefully, I take Kye's hand from my arm. "I can assure you, there's nothing wrong with my hearing."

"Just your common sense, then," Lira says.

I watch her swipe the hair from her face. "How's that?" I ask.

"If you had any, then you would have killed her by now." Lira points to the siren. "Her heart could be cold in your hands."

Kye arches an eyebrow. "Damn," he says. "What sort of ship did she get thrown off of?"

Beside him, Madrid adjusts her stance, weapon never wavering as her feet shift. She's anxious, and I can feel it as much as I can see it. Madrid never wants to kill, whether it's monsters or men. In Kléftes she killed enough to last a lifetime, and in some reverse twist of fate it instilled her with more morals and scruples than before. Neither of which have a place on the *Saad*. But she is the best marksman I have, and if I ignore her principles, then it makes her one of my best chances at not dying.

"It's the sirens who take the hearts," Madrid tells Lira. "Not us."

The knife gleams in my hand. "I've taken plenty of hearts."

I watch the siren, getting as close as I can without slicing my boots on the net. I think of Cristian drowning in the ocean, the lie of a kiss on his mouth. For all I know, this could be the siren who did it. There was another one with the Princes' Bane; I've gathered that much from the tales that spread throughout my kingdom. Cristian's murderer could be on my ship.

The siren says something to Lira, and I wonder if she's begging again. If Cristian begged, or if he was so far under the siren's spell that he died willingly.

"Hold her down," I say.

A spear shoots from Madrid's gun, piercing through the center of the siren's fin. Pinning her to my ship. I resist the urge to look at Madrid, knowing the grim look of resignation she'll be wearing. As good a shot as she is, Madrid is an even better person.

I kick pieces of netting away and crouch down beside the imprisoned creature. This part always makes me feel less human, as though the way I kill draws a moral boundary.

"I want you to tell me something," I say. "And I'd appreciate your doing it in my language."

"*Poté den tha.*"

The siren writhes beneath the spear that staples her to the *Saad*. It's dipped in silver thinite, which is deadly to their kind. Its slow poison coagulates at the entry point, stopping the wound from seeping onto my ship and, given enough time, stopping what scraps of a heart she might have.

"That's not Midasan," I tell her. I clasp my compass, eyeing the steady points of the face. "What do you know about the Crystal of Keto?"

The siren's lips part and she looks at Lira, shaking her head. *"Egó den tha sas prodósei."*

"Lira," I say. "I don't suppose you'd be kind enough to translate?"

"I've never been accused of kindness before."

Her voice is closer than I would like, and I shift when I see her shadow hovering next to mine. She's as quick as she is quiet, capable of sneaking up on even me. The thought is unsettling, but I push it to the back of my mind before I consider it too much. It's a dangerous thing to be distracted with a monster so close.

Lira crouches beside me. For a moment she's quiet. Her storm-blue eyes narrow at the spear in the center of the siren's fin. She's trying to decide something. It could be whether she's disgusted by our violence and if she should hide it, but I can't see any sign of repulsion. Then again, a mask is the easiest thing to slip on. There's nothing in my own eyes, despite the sick feeling creeping up in my stomach with the siren's screams. I push it away, as I do everything. A captain doesn't have the luxury of guilt.

Lira stands and she's newly steady as she looks down at the dying creature. "Maybe it would be helpful," she says, "if you take out her other eye."

I flinch and a smile presses to the corner of Lira's pale lips. I don't know if it's because the siren is so scared, or if Lira is simply pleased by the look on my face. If she said it just to see how I'd react.

"I'd be depriving her of your winning smile," I say.

Lira cocks an eyebrow. "She's your enemy. Don't you want her in pain?"

She looks at me as though I've lost all sense. My crew tends to look at me the same way, though not usually on the days when I refuse to torture. There are many things the world can say about the siren hunters of the *Saad*, but one thing that could never be true is that we enjoy this life. The ocean, yes, but never the death. It's a necessary evil to keep the world safe, and as dishonorable as killing is, it has purpose. If I start to like it, then I become the very thing I'm trying to protect the world from.

"Soldiers don't enjoy war," I say.

Lira purses her lips, but just as she opens her mouth to say something, I'm thrown onto my back. My head cracks against the floor, and pain explodes in my temples.

The siren is on top of me.

She scratches and bites, making an ungodly howl. I dodge her attacks as she tries desperately to take a chunk out of me. Her fin is a mess of clotted blood, ripped straight down the middle. She must have torn herself free.

"I can't get a clear shot!" someone says. "I'm gonna hit him."

"Me either!"

"Madrid!" Kye yells. "Madrid, shoot it now!"

"I can't." I hear the sound of a gun being thrown to the floor. "Damn thing is wedged again."

I struggle beneath the venomous creature. Her face is fangs and hate and nothing else. She is hungry for part of me. Heart or not, she'll take whatever piece she can.

The weight of her presses down, crushing my ribs. There's a crack, and then I can barely breathe through the pain. Around me, my crew shouts so loudly that it's almost incomprehensible. As their voices turn to noise, my arms burn with aching. The siren is too strong. Stronger than me, by far.

Then, just as suddenly as it came, the heaviness disappears. My breath rushes back.

Kye grips her devil shoulders and rips the siren from me. She skitters and slides across the deck before colliding furiously with the cabin wall. My crew jumps out of the way to let her body skim past them. The sound of her impact shakes the *Saad*.

The siren digs her fingernails into the deck, shoulders arched. She hisses and lurches forward. Quickly, I grab my knife. I ignore the furious pain in my ribs as I let the featherlight blade take aim in my hand and then hurl it through the air. It glides into what is left of her heart.

Most of the blood blisters onto her skin, but the remnants that threaten to spill onto my deck are quickly drunk up by my knife. The siren screams.

As Kye pulls me to my feet, I catch a discreet breath, not daring to show that I was surprised. Even if it's obvious. It's my job to expect the unexpected, and I was stupid enough to turn my back on a killer.

"Are you all right?" Kye asks, searching for wounds. He glares at the blood on my arm. "I should've been faster."

The look on his face rips through me as much as the siren did, and so I roll my shoulder, careful not to wince as the pain in my ribs intensifies with each moment. "All in a day's work," I say, and turn to Madrid. "Your gun jammed again?"

Madrid picks up her discarded weapon and studies the spear mechanism. "I don't get it," she says. "I'll have to bring it belowdecks for another service."

She starts to walk to the other side of the deck and then abruptly stops when she notices the siren's body blocking the doorway. Madrid swallows and waits patiently. They all do.

Perfectly silent until the moment the siren begins to fade. The sight is never anything less than a wonder to them, even after all this time. But I don't look at the lifeless creature turning to foam on my deck. I've seen a hundred monsters die. Instead I turn to the strange girl I pulled from the ocean.

Lira isn't smiling anymore.

18

Lira

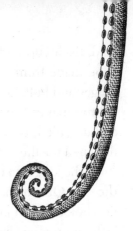

MAEVE DISSOLVES INTO NOTHING.

Killing a siren is not like killing a mermaid. Their rotting corpses stain the ocean floor and skeleton among the coral, while we dissolve into the very thing that made us. Into ocean and foam and the salt in our veins. When we're gone, there's nothing left to remember.

I thought I'd be glad when Maeve died, but the battle between our species wages on and I've just helped the humans in their bid to slaughter us. At the very least, the prince didn't cut out her heart before he killed her. I've never paid mind to legends, unless I'm the legend of discussion, but even I know the stories. Ones that warn of any human who holds a siren's heart being granted immunity to our song. It's said that's why we turn to sea foam when we die, that it's not a curse to erase us from the world but a blessing from Keto to ensure a human can never take our hearts.

After Maeve disappears, I'm taken belowdecks to a windowless room that smells of aniseed and rust. The walls are not walls but thick drapes that hang from a varnished ceiling. Their damp edges catch the floor, and as the ship pierces on, they sway and reveal endless lines. Of books, weapons, and gold. Each curtain has its own secret. In the center is a large cube made from black glass. It's as thick as I am long, with hinges and bolts that are heavy gold. The same kind that the eel-mermaid's brooch was made from. It's a prison of sorts and doesn't appear to be designed for humans. Or, if it is, it's designed for the worst kind.

In the kingdom of Keto, we don't keep prisoners. Betraying the Sea Queen means giving up your life, and so we have no choice but to be what my mother says we are. Deciding differently offers no second chances; my punishment is proof of that.

I turn to Elian. "Why am I down here?"

With each passing moment, he takes on more of the ocean. A brown leather tunic is slung over his shirt, frayed black string fastening it at the neck. His legs are half trouser and half long brown boots that catch at the knees. A strap crosses from his shoulder to his waist, and from it a large cutlass dangles. His knife is hidden behind, away from strange eyes. I can still smell Maeve's blood on it.

"You seem worldly," Elian says. "Can't you figure it out?"

Behind him, Kye and Madrid are resolute guardians. Less than a day on this ship and I already know who his most trusted are. Which means I already know his greatest weakness.

"I thought princes liked saving young women in need."

Elian laughs, teeth flashing white against his handsome face. "You're a damsel now?" he asks. "It's funny, because you didn't seem like one when you were trying to claw your way past me to attack a siren."

"I thought killing sirens was what people on this ship did."

"Usually not with their bare hands."

"Not everyone needs magical knives to do their dirty work for them."

"Not everyone can speak *Psáriin*," he says.

I keep a coy smile on my lips, playing my role well. "I have a talent for languages."

"Your Midasan says differently."

"I have a talent for interesting languages," I amend, and Elian's green eyes crinkle.

"What about your own language?" he asks.

"It's better."

"How?"

"It's more suited to me."

"I dread to think what that means."

Elian brushes past me and presses a hand to the cold glass of the cube. As his fingers spread over the would-be prison, I can almost feel the cold of it through him. The siren part of me aches to feel the frost beneath my fingers and know the cold like I used to. The human in me shivers.

"Where is your home?" Elian asks.

His back is to me, and I see his lips move through his reflection. He watches himself, keeping his eyes far from mine. For a moment I don't think he's asking me. That maybe he's asking himself. A prince who doesn't know which kingdom he should claim. Then Kye clears his throat and Elian spins back around. When he does, his face is all lights.

"Well?" he asks.

"I didn't think I was going to be interrogated."

"Did the cage not give it away?"

"I didn't see a cage." I arch my neck, peering behind him as if I hadn't noticed my looming prison. "Your charm must have masked it."

Elian shakes his head to hide the growing smile. "It's not just any cage," he says. "Back when I first started all of this and long before I knew better, I had it built with every intention of using it to hold the Sea Queen." He arches an eyebrow. "Do you think it can hold you?"

"You're going to throw me in a cage?" I ask.

"Unless you tell me where you're from," he says. "And why you left."

"It wasn't my choice."

"Why were you out in the middle of the ocean without a ship?"

"I was abandoned."

"By who?"

I don't hesitate when I say, "Everyone."

With a sigh, Elian leans back and presses a foot flat against the glass. He ponders my carefully chosen words, turning them over in his mind like the wheel of a ship. I dislike the silence that follows and the heavy weight that his quiet leaves in the room. It's as though the air waits for the sound of his voice before it dares to thin out and become breathable. And I wait too, trying to anticipate what his next move will be. The situation is unbearably familiar. So many times I've hovered in front of my mother, biting my tongue while she chooses how I live my life. What I will do and when I will kill and who I will be. Though it's strange to watch a human deliberate my fate, it's not such an odd thing to wait while it's decided by someone other than myself.

Hidden under my seaweed lies, there's truth. I was abandoned, and now I'm on a ship with humans who would see me dead if they knew what I was. Below the surface, my mother rules a kingdom that should be mine, and if anyone questions where I've gone, she'll spit whatever lies make me most forgettable. Harpooned by a passing sailor. Killed by a simple mermaid. In love with a human prince. It will leave my memory as more of a joke than a legend, and the loyalty of my kingdom will dissolve as quickly as Maeve did.

I will be nothing. Have nothing. Die as nothing.

I look at my necklace, still hanging from Elian's neck. I don't doubt that if I press my ear to the red bone, I'll hear the ocean and the sound of my mother's laughter rippling through it.

I turn, disgusted.

"We dock at Eidýllio in three days' time." Elian pushes himself from the glass. "I'll make my decision when we get there."

"And until then?"

A slow smile spreads across his face. He steps aside to reveal the full glory of the cage. "Until then."

In the wake of the unspoken order, Madrid grabs my elbow. To my other side, Kye's hands tighten around my arm. I struggle against them, but their hold is unbreakable. In moments I'm hoisted from the floor and dragged toward the cage. My writhing does nothing to steer them from their path.

"Let me go!" I demand.

I try to kick out with clumsy motions, but my body is squashed between them, leaving little room to breathe or move. I throw my head back wildly and thrash, furious at the lack of control. How frail and weak my body is now. In my siren form, I could tear them in half with a single movement. I bare my teeth and snap through the air, missing Kye's ear by half an inch. He doesn't even blink. I'm as powerless as I feel.

We reach the cage and they throw me in like I weigh nothing. I bounce off the floor, and when I rush back to the entrance, my palms meet a wall. My fingers spread over the surface, and I realize that it's not glass after all, but solid crystal. I pound relentlessly against it. On the other side, Elian crosses his arms over his chest. My human heart thumps angrily against my chest, stronger than my fists on the prison wall.

I point an accusing finger at him. "You want me to stay in here until Eidýllio?"

"I want you overboard," Elian says. "But it's not like I can make you walk the plank."

"Your chivalry won't allow it?"

Elian walks to a nearby wall and pulls back one of the drapes to reveal a circular switch. "We lost the plank years ago," he says. Then, in a voice much lower: "And I lost my chivalry around the same time."

He twists the switch and the shadows take over.

THERE'S ONLY NIGHT INSIDE the crystal cage. The room is coated in damp darkness, and though the prison seems impenetrable, I can smell the musk of soggy air from the world outside. Every so often, someone comes with food and I'm allowed a rare few minutes of lantern light. It's almost blinding, and by the time I'm done squinting, the lights are off and a tray of fish assaults my senses. It doesn't quite have the taste of salties and white pointers, but I devour it in moments.

I don't know how long I've been in the crystal cage, but the promise of Eidýllio weighs on me. When we arrive, the prince will try to throw me onto land with humans who know nothing of the ocean. At least in this place, I can smell the salt of home.

When I sleep, I dream of coral and bleeding hearts. When I wake, there's nothing but dark and the slow wash of waves against the body of the ship. The first time I killed a human, it was so bright, I couldn't go above water without squinting. The surface barely rippled, and in moments the sun melted any shards of my kingdom's ice that still lingered on my skin.

The boy was a prince of Kalokaíri and I was twelve.

Kalokaíri is not much more than a beautiful desert in the middle of a desolate sea. It's the land of endless summer, with wind that carries the smell of sand. In those days, my legend hadn't been born, and so royalty sailed with no more trepidation than any human.

The prince was cloaked in white, with purple cloth wrapped tightly around his head. He was gentle and unafraid, and he smiled at me long before I sang. When I sprang from the ocean, he had called me *ahnan anatias*, which was Kalokaírin for "little death."

The boy wasn't frightened, even when I bared my teeth and hissed in the same way I heard my mother do. Taking his heart had not been such a nasty business then. He almost came willingly. Before I began my song, he reached his hand out to touch me, and after the first few clumsy lines, he climbed slowly from the docked sailing boat and walked until he was deep enough to meet me.

I let him drown first. While his breathing slowed, I held his hand, and only when I was sure he was dead did I think of his heart. I was careful when it happened. I didn't want there to be too much blood when his family found him. For them to think he suffered, when he had died so peacefully.

As I took his heart, I wondered if they were looking for him. Had they realized he was missing from the boat? Above the water's edge, were they screaming for him? Would my mother scream like that if I never came back? I knew the answer. The queen wouldn't care if I was gone forever. Heirs were easy things to make, and my mother was the Sea Queen first and nothing second. I knew she would only care that I hadn't taken the boy's heart while he was still alive. That she would punish me for not being enough of a monster. And I was right.

When I arrived home, my mother was waiting for me. Surrounding her were the other members of our royal bloodline, arced in a perfect semicircle as they awaited my entrance. The Sea Queen's sister was at the forefront, ready to greet me, each of her six daughters looped behind her. Kahlia was last, directly beside my mother.

As soon as the Sea Queen saw me, she knew what I had done. I could see it in her smile, and I was sure she could smell it on me: the stench of my regret for killing the Kalokaírin prince. And no matter how much I tried to avoid looking at her, the queen could tell I had been crying. The tears were long washed away, but my eyes remained bloodshot and I had done too good of a job trying to scrub the blood off my hands.

"Lira," she said. "My sweet."

I placed a trembling hand onto her outstretched tentacle and let her pull me slowly into her hold. Kahlia bit her lip as my mother regarded my clean hands.

"Have you come bearing gifts for mummy dearest?" the Sea Queen asked.

I nodded and reached into the netting tied around my waist. "I did what you asked." I cradled the young prince's heart, lifting it above my head to present it to her like the trophy she wanted. "My twelfth."

The Sea Queen stroked my hair, her smooth tentacle slinking from my scalp and along my spine. I tried not to blink.

"Indeed," the Sea Queen said. Her voice was soft and slow, like the sound of the dawn breeze. "But it seems you didn't quite listen."

"He's dead," I told her, thinking that was surely the most important thing. "I killed him and I took his heart." I held it a little higher, pushing it toward her chest so she could feel the stillness of the prince's heart against the coldness of her own.

"Oh, Lira." She cupped my chin in her hand, sliding the talon of her thumb over my cheek. "But I didn't tell you to cry."

I wasn't sure if she meant when I killed the prince, or not to do it now, in her grasp, with our royal bloodline watching. But my lips shook with the same fear my hands had, and when the first drop fell from my red eye, my mother breathed a heavy lament. She let the tear run onto her thumb and then shook it from her skin like it was acid.

"I did what you asked," I said again.

"I asked you to make a human suffer," the Sea Queen said. "To take its still-beating heart and rip it out." A tentacle slid over my shoulder and around my tiny neck. "I asked you to be a siren."

When she threw me to the ground, I remember feeling relieved. Knowing that if she was going to kill me, she would have crushed me under her grasp. I could take a beating. I could be humiliated and bloodied. If taking a few hits would quell my mother's temper, then it wouldn't be so bad. I would have gotten off easy. But I was a fool to think that my mother would choose to punish only me. What good was it to scold her daughter when she could shape her instead?

"Kahlia," my mother said. "Would you do me a favor?"

"Sister." My aunt swam forward, her face suddenly wretched and pained. "Please don't."

"Now, now, Crestell," my mother said. "You shouldn't interrupt your queen."

"She's my daughter."

I remember hating the way Crestell's shoulders hunched forward as she spoke. Like she was already preparing for a blow.

"Hush now," my mother cooed. "Let us not fight in front of the children."

She turned to me and stretched out her arm toward my cousin. It was like she was presenting Kahlia, the same way I had done with the Kalokaírin heart. I didn't move.

"Kill her," the Sea Queen said.

"Mother—"

"Take her heart while she still screams, like you should have done with the human prince."

Kahlia whimpered, too scared to move or even cry. She glanced over at her mother, then back to me, blinking a dozen times over. Her head shook violently from side to side.

It was like looking into a mirror. Seeing the horror on Kahlia's face was like seeing a rendition of myself, every drop of terror I felt reflected in her eyes.

"I can't," I said. Then, louder: "Don't make me."

I backed away, shaking my head so adamantly that my mother's snarl became a blur.

"You stupid child," she said. "I am offering you redemption. Do you know what will happen if you refuse?"

"I don't need to be redeemed!" I yelled. "I did what you asked!"

The Sea Queen squeezed her trident, and all the poise that remained vanished from her face. Her eyes grew to shadows, blacker and blacker, until I could only see the darkness in them. The ocean groaned.

"This *humanity* that has infected you must be quelled," she said. "Don't you see, Lira? Humans are a plague who murdered our goddess and seek to destroy us. Any siren who shows sympathy toward them – who mimics their love and their sorrow – must be cleansed."

I frowned. "Cleansed?"

The Sea Queen pushed Kahlia to the seabed, and I winced when her palms slammed against the sand.

"Sirens do not feel affection or regret," my mother seethed. "We don't know empathy for our enemies. Any siren who feels such things can never be queen. All she will ever be is defective. And a defective siren can't be allowed to live."

"Defective," I repeated.

"Kill her," my mother said. "And we'll speak no more of it."

She said it like it was the only way I could ever make up for my sins against my kind. If Kahlia died, then I'd be a true siren worthy of my mother's trident. I wouldn't be impure. The emotions I was having were a sickness and she was offering me a cure. A way out. A chance to rid me of the humanity she claimed had infected me.

Kahlia just needed to die first.

I moved closer to my cousin, clasping my hands behind my back so the Sea Queen couldn't see how much they were shaking. I wondered if she could smell blood from the crescents I had stamped into my palms.

Kahlia cried as I approached, great howls of terror spilling from her tiny lips. I wasn't sure what I planned to do as I got closer to her, but I knew I didn't want to kill her. *Take her hand and swim*, I thought. *Get as far away from the Sea Queen as we can.* But I knew I wouldn't do that, either, because my mother's eyes were the ocean and she would see us wherever we hid. If I took Kahlia, we'd both be killed for treason. And so my choices were this: to take my cousin's heart. Or to take her hand and let us die together.

"Stop," Crestell said.

She swooped in front of Kahlia, creating a barrier between us. Her arms were spread wide in defense, fangs bared. For a moment I was sure she would attack, slicing her claws through me and putting an end to this madness once and for all.

"Take me," she said.

I paled.

Crestell grabbed my hand – it looked tiny in hers, but nowhere near as delicate – and pressed it to her chest. "Take it," she said.

My cousins gasped around us, their faces contorted in terror and grief. This was their choice: watch their mother die or see their sister killed. I stammered before my aunt, ready to scream and swim as far away as I could. But then Crestell shot a look to Kahlia, who trembled on the seabed. A worried, furtive glance, quick enough for my mother to miss. When her eyes returned to mine, they were filled with begging.

"Take it, Lira," Crestell said. She swallowed and raised her chin. "This is the way things must be."

"Yes," my mother cooed from behind me. I didn't have to turn to know there was a smile cutting across her face. "That would be quite the substitute."

She placed a hand on my shoulder, her nails scraping over my skin, clamping me into place before she lowered her lips to my ear and let a whisper form between us.

"Lira," my mother said so quiet that my fin curled. "Cure yourself and show me that you truly belong in the ocean."

Defective.

"Any last words, sister?" the Sea Queen asked.

Crestell closed her eyes, but I knew it wasn't to keep from crying. It was to seal the fury in so that it didn't burnish her irises. She wanted to die a loyal subject and keep her daughters safe from my mother's revenge. From me.

When Crestell opened her eyes again – one such a pure blue and the other a most miraculous shade of purple –

she looked nowhere but at me.

"Lira," she said. Her voice rasped. "Become the queen we need you to be."

It wasn't a promise I could make, because I wasn't sure I was capable of being the kind of queen my mother's kingdom needed. I had to be without emotion, spreading terror rather than feeling it, and as my breathing trembled, I just didn't know if I had it in me.

"Won't you promise?" Crestell asked.

I nodded, even though I thought it was a lie. And then I killed her.

That was the day I became my mother's daughter. And the moment it happened was the moment I became the most monstrous of us all. The yearning to please her spread through me like a shadow, fighting against every urge I knew she'd perceive as weakness. Every flash of regret and sympathy that would lead her to believe I was impure.

Abnormal. *Defective*. And in a blink of an eye, the child I was became the creature I am.

I forced myself to think only of which princes would please my mother most: the fearless Ágriosy, who tried for decades to find Diávolos under the misguided notion they could end our kind, or a prince of Mellontikós. Prophets and fortune-tellers who chose to keep themselves apart from the war, rarely daring to let a ship touch the water. I toyed with the thought of bringing them to my mother as further proof that I belonged by her side.

Over time, I forgot what it was like to be weak. Now that I'm trapped here in a body that is not my own, I suddenly remember. I've gone from being my mother's least favorite weapon to a creature who can't even defend herself. A monster without fangs or claws.

I run a hand over my bruised legs, paler than a shark's underbelly.

My feet arch inward as an awful cold snakes through me and small bumps begin to prickle over my new skin. I don't understand what it means, and I don't understand how I could have gone from darting through the ocean to stumbling among humans.

I heave a frustrated breath, turning my caress to the skin on my ribs. No gills. No matter how deep I breathe, the skin doesn't part and the air continues to fog in and out of my lips. My skin is still damp and the water no longer runs off it, seeping instead into every pore and bringing with it an unbearable cold. The kind of cold that sends more bumps along the surface of my skin, crawling from my legs to my frail arms.

I can't help but start to fear the water outside of this cage. If Elian were to throw me overboard, how long would it take for me to drown?

The lanterns glow, faint enough to give my human eyes the time to adjust. Elian presses a key into the crystal cage, and a section of wall slides open. I ignore the instinct to rush him, remembering how easily he pinned me to the wall when I tried to attack Maeve. He's stronger than I am now and more agile than I gave him credit for. In this body, force is not the way.

Elian sets a plate down in front of me. It's a thick broth the color of river water. Pale meat and sea grapes float curiously at the top, and the overwhelming smell of anise climbs through the air. My stomach aches in response.

"Kye and I caught sea turtles," he explains. "It stinks to high heaven, but damn if it tastes good."

"I'm being punished," I say in a cold rendition of Midasan.

"I want you to tell me why."

"You're not being punished," he tells me. "You're being watched."

"Because I speak *Psáriin?*" I ask. "Is speaking a language a crime now?"

"It's banned in most kingdoms."

"We're not in a kingdom."

"Wrong." Elian leans against the door arch. "We're in mine. The *Saad* is my kingdom. The entire ocean is."

I ignore the insult of a human trying to lay claim to what is mine and say, "I wasn't given a list of laws when I boarded."

"Well, now you know." He twists the key around on his finger. "Of course, I could arrange for a more comfortable sleeping arrangement if you'd just stop being so evasive."

"I'm not being evasive."

"Then tell me how you can speak *Psáriin.*" The curiosity in his voice betrays his lax movements. "Tell me what you know about the Crystal of Keto."

"You saved my life and now you're trading comforts for information? It's strange how fast kindness disappears."

"I'm fickle," Elian says. "And I have to protect the *Saad*. I can't just go trusting anyone who climbs aboard. They need a good enough story first."

I smirk at that.

If a story is all I need, then that's easy enough. The Second Eye of Keto is a legend in our waters, too. The Sea Queen hunted it for years when she began her reign. Where previous queens dismissed it as a lost cause from the outset, my mother was always too hungry for power. She rehashed the stories of the ritual to free the eye, over and over, in a bid to find some clue to its location. Tales that generations had ignored, my mother made sure to memorize. And her obsession meant that I knew them, too. She once told me that the eye was the key to ending all humans, as much as it was the humans' key to ending all of us. I think of her charcoal bone trident and the beloved ruby that sits in the center, the true source of the Sea Queen's magic. The eye is said to be its twin, stolen from my kind and hidden where no siren can follow.

My mother knows everything about the eye, except for how to find it. And so, after many years, she gave up on the hunt. But her failure to succeed where her predecessors failed has always irked her.

I pause, an idea sparking inside me.

The eye is hidden where no siren can follow, but thanks to my mother, that no longer applies to me. If Elian can lead me there, then I can use the eye to make the Sea Queen's greatest fear come true. If she truly thinks I'm unworthy of ruling, I'll prove just the opposite by using the Second Eye of Keto to overthrow her. To destroy her, the way she tried to destroy me.

I lick my lips.

If Elian is truly hunting the eye, then he's doing so on the faith of stories. And if a man can hunt them, then he can hear them. All I need is to convince the prince that I'm useful, and he might just let me above deck and away from the shackles of my cage. If I can get close enough, I won't need my nails to rip out his heart. I'll do it with his own knife. Just as soon as he secures my place as the ruler of the ocean.

"The Sea Queen stole my family," I tell Elian, layering my voice in the same melancholy I've heard in the calls of sailors as they watched their rulers die. "We were on a fishing boat and I was the only one to survive. I've studied them ever since I was a child, learning everything possible from books and stories." I bite down on my lip. "As for the language, I don't pretend to be fluent, but I know enough. It was easy to pick up with one of them as my prisoner. My father managed to cripple it before he died, and that meant I was able to keep it captive."

Elian sighs, unimpressed. "If you're going to lie," he says, "do it better."

"It's not a lie." I pretend to be wounded by the accusation. "One of them was injured during the attack on my family. We're from Polemistés."

At the mention of the warrior land, Elian takes a step forward. He reaches into his pocket and pulls out a small circular object. The same compass he palmed when we spoke above deck. A thin gold chain hangs delicately from the hilt, and when he flips it open, the ends chime together.

"Do you really expect me to believe that you're from Polemistés?" Elian asks.

I try not to take offense at the question – right now I wouldn't believe I was a warrior either – but I don't argue my case. I don't like the way Elian glances down at the compass, as though he's relying on it to discern something. With every lie that crosses my thoughts, I can almost feel the object reaching out to crawl into the watery depths of my mind. Pluck out the lies like seaweed roots. It seems impossible, but I know how much humans like their trickery.

"My family are hunters," I say carefully. "Just like you. The Sea Queen wanted revenge because she felt she was wronged."

The space between us cloys with the compass's phantom magic, and I conjure an image of Maeve's face to prove to the strange object that this is not technically a lie.

"I tortured one of her sirens to get what I needed," I say.

"What happened to the siren?"

"Dead," I tell him.

Elian glances down at the compass and then frowns. "Did you kill it?"

"Do you think I'm not capable?"

He sighs at my evasive answer, but it's difficult to miss the intrigue in his eyes as he toys with the possibility of believing me. "The siren," he says. "Did she tell you about the crystal?"

"She told me a lot of things. Make me an offer worth my while, and perhaps I'll tell you, too."

"What kind of offer?"

"A place on your ship and this hunt."

"You're in no position to bargain," Elian says.

"My family has studied sirens for generations. I guarantee that I know more about them than you ever could hope to. And you've already seen that I can speak their tongue," I say. "This isn't a bargain, it's a deal."

"I'm not in the business of striking deals with girls in cages."

I twist my lips into a cruel smile. "Then by all means, let me out."

Elian laughs, pulls a pistol out, and shakes his head once again.

"You know," he says, approaching the cell, "I think I might like you. Thing is" – he taps his gun against my prison – "there's a difference between liking someone and trusting them."

"I wouldn't know. I've never done either."

"When we get to Eidýllio," Elian says, "we can drink to that."

The thought is enough to make me wince. Eidýllio is a land devoted to romance. They celebrate love as though it's power, even though it has killed far more humans than I ever have. I would rather be surrounded by the blinding gold of Midas than be in a kingdom where emotion is currency.

"You trust me enough to buy me a drink?"

Elian pockets his pistol and heads back to the switch. "Who said I'd be the one buying?"

"You promised that you would set me free!" I shout to his retreating figure.

"I promised you more comfortable living arrangements." Elian's hand flickers over the switch. "I'll get Kye to bring you a pillow."

I catch one last look at his angled smirk before the lantern dims and the last speck of light is pulled from the room.

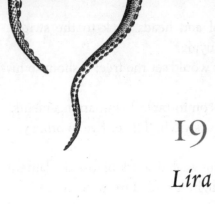

19

Lira

WHEN THE LIGHT BREAKS across the shore of Eidýllio, there's a flash of pink that shatters the sky. The sun gleams against the horizon, encircled by a miraculous hue of diminished red, like melted coral. I'm pulled from the depths of my cage and into the light, where there's an explosion of warmth and color, like nothing I have ever witnessed. There's light in every corner of the earth, but in Eidýllio it seems closer to magic. The kind that's crafted into Elian's blade and my mother's ashen trident. Dreams shaped into something more powerful than reality.

Across the docks, the grass is the color of neon gobies. A meadow floating on the water. Stems of juniper sprout like fireworks, rain beads clinging to their tips in indestructible droplets. They are orbs of light guiding the way back to land.

I realize that I'm warm. It's a new sensation, far from the tickle of ice I loved as a siren and the sharp frost I felt in my human toes aboard the *Saad*. I've shed Elian's damp shirt, which clung and dried against me like a second skin. Now I have a ragged white dress, pinched at the waist by a belt as thick as either of my legs, and large black boots that threaten to swallow my new feet whole.

Madrid takes a step beside me. "Freedom's in your grasp," she says.

I throw her a disparaging look. "Freedom?"

"The cap planned to cut you loose once we arrived here, didn't he?

No burn, no breach."

I recognize the saying. It is a Kléftesis phrase from the kingdom of thieves – *no harm, no problem* – used by pirates who pillage passing ships and any land they dock on. If nobody is killed, the Kléftesis don't believe a crime has been committed. Their pirates are true to their nature and pay no mind to noble missions and declarations of peace. They sail for gold and pleasure and the pain they cause when taking it. If Madrid is from Kléftes, then Elian chose his crew well. The worst of the worst to be his best.

"How trusting you are of your prince," I say.

"He's not my prince," Madrid says. "He's not any sort of prince on this ship."

"That I can believe," I tell her. "He wasn't even civil when I offered help."

"Let's be straight," Madrid says. "You're only looking to help yourself."

"Is there anyone alive who isn't?"

"The captain." Her voice holds a spark of admiration. "He wants to help the world."

I laugh. The prince wants to help a doomed world. As long as my mother's alive, war is all we will ever know. The best thing Elian can do for his safety is kill me and anyone else he can't afford to trust. Instead he kept me prisoner. Suspicious enough to lock me away, but not brutal enough to take my life. He showed mercy, and whether it's weakness or strength, it's jarring all the same.

I watch Elian descending the ship, paying no mind to the shipwrecked girl he could easily abandon. He takes off in a run and jumps the last of the way, so that when his feet touch the tufts of grass, small droplets explode into the air like rainfall. He pulls his hat off and takes a sweeping bow at the land. Then he reaches up a tanned hand, ruffles the wisps of his raven hair, and slips the hat back onto his head in a flourish. He takes a moment, surveying the canvas, his hands hitched on his hips.

I can hear the exhale of his breath even from high on the deck of the *Saad*. His joy is like a gust of unfamiliar wind sweeping up to us. The crew smiles as they watch him stare into an ocean of grass and juniper and, in the distance, a wall made of light. A castle peeks out from the city lines like a mirage.

"He always does this," Kolton Torik says.

His presence casts a shadow beside me, but for all the foreboding Elian's first mate could bring, he's nothing of the dire pirate he could be. His face is gentle and relaxed, hands shoved into the pockets of frayed shorts. When he speaks, his voice is deep but soft, like the echo after an explosion.

"Eidýllio is one of his favorites," Torik explains.

I find it hard to believe the prince is a romantic. He seems as though he might find the notion as ridiculous as I do. I would know in an instant that Midas isn't his favorite kingdom; men don't make homes if they have them already. But my guess would have been Ágrios, a nation of fearlessness. Or the warrior kingdom of Polemistés that I chose for my origin. Lands for soldiers on the precipice of war. Fighters and killers who see no use in pretending to be anything else.

I would not have guessed that the infamous siren hunter

had humanity in him.

"It's one of my favorites too," Madrid says, inhaling the air. "They have streets of bakeries, with chocolate hearts oozing toffee on every corner. Even their cards smell sweet."

"Why is it *his* favorite?" I point to Elian.

Kye arches an eyebrow. "Take a wild guess."

"What else do you need in life when you have love?" Madrid asks.

Kye snorts. "Is that what the kids are calling it nowadays?"

Madrid swipes at him and when Kye sidesteps her blow, she narrows her eyes. "This is supposed to be the land of romance," she tells him.

"Romance is for royals," Kye says just as Torik throws an empty bag in the middle of their makeshift circle.

He has shed his shirt, and I see that his bare arms are covered in tattoo mosaics, not a single piece of skin spared from the patchwork quilt of color. On his shoulder a snake stares down. Yellow, teeth bared, hissing as his biceps flex.

"And what's the captain, then?" he asks.

"A pirate." Kye throws his sword into the bag. "And we all know why pirates come to Eidýllio."

Madrid shoots him a withering look.

I dare another glance at the prince. The warm wind bellows the tails of his coat, and as it pulls back, the point of his knife catches my eye. It splinters the sun's growing hue, and then a small vein of black crawls up the metal and snatches the light. Drinks it until there isn't a glimmer left on the blade. I bite down on the corner of my lip and imagine holding something that powerful.

A knife that absorbs life and light.

Elian's stance goes rigid. His knuckles whiten on his hips, and his head tilts ever so slightly back toward the ship. To me. As though he can sense my thoughts. When he turns, it's slow and meaningful, and it takes a few moments for his eyes to find mine among his crew. He stares, unblinking, and just when I think he's going to raise his hand and signal for Madrid to shoot me, or for Kye to throw me back into the crystal cave, he smirks. The left side of his mouth tugs upward, and the action, somehow, feels like a dare.

Then the look is gone and Elian turns to survey the rest of his crew. When he does, his smile becomes real and wide enough to dimple his bronzed cheeks.

"You know the routine," he tells them, climbing back onto the deck. "Everything sharp or deadly in the bags." He looks at me. "Think you'll fit?"

I shoot him a feral look, and his crew reluctantly pulls their swords from their belts. Drags arrowheads from their shoes. Reveals knives in the folds of their trousers. Hoists guns that were tucked into their waistbands. At one point, Kye takes off his boot and throws it in. The inked sun reflects the light from a hidden dagger in the heel before it's buried beneath a mass of weaponry.

There are pirates unarming in front of me. Layer by layer they throw down their protection, shedding it like a second skin. When they're done, each of them shuffles, placing awkward hands on their hips or reaching for weapons that are no longer there.

Madrid brings her thumb to her mouth and bites down hard on the nail, while Kye cracks his knuckles. The pops are as rhythmic as waves.

"Why are you doing that?" I ask, eyeing the stash of weapons.

If I can swipe one, then I can use it on the prince if he tries anything, but in this gown, there's nowhere to hide it. I sigh in frustration, knowing I won't be able to get close enough with a weapon in plain sight.

"No weapons in Eidýllio," Madrid explains. She flicks the last two twin blades from either of her sleeves.

"It's law," Kye continues. "You can't touch the ground if you're carrying, so we pack up our arms and take them to the wall. Then drop the bag with the scouts."

"Why not just leave them on the ship?"

Madrid looks down to her discarded speargun, horrified. "Don't worry," she whispers to the deadly contraption. "She didn't mean it."

Kye smirks and kicks one of the bags somewhat fondly. "Can't risk leaving our best metal on the ship. If another lot docks here, they might decide to have a rummage. Of course," he says, casting a meaningful look my way, "it'd be really stupid for anyone to try to get on the wrong side of the *Saad*'s captain."

Elian claps a hand on Kye's shoulder. A straw of black sugar is nooked inside his mouth, carrying the familiar aniseed smell. "But you can't bet your life on people not being stupid," Elian says. "That's how you end up with a knife in your gut."

Torik hoists the weapon-filled bag from the floor and grunts. "Okay then," he says. "Heads or tails on which of you gits wants to help carry these."

Kye pulls a gold coin from his pocket. A pyramid is etched onto the front face, and so I immediately know that it's Midasan. The royal crest is unmistakable.

"Heads you lose, tails I win." Kye throws the coin into the air but brushes past Torik before it has a chance to land. As soon as the coin hits the deck by Torik's feet, Kye calls over his shoulder, "Guess it's my lucky day!"

"I'm keeping that gold, you little shit," Torik tells him, picking up the coin and polishing it on his shirt before pocketing it.

Elian gestures for Madrid to help Torik with the bag and takes a bite from the tarry sweet. As his arm moves from his side, I see the knife still secured under the billow of his coat.

I gesture to the blade. "You don't follow your own rules?"

"They're not my rules," Elian says. "And besides" – he taps the handle of his knife, the mockery crisp in his voice – "I have diplomatic immunity."

Kye laughs from the grass below. "Is that what we're calling Queen Galina now?" he asks. "You might want to tell Her Royal Highness that her title has changed."

"I think I'd rather not."

"When are you going to go see her?" Madrid asks, slinging the other arm of the weapons bag over her shoulder. "You just know that as soon as she hears we've docked, she'll send guards to escort you over to the palace."

"She always wants to make sure we settle in okay," Elian says.

Madrid snorts. "You mean she always wants to keep an eye on us."

Elian shrugs noncommittally and presses a hand to the seashell.

I try to be indifferent, but the thought of it being in his grasp makes me dizzy with anger. The sea kingdom of Keto has remained hidden from humans since the dawn of time, lost in a maze of ocean and magic woven by the goddess herself. The secret of its whereabouts is our best line of defense in this ongoing battle, and to have that advantage destroyed by him – because of me – would be unthinkable.

Even if the seashells do not work for humans, Elian isn't

like most humans. There's no telling how much havoc he would leave in his wake if he captured a siren and forced her to use its power to lead him to our kingdom. I doubt there are any limits to his desire to rid the world of my race. His movements are as unpredictable as his motives, and if there's anything I've learned these past few days, it's that the prince has a way of getting what he wants. I'm not prepared to let him hold the key to my kingdom for long enough to realize that it is one.

Elian leads me from his ship and onto the floating meadow, the seemingly perpetual smudge of dirt creasing on his forehead. He never seems to be quite perfect. Every glimpse of him is tarnished with an odd dishevelment, noticeable even as he stands among such a makeshift crew. It seems to be a way for him to fit in with the thieves and rogues he has collected, in a similar way that I was fashioned into my mother's vision of a true siren. And because of this, I know his attempts are fruitless. Royalty cannot be unmade. Birth rights cannot be changed. Hearts are forever scarred by our true nature.

"When we reach the wall, we can discuss your future," Elian says.

I clench my fists, appalled at his audacity and the fact that I'm being forced to tolerate it. Never the queen, always the minion.

"Discuss it?" I repeat.

"You said you wanted to come with us, and I want to make sure you're useful. You can't just be a prisoner taking up space on my deck."

"I was belowdecks," I remind him. "In a cage."

"That was this morning," he says, as though it's far enough in the past to be forgotten. "Try not to hold a grudge."

The grin he gives me is beyond taunting and I sneer, not deigning to reply. Instead I breeze past and make sure to knock my shoulder as hard as I can into his. The sooner I have his heart, the better.

THE WALL IS NOT made of light, but of rose petals. They are pure white and when the sunlight bounces off the delicate leaves, they glisten like stars. At first, it's hard to tell whether they are part of the wall, or if they are the wall itself. Tiny flower shavings somehow creating a barrier around the border to Eidýllio's capital. As we approach, I see the solid marble drawbridge begin to fall, parting flowers through the middle.

Once we step inside the city, I'm hit by the smell of sugar bread and peppermint. Market stalls line the curved cobble streets, each stone like a ripple. By the entrance, a trader leans over a barrel of thick chocolate and stirs it with a spoon that's almost the same height as him. Customers lick warm honey from their fingers and drip milk onto satin dress shirts.

When I open my mouth to sigh, the air caramelizes on my tongue.

I've never been inside a human city and I marvel at its abundance. How many people. How many colors and smells and tastes. The way their voices blur into whispers and roars while their feet clap against the cobblestone. So many bodies moving and crashing. There's an unnerving madness to it. How do they breathe, with so little space? How do they live, with so much mayhem? In spite of myself, I edge closer to Elian. There's comfort in his presence and how relaxed he disguises himself to be. As though he could belong anywhere if he truly wanted to.

The scouts seem to recognize him. They smile and greet

the prince with swift bows before opening the weapons bag Torik slaps onto their station. Though Elian's knife is covered by his jacket, it's not completely unnoticeable and he makes no real attempt to hide it.

The scouts approach his crew, albeit warily, and begin to pat the first of them down. They feel their pockets and run their hands over the linings of their clothing, checking for any hidden weaponry. When it comes to Madrid's turn, she wags her eyebrows mockingly and Kye rolls his eyes.

The scouts continue along the group, passing Elian by. It seems he was right about his so-called immunity. Either Elian's sway extends far beyond his own Midasan kingdom, or Queen Galina of Eidýllio really does have a weakness for pirates.

A scout approaches me and gestures for me to hold out my arms. He towers over me by at least two heads, with a patchy orange beard that trickles down to his neck. His skin is fish-bone white, a less immaculate version of my own. Or what it once was, before my mother's curse. I still haven't seen my new self. I would rather stay blind to how humanity has tarnished a face that once sunk ships.

The scout takes a step closer and I smell stale smoke on his uniform.

"Touch me," I tell him, "and I will break every one of your fingers."

His eyes roam over my body, taking note of how the wrinkled white dress clings awkwardly to my sharpened shoulders. He must decide that I don't pose much of a threat, because he quickly grabs my arms and spreads them out like wings.

I use his disregard to my advantage, confident that even without my strength, I'm still deadly. I may not have my fins, or even my voice, but I am my mother's daughter. I am the most murderous creature in the hundred kingdoms.

I twist my outstretched arm back underneath the scout's hands and pull on his wrist, then angle my elbow up and make to crack it across his smug face. When I move, there's a satisfying thump, but it's not the sound of bone crunching.

It's the sound of me being flung to the ground.

The guard has snatched my arm and thrown me with enough force for my elbow to scrape against the gravel. The pain sears across my skin and I feel fury like never before. I could have killed him with one hand if this was the ocean. One song. Yet now I'm cowering as my arm throbs under my weight. How can I expect to take down a trained siren killer when I can't handle one pitiful guard?

I glare and the scout moves his hand to his hip, half-pulling his sword from his belt. His comrades reach for pistols. I can see the anger in their eyes, as they think about repaying me for trying to attack one of their own. But they don't draw. Instead they look to the prince.

Elian stares back with an indifferent expression. He's sitting on the counter of the scout station, one leg hoisted onto the wooden varnish, knee resting in the crook of his elbow. In one hand, he holds an apple the color of rose blossoms.

"So much for a warm welcome," he says, and hops down from the counter.

The scout wipes his nose with the back of his hand. "She tried to *hit* me," he snarls.

Elian takes a bite from the apple. "She also threatened to break your fingers," he says. "You should grab her again and find out if she was bluffing."

"I was just trying to search for weapons. We need to check everyone coming into the kingdom. It's law."

"Not everyone." As Elian moves his hand back to his waist, there's a flash of the knife he never seems to let out of his sight. If the guards didn't notice it before, they have now. And it's obvious that's exactly what Elian wants.

The scout wavers. "She could be hiding a weapon," he argues, but there's less conviction in his voice.

"Right." Elian nods. "So many places she could have stashed it." He turns to me and holds out his hand. "Give up that crossbow you've got under your skirt and they'll let you off with a slap on the wrist."

His voice is deadpan and when I only glare in response, Elian turns back to the scout and throws his arms up, like I'm being difficult.

"You'll just have to throw her in the dungeons," Kye says, appearing by Elian's side. I'm not entirely sure if he's joking. "She's clearly part of some elite smuggling ring."

Elian turns to him and gasps, placing a hand to his heart. "Gods," he says, lowering his voice to a conspiratorial whisper. "What if she's a *pirate*?"

Kye snorts, and after a moment I realize that I'm smiling too.

I can't remember the last time I truly laughed. I've been so set on pleasing my mother that finding any joy of my own seemed unreasonable. Not that it mattered; I could be the perfect monster and it wouldn't change a thing. If I disappoint her, I'm a failure. But if I excel, I prove my worth as a ruler and that's a far greater sin.

I think of what look she'll have when I present the Second Eye of Keto to her and throw it down like a gauntlet.

The scouts let us pass and when they move aside, the city opens its arms. Nobody takes a second look at me. I blend into the stone, merging with every other face in the market.

I'm utterly insignificant for the first time. It's both freeing and maddening.

"Take a good look," Elian says. "This could be your new home."

His hat hangs at his side, hooked onto the handle of his knife. Concealing the weapon and drawing attention to it all the same. He wants to be noticed. He's incapable of being forgettable.

I cross my arms over my chest. "You'd really just leave me here if you don't think I'm useful enough?"

"I prefer abandon," he says. "Desert. Dump. Push heartlessly to the wayside." He sweeps a lock of thick black hair out of his eyes. "You have to admit that Eidýllio is better than the plank," he says. "Or a cage."

At this moment I think I'd prefer either of them. The feel of land under my feet is strange, and its steadiness tugs my stomach in too many directions. I long for water gushing against my fins or even the rock and sway of the *Saad*. Everything on land is too still. Too permanent.

"Don't you miss it?"

I don't know why I'm asking, as though Elian and I have anything in common. I should leave while I can. I should kill him while I can. Forget waiting until he leads me to the eye. Forget trying to overthrow my mother, and just take his heart like she demanded, securing my place as her heir again. If I come back with enough human weapons, surely I can take him on.

Instead I simply say, "The ocean," and Elian's eyes crinkle.

"It's still out there," he says.

"So far. We've walked for three hours."

"It's never too far. You're forgetting that this whole place is a river delta."

There are limits to my Midasan and when I stare blankly at the mention of a river delta, Kye releases a loud sigh from a nearby market stall.

"Oh, come on." He licks chocolate from his finger. "Don't tell me you're not up on centuplicate geography."

"It's how Kardián was made," Madrid explains. Her hair is in two high ponytails now, and when she speaks, she reaches up to tug them tighter. "A river delta formed from Eidýllio, and cousins of the royal family decided they deserved a nation of their own. So they took it and named themselves king and queen."

"My kind of people." Kye raises his fist in the air like a toast.

"Your kind of people aren't anyone's kind of people," Madrid says. "You're uniquely idiotic."

"You had me at *unique*," Kye says, and then turns to me. "All that separates Kardián and Eidýllio are rivers and estuaries. They're everywhere you look in this place."

I remember Torik's comment on the *Saad*, about how Eidýllio was Elian's favorite kingdom. At the time I couldn't fathom why – the rogue prince enamored with a land of love seemed odd at best and ridiculous at worst – but now, understanding dawns.

"That's why you like it here," I say to Elian. "Because the ocean is never too far away."

He smiles, but just as he is about to respond, Torik places a hand on his shoulder. "We got to get movin', Captain. The Serendipity only holds our rooms for two hours after sunrise."

"You go," Elian tells him. "I'm right behind you."

Torik gives a swift nod and when he turns to leave, the rest of the crew follows his lead. Except for Kye, who lingers on the edge of the crowd with an unfathomable expression. He squeezes Madrid's hand – just once – and then watches until she disappears. When she's no longer in sight, he turns back to Elian and me, his face adopting a sudden severity.

It seems the prince is so rarely left unguarded.

"I owe you something," Elian says. "Or, technically, you owe me, since I saved you from drowning. But I'm not one for holding life debts." There is a flicker of a smile on his lips as he unloops my seashell from his neck. Something like hope takes ahold of me. My fingers twitch by my side. "Here," he says, and throws it to me.

As soon as the scarlet shell touches my hand, power floods through me. My knees almost give way as I feel an ungodly strength return. My bones harden, my skin crystallizing. For a moment my heart withers back to what it was. Then there's a whisper that slowly turns to a hum. I can hear the call of the Diávolos Sea and the kingdom of Keto. I can hear my home.

And then it's gone. Just like my powers.

The rush disappears as quickly as it came. My body slackens and my skin turns warm and soft. Bones so easily broken. Heart red and pounding once more.

The ocean is silent.

"Lira."

I snap my eyes up to meet Elian's. I still can't get used to the sound of my name in his accent. Like one of the songs I used to sing. A melody as sweet as it is deadly.

"If you miss the ocean," he says, "then Reoma Putoder is the closest water you'll find. On the holy day, locals throw stones in the waterfall to wish for their lost love. Access is forbidden the rest of the week, but I don't doubt you'll be able to find a way around that."

He makes to move by me and I sidestep. "Wait," I say. "I thought you said you wanted me to prove myself worthy of going with you. I told you that I have information on the crystal you're looking for and now suddenly you won't even consider a deal?"

"I've made enough deals lately," Elian says. "And the last thing I need is a straggler on this mission. Especially one I can't trust. Besides, you can't offer me anything I don't already know." Elian settles his hat back onto his head with a graceful twirl and tips it forward in my direction. "If you go to the Reoma Putoder," he says, "try not to drown this time."

He doesn't look at me again before he turns to weave his way through the market and toward Kye. I catch a brief glimpse of them standing together and then, just like that, they disappear into the crowd.

It takes me the better part of an hour to find the Reoma Putoder. I don't ask for help, partly because my pride can't take another human rescuing me. Mostly, because my patience can't take another human talking to me. I've already been stopped over a dozen times by locals offering me food and warmer clothing, as though I need it in this sweltering heat. There's something about a girl wandering alone in a wrinkled dress and old pirate boots that unnerves them.

I bet ripping out their hearts would be more unnerving.

The Reoma Putoder is a waterfall with a pure white lagoon that, somewhere far in the distance, leaks into the ocean. I heard it before I saw it, lost in the endless bakery alleyways, the smell of pastries clinging to my skin like perfume. It sounded like thunder and there were a few hesitant seconds when I thought for sure that was what it was. But the closer I got, the more recognizable the sound was. Water so powerful that it sent shudders through me.

I sit quietly at the base of the waterfall, my legs hanging over the edge of the lagoon. It's so warm that every now and again I have to take my feet out and let them rest against the dewy grass. At the bottom of the water, sitting on sand that looks akin to snow, there are thousands of red metal coins. They peek out from the shingle like tiny droplets of blood.

I thumb the seashell. Pressing it to my ear brings nothing but unbearable silence. I've been trying ever since Elian left me in the marketplace. On the walk to the waterfall, I held it against me desperately, hoping that with time it would speak to me again. There were a few moments when I almost tricked myself into thinking that I could hear the echo of a wave. The rumble of a sea storm. My mother's bubbling laughter. Really, the only sound was the ringing of my ears. All of that power, gone. A tease of my own self dangled in front of me just long enough for the thirst to return. I wonder if it's another one of my mother's tricks. Let me keep the shell so she can taunt me with the echoes of my destroyed legacy.

I grip it tighter. I want to feel it splinter into my skin. Crack and crumble to nothing. But when I open my hand, it's intact, undamaged, and all that remains is an indent in my palm. With a scream, I raise my arm high above my head and throw the shell into the water. It lands with an anticlimactic plop and then sinks leisurely to the bottom. I can see every moment of its slow descent until it finally settles against the water bed.

Then there is a glow. Faint at first, but it soon scatters into orbs and embers. I inch back. In all the time I've used the seashells to communicate with sirens, or even as a compass to my kingdom, I've rarely seen this. It calls out as though it can sense my desperation, reaching into the waters to search for another of my kind. Instead of a map, it's acting as a beacon.

And then, in almost no time at all, Kahlia appears. My cousin's blond hair is swiped across the water, falling into her face so that her eyes fail to meet mine.

I jump to my feet. "Kahlia," I say with astonishment. "You're here."

She nods and holds out her hand. Resting against her long, spiny fingers is my seashell. She throws it onto the grass by my feet. "I heard your call," she says quietly. "Do you have the prince's heart yet?"

I frown as her head stays bowed. "What's the matter?" I ask. "Can't you look at me now?"

When Kahlia does nothing but shake her head, I feel a pang. She once admired me so venomously that it drove my mother to hate her. My entire life Kahlia remained the only one in our kingdom who I thought to care about and now she can't even look me in the eye.

"It's not that," Kahlia says, like she senses my thoughts.

She lifts her head and there's a tenuous smile on her thin pink lips as she fiddles uncharacteristically with the seaweed bodice around her chest. She takes in my human form and rather than look scared or disgusted, she only looks curious. She cocks her head. Her milk-yellow eye is wide and glistening. But her other eye, the one that matches my own so perfectly, is shut and bruised black.

I grit my teeth, grinding bone on bone. "What happened?"

"There had to be a punishment," she says.

"For what?"

"For helping you kill the Adékarosin prince."

I take an outraged step forward, feet teetering on the edge of the lagoon. "I took that punishment."

"The brunt of it," Kahlia says. "Which is why I'm still alive."

A chill runs through me. I should have known my mother couldn't be satiated with punishing one siren when she could have two. Why make me suffer alone? It's a lesson she's taught me so often before. First with Crestell and now with her daughter.

"The Sea Queen is entirely too merciful," I say.

Kahlia offers me a meek smile. "Does the prince still have his heart?" she asks. "If you bring it back, this will be over. You can come home."

The desperate hope in her voice makes me flinch. She's scared to return to the Diávolos Sea without me, because if I'm not there, then nobody will protect her from my mother.

"When we first met, I was too weak from almost drowning to kill him."

Kahlia grins. "What is he like?" she asks. "Compared to the others?"

I consider telling her about Elian's truth-discerning compass and the knife he carries that's as sharp as his gaze, drinking whatever blood it draws. How he smells of anglers and ocean salt. Instead I say something else altogether. Something she will find far more entertaining.

"He locked me in a cage."

Kahlia splutters a laugh. "That doesn't sound too princely," she says. "Aren't human royals supposed to be accommodating?"

"He has more important things to worry about, I suppose."

"Like what?" Her voice is eager as she swipes a string of seaweed from her arm.

"Hunting legends," I explain.

Kahlia shoots me a teasing look. "Weren't you one of those?"

I raise my eyebrows at the jab, pleased to see some of the spark return to her face. "He's looking for the Second Eye of Keto," I say.

Kahlia swims forward, throwing her arms on the damp

grass by my feet. "Lira," she says. "You're planning something wicked, aren't you? Do I have to guess?"

"That depends entirely on how much you enjoy playing minion to your beloved aunt."

"The Sea Queen can't expect devotion if she preaches the opposite," Kahlia says, and I know she's thinking of Crestell. The mother who laid down her life for her in an act of devotion my own mother could only scoff at.

It doesn't surprise me that Kahlia would be eager to turn against the Sea Queen. The only thing that has ever surprised me is her continued allegiance to me. Even after what I did. What I was made to do. Somehow Crestell's death bonded us rather than tearing us apart as my mother had hoped it would. I can't help but feel smug at the look of cunning in Kahlia's eyes. Expected or not, the display of loyalty is all too satisfying.

"If the prince leads me to the eye, then the power it holds would make me a match for the Sea Queen." I hold my cousin's gaze. "I can stop her from ever daring to touch either of us again."

"And if you fail?" Kahlia asks. "What becomes of us then?"

"I won't fail," I tell her. "All I need to do is share enough of our secrets to get the prince to trust me and he'll welcome me on board."

Kahlia looks doubtful. "You're weak now," she says. "If the prince finds out who you are, then he could kill you like he killed Maeve."

"You know about that?" I ask, though I shouldn't be shocked. The Sea Queen can feel the death of every siren, and now that she's keeping Kahlia so close to her side in my absence, no doubt my cousin would have been there when she felt it.

Kahlia nods. "The Sea Queen waved it off as though it were nothing."

The hypocrisy of that strikes me. My mother showed more emotion when I killed a lowly mermaid than when one of our own kind was gutted on the deck of a pirate ship. Our deaths are nothing but a minor annoyance to her. I wonder if the real reason she wants to kill the humans is not so much for the good of our kind, but so she can stop experiencing the inconvenience of our deaths. We're expendable in this war. Every last one of us so easily replaced. Even me.

Perhaps, especially me.

"That will change soon," I say. I reach over and place a hand on Kahlia's arm, my palm an odd blanket of warmth over the frost of her skin. "I'll take the eye and the Sea Queen's throne along with it."

20

Elian

IN THE PALACE, IT'S always hard to tell who's in their right mind.

I stand alone in the entrance hall and fasten my black waistcoat. I look princely, which is exactly how I hate to be and, always, how Queen Galina wants me. The sun of Eidýllio has long vanished, and with it the paint-blotted sky has dimmed to midnight hues. Inside the palace, the walls are a soft red, but under the light of so many chandeliers they look almost orange. Like watered-down blood.

I try not to reach for my knife.

Madness moves at inhuman speed here, and even I'm not quick enough to stop it. I feel unsettled in this place, without my crew beside me, but bringing them would mean breaking a pact between the royal families of the world. Letting them in on a secret that should never be known, especially to pirates. So instead of bringing my crew, I lied to them. I lie to everyone these days. Whisper stories of how mundane a pirate's life is to my sister. Wink when I tell my crew about Queen Galina and how she likes me all to herself.

Only Kye knows otherwise, which is the one favorable aspect to being a diplomat's son that either of us has been able to find. Being aware of royal secrets – or having dirt on the world's leaders to use when convenient – is something Kye's father specializes in. And Kye, who usually makes it a point to be a paradox to his upper-class bloodline, has kept that trait. It's the only thing he inherited from his father.

"Are you sure you don't want me there?" he asked on the way to the Serendipity.

I glanced back to see if Lira was still standing in the center of the market square, but it was far too busy and we were far too fast and she was far too elusive to stay prominent in a crowd.

"I need Queen Galina to trust me," I said. "And your being there won't help."

"Why?"

"Because nobody trusts diplomats."

Kye nodded as though that was a valid point, and shoved his hands into his pockets. "Still," he said. "It'd be nice for you to have backup in case Galina isn't fond of your plan to manipulate her kingdom."

"Your confidence in me is heartwarming."

"Nothing against your charm," he said. "But do you really think she's going to go for it?"

"Everything you just said is exactly against my charm." I knocked his shoulder with mine. "Either way, it's worth a try. If there's any hope that Queen Galina can help me sidestep a marriage alliance with someone fully capable of killing me in my sleep, then I'll take it."

"You say that like Galina isn't fully capable of killing you when you're awake."

He had a point, of course. Kye always made a habit of having points, especially where dangerous women were concerned. Still, I left him behind with the others, because as nice as backup would be, there's not a chance in hell Galina would let a pirate into her palace.

I look down at my shirt to check if my buttons are fastened, just in case – there are certain sins that won't be tolerated – and stand up a little straighter. Comb back my hair with my hand. I already miss my hat and my boots and everything else that keeps the *Saad* with me even when she's docked.

But Galina really does hate pirates.

She trusts me more when she can see the prince of gold rather than a captain of the sea. Though there are a lot of things I will never understand about her, that isn't one of them. I barely trust myself when I've got my hat on.

"She's waiting for you."

A guard steps out from the shadows. He is covered head to toe in red armor, not a single slice of skin on show. His eyes float aimlessly in a sea of red fabric. This is what it's like for most of the guards and household staff. Never any chance of being touched directly.

I eye him cautiously. "I was waiting for you," I tell him. "The door looks too heavy to open all by myself."

I can't tell if he smiles or glares, but he definitely doesn't blink. After considering me for a mere second, he steps forward and brings his hand to the door.

The room is different. Not just from the rest of the palace, but from how it was the last time I was here. The marble walls have turned charcoal and are thick with stale ash and the smell of burning. The ceiling sprawls to endless heights, ribbed by grand wooden beams, and the color is gone from everywhere but the floor. It's the only red thing, polished to shine.

And in the far corner, on a throne shaped like a bleeding heart, the Queen of Eidýllio smiles.

"Hello, Elian."

The guard closes the door, and Queen Galina beckons me forward. Her black hair glides down her waist and onto the floor in tight coils. It's woven with rose petals that shed from her like tiny feathers. Her deep brown skin blends into the satin dress that begins at her chin and ends far past her toes.

She holds out her hand for mine, fingers spread like a spiderweb.

I consider her for a moment and then raise an eyebrow, because she should know better. Or at least, be aware that I know better.

The legend of Eidýllio says that anyone who touches a member of the royal family will instantly find their soul mate. The secret of Eidýllio, which only the royal families of the hundred kingdoms – and Kye's family, apparently – are privy to, is a little different. Because the gift, passed down through the women of the family, does not help men find love, but lose their will completely. Overtaken by endless devotion and lust until they become mindless puppets.

I take a seat on the plush sofa opposite the thrones, and Galina drops her hand with a smirk. She leans back and stretches her legs out onto the tiles.

"You came to visit," Galina says. "Which must mean that you want something."

"The pleasure of your company."

Galina laughs. "Neither of us has pleasurable company."

"The pleasure of your company and a mutually beneficial bargain."

Galina sits up a little straighter. "A bargain, or a favor? I much prefer favors," she says. "Especially when they place princes in my debt."

Sakura's face flashes across my mind, and I think back to the bargain I made with her. My kingdom, for an end to the siren plague. "I'm in enough debt with royalty," I say.

"Spoilsport," Galina teases. "I won't ask for much. Just a region or two. Perhaps a kiss."

Usually I entertain this game of cat and mouse for a little longer. Let her toy with me through thinly veiled threats of skin on skin, as though she would ever dare turn me into one of her playthings. On a normal day, we would pretend. I, to be scared she would touch me. And Galina, to be brave enough to consider it. But the truth is, that for all of her faults – and the last I counted, there were many – Galina takes little joy in her abilities. It even caused the king to turn against her when he grew tired of protecting her secret for a marriage that offered no intimacy.

Galina didn't hold his hand or stand close enough for their skin to touch, nor did she share a bed with him on their wedding night or any other night that followed. They slept at distant ends of the palace, in separate wings with separate servants and ate very much the same way: at opposite edges of a table large enough to seat twenty. It was information we shouldn't have known, but once the king had a drink, he was more than vocal about such matters.

Unlike her predecessors, Galina has no desire to force love to secure heirs. She didn't want her husband to slowly lose his mind with devotion, and so instead he slowly lost it to greed. He wanted more than she could offer – her kingdom, if he could – and it resulted in a coup bloodier than most wars.

Since his betrayal, she seems to have chosen a life of even more solitude. *There is to be no second husband*, she told the other ruling families. *I have no interest in being betrayed again or passing my curse on to any children.* And so instead she takes in wards from Orfaná, which houses all of the world's unwanted children.

Not continuing her bloodline is bad enough, but choosing to rule alone has left her country suffering. With Kardiá gaining power, Galina needs someone by her side to do the things her gift prevents her from, like liaise with the people and offer the warmth she has grown too frightened to give. And I need someone who can get me out of my deal with Sakura.

I walk toward the throne and hold out a piece of parchment.

This time, I'm too anxious to play pretend. Galina's reluctance to remarry tells me all I need to know and, in a fortuitous turn of fate, presents a rather interesting solution to one of my many problems. So rarely does karma grant me such favors.

Galina takes the parchment from me and her eyes scan over the paper, first with a confused frown and then with an intrigued smirk. It's exactly the sort of reaction I was hoping for.

"Prince Elian," she says. "How did you get your hands on something like this?"

I take a step forward, as close as I can get without risking my sanity. "From the same place you can get everything you've ever wanted."

THINGS WERE GOING SMOOTHLY. Or rather, they had screwed themselves into a great mess, and I was getting closer to pressing out the wrinkles. Galina played coy, but there was undeniable thirst in her eyes that gave me hope. *Mutually beneficial*, she mused, quoting my words back to me.

Her support would mean one less thing to think about on this impossible mission. And with Lira finally off my ship, I've also got one less person to worry about trusting. All in a day's work.

I struggle to get Lira's face out of my mind as I walk through the sparse Eidýllion streets. When I returned the seashell, there had been an odd look in her eyes. Like I was idiotic and wonderful at the same time. Like I was a fool and she was glad for it.

I take in a long breath and press my palms to my eyes, trying to blot out the sleep. When she told me that the Sea Queen had taken revenge on her family, it seemed sincere enough, and the compass, though unsteady, had pointed north just the same. Still, I haven't been able to shake the feeling that something isn't right. That no matter what truths she may give, there are lies hidden within.

I stroll across the abandoned market street, which is thick with pastry crumbs. The night is warm and sweet, even with the moon blanketing the sky. The stars here are clearer than in most kingdoms, and it's a struggle for me to keep walking. Not to stand and marvel at them. Lie on the cobblestone and think about their stories, the way I do aboard the *Saad*.

I head toward the Serendipity. We stay there each time we dock in Eidýllio, because it's an inn and a tavern, and there are few things that can't be solved with both sleep and rum. As I make my way there, a symphony of footsteps trails behind my own. I slow my pace and slip into a nearby alley marked by abandoned trader stools. It's thin, and a line of stars hangs overhead like streetlamps.

I push myself against the wall, feeling warm brick against my back. The footsteps become uncertain, searching. There's a small moment of trepidation, when the world goes quiet and all I hear is a low gasp of wind. Then the footsteps follow me into the alley.

I don't wait for my attacker to strike. I step out of the darkness, hand poised over my knife. Ready to gut whoever would be stupid enough to try to jump the captain of the *Saad*.

A girl stands, half in the shadows, dark red hair clinging to her cheeks. When she sees me, she hooks her hands over her hips, exasperated. Her eyes flood through me like poison.

"Why are you hiding?" Lira asks. "I was trying to follow you."

I let out a long breath and sheathe my knife. "I'm pretty sure I got rid of you already."

Lira shrugs, unoffended, and I consider what it would take to get under her skin. She waves off each and every comment like they're barely an annoyance. As though she has far better things to do than worry about what me or any of my crew thinks.

Lira studies me. "Why do you look like a prince all of a sudden?" she asks.

"I am a prince," I say, and move to pass her.

Lira walks in stride with me. "Not usually."

"What would you know about being usual?"

Lira's face remains blank, and once again I fail to have any sort of impact. Then she rolls her eyes, as if in compromise. *Here, I'll act irritated. Just to please you, Your Highness.*

"You're right," Lira tells me.

She pulls on the fabric of her dress. It's an old raggedy thing that Madrid found shoved into a trunk belowdecks. A stowaway from a ransack of a pirate ship. I'm almost sure it was pretty once, just as I'm almost sure we've been using it to clean Madrid's speargun for the past year. It was the best that I could do on short notice, unless Lira wanted to be clothed like a pirate, which I doubted.

Still, looking at her now, the decent man in me feels a little ashamed.

Lira stops walking to clutch the ends of her dress in both hands and then lower to the ground in a sardonic curtsy. I, too, stop, shooting her a scathing look, and she scoffs, which is the closest thing to a laugh I've heard from her.

"Queen Galina isn't big on pirates," I tell her, as I turn away and begin walking again. Lira follows. "It's not like I enjoy dressing this way."

I tug at my collar, which suddenly feels tight around my neck. There's silence and Lira promptly stops walking. I turn to face her, a question in my eyes, but she just stares.

"Here," she says, and makes a grab for my knife.

I flinch back and grab her wrist before she has the chance. Lira shoots me a disparaging look, like I'm even more of an idiot than she thought. I can feel her pulse strumming under my thumb before she slowly pulls out of my grasp.

She reaches for my knife again, tentatively, and this time I let her. I can tell she's enjoying the fact that I'm wary, as though it's the greatest compliment I could give. When her hand touches the knife, there's a spark in my chest, like a cog being pulled loose from a machine. I've always been connected to it in a way that I struggle to explain. When Lira touches it, I feel a sudden coldness passing from the blade through to my bones. I watch her with steady eyes, not risking a blink. She hesitates with the blade in her hands, as though considering all the possibilities it could bring. And then she takes a breath and swiftly cuts a line down my shirtsleeve.

The blade grazes my skin but, miraculously, doesn't draw blood.

I snatch the knife back from her. "What do you think you're doing?" I ask, surveying the tear below my shoulder.

"Now you look like a pirate," she says, and continues walking.

Incredulous, I jog to catch up with her. I'm about to tell her that she's going to have to pay for that, either with coin – which I doubt she has – or her life, but she turns to me and says, "I saw the Reoma Putoder."

"Did you make a wish?"

"Maybe I stole one instead."

She says this with a biting smile, but as the sentence fades, she reaches up to toy with the seashell I returned. It looks unnaturally bright against her neck. She touches it contemplatively, and I recognize the gesture. It's something I've done a thousand times over with my family crest ring. Whenever I think of the people I've left behind, or the burdens of a kingdom I'll never feel ready to rule. If Lira's story is true, then the necklace probably belonged to the siren who killed her family. A talisman to remind her of the revenge she must carry out.

"I still want to come with you," Lira says.

I fight to keep walking with long, even strides. The Serendipity appears ahead, another building in a row of chess-piece houses. It's stacked three stories higher than the others, with orange brick and a sign that hangs from a silhouette of the Love God. Outside, a group of women smoke cigars on thick oak benches, large jugs of mulled wine by their feet.

We stop by the doorway and I raise an eyebrow. "To avenge your family?"

"To stop this war once and for all."

"We're at war?" I make a grab for the door. "How dramatic."

Lira snatches my torn shirtsleeve. "This needs to end," she says.

I flinch at the contact, resisting the urge to go for my knife. There's never a time when I don't have to be on guard.

I roll my shoulder out of Lira's grip and keep my voice low.

"Don't keep making the mistake of thinking you can touch me," I tell her. "I'm the crown prince of Midas and captain of the world's most deadly ship. If you do that again, a few nights in a cage will seem like a godsend."

"The Sea Queen took everything from me," Lira spits, ignoring the threat. There's a deep crease in the center of her brow, and when she shakes her head, it's as though she is trying to shake the wrinkle out. "You can't imagine the pain she's caused. The Crystal of Keto is the only way to fix that."

She hisses the last part. The raw and scratchy way her voice pounces on the Midasan, like the words aren't enough to convey what she's feeling, makes my head swim. So much inside of her that she can't get out. Thoughts and feelings there are never enough ways to show.

I swallow and try to pull myself together. "You said you know things that nobody else does. Like what?"

"Like the ritual you must perform if you want to free the Crystal of Keto from where it's hidden," she says. "I'd bet my life you don't have the first clue about that."

I don't let the surprise register on my face. Even Sakura didn't know the first thing about the ritual we need to conduct, and it's hidden in her kingdom. What are the chances a stowaway on my ship would be the one to have the last piece of my puzzle? There's no way I'm that lucky.

"You have a habit of using your life as collateral," I say.

"Does that mean you will take the deal?" Lira asks.

I'd be a fool to take it and trust a stranger who claims to know the one secret I don't. I haven't survived this long by putting my life in the hands of my ex-prisoners. But to not take it would make me even more of a fool. Lira can speak *Psáriin*. She has experience hunting sirens. What if I leave her behind and then can't even free the crystal once I have it? If

I make it all that way only to drown in the final wave. The ritual is the only part of my quest where I don't have an idea past winging it, and now Lira is offering up a plan of her own on a gold platter.

If Kye were here, he'd tell me not to even think about considering it. *Good riddance*, he said when we left Lira to the streets of Eidýllio, sure neither of us would see her again. *I've got enough to protect you from without adding deadly damsels to the list.* And he wasn't wrong. Kye had sworn to protect me – not just to my father, whose money he'd taken more for the heck of it than to seal any deal – but to me. To himself. And Kye has never taken that job lightly. But I have a job too, a mission, and without Lira's help, I could leave the world open to the evils of the Sea Queen and her race forever.

"Well?" Lira presses. "Are you going to take the deal?"

"I told you I don't take deals," I say. "But maybe I'll take your word instead."

I pull open the door to the Serendipity, and Lira pushes through ahead of me. I'm hit with the familiar smell of metal and ginger root, and there are a thousand memories that shift through my mind, each as dastardly as the next. For all the ideas a name can give, the Serendipity's tells nothing of its true nature. It's a den for gamblers and the kinds of men and women who never see the light of day. They stick to moonlight, far from the ornate colors of the town. They are shadows, with fingers made sticky by debt and wine strong enough to knock a person dead from a single jug.

Some of my crew takes the large round table at the back and I smile. When I left to visit Queen Galina and strike a deal for my future, an odd wave of nausea crept up into my stomach. Like ocean sickness, if I could ever feel such a thing. Land sickness, maybe. Being separated from them, especially for such an important task, left me drained. Seeing them now, I'm revitalized.

"Just so you know," I say to Lira, "if you're lying, I might kill you."

Lira tips her chin up, eyes defiant and too blue for me to look at her straight. At first I'm not sure if she's going to say anything back, but then she licks her lips and I know it's because she can taste the sweetness of whatever insult she's about to throw.

"Maybe," she says as the light whimpers against her skin, "I might just kill you first."

21

Elian

FOG POOLS BY THE open window, like the whirls of cigar smoke. With it comes the smell of dawn as the pink-lipped sky barely stays tucked behind the line of ocean. Time is lost here, in a way that can't be said for anywhere else in the kingdom, or the world. The Serendipity exists in its own realm, with the people who could never truly belong anywhere else. It deals in deals, and caters only to traders who could never set up stalls for their goods.

Torik breaks into a low whistle as he deals another hand. His fingers glide over the cards, slick as butter, swiping them across the table in perfect piles by the stacks of red coins. When he's done, Madrid fingers her deck blankly, like the cards themselves don't matter, only what she does with them. Madrid is very good at adapting and never satisfied with playing the hand she's dealt. I'd like to say I taught her that, but there are so many things Madrid was forced to learn before she chose the *Saad*. When you're taken by a Kléftesis slave ship, you quickly learn that to survive, you can't bend to the world; you have to make it bend to you.

Unfortunately for Madrid, her tell is the fact that she has no tell. She's never willing to end how she begins, and though that means I can't guess her hand like I can most people's, knowing that she won't settle makes it easy to guess what she's going to do next.

Lira watches us predatorily, her eyes darting each time a hand moves or a coin falls from the top of a pile. I can tell that she sees the same things I do; whenever someone scratches their cheek or swallows a little too forcefully. Minute beads of sweat and twitching lips. The intonation when they ask for another jug of wine. She notices it all. Not only that, but she's making notes of it. Filing their tells and ticks away, for whatever reason. Keeping them safe, maybe, to use again.

When Kye shifts a row of red coins into the center table, I watch Lira. She quirks her lips a little to the right, and even though she can't see his cards – there's no possible way she could – she knows his hand. And she knows he's bluffing.

Lira catches my eye and when she sees me staring, her smile fades. I'm angry at myself for that. I never seem quick enough when it comes to watching these moments for long enough to pick them apart and see how she works. Why she works. What angle she's working.

I push my coins into the center of the table.

"It's too quiet in here," Madrid says.

She grabs the wine decanter from the table and fills her glass a little higher, until red sloshes over the brim. If Madrid is a good shooter, she's an even better drinker. In all our years together, I've never so much as seen her lose balance after a night of heavy liquor.

Madrid sips the wine carefully, savoring the vintage in a way none of us have ever thought to. It reminds me of the wine-tasting lessons my father forced me to attend as part of my royal training. Because nothing says King of Midas like knowing a fine wine from something distilled in a back-alley tavern.

"Sing 'Shore of Tides,' " Torik suggests dryly. "Maybe it'll drown out the sunlight."

"If we're voting, 'Little Rum Ditty' will do. Really, anything with rum."

"You don't get a vote," Madrid tells Kye, then quirks an eyebrow at me. "Cap?"

I shrug. "Sing whatever you want. Nothing will drown out the sound of me winning."

Madrid pokes her tongue out. "Lira?" she asks. "What do they sing where you're from?"

For some reason, Lira finds this amusing. "Nothing you would appreciate."

Madrid nods, as though it's more a fact than an insult. " 'Siren Down Below,' " she says, looking at Kye with a reluctant smile. "It's got rum in it."

"Suits me then."

Madrid throws herself back onto her chair. Her voice comes out in a loud refrain, words twisting and falling in her native Kléftesis. There's something whimsical to the way she sings, and whether it's the tune or the endearing grin drawn on Kye's face as she bellows the melody, I can't help but tap my fingers against my knee in rhythm to her voice.

Around the table, the crew follows on. They hum and murmur the parts they can't remember, roaring out each mention of rum. Their voices dance into one another, colliding clumsily through verses. Each of them sings in the language of their kingdom. It brings a piece of their home to this misshapen crew, reminding me of a time, so long ago, when we weren't together. When we were more strangers than family, belonging nowhere we traveled and never having the means to go somewhere we might.

When they've sung through three choruses, I almost expect Lira to join in with a rendition from Polemistés, but she remains tight-lipped and curious. She eyes them with a tiny knot in her brow, as though she can't quite understand the ritual.

I lean toward her and keep my voice to a whisper. "When are you going to sing something?"

She pushes me away. "Don't get too close," she says. "You absolutely stink."

"Of what?"

"Anglers," she says. "That oil they put on their hands and those stupid sweets they chew."

"Licorice," I tell her with a smirk. "And you didn't answer my question. Are you ever going to grace us with your voice?"

"Believe me, I'd like nothing more."

I settle back in my chair and open my arms. "Whenever you're ready."

"I'm ready for you to tell me everything you know about the Crystal of Keto."

It always comes back to that. We've been in Eidýllio for two days, and Lira has been relentless in her questions. Always wanting answers without ever revealing any herself. Someone, of course, has to go first. And I'll admit that I've grown bored waiting for it to be her.

"All I know is that it's in Págos," I tell her, wary of the glares Kye is sending my way. If it were up to him, the only way Lira would come aboard the *Saad* is if she were back in the cage.

"It's at the top of the Cloud Mountain," I explain. "In a sacred ice palace."

"You have a great ability to disguise knowing a lot as knowing a little."

"And you have a great ability to disguise knowing nothing as knowing everything," I tell her. "You still haven't told me about the ritual."

"If I tell you, then there's no use in you keeping me around. And I'm not going to spill the best leverage I have so you can leave me stranded here."

She has a point. The best habit I have is keeping only what I can use. And Lira is definitely something I can use. Even thinking it makes me sound too pirate-like for my own good, and I imagine my father's crude disappointment at how I've come to regard people as a means to an end. Bargaining chips I trade like coin. But Lira is in the unique position of knowing what she is and of being more than happy to play along if it gets her what she wants.

"Tell me something else then." I swap a card from the deck. "What do you know about the crystal?"

"For starters," she says, chastising, "it isn't a crystal, it's an eye. The ruby eye of the great sea goddess, taken from the sirens so their new queen and her predecessors would never be able to hold the power that Keto did."

"Tell me something I don't know."

"Okay," she says, like it's a challenge I've thrown down. "The Sea Queen's trident is made from Keto's bones and Keto's second eye is what powers it. When the goddess was killed, her most loyal child was nearby. She couldn't prevent Keto's death, but she did manage to steal one of her eyes before the humans could take both. With that and the few pieces of Keto that remained, she fashioned the trident and became the first Sea Queen. That trident has been passed down from generation to generation, to the eldest daughter of every Sea Queen. They use it to control the ocean and all of its creatures. As long as the queen has it, every monster in the sea is hers. And if she finds the other eye, she'll use it to enslave humans in the same way."

"What a thrilling story." Kye stares at his deck. "Did you make that one up on the spot?"

"I'm no storyteller," Lira says.

"Just an outright liar, then?"

I press my fingers to my temples. "That's enough, Kye."

"It'll be enough when we leave her stranded here like we planned."

"Plans change," Lira says.

"Let's get one thing straight," Kye tells her. "If you think that just because you've manipulated your way into this mission that it means you're part of our crew, then you're wrong. And as long as you're on the *Saad*, there's not a step you're going to take that I won't be watching. Especially if it's near Elian. So put just one foot wrong and it'll land you back in that cage."

"Kye," I warn.

Lira clenches the corner of the table, looking about ready to come undone. "Are you threatening me right now?" she asks.

"Nobody is threatening anyone," I say.

Kye throws his deck down. "Actually, that's exactly what I was doing."

"Well, great," I tell him. "Now that you've let her in on the fact that you're my hired protection, maybe you can be quiet for five seconds so I can ask her a question." I turn back to my glaring new crew member, ignoring the irritation on Kye's face.

"What did you mean, *enslave humans in the same way*?" I ask.

Lira releases her grip on the table and turns her stony eyes from Kye. "Sirens are not a free species," she says.

"Are you trying to tell me that they're just misunderstood? No, wait, let me guess: They actually love humans and want to be one of us but the Sea Queen has them under mind control?"

Lira doesn't blink at my sarcasm. "Better to be a loyal warrior than a treacherous prisoner," she says.

"So once I kill the Sea Queen, they can hunt me of their own free will," I say. "That's great."

"How are you even going to navigate up the Cloud Mountain of Págos to get to the eye?" Lira asks.

"We," I correct her. "You wanted in on this, remember?"

She sighs. "The stories say that only the Págese royal family can climb it." She eyes me skeptically. "You may be royal, but you're not Págese."

"Thanks for noticing."

I slide more red coins into the center of the table, and Torik throws his hands up.

"Damn you all," he relents, folding his cards over in a dramatic declaration. "Sweep my deck."

I grin and slip two of his cards into my own deck – one that I want, and another that I want them to think I do. I split the rest between Kye and Madrid, and they don't hesitate to shoot me disparaging looks at having ruined their hands.

"I have a map," I tell Lira.

"A map," she repeats.

"There's a secret route up the mountains that will shave weeks off our journey. There are even rest sites with technology to build quickfires to stop the cold. It shouldn't be a problem."

Lira nods, slow and calculating, as though she's trying to piece together a puzzle I haven't given her. "How did you get the map?" she asks.

"My charm."

"No, really."

"I'm really very charming," I say. "I even roped this lot into sacrificing their lives for me."

"Didn't do it for you." Madrid doesn't look up from her deck. "Did it for the target practice."

"I did it for the hijinks of near-death experiences," Kye says.

"I did it for more fish suppers." Torik stretches his arms out in a yawn. "God knows we don't have enough fish every other day of the year."

I turn to Lira. "See?"

"Okay, Prince Charming," she says. "Whatever it is, I'm sure it'll come around to bite you later on. I'd rather enjoy that then than hear it now."

"Ever the cynic."

"Ever the pirate," she retorts.

"You say that like it's an insult."

"You should assume," she says, "that everything I say to you is an insult. One day the world is going to run out of luck to give to you."

She folds her arms over her chest and I paint on my most arrogant smile, like I'm daring the world, and fate along with it, to catch up with me. Even though I know it will someday, I can't let anyone else see that. Either things fall into place, or they fall apart, but either way, I have to keep up pretenses.

22

Lira

KAHLIA'S FACE IS HAUNTING me. I picture her on the edge of Reoma Putoder, head bowed as she tried to hide her wounds. Ashamed that I'd see the pain my mother inflicted on her in my absence. I can taste it like a sickness in my mouth. Kahlia's anguish lingers at the back of my throat the same way it did on the day I held Crestell's heart in my hand.

I prowl the deck, watching the crew settle into their routines. They laugh as they scout the water and play cards as they load their guns. All of them seem so at peace, no hidden aches for home behind their eyes. It's as if they don't mind being ripped from their kingdoms over and over, while I miss mine more each day. How can they claim a nomad home so easily?

"You're thinking too much," Madrid says, settling beside me.

"I'm making up for the people on this ship who don't think at all."

Madrid hooks her arm around a cobweb of rope and swings herself onto the ledge of the ship. Her feet dangle off the edge as the *Saad* glides forward. "If you're talking about Kye," she says, "then we can agree on that."

"You don't like him?" I press my palms flat on the edge of the ship. "Aren't you mates?"

"*Mates*?" Madrid gapes. "What are we, horses? We're partners," she says. "There's a big difference, you know."

The truth is, I don't. When it comes to relationships, I don't know much at all. In my kingdom, there's no time to get to know someone or form a bond. Humans speak of *making love*, but sirens are nothing if not regimented. We make love the same way we make war.

In the ocean, there are only mermen. Most serve as guards to my mother, protecting the sea kingdom of Keto. They are the strongest warriors of us all. Vicious and deadly creatures, more vile than their mermaid counterparts. More brutal than me.

Unlike sirens, mermen have no connection to humanity. Sirens look like humans, and so there's part of us that's connected to them. Or perhaps, they look like us. We're born half of sea and half of them, and sometimes I wonder if that's where our hatred really comes from.

Mermen don't have this problem. They're crafted more from the ocean than any of us, made from the most deadly mixes of fish, with tails of sharks and sea monsters. They have no desire to interact with land, even for the purpose of war. They exist, always, under the sea, where they are either solitary and disciplined soldiers of the guard, or rampant creatures who live wild on the outskirts of the ocean.

Under order of the Sea Queen, these are the creatures we mate with. Before I was thrown into this curse, I was promised to the Flesh-Eater. Mermen have no time for names and other nonsenses and so we call them as they are: Phantom, Skinner, Flesh-Eater. While mermaids are fish through and through, laying eggs to be fertilized outside of their bodies, sirens are not as lucky. We must mate. And it's the brutality and savagery of the mermen that make them a worthy combination to create more of our murderous race. At least, that's what my mother says.

"I'm glad the captain agreed to let you stay," Madrid says.

I shake the thoughts of home and look at her questioningly. "Why would you be glad?"

"We need to start outnumbering them."

"Who?"

"The men," she says. "Ever since we pulled down to skeleton crew, there's been too much testosterone aboard."

"It seems safer to have a full crew for this mission."

She shrugs. "The captain didn't want to risk them."

"Or he couldn't trust them."

Madrid heaves herself back onto the ship's deck, her fairy-like boots stomping against the wood grain. "He trusts us all."

There is something defensive in her voice, and her eyes narrow ever so slightly.

"Are you upset?" I ask, raising an eyebrow. Humans are so sensitive.

"No," Madrid says. "You just shouldn't say things like that. Someone might hear."

"Like who?"

"Kye."

"Because he and Elian are good friends?"

"We're *all* good friends." Madrid throws her hands in the air. "Quit doing that."

"I'm not doing anything."

"You're trying to meddle."

It seems like such a silly thing to be accused of in the grand scheme of things. I'm plotting to steal back my birthright, betray my mother, and then rip out Elian's heart so no human can be a worthy threat to us. Yet somehow Madrid thinks my comments on her friendships are troublesome. Will they have a word for what I'll be when I turn on them?

"What are you talking about?" Kye asks, stepping out from the cabin belowdecks.

He looks at me with a mix of mistrust and curiosity. It's a drastic change from the carefree rapport he shares with everyone else aboard the *Saad*. If there's anyone on this ship I've failed to convince of my usefulness, then it's Elian's pseudo-bodyguard. I could leak every bit of information I have on the Sea Queen – I could even tell him where the Diávolos Sea is – and Kye still wouldn't think I'm worth keeping around. His earlier threats in Eidýllio play in my mind. He looks at me like he's just waiting for me to slip up and reveal any number of things he could use to sway Elian further into the notion that I can't be trusted. Whether it's on this ship or in my mother's ocean, there never seems to be a time when I don't have to prove myself, or worry that anything I do could lead to my downfall.

"Apparently, I'm a meddler," I tell Kye.

Madrid snorts. "At least she's open to criticism."

"Good," Kye says. "I have a lot of that to go around."

"Speaking of things to go around." Madrid looks at my dress with a grimace. "Don't you want to change your clothes sometime soon? You can't honestly want to be stuck in that thing for the rest of the trip."

"It isn't a trip," Kye says. "It's a sacred quest to save the world and destroy the Sea Queen and we shouldn't be bringing along stragglers."

Madrid nods. "Sure," she says. "But we also shouldn't be making Lira wear my cleaning rag."

I finger the hem of the white dress. It's fraying toward the bottom, string peeling from the fabric like skin. The material isn't so much white anymore as it is a muted gray, thick with the charcoal of smoke and grime that I don't want to imagine the origin of.

"She can dress herself," Kye mutters. His eyes cascade over the wrinkled dress, to the shabby ends of my red hair. "If you were planning something though," he says, "start by giving her a shower."

"A shower," I repeat.

He sighs. "Warm water and soap. I'm assuming they have that where you're from?"

Madrid tugs her shirtsleeves up to her elbows, revealing sundials and poetry painted onto every inch of her skin. The tattoos on her hands and face are simple enough, but there's no mistaking the ones that circle her arms, past her elbows and probably winding over her shoulders, too. The mark of Kléftesis pirates. Killers by trade. Though I assumed she was from Kléftes, I never dreamed Elian would choose an assassin to be on his crew. For a man who denies being at war, he certainly picks his soldiers well.

Madrid nudges me and lowers her voice. "The water isn't warm," she says. "But Kye wasn't lying about the soap."

"It beats jumping in the ocean," Kye argues. "Unless you want me to fashion a new plank?"

"No," I say. "We'll save that for the next time you threaten me."

He scowls. "If the captain wasn't watching, I really would pitch you overboard."

I roll my eyes and look over to the upper deck, where Torik is currently steering the ship. Elian leans on the railings beside his first mate. The same railings I was tied to. His hat hangs low over the shadows of his eyes, stance loose and casual. His left foot is hooked behind his right and his arms crisscross over his chest, but even I can recognize the difference between appearing relaxed and actually being so. It's the mark of a true killer, to never show the fire within.

He watches us with hawk eyes, glancing back to Torik every now and again to continue their conversation. Mostly, he talks with me in his sights. He makes no qualms about surveying me because he clearly wants me to know that my every move is being watched. I'm not trusted, and Elian doesn't want me to forget that. It's smart, if not a little annoying, but the more he watches me and sees that I'm not doing anything, the more complacent he'll get. And eventually he'll forget to look at all. Eventually he'll trust me enough that he won't think he needs to.

"He doesn't care that I can see him," I say.

"It's his ship," Kye says.

"Aren't I a guest?"

"You're not a prisoner." I don't miss the disappointment in his voice.

For some reason, this makes me laugh. "He's going to get bored watching me all the time."

Madrid frowns, lines creasing through her tattoos. "The captain doesn't get bored," she says. "It's not in his bones."

I take in a long, cold breath and look back at the water. "What's our next destination?"

"Psémata," Kye says.

"The land of untruth."

"Something you're familiar with?" he asks, and Madrid smacks him on the shoulder.

"Actually, my mother made me learn about most of the kingdoms," I answer truthfully. "She thought it would be useful for me to know about my" – I stop short before the word *prey* leaves my lips – "about history."

"What did you learn?" Kye asks.

I cast a quick glance over my shoulder to Elian, who reclines farther against the railings, pitching his elbows onto the wood. "Enough."

"And how many languages do you speak?"

I eye Kye carefully, aware that this is starting to sound like an interrogation. "Not many."

There was never a reason for me to learn more than Midasan and a few other lingering dialects common throughout the kingdoms. My own language, for all its jagged edges, more than sufficed. Really, I could have chosen not to speak Midasan at all. There are many sirens who don't learn the language, even if it's so widely used in the human world. Our songs steal hearts no matter what tongue they're in.

Still, I feel lucky knowing such things now. If I hadn't, the prince would have killed me as soon as I opened my mouth. A human who can only speak *Psáriin* is not exactly the best disguise.

"The captain speaks fifteen languages," Madrid says admiringly.

"Don't forget to wipe the drool off your shoulder." Kye points to her arm. "Right there."

Madrid slaps his hand away. "I meant that it's impressive because I only know two."

"Right," he says. "Of course you did."

"Why would anyone want to know fifteen languages when most of the world speaks Midasan?" I ask.

"Don't let the cap hear you say that," Madrid warns. "He's all for *preserving culture*." She says the last bit with a roll of her eyes, as though there's nothing she would like more than to watch her own culture wither to flames. "He studied in

Glóssa, but in the end he realized nobody can master every language, except one of their royals."

"Lira doesn't need a backstory of the captain's life," Kye says guardedly. "Not when she could be trying on something that doesn't stink of weapon grease."

Madrid smiles. "Right," she says, and snaps her fingers at me. "How do you feel about something a little bolder?"

"Bolder?"

I hesitate, and the beginnings of a smile drift over Madrid's warrior features.

"Don't panic," she says. "I just mean far less damsel and far more buccaneer."

I nod slowly. I couldn't care less what she dresses me in, so long as it warms my fragile bones, because right now the cold is pressing against them with the weight of a hundred sirens.

I dare another look at Elian. His hat shields his eyes from the midday sun, but I can still feel them on me, watching. Waiting. For me to slip up and reveal my true intentions or, just maybe, for me to do something to earn his loyalty. Let him watch. If Madrid has her way, the next time he sees me, I'll be as much of a pirate as he is.

23

Elian

I DON'T REALIZE HOW restless I am until Lira emerges from below the forecastle deck, dressed in everything but a peg leg.

The crew is humming something soft and off-kilter, while Kye speaks animatedly with Torik about old debts dying hard. Yet there's silence when we see her.

Lira's hair is pulled to one side in sweeping strands, with braided string running through odd sections. Large gold hoops hang from her ears, stretching her lobes. Even from the quarterdeck, I can see the dried blood around the loops. She's dressed in a pair of dark teal trousers with an ornate jacket to match, ridged by oval button twists. Her shoulders are a flourish of gold tassels, and the ends of a white dress shirt poke out from her wrists. There are patches on her elbows, hastily stitched together with black string.

Lira places a hand on her hip and tries to pretend she doesn't feel self-conscious, but it's the first true thing I've seen on her face since we met. She may look like a pirate, but she's got a way to go before she can pass for one.

"You've got to me kidding me," Kye says. "I told Madrid to give her a shower, not dress her up like a pirate princess."

"It's sweet that you think she looks like a princess," I say.

"I'll be sure to tell her that later."

"I'm serious," Kye tells me, like I couldn't have worked that one out for myself. "First she weasels her way onto this ship and now she's even trying to look like one of us? It's like she wants us to forget that's she's an outsider so we'll turn our backs on her."

"You're getting an awful lot of conspiracy from a dress shirt and a new pair of boots."

"Don't be naïve," Kye says. "You know better than to trust strangers."

I half-smile, grinding my teeth together. Advising me to be cautious is one thing, but lecturing me on the deck of my own ship like I'm a child is another altogether. *Naïve*. The word is too familiar not to get under my skin.

"You sound like my father," I say. "If I want a lecture, I'll ask for one."

"I'm trying to give you some advice."

"You're trying to second-guess me and it's getting old fast." I sigh, feeling the tiredness creep back in – the one usually reserved for my trips to Midas. "I'm not some novice setting sail for the first time," I tell him. "I'm the captain of this ship and I'd appreciate it if you stopped treating me like an inexperienced little prince who needs to be *advised*."

Kye's shoulders go rigid, but I'm too frustrated to care about the way his face blankets over in practiced calm. On this ship, I'm not supposed to be a Midasan royal with a legion of bodyguards and counsels. I'm supposed to be a damn pirate.

It's times like this I'm reminded of the bargain my father offered him: to stay by my side as a guardian rather than a friend, protecting me from the world I'm eager to explore. Even if Kye denies that's why he's here, having him doubt my decisions and question my moves just makes me think of my father and his court. It reminds me that Kye's a diplomat's son, used to *handling* royals. And I'm just another prince, getting adventure out of my system before I become king.

I slide down the ladder and onto the main deck. Lira has a gun holster attached to her thigh, above the folds of her knee-length boots. From the red fabric belt that clinches her waist, there's also a golden cuff just big enough to pull a sword through. Thankfully, Madrid didn't give her the weapons to match.

"You almost blend in," I say.

Lira's nose crinkles. "That's not a compliment."

I pull off my hat and step toward my sword, which rests against the ladder. It's a saber that begins in strong gold and fades to ashen black. The handle is an elaborate cuff with a map of Midas swirled into the metal, and the blade itself curves up ever so slightly at the tip, for the most deadly strike.

I point the weapon at Madrid and say, "Lend Lira something."

I ask Madrid, because she's more attached to her speargun than anything else. And because I know the rest of the crew would be hesitant to oblige. Trying to separate a pirate from his sword doesn't bear thinking about.

"Elian."

Kye's voice gives me pause. It's a warning not to do anything stupid or reckless, especially if it's only to prove a point.

"Madrid," I say, gesturing to her cutlass.

She hands it over without pause, deliberately avoiding a glance in Kye's direction. She's eager to see what will happen, just as the rest of my crew is. I can feel their eyes circling us, hear the quiet as their voices drift off and they stop singing to take in the sight.

"I didn't realize you could smile," I say as Lira studies her new blade.

"You're going to teach me how to fight."

It isn't a question, any more than it's a request. She's demanding it, as though I haven't so much as offered and it's her feminine charm that's spurred this whole thing on.

As though she has any sort of charm.

I don't make a habit of teaching strangers my tricks, but if Lira's going to survive among my crew, then she's going to need to know how to carry a blade. Watching her grapple with the guard in Eidýllio was embarrassing enough, and I need her if I'm going to be able to take down the Sea Queen. Lira isn't going to offer any of her secrets – not the intimate details of the ritual or any other nuances – until we reach the mountain peak. Which means I need her alive and able to defend herself if I'm not there. Especially when we arrive at our next destination. If Lira thinks my crew is rough around the edges, then she's going to be in for a shock when she meets the Xaprár.

"I'm going to teach you how to survive," I correct. "First lesson being: Don't stand like that."

I gesture to her feet, which are pressed closely together, knees as straight as nails. If Lira really was telling the truth about her family, then I'd expect her to know better. Warriors from Polemistés are nothing if not natural mercenaries. But then, she said her family died when she was just a child, and that could mean she was too young to be properly coached.

I adjust my position and Lira widens her stance to match. She's like a mirror, even raising her arm to mimic the bend in my elbow.

"If I beat you, what do I win?" she asks.

"The ability to defend yourself."

Her smile is lethal. "And if I kill you?"

"False confidence is nobody's friend," I school in a faultless echo of my father's voice.

And then I attack.

Lira swoops her sword up in a high arc, blocking my first blow. She's quick, but uncertain. Her feet are clumsy and when she sidesteps, her knees knock against each other. She doesn't seem used to walking, let alone have the right footwork for a duel. I swing again, slower and softer than before. Our swords clink together.

I twist away and bring my sword above my head, giving Lira an opening to attack. She doesn't hesitate. Her blade comes down on mine, hard. If she's not going to win by skill, she's going to do it with brute force. Never mind that I'm actually trying to teach her something. All she wants to learn is how to win.

I crouch down and sweep my foot under hers, but she jumps at the last minute and I miss. "That's good," I say. "How did you know I was going to do that?"

"You're highly predictable."

I roll my eyes. "Stop retreating, then. When I attack, it's your job to get me on the defensive. Always switch your position so your opponent needs to be the one to get away."

"Wars aren't won by running," she says.

"You can't win a war," I tell her. "Someone else just loses."

Lira's sword wavers and a look of confusion passes over her severe features. Like she expected another kind of reply from the siren-slaying prince. When she doesn't speak, I point my sword at her, uneasy with the lingering silence. "Attack me," I say.

She lurches forward with enough power that our blades smash against each other. The noise ricochets on long after I step away. Lira strikes again, repeatedly, and with no real purpose other than to do any kind of harm. It's the same misguided mistake that all novices make. Attacking with no goal but death.

"Have a purpose," I tell her, blocking another attempt.

Lira's breath is quick and heavy. "What does that mean?"

"You have to decide what you want. What's going to cause the most harm and how you can achieve it. You have to *think* before you attack."

I press forward and Lira withdraws, then steps toward me. Her feet jabbing and dancing across the deck. It's not exactly graceful, but it's better. At the very least, she's a fast learner.

I bring my arm down on hers, harder this time. A little more force with each blow, until I can see her arms begin to falter. Just when I think her sword is going to drop, she twists to the side and brings her left elbow up. I block it just in time, inches before my nose is shattered. She's adapting, using whatever she has to win. It would be admirable if it wasn't so shrewd.

I push Lira away and she falls to the floor with a grunt. She flips onto her back, elbows digging into the wood of the deck, and lets out a long breath.

"Gallantry is not your strong point," she says.

"I'll remember that the next time you're drowning."

"I wasn't drowning." Lira heaves herself off the floor. "I can't drown."

"No," I say. "You can't swim."

She glowers and then raises her sword, gesturing for me to do the same. I'm more than happy to oblige. It seems I can get under her skin after all.

Lira pierces the blade forward, aiming for my heart. I jump out of the way and slam the handle of my sword into her stomach. She stutters back, but her teeth are ground together. There's no scream or sign of pain aside from the devilish flicker in her eyes. I think about stopping, but I don't have the chance before she's surging toward me once more.

She throws her weight into the next blow and I struggle to bring my sword up fast enough. It's unexpected, and I take a moment too long to process it, giving Lira the perfect opening.

Her fist cracks against my cheek.

The pain is intense but fleeting, and Lira blinks, surprised at herself. I'm less shocked at her for taking the opening than I am at myself for giving it. I kick my leg up, sending Lira's sword flying across the deck. She tries to copy the gesture, aligning her foot directly with my heart. But she can't keep her balance, and as soon as her ankle is in the air, I grab it and twist. She whirls over and crashes onto her hip.

I take a step toward her. Her palms are flat on the deck, but when she sees me nearing, her head whips up and she curls her leg out. I feel my feet being swept out from under me, but catch myself before I slam beside her.

I step back and Lira pounces to her feet again. We eye each other like hunter and prey, and I cock an eyebrow, daring her to move toward me. Lira smiles impishly in return and picks up her fallen weapon.

We continue on that way, swords arcing through the air, our breath ragged. Soon there's sun in the distance, or perhaps even moonlight. Everything is muted and as Lira swoops her blade down on mine once more, I let it all fall away. My mission, my kingdom. The world. They exist somewhere other than in this moment, and now there is only this. Me, my ship, and a girl with oceans in her eyes.

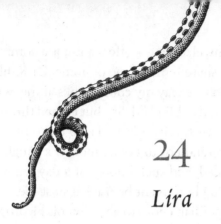

24

Lira

I HUM IN SYNC with the ocean, one hand hitched to the empty sword loop on my waist and the other closing over the edge of the *Saad*. Night quilts the sky with stars sown like the uneven stitching of my jacket.

A new land lies somewhere in reach – the next plotted point in Elian's quest – and the crew sleeps peacefully below while we sail toward it. Above where I linger, the ship's wheel stands firm, twitching ever so slightly to steer the *Saad* onward. Even without a pirate awake to command it, Elian's mighty vessel navigates knowingly along his chosen course.

I fasten my jacket over my chest as the wind picks up speed and quicken my song to match the pace. It's an odd sensation to be able to sing and have nobody suffer a consequence for it. To use my voice in the complete opposite way it was intended, with neither death nor sorrow in its wake. Leaving behind nothing but a melody.

I feel at peace.

There's something about the easy routine of the *Saad* that settles the awful parts holding true inside my heart. Nights are spent taking in the uncanny tranquility of the ocean, far from my mother's wrath, and the crew – even Kye, who isn't at all afraid to be entirely unwelcoming – offers a unique comfort. The easy rapport they share reminds me of home. Of Kahlia. They look at Elian the same way my cousin looks at me: with devotion that isn't offered in blind fidelity, but earned through something far deeper. Trust. Friendship. Maybe even love. At the very least, I can pretend not to be my mother's daughter. Live like I've never killed, and spend hours of a day without worrying that everything I do might be used against me.

I can almost see why Elian chose to abandon his birthright in favor of such a nomadic life. Though I plan to return to the Diávolos Sea and take my mother's place, I can't deny the appeal of a life spent far from the weight of kingdoms. It definitely isn't the worst idea the prince has had. Most likely. At least he knows what he wants.

My mother's voice boomerangs inside my mind, commanding me to give up the hope of trying to overthrow her and just take Elian's heart before it's too late. If I fail at getting the Second Eye of Keto, then not only will I die, but I'll die a traitor to the ocean. But what's the alternative? Bowing and praying that one day she gives me the throne, all the while watching Kahlia wince in her presence? If I follow my mother's orders, then I'm condemning Kahlia and the rest of the ocean to her rule. But if I don't follow them, if I dare to go through with my plot, then I risk proving just how defective I really am.

I grip the ship more tightly, inhaling the slick salt in the air.

If only my quest were as simple as Elian's, singularly focused on being the savior of humanity. It might seem like a big undertaking, but it's not like it requires him to betray everything he's ever known. If he succeeds, his mother might be proud. If I succeed, mine might die.

Thinking of Elian makes the night seem colder. I know

whichever plan I go with will lead to his death. Either I try to kill him now, or I wait to kill him after, but there's no path I've mapped out for myself that doesn't end alongside his life.

Every action will betray. Every choice will slaughter. Despite what my mother says, I seem to be the exact kind of monster she wanted.

The very moment I think that, a soft melody slips through the air. A distant lullaby, too far to make out, but familiar all the same. It's drowsing and seductive. So much so that it takes me a few moments to realize the ship is quaking. It's like the ocean hears the treachery of my thoughts and sends a mighty force crashing into the side of the *Saad*. I hurl forward and my hands slam over the edge of the ship's body.

I barely stop myself from plummeting overboard. I hold back a scream and look down at the peaceful ocean below. There's not a wave in sight, or the slow bubble of froth that comes after such a powerful surge. But there is a shadow.

I blink.

It lingers in the pooling darkness, half-swallowed by water and gripping firmly on to the *Saad*. I squint, leaning farther over the edge to get a closer look.

From the darkness, a skeleton claw rises.

The shadow scrambles toward me, scurrying up the side of the *Saad* with nefarious speed. I jump back just in time for the creature to pounce onto the deck and shake the sails.

Ridges crisscross down its body like scars, patched by motes of gray that seep into its flesh. Each of its fins are set apart in razors, and its large torso is carved into endless folds, leading to arms that end in inky talons. Half-shark, half something far more demonic.

The Flesh-Eater.

I drop to my knees and my mother's monster roars. He

skitters toward me, reaching out with slick palms to drag a hand down my cheek.

"*Pórni mou,*" he gnarls.

I don't react to the possessive claim, or the repulsive way he phrases it, his claws scraped against my skin in warning. I was wary of the Flesh-Eater even when I was a siren, but now that I'm human, he could easily tear through me. Perhaps that's why my mother sent him. I wonder why Elian and his crew haven't come running. Is it possible they didn't feel the ship lurch? I focus again on that familiar lullaby gliding through the wind, making my eyes heavier with each verse.

A siren's song. Making sure the crew stays in their slumber.

"*Anthrópinos,*" the Flesh-Eater barks.

Human.

The word croaks from deep within his throat, splintering through the cracks in his fangs. Disgusted. Curious. Perhaps amused, if it's possible for mermen to feel something so closely related to joy. The Flesh-Eater takes ahold of my chin and jerks my face to his so I can smell the sour blood on his breath. When he slides his viscous lips against mine, I keep deadly still. My teeth grate together, but it's only seconds before I feel flesh crawling along my tongue. I can taste the decay in him.

The Flesh-Eater rips away from me and spits. He swipes his shark tail in the air and bares his saliva-stringed fangs. He can taste the humanity in me just as I can taste the demon in him. At his outburst, a call of laughter spills from the ocean, ricocheting off the *Saad* and blowing through her sails. The music climbs and my heart clinches.

My mother's long tentacles spill over the deck like oil, familiar tribal tattoos cutting across her skin. Her crown sits gloriously sharpened, crawling down the length of her back in a magnificent headdress. She grasps the trident and stares at me with eyes like pits.

"Don't look so frightened, darling." The Sea Queen bears her fangs to a smile. "Mother's here."

I pull myself up from my knees and stare hard at the floor, to give the appearance of bowing. The longer I glare at the wood grain, the more my skin heats, sweat pasting through my clothes as the anger boils beneath. I can hardly bear the thought of looking at her. After everything she's done, for her to show up here – on Elian's ship, of all places – is the worst kind of insult.

A terse silence gathers between us, and for a moment I wonder what the next sound will be. The Flesh-Eater's roar; my mother's laughter; the erratic pounding of my furious heart.

Instead I hear my song.

The deadly lullaby from before grows louder, and I snap my head up in sudden recognition, stumbling backward. It crawls across the deck, reaching out with delicate hands to sway the *Saad*. The melody is as opiate as ever, and even I'm barely able to keep my footing as it grows. Hearing it feels like being lost in a memory, or a dream that's impossible to wake from. It feels like being born into a world imagined.

With the lie of my song, there's no chance any of the crew will wake from their sleep.

My mother presses a long webbed finger to her chest, and her seashell flickers against my voice. When my eyes begin to fog, her mouth tugs up. "It's only a keepsake," she says. "I'll return it if you succeed."

I try desperately to blink the sorrow from my eyes. "Have you come to taunt me?" I ask.

"Not at all," the Sea Queen says. "I've come to see how the

Princes' Bane is faring." She arches her neck. "Do you have the prince's heart hidden somewhere in those unsightly rags?"

It doesn't surprise me that she's come to check if I'm sticking to her plan. Being punished and pushed in the exact direction she's plotted, like Elian's ship following his course even while the captain sleeps. I am my mother's vessel. Or so she thinks.

"It's not that simple," I say.

"Oh, Lira." She swipes a string of seaweed from her trident. "Queens do not make excuses. I suppose this is just further proof of why you can't become one."

"I deserve to be queen," I say. "I'm strong enough to lead our kind."

"You're weak," she accuses. "You've always been weak. Look at you now, dressed in your human clothes, with your human emotions. Do you know what I see in your eyes, Lira? It's not death or darkness or even anger. It's tears."

I swallow. "I don't know what you're talking about."

"I'm talking about the look on your face," she says. "Your human grief."

I want to argue, but even I can't deny the sadness pricking the backs of my eyes. I felt anger as a siren, but never sorrow. Not since I took Crestell's heart with my mother's hand steady on my shoulder. But hearing my song cleave through Elian's ship, knowing that at this very moment my mother is still able to use me as a weapon without my consent, feels like being speared. And the way she looks at me, not at all concerned, so entirely contrasted by the worry I felt when I saw Kahlia's wounds. Or that Kye had when Maeve attacked Elian. Or even the look on the prince's face when he pulled me from the ocean my mother left me to drown in. How can the Sea Queen see it as a weakness when it's the very thing that binds the humans together, ensuring their strength as a unit? A family.

The Flesh-Eater snarls and my mother reaches out to run a talon over his face. She slices a line across his cheek slowly, soothingly, and the Flesh-Eater growls in satisfaction.

"Your time is running out, Lira," she says, bringing her finger to her lips. "And if you don't bring me the prince's heart soon, then I'm going to take yours."

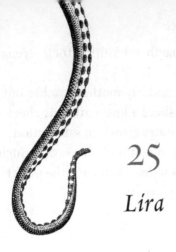

25

Lira

WHEN I LOOK IN the mirror, a stranger stares back. She takes in my newfound piracy and my newfound humanity – the face the Flesh-Eater still claimed for his own – and frowns in a way that marks her innocent features with a curious dent, deep in the center of her brows. Her lips thin and she roughly irons the wrinkle out with the palm of her hand.

My skin is flushed red from sun and my hair is stiff with the saltwater breeze. I step forward and touch the glass with spiny fingers, blinking rapidly as I take in this version of myself. Legs and feet. Eyes, each the same color. A human heart beating somewhere underneath it all, ready for my mother to take.

In the reflection, I see Elian. He stands behind me with an amused expression, leaning against the doorway, his arms tangled over his chest. He doesn't say anything, and we continue to watch each other through the pathway of glass until an odd feeling washes over me, worse than dread.

Soon we'll be in Psémata, and that means Págos won't be far off. Then the Cloud Mountain. The Second Eye of Keto. Elian's certain death. Each point of my deception is so seamlessly plotted that I should feel prepared. But I don't. Everyone I'm going to betray is too close. My mother may even be watching, and that means there's a chance she could discover my plan. It feels like a miracle that she didn't smell it on me before, or hear how fast my human heart beat. And then there's Elian, who gave me a blade instead of stabbing me with it, standing behind me now. The mercy he practices and the loyalty he has earned are both ideals that my mother would sooner burn out of me – because mercy is never an option, and loyalty is always taken – but those very emotions my mother said made me weak seem to make him strong. He's a warrior who is my opposite in every way and yet, in some ways, maybe fierceness alone, we seem to be the same.

In the mirror, Elian continues to stare. I frown when I realize that my back is to him. I've never been able to turn my back on my mother before.

I spin to face him. "What?" I ask.

"Are you done admiring yourself?"

"Never," I say, though truth be told, I'm glad to be distracted from my thoughts.

"We're about to dock at Psémata. Try to remember what I told you."

As though I could forget. What he told me was to lie, which I had enough practice in to not think of it as something that needed to be done, but something that always was.

"If Psémata is so dangerous," I say, "then why are we stopping there?"

"Because we need to get something."

I shoot Elian a skeptical look. "You mean we need to steal something."

"Good," he says. "You're learning."

I follow him out onto the main deck, where the crew is gathered. Kye tucks his sword into the strap across his chest and slips a pistol under his coat. Rather than go to his side,

Elian avoids eye contact with his bodyguard, choosing to stay beside me. Kye doesn't move to shadow him either, suddenly preoccupied with adjusting his coat collar.

"You'd think the land of lies would be a little more forgiving when it came to thievery," Madrid says. "But apparently not."

I give Elian a scathing look. "You stole something last time you were here," I say. "And now you're going to do it again?"

"Who said I was the one who stole something the first time?"

His voice is indignant, which doesn't fool me. I roll my eyes to illustrate this, and Elian sighs.

"Look," he says, "all that matters is that the *Saad* isn't welcome."

"The *Saad*," I repeat. "Or you?"

"You say that like there's any sort of difference."

"I suppose there isn't." I twist my seashell between my fingers. "You're both equally dense."

Elian laughs. Loudly, monotone, and in a way that's nearly as mocking as my comment. "Come on," he says. "We don't have time for you to learn how to be funny."

PSÉMATA IS A VERY peculiar shade of gray.

There's color, but it's diluted into an eerie film of black. Like a just-visible cloud coating the land in a tint of shadow and dust. It reminds me of looking through murky ocean water at twilight, or the feeling of staring straight into my mother's eyes. A darkness that seems ever-present.

I rub a knuckle in my eye and when my vision refocuses, everything seems darker than it was before. The more I try to make the shade disappear, the stronger it gets. It's no wonder this is the land of lies and treachery, with air as gray and smog-like as the scruples of the people who breathe it.

The wind sweats as we weave through the streets, avoiding eye contact and the usual noise Elian and his crew enjoy making. Only a dozen of them are with us, the others waiting on the *Saad*. They move like wraiths, floating instead of walking. Gliding across the hardstone pavements. I stumble to keep in step with them, nowhere near as graceful, but every bit as invisible.

As we make our way across the square, I tip my hat farther down my head. It's ridiculous, I realize, because there isn't a human alive who can recognize me. If anything, I'm the most ghostlike of us all. Still, I do it anyway, thrilled by the slight jump of my heart when someone lingers their stare on our group for too long. When I look to Elian, his face is blank and stoic, but his eyes are nowhere near as dead. They flicker with the same dirty pleasure. It's this, I realize, that draws the crew as much as the ocean. The pleasure of becoming as elusive as they are notorious.

We turn into an alleyway, where a man waits for us. He's dressed in a long black coat with a white pressed-down collar, and his heavily ringed hand rests upon a cane that is the same sandy shade as his hair.

Elian flashes him a smile, and when the man doesn't return it, he flashes him a pouch of coin instead. A toothy grin slides onto the stranger's face, and he presses his palm flat against the gray stone wall. It slides out from under him, drawing back like a curtain.

He hands Elian a small key and gestures for us to step inside. Once we do, the wall closes behind us and leaves nothing but shadows in our midst. The torchlight flickers as wisps of air blow through the stone entrance. We hunch together at the foot of a staircase the narrow room can barely contain. I reach up to fiddle with my seashell. The space is too small, and I realize quickly that it's the smallest space I've ever been in. Even the crystal cage seems commodious in comparison.

"What is this?" I ask.

Elian casts a glance over his shoulder. "Stairs," he says, and begins to climb them.

I don't waste good breath on a retort. Staring up at the never-ending spiral, I have a suspicion that I'll need to save it. I can't imagine the climb up the Cloud Mountain of Págos being this arduous.

I keep my silence as we ascend, wondering if we'll reach the top before my legs buckle out from under me. But just as it seems I won't be able to take another step, Elian comes to a halt and a large oak door emerges from the barely there light.

"This is dramatic," I say, squashing myself into the space beside him. "Is someone on the other side going to try to kill us?"

"Since when did you become one of us?" Kye asks, and Madrid jerks him in the ribs. He grunts and then says, "Fine. I look forward to you laying down your life for mine, comrade," at which point I debate whether or not to push him back down the stairs.

I watch Elian pull the key from his pocket and twist it into the slanted lock. When the door pushes open, I expect to be hit with a rush of dust or the smell of dying embers and decay. Instead I'm hit by light. It flashes away gray and echoes from dozens of sphere-shaped torches that blink with deep yellow flames.

The room is large and accommodating enough for a hidden attic, with an alleyway of doors that lead off to separate rooms. A low chandelier slices through the middle, with beads that graze the polished floors.

"This is not what I expected," I say, taken aback by the misplaced opulence.

Elian steps farther into the room. "As you like to remind me," he says, "I am a prince. This is where royalty who don't want to be found go to never be found."

"This is where we should always stay." Kye throws himself onto a plush fur chair that leans against the farthest wall. "There's no rum, but damn if the beds aren't good."

"Like you're going to find out," Madrid says with a smile. "Only enough beds for half of us, remember? And I think it's your turn for floor duty."

"We can't share?" He presses an injured hand to his chest. "Plenty of women would kill to climb into bed with me."

Madrid bristles. "They're single beds," she says sharply.

Undeterred, Kye places a hand on her knee. "I'll flip you for it."

Madrid pushes his hand from her leg. "Heads I win, tails you're an idiot?"

"Torik should sleep on the floor," Kye says, settling back into the chair. "He's always on about home comforts being dangerous for making us believe we actually have a home."

Torik casts him a side-eye. "I know enough about knives to stick them where the sun don't shine if you aren't careful." Kye smirks. "It's not good form for someone like me to sleep on the floor. I'm practically an aristocrat."

Torik casts him a blank, unimpressed stare. "You're an aristoprat," he says.

I look to Elian, who stands like a statue beside me. It's surprising not to hear him chime in with his crew's tender insults, or smile as they carelessly throw cheers around. He brings his hand to the back of his neck, unsure what to do with himself when he's not smiling.

"So our next step is to hide out here?" I ask.

"Our next step is to try to think of how we're going to get our hands on an ancient artifact without revealing who we are," Elian says.

"Steal," I correct. "How you're going to steal an ancient artifact."

"It's not stealing if you're stealing it back." Elian slips out of his jacket and throws it onto the table behind him. "The necklace belongs to the Págos family. I bargained a lot to get my hands on the map that shows their route up the mountain, but without the necklace, all of it is for nothing. She told me it was the key to the hidden dome."

"She," I repeat. "Who are you talking about?"

"The Princess of Págos," Elian says.

His eyes dart to Kye, and a strange look passes between them. Kye clears his throat.

"You mean she sacrificed her family's secrets for jewelry?" I scoff. "How trite."

Elian raises an eyebrow. "If I remember rightly," he says, with a look that is far too smug, "you were willing to sacrifice your life for a necklace."

"I was willing to sacrifice yours first," I say.

LONG AFTER THE REST of the crew disappears into sleep, Elian and I sit together. We plot in the most ghastly ways, scheming through each detail of his plan, including how to get the princess her family's necklace without getting a bullet in our hearts. Key points I'm keen to clarify.

Sunlight threatens to spill through the tiny round window above us, buried in the arch of the ceiling. The candles have died down to withering embers, and their faint afterglow casts blurry shadows around us. The smell of dawn smokes through the air, and with it the grayness seeps in from the outside world.

"I still don't understand how you know that these pirates have the necklace," I say.

"The Xaprár are infamous for stealing from royalty," Elian explains, palming a licorice stick. "If there's a precious heirloom missing anywhere in the world, you better believe that Tallis Rycroft and his band of pirate thieves have it in hand."

"Even if that's true, wouldn't they have sold it by now? What use would it be to keep something like that?"

"You're assuming that Rycroft needs to steal to survive," Elian says. "Maybe he did once, but now he steals just to prove that he can. A necklace like that carries prestige. It would be more of a trophy to him than a treasure. Just another artifact to prove how good he is."

"If he's that good," I say, "how are you going to steal it from him? I think he might notice your hand running through his pockets."

"Misdirection." Elian takes a bite out of the licorice stick. "They look over here" – he waves a hand theatrically – "while I'm pilfering over here." He wags his other hand at me, looking all too satisfied. "As long as you can manage to look innocent and above suspicion."

"And if that doesn't work?"

"I have a backup plan." Elian produces a small vial from his pocket with a flourish. "It's less wily, but equally duplicitous."

"Poison?" I muse. "Were you keeping that around for your future wife?"

"It's not lethal," Elian says. For a killer, he seems oddly offended at the idea. "And no." He pauses, then turns to me with a half-smile. "Unless you were my wife."

"If I were your wife, then I'd take it."

"Ha!" He throws his head back and pockets the vial once more. "Thankfully that's not something we have to worry about."

"Because you're betrothed?"

He hesitates. "Why would you say that?"

"You're royal," I tell him. "That's what royalty does. They marry for power."

I think back to the Flesh-Eater and the way my mother's voice turned into a song when she told me she had chosen her finest warrior to continue our line. The orange rusted blood in the corners of his lips as he regarded me with a mix of hunger and regimented disinterest. And on the *Saad*, just nights before, when he claimed me even in my human body. An uneasiness creeps through me at the memory.

"I don't want it to be that way," Elian says. "When I marry, it won't be about power."

"What will it be, then?"

"Sacrifice."

His voice is crisp. There's a certainty to it, as though he's resigned to the fact rather than proud of it. He swallows, just loud enough to catch me off guard, and the action makes me shift, his discomfort snaking through the air toward me.

Elian's eyes drop to the floor, and I feel as though I've exposed him or he's laid himself bare and suddenly regrets it. Either way, I'm not sure what I'm supposed to say, and something about the moment seems so personal – too personal – that I find myself searching for anything to fill the quiet.

"You're right," I tell him, trying to shake the melancholy from my voice. "Spending a lifetime with you would be a sacrifice."

"Oh?" A glow returns to Elian's eyes and he smiles as though the last few seconds didn't happen. Erasing whatever parts of his past he doesn't want to remember.

"What would you be losing?" he asks.

"If I married you?" I stand to tower above him, pushing away the unraveling thing inside me. "I suppose it would be my mind."

I turn, and the ricochets of his laughter follow me out of the room. But even with that infectious melody, I can't shake the look that crossed his face when I mentioned marriage. It makes me more curious than I ought to be.

I think sinister thoughts, but I know the most likely of them is an arranged marriage, ordered by the Midasan king to bind their kingdom to another. Maybe the weight Elian carries is born from the shackles of a royal life and a kingdom that is unwanted but needed all the same. It's something I can understand. Another similarity between us that I'd be blind not to note. In the pits of our souls – if I amuse myself with the notion that I have a soul – Elian and I aren't so different. Two kingdoms that come with responsibilities we each have trouble bearing. Him, the shackles of being pinned to one land and one life. Me, trapped in the confines of my mother's murderous legacy. And the ocean, calling out to us both. A song of freedom and longing.

26

Elian

STEALING IS SOMETHING I first mastered when I was sixteen and spent the better part of the year in the northern isle of Kléftes. Everything was new and it was all I could do not to beg everyone I met for a piece of their history. A skill or a story only they knew. I wanted it all.

My crew was barely a crew and I was barely a man, let alone a pirate. After Kye, Torik was one of the first men I recruited, and with his addition, my father insisted on a ship capable of the task I set myself, while I insisted on something that was more weapon than boat.

I gained Torik's unyielding loyalty in his home country of Ánthrakas, where the mines run deep and coal travels through the wind in a song. But though he was great with a pistol and even greater with a sword, even he didn't have the stomach for the brute force that was needed to kill a siren. And as the days went on, I found I was the same. I needed to be more agile.

Kléftes breeds thieves, but more than that it breeds ghosts. Men and women traded like cattle, reared to be demons and killers and whatever else their masters demand. Subject to the whims of slavers who would sooner sell their own people than lose a trinket. They are trained to be as invisible as they are deadly, able to sweep in through the night unnoticed and carry out deeds that never could be done in the true light of day.

I wanted to learn from them, and one day, when the mantle of king was forced upon me, inflict the same suffering on them that they inflicted on the world. Sirens weren't the only enemy. Humans could be just as demonic, and it was a wonder to me that my father and the other kingdoms hadn't banded together to wage war on Kléftes. What good was a global peace treaty if the kingdoms were savaging themselves?

Of course, Madrid changed that. When I strode into Kléftes and saw her – tattooed and bleeding from so many wounds, it was hard to make out her face beneath it all – I realized that some things couldn't be fixed. In a world that bred killers as easily as ours, the best I could hope for was to make them mine. Killers couldn't undo death, but they could find new prey. They could find a different kind of pain to inflict.

I stare at the Xaprár as they prepare their ship for sail. They're Kléftesis snatchers known for sleuthing into kingdoms and leaving with the most precious jewels. Masters of disguise who have stolen heirlooms from too many royals to count. They would be legends if they weren't so reviled by the ruling families. It would be easy enough to declare a bounty on their heads, but nobody would be brave enough to try their hand at it. Going after one of the Xaprár would be like going after a member of the *Saad*. Which means that it would be suicide. Not to mention that the Xaprár are good at stealing from royalty but even better at stealing *for* royalty. Thieves for hire who most of the families don't dare think of crossing, for fear they may need their services one day.

Luckily, I don't have that fear.

I watch Tallis Rycroft lounge at the base of the mighty dock steps. He counts his loot brazenly, fingers slick with the kind of speed that comes only from years of earning nothing and taking everything.

I'm not one to listen to the stories that filter through our world like grains of salt through open hands, but there's something about Rycroft that has always set me on edge. He owns a slave ship in the northern isle. I can't be sure which, and I know it's unlikely to be the same vessel Madrid had to murder her way out of, but there isn't a member of my crew who doesn't bristle at his name. Politics prevail, though, and declaring a feud with the Xaprár wouldn't be worth it.

I look to Madrid and Kye, who tuck themselves behind the shrubs beside me. While Kye turns to me with a questioning stare, Madrid's eyes stay focused on Rycroft, unblinking. She won't risk letting him out of her sight; she doesn't risk anything when it comes to her countrymen. It's why Kye insisted he be in her squad, if for nothing else than to hold her back if the time comes.

Torik has taken flank across the way with more of the crew, weapons poised for whatever could go wrong. To approach Rycroft with my crew, in any place outside of a tavern, would arouse suspicion. I have to be cautious and clever, which is lucky because I like to think I'm always both of those things at any given time.

I turn to Lira. She looks like a portrait, with deep copper hair pulled from her star-freckled face, only confirming the fact that she isn't capable of lying low. Not saying whatever crosses her damned mind. Lira can keep secrets but she can't, by any stretch of the imagination, keep peace. While I have ample practice in pretend, there's too much fire in Lira's eyes for such things. Some people burn so brightly, it's impossible to put the flames out. Thankfully, that's just what I need.

The captain of the *Saad* approaching another pirate ship with his league of siren killers would only end in death, but Elian Midas, prince and arrogant son of a bitch, strolling through the docks with a new woman on his arm, too brazen to be a sleuth or a spy . . . that just might work. Rycroft might just let enough of his guard down to let us aboard his ship. And once we're on board, all I need is for Lira to confirm he has what we're looking for.

"If you're ready," I say to Lira, "I give you permission to risk your life for me."

She lifts her chin. There's something about the way she carries herself that reminds me of the women at court. She has the air of someone with a lifetime of never knowing anything but her own way. I know because I have an identical look. Though I try to hide it, I know it's still there. The entitlement. The stubbornness that can never truly be lost.

It's not a look that belongs on the face of a lost orphan girl.

I make to take her hand and head toward Rycroft's ship, when Kye grabs on to my shirtsleeve. He doesn't need to say anything; I can read the look in his eyes telling me that he'd rather be the one by my side if we're going to go head-on with Rycroft. Truth be told, I'd feel better having him there too. Thing is, as pretty as Kye might find himself, I don't think Rycroft would agree, and what I need right now is an inconspicuous companion, not a pirate-shaped protector.

"Just trust me," I tell him.

"It's not you I don't trust."

Lira laughs, like someone worrying about my safety is the funniest thing she's heard all day. "Better be careful," she tells me. "I could strike a bargain with the Xaprár and use those three days of sword training to stab you in the back."

"As though you'd ever abandon the luxuries of the *Saad* for Rycroft's rust boat," I say, gesturing to Rycroft's ship.

It isn't a bad vessel, but it's no match for the deadly beauty of the *Saad*. With a redwood body and sails the color of ash, it's more than worthy for looting, but to hunt the Princes' Bane and her sea witch mother, or hold a prince whose heart does not beat but crashes like ocean waves . . . well, it's not quite capable of that.

"I don't see much difference," Lira says. "Paint the wood a shade darker, give the captain a large chip for his shoulder, and I wouldn't notice a thing."

I widen my eyes, outraged, but Lira only smiles.

"Just remember," she says, blue eyes glistening, "if you want this scum to believe you and I could be *together*" – her voice echoes with shameless disbelief – "then you need to take off that ridiculous hat."

"Just you remember," I say as we step out from behind the shrubs and approach my lounging rival, "if we're caught, there's no way in hell I'm risking my neck to save you."

Rycroft spots us the moment we maneuver out of the dark and into the unforgiving light of the star-dappled sky. He doesn't speak as we approach, or move from his sprawling position on the dock steps that lead to his ship. But I know he sees us. He continues counting his riches, but his moves are more precise. It's not until we're directly above him that he deigns to look up with a gold-studded grin.

Objectively speaking, Tallis Rycroft isn't a handsome man. His features don't quite seem to belong to him, just another thing he's stolen. His eyes are dark pits that bore into his ashen skin, and his lips are pale brown – thin and curved upward in a permanent smirk, hooded by a slender mustache. A deep burgundy turban wraps around his head, and from it large pieces of gold and silver hang like droplets, falling into his face and down his neck. When he looks at me, he runs his tongue over his lips.

"Where's your guard dog?" he asks in heavy Kléftesis.

"Which one?" I reply in Midasan, not willing to give him the satisfaction of making me use the tongue of thieves and slavers.

Rycroft stands and leans against the rope of the dock steps. "If you're here, Kye and that tattooed whore can't be far off. And let me guess: She has a target on my head? Like a pissant prince would dare take me out."

I school my features into surprise. "Such paranoia," I say. "It's just me and my lady friend, alone and unarmed. Really, you can't be scared of a single pissant prince, can you?"

Rycroft narrows his eyes. "And this one?" He casts a lecherous grin toward Lira. Though I'm sure she doesn't speak the language – there aren't many outside Kléftes who do – her face twists in measured disgust.

"Not a guard dog," I tell him.

"Really?" He slips into Midasan and lets an alley-cat grin loose on his face. "Looks like a bitch to me."

I keep a lofty smile on my face. "You're as pleasant as ever." I slip a lazy arm around Lira's waist. She bristles and then eases herself rigidly into my grip. "And after my new friend and I came to admire your ship."

"Admire it," Rycroft repeats. "Or steal it?"

"An entire boat?" I give him my most shit-eating grin. "It's nice to know you have such a high opinion of me." I turn to Lira. "Do you think it could fit in your purse?"

"Perhaps," she says. "Nothing here looks very big."

She casts a meaningful look at Rycroft and I cough, covering my mouth to hide the possibility of laughter.

Rycroft snarls. "Okay," he says. "I'll play this out." He opens his arms in a dangerous welcome, revealing the full mass of the ship behind him. "Come aboard. We'll talk over rum fit for a king."

It's a jab. A double-edged sword to point out what I've not yet become and mock me with what I will one day be. Never a pirate, always a prince.

I accept Rycroft's invitation with a curt nod and keep my arm wrapped protectively around Lira. My every instinct is on edge, telling me to walk behind him and not in front. Watch his hands and his eyes and the two dozen men who are leering down at us as we settle around a table on the ship deck. To never, for a single second, think that he doesn't wish me dead. And that he's not going to try to make that wish come true when I steal the Págese necklace.

The rum Rycroft offers us is from Midas, which wouldn't bother me half as much if it wasn't also from the royal cellar. The bottle is blown glass, twisted into the shape of our crest, with liquid gold printing the intricate details. The drink itself is littered with gold dust that glistens against the reflection of the glass. I don't know when he stole it, or why – if he did it just because he could, or if he did it just because he wanted me to know that he could – but my hands clench into fists under the table.

I pray to the gods that Madrid's finger slips on her trigger.

"How's it taste?" Rycroft asks.

Lira brings the goblet to her lips and inhales. I'm not sure if she's smelling for poison or if she actually wants to savor the drink, but she closes her eyes and waits a few moments before bringing the goblet to her mouth. There is a spot of blood on her tongue when she licks her lips, from the shards of gold that dance inside the bottle.

When Lira runs her tongue over her lips, my hands unclench and the anger seeps from me. Everything she does is sensual, playing her part as perfectly as she can. Or maybe she doesn't need to act and simply enjoys the lustful way Rycroft's teeth scrape his lip when he watches her.

"It's perfectly lovely," Lira says, her voice almost unrecognizable.

"Good." Rycroft's smile could cut through steel. "I wouldn't want you to be unsatisfied."

"Oh, I wouldn't worry about that," Lira says. "Not now that I'm in such good company."

Rycroft's eyes fill with a calculating lust. He blinks at her, then turns to me. "Are you gonna tell me the reason for your visit?" he asks. "Or shall we keep playing this game?"

There was never an option to stop playing. String him along and let his suspicions get the better of him. Let him think that I'm up to no good while Lira plays to his ego and swoons on his every senseless word. Let him think that he needs to watch my every move and scour the docks where my crew waits. Let his attention be on everything but the newly demure Lira. The harmless arm piece I'm flaunting in front of him like the jackass prince I am.

"Actually," I say, swirling the goblet of rum, "there is something."

Rycroft leans back and hoists his feet onto the table. "Spit it out," he says. "If it's a trade you want, we can come to an agreement."

His eyes flicker to Lira and she smiles coyly. I didn't realize she was capable of looking coy, but it seems I've underestimated her skills of deceit. She wraps a winding piece of hair around her finger, so convincing that I have to do a double take to catch the clamped fist she's concealing under the table. Her face betrays nothing of it.

"A yellow sapphire amulet disappeared from the Midasan royal vaults," I say, recalling the lie verbatim as we practiced. "I was hoping you might know something."

Rycroft's strange features fill with delight. He arches his arms behind his head. "So you've come slinging accusations?" He looks far too pleased by it.

"It's precious to me," I tell him. "If it were to suddenly reappear or if you caught word of where it might be, the information would be very valuable. Priceless, one might say."

I can almost see Rycroft weigh the options of whether he should pretend he has something of mine, just to watch me squirm, or offer to help me find it for a fee as large as he would like.

"I don't have it," Rycroft tells me, like a moth to the flame. "But I've heard whispers."

Lies, I think. *Such bullshit lies.*

"It's possible I know where it is."

I swallow my smirk and feign intrigue at the chance that he could have the location of my imaginary Midasan heirloom. "What would that information cost me?"

"Time," he says. "For me to check my sources are correct." For him to actually gather sources. "And I think I'd also like your ship."

I knew it was coming. For every unpredictable thing Rycroft did, there were a hundred more easily guessed. What better way to make a prince suffer than to take away his favorite toy?

I let a flicker of practiced irritation cross over my features. "Not going to happen."

"It's your ship or your amulet," Rycroft says. "You have to decide."

"And how do I know you're not the one who has it?" I time my anger in perfect pulses. "I'm not paying you to give me back something you've already stolen."

Rycroft's eyes go dark at the insinuation. "I told you I didn't have it."

"I'm not going to take your word for it."

"So, what, you want me to take you belowdecks and let your sneaky shit fingers trawl through my treasure?" he asks.

Which is exactly what I want. The entire reason we came here and talked our way onto his ship was to get a look at his spoils and confirm that Sakura's necklace is among them.

"If you think that's happening," Rycroft says, "then you're stupider than you look."

"Fine." I glare. Spoiled, impatient. Playing my part just as he would expect. I wave a dismissive hand over to Lira. "Let her look instead. I don't care either way, but unless one of us has a peek at the unmentionables you're hiding, you can keep your ship and watch the *Saad* sail off into the sunset without you."

It was always going to be Lira, of course. I knew there wasn't a chance in hell Rycroft would let the captain of the *Saad* into his treasure trove. But to let one of the Midasan prince's captivating floozies take a quick look around? Maybe.

"Her," Rycroft repeats with a snake smile. "How will she know what she's looking for?"

"It's yellow sapphire," I tell him. "She's not a complete idiot."

Lira kicks me under the table, hard. Rycroft shoots her a devil's smile and turns to one of his approaching shadows. The man is older than I am, his skin brandished by the sun, and I can't help but think he looks familiar. A cleaver is sheathed to his belt, and large earrings stretch chasms into his lobes.

When he leans down to whisper into Rycroft's ear, he sweeps a long velvet coat out of the way.

I straighten, knowing where I've seen him before. The man from the Golden Goose. The one who started this quest by pointing me in the direction of the Sea Queens's weakness.

He's one of the Xaprár.

It was Rycroft who sent me after the crystal.

"I have a new bargain for you," Rycroft says, all teeth. "Now that my men have sights on your crew, how about we both be a little more honest? Your guys are good at hiding, but they're not Xaprár. What they are, is screwed. And they'll be dead if you don't tell me exactly how you plan to get the Crystal of Keto."

I don't blink. "Never heard of it."

"Whose life should I bring you to get your memory going?" Rycroft slides his finger across the rim of his goblet. "The tattooed bitch with the gun? Or maybe I'll slice the giant a new smile? Pick a person and I'll pick the body part."

I arch an eyebrow. "That's very dramatic."

"I like dramatic," he says. "How about Kye's head on a platter?"

"How about me killing you before your crew can even blink?"

Rycroft smiles. "But then where would your friends be?" He gestures to one of the Xaprár, who pours him another measure of rum.

"So you kill me as a trade for their lives?" I ask.

Rycroft throws his head back. "Now who's dramatic? I wouldn't risk starting a war with your daddy." He waves a hand. "Just tell me what I want to know."

"How about you tell me why you're suddenly so interested in the crystal?"

Rycroft leans back in his chair, letting his gold teeth track to a lazy smile. "I've had my sights on it for a while. Every pirate likes hunting for lost treasure, and the more elusive it is the better. You know that, don't you, Your Highness?" Rycroft pulls aside his collar. The necklace is not quite like it was in the stories. The stone is not a stone, but a droplet of blue that teeters from the chain like it's ready to fall. Each fragment of it dances as though it's made of water, with small ornate fangs latching around the diamond.

The lost Págese necklace. I was right. Rycroft does have it.

"I got my hands on this straight after hearing it was the key," Rycroft says, folding his collar back over to hide the necklace.

"How did you even find out about that?"

No way had Rycroft gotten the information easily when I had to sell my country – and my damn soul – for it.

"I'm a man for hire," Rycroft says. "And the Págese are always looking for someone to do their dirty work. I had a few words with one of their princes a few years back after completing a job. You'd be surprised how loose his lips got after a few whiskeys and some sweet nothings."

I bristle. Rycroft had played the seducer, using a charm conjured from hell knows where, while I had put my country on the line. He had nothing to lose, so he'd traded nothing. Whereas I had an entire kingdom to lose and I'd offered it at a bargain price. Too caught up in my own crusade to even stop to think. Pathetic. I was starting to feel really damn pathetic.

"Why do you want to kill the Sea Queen?" I ask. "Hero isn't exactly your color."

Rycroft rolls his shoulders back. "I don't give a damn about your little war with the octobitch," he says. "I care less about her life span than I do yours."

"Then what?"

Rycroft's eyes are hungry. "All the power of the ocean," he says. "If I get that crystal, then I control the oldest magic there ever was." He takes a swig of rum and then slams the goblet back onto the table, hard. "And if the Sea Queen gives me any trouble, I'll put her and her little bitches back in their place."

Lira's lips curl. "Is that so?"

"It's a fact," he tells her. "Let them try to come for me."

The fabric of Lira's dress is bunched between her fists, and when she makes like she's going to stand, I place a hand on her knee. We're far too outnumbered to start throwing punches.

"Why the charade of having your man come to Midas and feed me information?" I ask. "Why get me involved at all?"

"I'm not an idiot," Rycroft says, though I beg to differ. "Nobody can make the climb up the mountain and live to tell the tale. The ice prince may have been willing to tell me about some ancient necklace nobody had seen in a few lifetimes, but he wasn't going to give up the most carefully guarded secret of their bloodline."

"And you knew that it was information I could get."

"You're the prince of Midas," he says. "Royalty sticks together, doesn't it? I knew you'd all be in on one another's dirty secrets. Or if you weren't, you could be."

And he was right. I managed to weasel my way into the secrets of Sakura's family just like Rycroft knew I would, learning things I had no right to, for a mission he had planned. All of my talk about being a captain, telling Kye I wasn't some naïve prince to be advised and influenced, and all the while I was playing into the hands of Tallis Rycroft and his merry band of miscreants.

"So you planned to use me to find out the way up the mountain."

"Not just that," Rycroft says. "I need entry, too. I'm not about to start a war with the Págese by trespassing on their mountain. They'd know I was there the second I started the climb, and they'd be on me and my guys before I got anywhere near the ice palace. A pirate isn't gonna get close to that crystal."

Lira slinks back into her chair, realization dawning on her face the moment it does mine. "But a prince might," she says.

Rycroft claps his hands together. "Smart girl," he says, then turns to me, his arms wide and welcoming. "Your diplomatic connections are gonna come in handy, golden boy. If my bets are right, you've already talked your way into some kind of deal with them. Offered them something in exchange for entry. If I'm with you, I can stroll right on up there with nobody on my back and then loot the whole damn place. By the time they realize what me and my lot are doing, I'll already have the power of the ocean in my hands."

"Great plan," I say. "Only problem being that I'm not telling you a thing and my schedule is a little packed to take you on a guided tour of a mountain."

"Not like I thought you'd be easy," Rycroft says. "But you don't have to take me anyway; we're taking you."

The Xaprár inch closer, creating a circle around us.

"As for the information, I can torture that out of you and your little lady on the way. It'll be a time-saver."

I smirk and look over at Lira. She blinks, not in shock, but as though she is considering what he's saying like a proposition rather than a threat. If she's scared, she does a good job of hiding it.

She lifts her rum from the table with a slow and steady hand. "Just so we understand each other," she says, swirling the goblet indifferently, "I'm not his lady."

Before I can register the look on Rycroft's face, Lira lurches forward and throws the golden liquid straight into his eye. Rycroft lets out an ungodly howl, and I jump to my feet, knife drawn as the pirate clutches his face where the gold dust slices with every blink.

"You *bitch*," he snarls, blindly drawing his sword.

Lira pulls out the small dagger she slipped into her boot earlier, and I press my back to hers. Rycroft's shadows surround us, and from the corner of my eye, I see snipers gather on the quarterdeck. I can take a dozen men, maybe, but even I'm not bulletproof. And Lira, for all the fire that runs through her veins, is not invincible.

"You think that was clever?" Rycroft wipes his eyes with the back of his sleeve.

"Maybe not," Lira says. "But it was funny."

"Funny?" He takes a step closer, and I see the anger rolling from him like smoke. "I'll show you funny."

I arch my body, turning our positions so Lira squares off with the Xaprár and I come face-to-face with Rycroft. "No point crying over spilled rum," I tell him.

For a moment Rycroft stares at me, deathly still. His lips curl upward and he blinks back a dribble of blood from his left eye. "To think," he says, "when I tortured you, I was going to let you keep your most precious appendage."

When he lunges, I push Lira to the side and dart back. The Xaprár clear a path for us and then circle like vultures, ready to peck at the leftover carcass of the kill. Rycroft brings his heavy sword down, and when my knife meets it, the sparks are blinding.

I kick at his knee and Rycroft stumbles back with a hiss, but it's only seconds before he's on me again, slashing and swiping with his sword. Lethal blows primed to kill. I jump back and his blade slices across my chest.

I don't take my focus off him to register the pain. He's mad to try this. To attack not just a prince, but a captain. Spilling royal blood is punishable by death, but spilling mine . . . well, my crew would think death was too kind.

I thrust my arm forward, aiming my dagger for his stomach. Rycroft twists out of the way, barely, and I feel my ankle slip. Saving what little grace I have, I plunge the blade into his thigh. I feel the jar of bone as it settles inside his leg. When I pull, my hand comes away empty.

Rycroft clasps a hand around the knife. He looks inhuman, like even pain is too scared to touch him now. Without ceremony, he yanks on the handle, hard, and the blade oozes from him. It comes away clean and for a moment I worry that Rycroft will see the otherworldly shine of the steel, but the pirate barely glances at it before tossing it across the ship.

"What now?" he asks. "No more tricks."

"You'd kill an unarmed man?" I raise a taunting finger.

"I think we both know that you're never unarmed. And that when I kill you, it'll be a damn sight slower than this."

He lurches his head in a gesture to someone behind me. I'm able to spare one last look to Lira, taking in the blinding light of her eyes, flared in warning, before a shadow pitches toward me. I whip my head back a second too late, and a blinding pain explodes against my skull.

27

Lira

I BRING MY TONGUE to the cut on my lip. My hands are secured to a large beam, and on the other side of the room, tied to an identical shaft, Elian sags on the floor.

He looks every bit the handsome prince, even with his head slumped against the splintered wood, his injury matting his hair. His jaw ticks as he sleeps, and when his eyes flutter as though they're about to open, something snags in my chest.

He doesn't wake.

His breathing is hitched, but I'm surprised he's even breathing at all. I heard the crunch as the bat connected with the back of his head. A coward's blow. Elian was winning, and in just a few more minutes – even without that knife he loves so damn much – he would have killed Tallis Rycroft. With his bare hands if he had to. And I would have helped.

If I had my song, I wouldn't have even wasted it on a man like Tallis. Let him drown knowing the horror of death, without the comfort of beauty or love. Elian has an army and we should have used that to attack Rycroft, but the prince prefers trickery to war.

Get away clean, he said. *Before anyone can notice what we've taken.*

I look to my hands, smeared with Elian's blood. This is not getting away clean.

In the sea, mermaids sing songs about humans. There's one they hum like a child's lullaby, which weaves the story of Keto's slaughter. In it, the mermaids speak of human bravery and how they claimed victory against all odds, but until I was dragged onto Elian's ship, I'd never seen courage from a human. Even the strongest men fell under my spell, and those I didn't lure were too scared to challenge me. Elian is different. He has courage, or recklessness masked as something like it. And he also has mercy. Mercy even for creatures like Maeve, whose life he took as a last option. He didn't want to savor it; he just wanted it over with. Like I had with the Kalokaírin prince. With Crestell.

I wonder if I'd be that sort of a killer if I had been raised human. Merciful and hesitant to shed blood. Or, perhaps, if I wouldn't have been a killer at all. If I would have just been a girl, like any other who walked the world. Keto created our race in war and savagery, but it was the sea queens who took her hate and made it our legacy. Queens like my mother, who taught their children to be empty warriors.

Elian's family taught him to be something else. The kind of man willing to throw a strange girl out of harm's way and battle a tyrannical pirate in her place. The chivalry I used to scoff at has saved my life twice now. Is that what it means to be human? Pushing someone else out of danger and throwing yourself in? Every time I protected Kahlia, the Sea Queen chided me for my weakness and punished us both as though she could beat the bond out of us. I spent my life rethinking every look and action to be sure there wasn't any visible affection in either. She told me it made me inferior. That human emotions were a curse. But Elian's human emotions are what led him to save me. To help me. To trust that I'll do the same when the time comes.

Elian stirs and lets out a low groan. His head lolls and his eyes flicker open. He blinks in his surroundings, and it only takes a few moments before he notices the restraints binding his hands. He tugs, a halfhearted attempt at escape, and then cranes his head toward me. From across the room, I see his elegant jaw sharpen.

"Lira?" His voice is as coarse as sand. He must see blood somewhere – it seems to be everywhere – because the next thing he asks is, "Where are you hurt?"

Again, I lick the crack in my lip where Tallis struck me.

The blood is warm and bitter.

"I'm not." I angle my face away so he doesn't see otherwise. "You bled all over me."

Elian's laugh is more of a scoff. "Charming as ever," he says.

He takes in a long breath and closes his eyes for a moment. The pain in his head must be getting the best of him, but he tries to swallow it and appear the brave warrior. As though it would be an offense for me to see him as anything else.

"I'll kill him for this," Elian says.

"You should make sure he doesn't kill us first."

Elian tugs at the rope again, twisting his arm in the most bizarre angles in an attempt to slip the restraints. He moves like an eel, slippery and too quick for me to see what he's doing from where I'm sitting.

"Enough," I say, when I see the rope begin to redden his skin. "You're not helping."

"I'm trying," Elian tells me. "Feel free to yank your own thumb out of its socket anytime now. Or better yet, how about you use that *Psáriin* to call some sirens here and let them kill us before Rycroft has a chance?"

I flick my chin up. "We wouldn't be here if you hadn't insisted on such a ridiculous plan."

"I think getting my head smashed in may have affected my hearing." Elian's voice loses its usual musicality. "What did you just say?"

"You didn't even realize he was tricking you," I say. "And you walked right into his hands."

Elian's shoulders twitch. "He has the necklace, so whether I knew about his ambush or not, I still would have come. I've sacrificed too much to fall at the last hurdle."

"As though you've ever had to sacrifice anything," I shoot back, thinking of the kingdom I have hanging on the line. "You're the prince of a kingdom that's full of brightness and warmth."

"And that kingdom is exactly what I've sacrificed!"

"What does that mean?"

Elian sighs. "It means that my deal with the princess was about more than just a map and a necklace." His voice is rueful. "I promised she could rule alongside me if she gave me her help."

My lips part as the weight of his words sink through the air. While I'm trying everything I can to steal my throne from my mother, Elian is busy bargaining his away for treasure.

Just like a pirate.

"Are you stupid?" The disbelief shoots like a bullet from my mouth.

"Finding the crystal could save lives," Elian says. "And marrying a Págese princess wouldn't exactly be bad for my country. If anything, it'll be more than my father ever dreamed of me achieving. I'll be a better king than he could have hoped for."

Though the words should be overcome with pride, they

are rough and bitter. Tinged in as much sadness as they are resentment.

I think about how much time I spent trying to make my mother proud. Enough that I forgot what it was like to feel content or anything I wasn't ordered to feel. I let her gift me to a merman like I was nothing but flesh he could devour, all the while reasoning that it was something I had to do for my kingdom. And Elian has thrust that own perdition onto himself. To fulfill the burden of the world and the duty of his title, he's willing to lose the parts of himself he treasures the most. The freedom and the adventure and the joy. Parts I barely remember having.

I look away, discomforted by how much of myself I see in his eyes.

Either way, you have to take his heart, I think to myself. *What other choice is there?*

"If the necklace is that precious," I say, "we should have just killed Tallis to get it."

"You can't just kill everyone you don't like."

"I know that. Otherwise you'd be dead already."

But it's not true. It almost surprises me how untrue it is. Because I could have killed him – or at least tried – and fulfilled my mother's orders a dozen times over.

The ceiling rattles before Elian can retort. There's a low rumble in the wind, and for a moment I think it might be the sea waves crashing against Tallis Rycroft's pathetic excuse for a ship, but then the rumble grows louder and a bang shakes the cabin. Dust rains from the ceiling, and beneath us the floorboards splinter.

There's a chorus of yells and then nothing but the sound of cannons and gunfire. Of screaming and dying. Of the world descending into chaos.

Elian pulls at the ropes with a new ferocity. He shuts his eyes and I hear a resounding pop. I stare in disbelief as he tries to pull his hand from the restraints, his left thumb now slack. Miraculously, it slips halfway down before the rope lodges against his skin.

"Damn," he spits. "It's too tight. I can't slip out."

The cabin groans. A large split slivers up the wall and the window frame cracks with the pressure. Above us, footsteps pound the deck and the thunderous clashing of swords is second only to the deafening snarl of cannon fire.

"What is that?" I ask.

"My crew." Elian jerks at the rope again. "I'd recognize the sound of the *Saad* cannons anywhere." He gives me a smile to light up nations. "Listen to my girl roar."

"They came for us?"

"Of course they came for us," Elian says. "And if they've battered up my ship doing it, then there's going to be hell to pay."

As soon as the words leave his lips, a cannonball crashes through the window. It shoots past me and collides with the wooden beam that holds Elian. He ducks his head with siren speed, and wood shavings rain down his back. My breath lodges and a feeling of nausea rises up through my stomach. Then Elian lifts his head and shakes the dust from his hair.

I let loose a long breath and my frenzied human heart returns to its normal rhythm. Elian surveys the massacre of wood around him. And then slowly, almost wickedly, he smiles.

He rises to his feet and slips out from beneath the shattered beam. He jumps, bringing his bound hands under his feet and to his chest in one swift motion. Briefly, he scans the dank room for something to cut the rope, but the cabin is desolate save for its two prisoners.

Elian glances at me and his smile fades as he takes in my restraints. The undamaged beam ready to take me down with the ship. He looks at his tied hands, his thumb still painfully dislodged from the socket. The room that is too bare to make use of. The girl he can't seem to save.

"Go," I tell him.

Elian's eyes harden. Darken. That green disappearing under a whirlpool of anger. "Being a martyr doesn't suit you," he says.

"Just *go*," I hiss.

"I'm not just going to leave you here."

The sound of gunfire pierces the air. And a scream – a roar of fury – so loud that I wince. Elian turns to the doorway. Outside, his crew could be dying. The men and women he calls family marking their lives as forfeit to save their captain. And for what? For him to surrender his own life to save the very monster he has been hunting? A girl who has been plotting to steal his heart from under him? A traitor in every sense of the word.

Both of us have put our lives and our kingdoms on the line to find the eye and overthrow my mother. If nothing else, I won't stand by and watch someone else lose their kingdom just so I won't be alone when I lose mine.

"Elian." My voice takes on a murderous calm.

"I—"

"*Run!*" I scream, and to my surprise, he does.

His teeth grind for a moment before, jaw pulsing under the weight of the decision. And then he turns. Quick as an arrow, the young prince darts from the cabin and leaves me to my doom.

28

Lira

I WAIT FOR DEATH to come.

There's a chance that when I die, I'll return to my siren form. The corpse of the mighty Princes' Bane, stuck inside a pirate's ship. Perhaps, a sunken ship. Perhaps, where nobody but the mermaids will find me. My mother might even feign mourning at the loss of her heir, or simply command the Flesh-Eater to help make her a new one.

I'm feeling a bit too sorry for myself when Tallis Rycroft bursts through the door. His eyes scratch over the cold and empty cabin, and he rips a wooden plank masquerading as a shelf from the wall, its rusted nails snapping with the force.

His trousers are stained red from where Elian's knife went in. Through the tear I can see thick black stitches crisscrossing his skin back into place. A rush job, but it seems to have done the trick. Elian must have missed any arteries.

Tallis's knuckles are raw and scratched pink. When he charges across the room, it's in a jagged limp. He spots the broken beam where Elian was and snarls, kicking the splinters at me.

I don't flinch.

"Where is he?" he barks.

I cross one leg over the other and slump my shoulders indifferently. "You are going to have to be a little more specific."

In two strides, Rycroft crosses the room and wraps his thick hands around my neck. He pulls me to my feet and growls.

"You tell me where he is," Tallis hisses. "Or I'll snap your pretty little neck."

The weight of his hands around my throat reminds me of my mother's hold. I want to cough and splutter, but there doesn't seem to be enough air. There's a fury without measure in my veins, pushing and pulling my insides until all that's left is a deep pit of loathing.

I twist my lips into a snarl of my own. "You seem upset," I say.

Tallis wrenches his hands from me. "They're ripping my ship to shreds," he seethes. "When I find that bastard, there aren't words for what I'll do. He's declared war."

"I think you did that when you attacked the Midasan prince and took him prisoner. If you think this is bad, imagine the entire might of the golden army devoted to hunting you down."

Tallis narrows his eyes.

"What do they call it when someone attacks a member of one of the royal families? Ah, yes." My smile could cut through flesh. "Treason of Humanity. Is it still the drowning they go for?"

Tallis's face goes slack at the mention of it.

The last punishment was long before my time, but sirens still tell stories. Humans who took arms against royalty, breaking the pact of peace among the kingdoms. They were anchored into the ocean and left for my kind. But no siren attacked. Instead they watched the traitors lose their breath and clutch at their throats. Then, in their final moments, approached so that the humans could drown in fear. According to my mother, it was only when the humans' hearts pumped for the final time that the sirens ripped them from their chests.

From the look on Tallis's face, he's heard the same nightmarish tales.

He draws his sword in a clumsy arc and presses the blade to my cheek. "What do you care?" Tallis whispers. "He left you here, didn't he?"

He says it like I should feel betrayed, but nothing in the accusation stings. Elian left because I told him to and he would have stayed if I had asked. He would have died, perhaps, if I would have let him. But I didn't. I salvaged some small part of myself that I forgot existed – a part I was so sure my mother had gutted from me – and I let him go.

"Could we continue this conversation after you kill me?" I ask.

Tallis strokes my cheek with his blade. Then, before I have time to flinch, he lifts the sword into the air and brings it swiftly down.

I look at my freed hands and the cleanly sliced rope falls to my feet.

"I like my women with a little fight," Tallis purrs. "Let's see how much of one you put up."

I don't waste time on a smile before I bear my nails to claws.

Whatever Tallis expects, it's not for me to try to tear his heart out. Like a vulture, I swoop down and scratch until my arms feel heavy. His chest. His eyes. Anything I can get my hands on. When he pushes me off, I barely stay on the ground for a second before I'm on him again.

I'm an animal, slicing my teeth into his delicate human flesh. I can taste him in my mouth. Acrid. A strange mix of metal and water. I bite harder, until he tears me from his arm and a slice of his skin goes with me.

"You filthy whore!" he screams.

I wonder how much I resemble the Flesh-Eater now, with a piece of Rycroft inking the corner of my lips and a smile like the devil goddess who made us all. I swipe my tongue across my lips, snarling as his filthy blood clots in the edges of my teeth.

Tallis strides over to me, each footstep like thunder against the decrepit floorboards. When he reaches me, he hoists me up by the ruffles of my dress and smashes me into the wall. His legs pin mine in place, knees digging into my thighs.

He slams my face to the side with the heel of his palm and my cheek scrapes against a twisted nail. "I'm going to make you pay for that," he says, breath warm in my ear.

"Sure you are." I shift my hips into place, keeping my hands steady as I reach under the fabric of his cloak. "But first, I would appreciate it if you didn't get your blood all over me."

As soon as I feel the knife hilt under his clothes, I pull my hand back and then lurch it violently forward. My wrist twists to the left and Tallis blinks. When I lurch my hand upward, he swallows, a choked and ragged sound.

His hands drop from my clothes and he stumbles backward.

I slink down the wall and let out a breath.

Misdirection, Elian said. *Be too quick for them to notice.*

I look at Tallis. His demon eyes and bone-gray skin. The look of fear and surprise that rolls over him like a sea storm. And the knife – his own knife – spearing his gut. It wasn't hard to lift. Apparently, it's difficult to notice someone stealing a weapon from your waistband when they also happen to be tearing their teeth through your skin.

The blade is so deep that the handle barely surfaces through his shirt. It takes a moment before he falls. Seconds of him frowning and gasping before his head finally hits the floor.

I stand over his body and swallow. There's a hollowness in my chest, and the rush that usually comes with death is replaced by a deep pit that sits beside my erratically beating heart. This is the first kill I've made since becoming human, and somehow I thought it wouldn't matter, but there's blood all over me and Tallis's face is slack and I don't know why but I'm shaking.

I look down at him and all I can see is Crestell, dying over the sound of Kahlia's cries. My hands so wet with her blood, a promise begged between us.

Become the queen we need you to be.

I close my eyes and wait for the moment to pass. Hope that it will, or else I might just go crazy in this cabin. It doesn't make sense for me to think of her now; it's not like Tallis is the first kill I've made since. I squeeze my fists and feel the blood cloy under my nails. But Crestell was the start of it, the one my mother used to pull me over to her edge. As a human I could pretend I had some kind of a clean slate if I wanted to. At least for a little while. But not now. Not anymore. I'm a killer in every life.

I open my eyes and when I look back down, Tallis is Tallis again, and my aunt's face returns to a memory. I sigh in relief and then squint as something shines in the corner of my eye. In the growing sun, I catch the string of metal around Tallis's neck. The light blinks from it, like a tiny star fighting to stay ablaze. Unsteadily, I crouch down beside the pirate's body and pull back his collar.

The Págese necklace is still latched around him. The key to freeing the eye. I smile and twist the clasp free, careful, as though I might wake the sleeping pirate, and then pocket the stolen artifact.

When the door to the cabin crashes open, I jolt. My

shoulders tense, fingernails ready to become weapons once more.

Elian doesn't even glance at Tallis Rycroft.

He crosses the room toward me, eyes bright and so green and flickering with relief. His hair is swept in every direction, ruffling across his forehead, streaking his face. His shirt is torn, but I breathe a sigh when I see there are no new injuries. Just dirt and the splatters of gunpowder. I don't think about whether I'm relieved because I still need him if I'm going to overthrow my mother or whether it's something else entirely.

Elian's knife is secured in his belt, the magic of it still so strong to me, and in his hand is a sword – his sword – gold and ash glimmering against the shattered glass. When he reaches me, he throws it to the floor and braces my shoulders. His smile is like nothing I have ever seen.

I say the first thing I can think of, mirroring his words to me from Eidýllio. "I'm pretty sure I got rid of you already."

Elian's cheeks dimple and he casts a look over his shoulder. Kye, Madrid, and Torik are gathered in a tightly grouped line behind him. They came. Not just for their captain, but for the stowaway. The strange girl they found floating in the middle of the ocean. They came for me.

When he turns back to me, his eyes flicker over my face. His lips tense to a thin line as he notices the scrapes burning into my cheek. The blood that covers me, so much of it my own and so much of it not mine at all.

"What are you doing here?" I ask.

He shrugs. "What I do best."

"Getting on my last nerve?"

"Saving you," he replies, picking up his sword. "This is the second time. Not that I'm counting."

It's the third, actually, if we count how he pushed me

from Rycroft's path on the deck of the ship. Elian may not be counting, but I am.

"I can't believe you came back for me," I say.

I don't bother to keep the gratitude from my voice.

Elian taps his belt, where his knife sits happily. "I actually came back for this," he says. "Rescuing you was mostly an afterthought."

I level a glare. "I don't need rescuing."

For the first time, Elian glances down to the body sprawled across the decaying floor. It's like he only just realizes that the leader of the infamous Xaprár, kidnapper of pirates and princes alike, is bleeding out by his feet.

"Remind me not to get on your bad side," Elian says.

"Too late."

He grins. He's still grinning when I see Rycroft's head rise from the floorboards. The pirate's hand is at his waist in barely any time at all, and when he lifts it into the air, I'm surprised to see that the pistol is as black as squid ink. Just as Elian turns his head – as his crew lurches forward in panic – a shot fires out.

It's not the first time I've heard a gun fired, but the sound seems louder. It shudders through my bones and drums in beat with my heart. Everything is a rush of sounds. The smell of gunpowder and the awful scream of warning that shoots from Kye's lips. And then Elian. The way his smile drops when he notices the dread in my eyes. Three life debts.

It's almost a reflex when I push him out of the bullet's path.

There is an instant quiet that blankets the room. A fragment of a second when the world seems to have lost all sound. And then I feel it. The pain of scorching metal tearing through my human skin.

29

Elian

I DIED ONCE AND I haven't been able to do it again since.

I was thirteen at the time, or some other number just as lucky. About a mile out from the Midasan shore, there's a lighthouse on a small stretch of floating meadow. The sea wardens use it as a vantage point, while my friends and I used it to prove our bravery. The idea was to swim the mile, touch the soaking tufts of grass, and stand on top like the proud victor.

The reality was not drowning.

Nobody ever made the swim, because anybody stupid enough to consider it was too young, and anyone old enough had learned the usefulness of boats. But the fact that nobody had done it – that if I could, I'd be the first – only made the idea more appealing. And the roar of my brain begging me not to die turned to a quiet whisper.

I made it to the lighthouse, but I didn't have the strength to pull myself up. I did, however, have the strength to scream before my mouth filled with water and I let the gold wash me away.

I'm not sure how long I was dead, because my father refuses to speak of such things and I never asked my mother. It felt like an eternity. After, the world must have felt particularly sorry for me, because of all the crazy, deadly things I've done since – which far outweigh a mile-long swim – I'm still alive. Untouched by another brush of mortality. Made invincible, somehow, by that first fatality.

The moment the bullet whizzes through the air and I feel Lira's cold hands at my back pushing me to the ground, I'm angry at that. At my invincibility. My flair for survival while those around me continue dying.

"No!" Madrid screams, pitching forward.

She cracks her boot against Rycroft's chin and sends teeth in so many directions, I can't focus. Kye grabs her by the waist, holding desperately as she tries to tear herself from his grasp and finish off the pirate. The one who stole her captain. Who may or may not have sold her into slavery. Who just shot a girl right in front of her.

Madrid screams and curses, while Lira makes no sound at all.

She frowns, which seems louder, and presses her hand to the hole in her side. Her palm comes away wet and shaking.

She looks down at the blood. "It doesn't burn," she says, and then buckles to the floor.

I rush to her, skidding underneath her frail body before it cracks onto the wood. I catch her head in my hands and she lets out a choked sound. There's blood. Too much blood. Every time I blink, it seems to pool farther and farther until the entire right side of her dress is soaked through.

I lay my hand on her rib and press down. She's right: it's not warm. Lira's blood is like melted ice running between my fingers. The harder I press, the more she shudders. Convulsing as I try to stop any more of the cold seeping from her.

"Lira," I say, the word more like a plea than a name. "You're not going to die."

I resist looking at the wound again. Not wanting to, for fear that she might actually die and my last words to her might be a lie and what a jackass thing that would be.

"I know," Lira says. Her voice is steadier than mine, like the pain is nothing. Or at least, it's something less than she's felt before. "I've still got a mountain to climb."

Her head lolls a bit and I steady my hand, propping her up. If she loses consciousness now, there's no knowing if she'll wake up.

"This evens the score, you know," I say. "But I'm still a point up."

Lira shifts. "Quick," she says. My fingers are webbed by her blood, shirttails damp against my hip. "Take this to make up for it."

She lifts a shaking arm and a small pendant falls from her hand to mine. Bluer than her eyes and far too delicate to hold so much power. The Págese necklace.

She got it.

I laugh and consider what smart comment I could make – telling her that it's not really my style, or that maybe I already have it in gold – but then Lira's eyes quiver back and there doesn't seem to be much point in being funny if she isn't the one to hear it.

"Captain!" Madrid yells, Kye's hands still clinched to her waist. "She needs a medic."

Torik shadows over me, squeezing my shoulder with his mighty hands and bringing me back to reality. I swallow. Nod. Stand with Lira far too light in my arms. Run from the dregs of Rycroft's shitty ship, leaving a trail of blood in my wake.

"Get moving!" I shout, once I step foot back onto the *Saad*.

"And blow that ship to hell in our backwash."

The *Saad* lurches and my crew jumps into anarchy. They run from one end of the deck to the other, pulling the lines from their winches and recleating the boom. Trimming sails and scanning for the wind. I cleave forward, pushing past the ones who stop dead, noticing the blood-soaked girl in my arms and offering their hand.

"Elian," Kye says. "You're injured. Let me carry her."

I ignore him and turn to Torik. His face is wretched as he stares down at Lira. She may not have been one of us before, but dying in the line of duty has a way of securing people's loyalty.

"Make sure the medic is ready," I say, and my first mate nods.

Rycroft is slung carelessly over his shoulder, his blood dripping down Torik's back. He's alive, but barely, and if I get my hands on him, then he won't stay that way for long. With Lira still limp in my arms, I yell for Torik to get a medic and he throws Rycroft to the floor without hesitation before rushing belowdecks.

Really, we don't have a medic, but my assistant engineer traveled with a Plásmatash circus and that's close enough. As I carry Lira toward him, through the twists and tunnels of my ship, I'm caught off guard by the notion that out of all the princes and pirates and killers and convicts, a small boy from a circus is the only one who can help. It seems funny, and I think how Lira might laugh, knowing that a rookie engineer will be stitching her skin back together. What biting comment she would come back with and how it would sink into me like a perfectly wonderful kind of poison. Like a bullet.

I push my way into the cramped room, Kye rushing in behind me. The would-be medic gestures to a table in the middle of the engineering room. "Put her down there," he says in a panicked breath. "And open her dress."

I do as he says and grab my knife. The strange thing is that at first I don't think I can see any more blood gushing from the wound – it seems to all be on her dress and on me – and then when I do see blood, it doesn't seem like enough. Or perhaps it's all already come out. Maybe there just isn't any left.

"Gods." Kye recoils as I slash open Lira's dress. "Is she going to live?"

"Do you care?" I snap back.

It isn't his fault, but yelling at Kye feels a little like yelling at myself, and I need to be yelled at right now. Because this is on me. If Lira dies, then it's on me.

I can't believe you came back for me.

But I left her first.

"I don't want her to die, Elian." Kye squeezes my arm, keeping me steady as the fraying parts inside threaten to dismantle me. "I never did. Besides" – Kye shoves a hand into his pocket and sighs through the next words – "she protected you when I couldn't."

"It looks like a clean shot," the medic says, and I turn, the irony of it gnawing at me. It was a dirty shot, through and through.

"It just scraped her ribs," he says. "I have to check no organs were damaged though." He points a gloved finger at Kye. "Don't just stand there shadowing my light. Get me some towels."

Kye doesn't bristle at the order, or argue that we should let Lira die to be sure she can't betray us. He turns, hurries from the room, and doesn't even waste the time to glare properly.

"She didn't nick anything important," the medic says.

He phrases the last part as an afterthought, but when he turns to me, his eyes are expectant.

"I'm not sure," I tell him. "There was a lot of blood."

He shrugs and grabs an instrument that does not look entirely legitimate from a nearby toolbox. "Haven't met an engine I couldn't fix yet," he says. "The human body's just another machine." He looks at me with assuring eyes. "I saved a monkey with a knife wound to the ribs once. There was an accident with a balloon bursting. It's not that different."

I think this is supposed to be reassuring, so I nod just as Kye bursts back into the room with a handful of fresh towels. After, we're both ushered back out the way we came, and I don't argue. I'm glad to be sent away so the medic can work, free from staring at Lira's limp body and thinking about how I've never seen her look so vulnerable. So capable of being finite.

I don't give myself a moment to breathe before I walk back onto the deck and toward Rycroft's body. My crew flares their nostrils, waiting to be let loose. Beside me, I sense the rigid way Kye stands. Barely able to restrain himself and hoping desperately I don't ask him to restrain the others. That's the thing about my crew. They don't need to be friends. They don't even need to like one another. Being on the *Saad* is the same as being family, and by saving me, Lira has proven something to Kye. I locked her in a cage and made her barter her way onto my ship, and she saved me all the same, believing that it was the right choice. A life for a life. Trust for trust.

Tallis Rycroft stares at me and he's not alive enough to make it look menacing. His left eye is closed, a lump stretching out like a mountaintop, and the wounds on his face make his lips indistinguishable. The hole in his stomach bleeds on.

"What are you going to do with him?" Kye asks. His voice is

not altogether calm, something unbalanced on those usually carefree tones. He wants revenge as much as I do. And not just for taking his captain, but for the broken girl lying in the dregs of our ship.

"I don't know."

Madrid walks a small pocketknife between her fingers. When it nicks her, she lets the blood drip onto Rycroft's injured leg. "He doesn't deserve to live," she says. "You don't have to lie to us."

One of Rycroft's eyes blinks, slowly, as he comprehends the storm he has created. The young prince in me wants to feel sorry for him, but I keep looking at the half-moons and long, serrated lines that crease into his biceps. Wounds made trying to fend him off. Nail marks so similar to the ones along my own chest.

I hesitate, caught off guard as a distorted image of the Princes' Bane flashes across my mind. She could have snapped my neck or done any manner of things to disable me, but she let her claws tear slowly through my chest instead. That was the thing about sirens. They always went straight for the heart.

"Captain," Madrid says, and I blink away the image.

"I'm going to find some shark-infested waters," I tell her, regaining my composure. "And then drop his favorite appendage in."

There is a phlegmatic silence, while everyone within earshot considers those words. Rycroft half-blinks again.

"Next time," Kye says, clearing his throat, "lie to us."

"What about Lira?" Madrid asks.

I shrug. "Depends on how pleasant she is when she wakes up."

"I meant," she says, "is she really going to be okay?"

I stare down at Rycroft, and it takes every scrap of strength I have to smile. "My crew is not so easily killed."

It's a bullshit line, but I need everyone to believe it. I need to believe it myself. I picture Lira, and it's like I can feel her cold blood dripping through my hands like melted ice. If she dies, then my plan and this entire mission dies with her. More than anything, I'm counting the minutes until our rookie engineer emerges and tells me that everything is fine. That Lira didn't die for me and that she can still offer the last piece of the puzzle to free the Crystal of Keto from its cage.

That maybe – just maybe – I don't need to rip Rycroft into any more pieces.

30

Lira

I WAKE AND THEN immediately wish I hadn't.

There's a raw pain in my ribs, like there's a creature gnawing at my skin, and I feel groggy in a way that tells me I've had too much sleep.

The room I'm in is as jumbled as my thoughts. I brush my open shirt out of the way and brace my heavily bandaged ribs. My teeth grind against one another as I let my legs swing over the side of the bench. It's a mere second of being upright before the gnawing turns into a bite.

"There's something about a bullet wound that makes me want to jump out of bed too."

Kye is washing his hands in a nearby sink. It's thick with oil and grease. When he's finished, he shakes the water from his hands and turns to me with a condemning look.

"This is supposed to be a bed?" I ask.

He places a wet hand against my forehead, and I resist the urge to retract from the cold.

"I don't think you're dying now," he says.

"Was I dying before?"

He shrugs. "Maybe. But the little circus medic fixed you up okay. He even taught me how to dress your wound so he could focus on helping the ship stay afloat." Kye nods to the bandages with a smug look. "Pretty perfect, aren't they? My first."

"Could you not have given me a bed, too?" I ask, not failing to notice that someone – I hope Madrid rather than Kye – has also dressed me in something more plain and comfortable than the dress I was in.

"Madrid fetched you pillows." Kye wipes his hands on a nearby rag. "It's the best we could do since moving you wasn't an option."

I glance down at the stained sheet draped thinly over me. There's a black velvet pillow where my head was, plush enough for me to have slept comfortably for however long, and a thin oval cushion is pressed into the shape of my feet. It's not exactly fit for a queen, but for a gunshot victim aboard a pirate ship, it might be considered luxurious.

"How are you feeling?" Kye asks, and I smirk.

"Were you worried?" When he doesn't reply, I test my ribs with a deep sigh. "Fine," I say.

The bandage is tight around my body, and the dressing feels fresh and crisp against my clammy skin. It must have been changed recently, I realize, which means that Kye has been watching over me.

"I expected Madrid," I tell him. "Of all people, I didn't think it would be you."

"She was here for a while," he says. "Longer than a while, actually. I had to send her off to get some sleep before she resorted to stapling her eyes open." He looks down at his hands. "She was worried you'd be just another girl who couldn't escape."

"Escape what?"

"Rycroft," he says, and then shuffles uncomfortably. "I'm glad you're awake."

The comment isn't as throwaway as he might want it to be. For all the distrust between us, Kye and the rest of the crew risked their lives to come back for me, and while I lay bleeding on their ship, they didn't leave me to sleep in solitude. They stayed. They came for me and they stayed.

"So you trust me now?" I ask.

"You nearly died trying to save Elian." Kye clears his throat as though it's a struggle to get the words out. "So like I said, I'm glad you're awake."

"I'm glad that you didn't kill me while I was unconscious."

Kye snorts a smile. "I like the way you say thank you."

I laugh and then wince. "How long was I asleep?"

"A few days," he tells me. "We had some strong sedatives and we all thought it would be a good idea for you to get some rest." He grabs the rag from by the sink and passes it uneasily between his hands. "Listen," he says gingerly. "I know I've given you a hard time, but that's only because Elian seems to like putting himself in death's hands a little too often and it's my job to stop that from happening whenever I can."

"Like a good bodyguard," I say.

"Like a good friend," he corrects. "And I think taking a bullet for him has earned you a break from me being shitty." He sighs and throws the rag onto my lap. "I guess this officially makes you one of us."

I take a moment to process that. The idea that I belong with them on a ship setting sail for everywhere and nowhere. It's what I wanted, isn't it? To gain the crew's confidence so that they wouldn't suspect me. And yet, the instant Kye says it, I don't think about how I've earned trust I plan to break. I think about how different it feels, to be a new kind of soldier, earning loyalty by saving lives instead of destroying them. Fighting a war on the other side.

"I didn't quite hear that apology," I say. "Could you repeat it?"

Kye glares, but it's different than before, lighter, nothing hostile grazing over it. A smile settles on his face. "Guess Elian's been teaching you his version of humor," he says.

At the mention of Elian's name, I pause.

He promised that he wouldn't come back for me if something went wrong, and then he did it anyway. The moment he freed himself from the restraints and was faced with the opportunity to leave, he didn't want to.

I squeeze my eyes shut as my head begins to pound. My entire purpose for being on this ship is to kill him, and when the opportunity came for someone else to do it, I stopped them.

I pushed him from the bullet the same way he pulled me from the ocean. Without thinking or weighing up what it could mean or how it might benefit me. I did it because it seemed like the only thing to do. The right thing to do.

In my world, Kahlia is the sole remnant of my lost innocence. The only proof that there's a tiny part of me I haven't let my mother get her hands on. I don't know why, but Elian has evoked the same feral feeling that used to be reserved only for her. The desire to allow sparks of loyalty and *humanity* in me to take hold. We're the same, he and I. Just as looking into my cousin's eyes feels like looking into a memory of my own childhood, being around Elian feels like being around an alternate version of myself. Reflections of each other in a different kingdom and a different life. Broken pieces from the same mirror. There are worlds between us, but that seems more like semantics than tangible evidence of how dissimilar we are.

Everything is murkier now. And Elian made it that way

in a single second, with an action as easy as breathing: He smiled. Not because I was suffering or bowing or making myself malleable to his every whim and decree like I've done with my mother. He smiled because he saw me. Free and alive, and already making my way back to him.

I've been so focused on putting an end to my mother's reign that I haven't thought about how I can put an end to her war. Even if I get my hands on the eye, I still planned to take Elian's heart, just as my mother ordered, thinking it would prove something to my kingdom. But what? That I'm the same as her, valuing death and savagery over mercy? That I'll betray anyone, even those who are loyal to me?

If I find the eye, maybe it's not just sirens who don't need to suffer anymore, but humans, too. Maybe I can stop the age-old grudge that began in death. Be a new kind of queen, who doesn't create murderers from daughters.

I think of Crestell, shielding Kahlia from me and laying down her own life instead.

Become the queen we need you to be.

"I should get the captain," Kye says, breaking me from my thoughts.

I slide from the bench, letting the pain soak through me and then drift away. I gather my footing and focus on this newfound urgency. "No," I tell him. "Don't."

Kye hesitates by the door, his hand already pressing down on the handle. "You don't want him to come?" he asks.

I shake my head. "He doesn't need to," I say. "I'll find him."

31

Elian

Págos draws near, and with every league the air grows thinner. We feel it each night, our bones creaking with the ship as she sweeps through water that will soon turn to sludge and ice. It doesn't matter how much farther we have, because Págos is something that is always felt from within. More and more with each fathom, it looms somewhere deep inside. The final part of our quest, where the Crystal of Keto waits to be freed.

Rycroft is as much a ghost now as he has ever been, hidden belowdecks with barely enough gauze and meds to stay alive. The minimum necessary to make the journey with us. I haven't been down there, delegating that responsibility to Torik and other members of the crew who can handle him well enough and show restraint even better.

Madrid can't be trusted. Not when it comes to one of her own countrymen. Her memories tend to taint her morals and I can understand it. Kye, equally so. There isn't part of me that trusts him to watch over Rycroft and deliver food that isn't laced with poison. And then, more than any of them, there's me. The person I trust the least.

Lira may be alive, but that doesn't put an end to things. The relief has layered over my anger like a film, masking the rage well enough that it can't be seen, though never enough for it to disappear. But whether I go down there or not, Rycroft can sense the fate that awaits him. Even he can hear the slow wolf call of Págos. From the depths of the crystal cage, where Lira once was, and where he will remain until I give him over to the ice kingdom. He can catch the whistles in the wind, in a room as dark as his soul. And when we finally arrive, he'll live with them as he rots in a jail as cold as his heart.

"You're not drinking."

Lira hovers on the ladder steps to the forecastle deck. A blanket is wrapped loosely around her shoulders, and when it slips, she shrugs it higher. I try not to notice the wince as she moves her arm too quickly, stretching her side and jarring the wound.

I reach out my hand to pull her up, and the look Lira gives me is nothing short of poisonous. "Do you want me to chop it off?" she asks.

I keep my hand hovering in the space between us. "Not particularly."

"Then get it out of my face."

She pulls herself up the rest of the way and settles next to me. The edges of her blanket skim my arms. It's always so cold these nights, enough that sleeping with my boots on seems to be the only way to keep my toes. But there's something about being up here, with the stars and the sound of the *Saad* swimming for adventure. It makes me feel warmer than I ever could be bundled up in my cabin.

"I'm hardly an invalid," Lira says.

"You are a little."

I don't need to face her to see that her eyes are burning through the air between us. Lira has a way of looking at people – of looking at me – that can be felt as much as it can be seen. If her eyes weren't such a surprising shade of blue, I would swear that they were nothing more than hot coals for the fire within.

I finger the Págese necklace, which hangs from my neck as Lira's seashell hangs from hers. The key to everything. To ending a war that's lasted lifetimes.

"If you get shot," Lira says, "I'm going to treat you like you're incapable of doing the simplest tasks." She cradles her arms around her knees to keep out the cold. "See how you like it when I hold out my arm to help you walk, even though you're not shot in the leg."

"I'd be flattered," I say, "that you would look for an excuse just to hold my hand."

"Perhaps I'm just looking for an excuse to shoot you."

I give her a sideways glance and recline on my elbows.

The deck of the *Saad* is littered with my friends, splashing drink onto her varnished wood and singing songs that knock against her sails with the gusts. Seeing them this way – so happy and at ease – I know nothing could ever be thicker than the ocean that binds us. Not even blood.

"Madrid said that you are going to hand Rycroft over when we get to Págos."

"There's been a price on his head for some time now," I say. "But the services of the Xaprár were too valuable for any kingdom to warrant attacking them. Now that the shadows have been decimated by us, I don't doubt he'll be a wanted man. If nothing else, it'll be some extra sway to make sure the Págese king grants us access to their mountain so we can get the crystal and finish this whole thing."

Lira leans back so that we're level. Her hair is more unruly than ever, and the wind from the approaching storm does nothing to help. It blows into her eyes and catches across her lips, clinging to the freckles of her pale cheeks. I clench my hands by my sides, resisting the impulse to reach over and push it from her face.

"Do you really hate the sirens that much?" she asks.

"They kill our kind."

"And you kill theirs."

My eyebrows pinch together. "That's different," I say. "We do what we do to survive. They do it because they want to see us all dead."

"So it's revenge, then?"

"It's retribution." I sit up a little straighter. "It's not as though the sirens can be reasoned with. We can't just sign a peace treaty like with the other kingdoms."

"Why not?"

The distance in Lira's voice gives me pause. The answer should come quick and easy: because they're monsters, because they're killers, because of a thousand reasons. But I don't say any of them. Truthfully, the idea of this not ending in death never crossed my mind. Of all the outcomes and possibilities I considered, peace wasn't one. If I had the opportunity, would I take it?

Lira doesn't look at me and I hate that I can't figure out the expression on her face.

"Why are you questioning this?" I ask. "I thought the Sea Queen took everything from you and you wanted to use the Crystal of Keto to end the war. You want revenge for your family as much as I do for Cristian."

"Cristian?" Lira looks at me now, and when she says his name, it freezes in the air between us.

"He was the prince of Adékaros."

I run a hand through my hair, feeling suddenly angry and

unfocused. For a man like Cristian to die while a man like Tallis Rycroft gets to live is more than unjust.

Lira swallows. "You were friends."

Her voice sounds wretched and it distracts me. I can't remember her voice ever sounding anything short of pissed off.

"What was he like?" she asks.

There are countless words I could use to describe Cristian, but a man's character is better seen in his actions than the laments of his loved ones. Cristian was full of proverbs and sentiments I never understood and enjoyed mocking as much as I enjoyed hearing them. There wasn't a situation we found ourselves in that Cristian didn't think warranted an adage. *Love and madness are two stars in the same sky. You cannot build a roof to keep out last year's rain.* He always had something ready to settle the rampant parts of me.

I think of what Cristian would say now if he knew what I was planning. Any other man would want revenge, but I know he wouldn't see the crystal as a weapon. He wouldn't even want me to find it.

If your only instrument is a sword, then you will always strike at your problems.

Instead of telling all of this to Lira, I clasp the Págese necklace and say, "Do you think she'll feel it?"

"Who?"

"The Princes' Bane," I say. "Do you think she'll feel it when the Sea Queen dies?"

Lira lets out a sigh that turns to smoke on her lips. The air is thin and perilous. Wind cuts between us like daggers while a storm rumbles closer. I can smell the rain before it's here, and I know within moments the sky will come weeping down on us. Still, I don't move. The night flashes and groans, thick clouds creeping toward one another and merging into an infinite shadow that blocks the stars. It grows darker with each moment.

"I wonder if she can feel anything at all," Lira says. She shifts, and when she turns to me, her eyes are vacant. "I suppose we won't need to wonder for long."

32

Lira

THAT NIGHT I DREAM of death.

Seas run red with blood, and human bodies drift along the foam of my fallen kin. When the waves finally ladder high enough to stroke the night, they collapse and the bodies mangle against the seabed.

The sand bursts beneath them, scattering my kingdom in golden flakes. Amid it all, my mother's trident liquefies. I call out to her, but I'm not part of this great ocean anymore, and so she doesn't hear me. She doesn't see me. She doesn't know that I'm watching her downfall.

She lets the trident wither and melt.

Elian stands beside her, and the newly sunlit water parts for him. He has eyes like vast pools and a jaw made from shipwrecks and broken coral. Every movement he makes is as quick and fluid as a tidal wave. He belongs to the ocean. He is made from it, as much as I am.

Kindred.

Elian stares at the seabed. I want to ask him why he's so fascinated by sand, when there is an entire world in this ocean that he can't begin to imagine. Why isn't he seeing it? Why doesn't he care enough to look? I've seen the world through his eyes; can't he see it through mine?

The urge to scream rips through me, but I can only remember the words in *Psáriin* and I don't dare speak the language to him.

I watch him turn toward the sand, his face as plainly broken as my mother's.

It's only when I'm certain I might lose my mind from the anguish that I suddenly remember his language. I sift quickly through the Midasan and find the words to tell him. I want to explain how full of magic and possibility my world could be if not for my mother's rule. I want to comfort him with the chance for peace, no matter how small. Tell him things could be different if I were queen. That I wasn't born a murderer. But I find the words too late. By the time they become clear in my mind, I see the truth of what Elian sees.

He is not staring at the sand at all, but at the hearts that rupture from it.

Don't look. Don't look.

"Did you do it?" Elian's eyes find mine. "Did you do it?" he asks again in *Psáriin*.

The razors of my language are enough to cut through his tongue, and I wince as blood slips from his mouth.

"I took many hearts," I confess. "His was last."

Elian shakes his head, and the laugh that escapes his lips is a perfect echo of my mother's. "No," he tells me. "It wasn't."

He stretches his hands out and I stumble backward in horror. I'm no longer in control when my legs buckle and throw me to the floor. I look at the heart in Elian's hands, blood gathering between his fingertips. Not just any heart. His own.

"Is this what you were after?" he screams.

He takes a step forward and I shake my head, warning him not to come closer.

"Lira," Elian whispers. "Isn't this what you wanted?"

I wake up gasping for air.

My hands clutch the thin white bedsheet, and my hair slavers over my bare shoulders. The ship rocks slowly to the side, but the motion that I used to find comforting makes me more nauseated by the second. My heart ticks madly against my chest, shaking more than beating.

When I unclench my fists from the bedsheet, there are scratch marks on my palm. Angry red streaks across the lines of my hand. No matter how hard I try, I can't seem to catch my breath.

The image of Elian's heart plays on an unsteady loop. The betrayal in his eyes. The punishing sound of my mother's laughter.

I spent my life hiding from the possibility of being different than what my mother told me I must be. Swallowing the child with a desire to become something else. I was a siren and so I was a killer. It was never wrong or right; it just was. But now my memories are cruel dreams, twisting into merciless visions and accusing me of a past I can't deny.

The truth of what I am has become a nightmare.

33

Elian

THE WATER IS SLUSH by the time the *Saad* makes her berth. Cold has a faithful presence here, and with dusk rapidly approaching, the air seems almost frozen by the impending absence of sun. Regardless, it's just as bright as if it were morning. The mirror of the frozen sky against the white water, flecked by tufts of ice and snow, makes for a kingdom that is beautifully void of darkness. Even in the dead of night, the sky turns no darker than a mottled blue, and the ground itself acts like a light to guide the way. Snow, reflecting the eternal tinsel of the stars.

Págos.

I feel the beat of the necklace against my heart as we step foot onto the snow. Finally the crystal is within reach. I have the key and the map to navigate the route, and all that's left is for Lira to tell me the secrets of the ritual.

The air is crisp on my skin, and though my hands are wrapped under thick gloves, I shove my fists into my pockets anyway. The wind penetrates here through every layer, including skin. I'm dressed in fur so thick that walking feels like an exertion. It slows me down more than I would like, and even though I know there's no imminent threat of attack,

I still don't like being unprepared in case one comes. It shakes me more than the cold ever could.

When I turn to Lira, the ends of her hair are white with frost. "Try not to breathe," I tell her. "It might get stuck halfway out."

Lira flicks up her hood. "You should try not to talk then," she retorts. "Nobody wants your words being preserved for eternity."

"They're pearls of wisdom, actually."

I can barely see Lira's eyes under the mass of dark fur from her coat, but the mirthless curl of her smile is ever-present. It lingers in calculated amusement as she considers what to say next. Readies to ricochet the next blow.

Lira pulls a line of ice from her hair, artfully indifferent. "If that is what pearls are worth these days, I'll make sure to invest in diamonds."

"Or gold," I tell her smugly. "I hear it's worth its weight."

Kye shakes the snow from his sword and scoffs. "Anytime you two want to stop making me feel nauseated, go right ahead."

"Are you jealous because I'm not flirting with you?" Madrid asks him, warming her finger on the trigger mechanism of her gun.

"I don't need you to flirt with me," he says. "I already know you find me irresistible."

Madrid reholsters her gun. "It's actually quite easy to resist you when you're dressed like that."

Kye looks down at the sleek red coat fitted snugly to his lithe frame. The fur collar cuddles against his jaw and obscures the bottoms of his ears, making it seem as though he has no neck at all. He throws Madrid a smile.

"Is it because you think I look sexier wearing nothing?"

Torik lets out a withering sigh and pinches the bridge of his nose. I'm not sure whether it's from the hours we've gone without food or his inability to wear cutoffs in the biting cold, but his patience seems to be wearing thin.

"I could swear that I'm on a life-and-death mission with a bunch of lusty kids," he says. "Next thing I know, the lot of you will be writing love notes in rum bottles."

"Okay," Madrid says. "Now I feel nauseated."

I laugh, but the sound is lost against the rhythm of nomadic drumbeats that barrel toward us. Up ahead, a line of warriors approach. There's at least a dozen of them, standing in a perfect military arrow, marching fiercely in our direction. Even with the blizzard, they're easy to spot. The snow does a poor job of obscuring their imposing statures and impressively systematic formation. They hike seamlessly in step with one another, feet crushing into the snow with the pound of every drumbeat. They look like giants, their uniforms so dark, they ink the empty landscape.

When they reach us, there's a momentary silence while we consider one another.

Even with the layers of fur and armor, it's not hard to tell the royals from their soldiers. The four members of the Págese family stand like titans, magnificent hunters' headdresses swooping down their backs in glorious coats. Their eyes peer through the jaws of their respective animals: polar bear, Arctic fox, wilderness wolf, and in the middle of the warriors and his brothers, the snow lion.

Each animal is a glorious shade of white that melts into the snow by their feet. It's a stark contrast to their black armor and weaponry – spears and swords that are all the darkest shade of ebony. They gleam in a way that's almost liquid.

The Págese brothers pull back the animal skins shielding

them from the cold. As expected, King Kazue is the snow lion. The most deadly of all creatures. Though it stands taller than some men, the Págese king seems to encompass the creature's size perfectly. He doesn't look at all dwarfed by the mammoth carcass.

"Prince Elian," Kazue greets.

His skin is so white, it's almost blue. His lips mingle with the rest of his face like a variant shade, and everything about him is as sharp as it is straight. His eyes are severe points that arch to the ends of his brows, and his hair is made from rays of sword-like strands that scrape against his weaponry.

Kazue brings his hand to his stomach and leans forward in a customary bow. His brothers follow suit, while the guardians around them stay firmly upright. In Págos, it's not customary for soldiers to bow to royalty. It's a greeting made only from one elite to another, and soldiers must stay still and impartial. Unnoticed until they're acknowledged.

"Your Royal Highness," I say, returning the greeting. "I'd like to thank you for receiving us into your kingdom. It's an honor to be welcomed here."

I turn to the princes, their headdresses matched according to their age and, so, according to their right to the throne. The second eldest, Prince Hiroki, is the polar bear; Tetsu, the wilderness wolf; and the youngest prince, Koji, is the Arctic fox. I formally greet them and they bow in turn.

I wonder which of them is Rycroft's naïve little source.

"Of course, it's not just my brothers who welcome you," Kazue says, "but our entire family."

He waves his hand behind him, and a new figure emerges from the soldiers, dressed as gloriously as the royal family. A fifth, standing shorter and with a far less military posture, but a similar sense of indignation. I don't need the unprecedented addition to pull back the animal skin to know who it is.

Sakura smiles when she sees my face tick, bright blue lips matching the ungodly color of the sky. Her hair is shorter than before, with a fringe cut bluntly to hide the tips of her eyes. A heavy bronze chain sweeps down from her forehead to a white-bone piercing on her left earlobe.

She doesn't look like a princess; she looks like a queen. A warrior. An adversary.

"Prince Elian," she says.

"Princess Yukiko."

She smiles at the use of her real name.

Kye stiffens beside me, his resentment growing. Now that my crew is faced with the very woman who manipulated me into giving up my time on the *Saad* – my time, and theirs – they can hardly be expected to smile.

Swiftly, I nudge Kye before he has a chance to say anything. Who knows how much Princess Yukiko has told her family about her time in Midas? Did she tell them she was the owner of the illustrious Golden Goose? That she traded as much in my royal secrets as she did liquor, gambling her nights away with the wretches of my kingdom? I doubt it. But even if she has, Kye addressing her informally won't go amiss. He may have been a diplomat's son once, but his disinheritance is no secret. Besides, she's a princess. A potential queen. *My* potential queen.

I flinch at the thought, hoping that my bargain with Galina is enough to make my bargain with Yukiko void.

I feel the stares of all one hundred of my crew on my back. But as much as they want to say to me, there's just as much I want to say to the princess. The deal I want to discuss and the counteroffer I'm desperate to present. Nevertheless, now's not the time. Not with so many prying eyes and pricked ears.

I bow in greeting.

"Look at you, trying to hide your surprise," Princess Yukiko says. "There's no reason for it, you know. The hiding or the surprise. Aren't we old friends? Isn't this my home? Where else should I be but with such dear friends and family?"

"Of course," I say tightly. "I'm just surprised by how quickly you made the journey."

"Not all ships float," Yukiko says. "Some prefer to fly."

Her voice is unduly self-assured, and unlike Lira's there's nothing I enjoy about her brand of arrogance. I resist the urge to roll my eyes and settle for a curt nod of understanding.

Págese airships are some of the best in the hundred kingdoms. They vary from the bullets – darting balloons with barely enough room for half a dozen passengers – to lavish ships that are opulent enough to be dubbed floating palaces. They have at least eight separate rotors and span up to three floors, depending on the cargo or, more often than not, the social standing of the passengers.

The Págese have always been on good terms with the Efévresic, who birth the world's greatest inventions. They're a kingdom at the forefront of nearly every technological triumph, and there's rarely an invention today that can't trace its origin back to Efévresi. Págos has been their ally for so long now that it doesn't even matter if they exist at opposite ends of the world. There's seldom anything stronger than two kingdoms drawn together by a decades-old marriage alliance. It means that Págos is privy to many of the technological advancements that Efévresi has, and so they're one of the few kingdoms with the means to confine most of their travel to air rather than sea. For the rest of the hundred kingdoms, airships tend to be unreliable. Malfunctions are not uncommon, and unless the journey spans longer than a month, it's more trouble than it's worth.

"You're the princess?" Lira asks.

As much as her contempt for everyone around her usually entertains me, I send Lira a pointed look, warning her not to say anything out of line. But she either doesn't notice or she doesn't care. I can guess which one is more likely.

Yukiko nods. "I didn't realize the prince was recruiting new members for the *Saad*."

"Oh, I'm not a recruit," Lira says. "I'm just here to kill him." She stares pointedly at the princess. "And anyone else who gets in my way."

Kye makes a poor attempt to muffle the sound of his laughter with the back of his hand.

I snap my gaze to Lira and clench my teeth. Has the cold gone to her head, or is she so used to our rapport that she thinks it can be the same with every royal? I try to catch her attention, but she's fixated on Yukiko.

Her eyes are as cold as the wind.

"She's joking," I say, pushing Lira behind me. "And probably drunk."

Lira scoffs and I squeeze my hand across her waist to silence her.

"Pay no attention to my crew," I say, giving the king a blithe smile. "When the food runs low, they tend to live off the rum."

King Kazue dismisses the comment with a laugh, though it's every bit as precise as his military stance. Beside him, Yukiko eyes my hand on Lira's waist.

"There are more important things to discuss," Kazue says. "Come, we must talk at the palace, away from the teeth of our weather. From what my sister has told me, there is a rather interesting bargain to be struck."

AFTER BEING SHOWN TO our guest chambers and given enough food to put Torik's mood to rest, I'm escorted to the grand hall. At the request of King Kazue, I'm alone, and yet there are seven guards who walk in step behind me as the royal concierge leads the way. I took it as a compliment when they came to fetch me from my new chambers, armed to the teeth with spears that looked like they may have actually been made from teeth. It's almost a testament to my reputation that they trust me so little.

The grand hall hides behind a set of iceberg doors that must be rotated via wheel mechanism. The cogs make an unreasonable amount of noise as they heave the great doors open to reveal the chamber inside. It's not a large space, but everything about it is grand and opulent. Chandeliers drip down in frozen teardrops, and icicles sprout up from the solid ice floor like weeds. I step on it, half-expecting to land with my legs in the air, but the surface is surprisingly dry under my feet.

The five siblings of Págos eye me from their thrones. Each of them is dressed in black finery that seeps from them like oil. From behind their lavish seats, there is a single window clawed with blue frost. It creeps across the pane like a flower, obscuring the last few minutes of sunshine that could penetrate the cavern.

"I trust your rooms are satisfactory," King Kazue says. "I must admit, I'm glad your crew is a little more downsized. A hundred pirates is enough; I dread to think what having an entire legion in my palace would be like."

"A lot of fun, I'd wager."

The young Prince Koji murmurs a laugh. "The stories speak for themselves," he says. "I'm a little sorry I won't get to experience them firsthand."

"Next time," I tell him, "I'll bring the whole horde." I turn back to the king. "Does our deal still stand?"

"I don't remember ever making a deal with you," King Kazue says. "But my sister seems to think she has the authority to." He casts an irate glance at Yukiko, but she waves him off with a flick of her eyes as though he's the nuisance.

Prince Hiroki leans over to his brother. "She gave him the map," he says. "I hope that means we got something equal in value."

"You did," I say, and pull the necklace from my pocket.

I let it dangle in the air between us, a beautiful drop of blue that dances from the chain. Still specked with Lira's blood.

King Kazue's fists tighten around the arms of his throne. "What a thing you present to us so casually," he says. "Where did you find it?"

"The same place I found that prisoner you've got locked away in your dungeons."

Prince Hiroki shuffles in his seat, and I stop wondering which of the king's brothers Rycroft was talking about.

"The Xaprár," King Kazue snarls. "Tallis Rycroft and his band of damned thieves. I should have known that anything lost would find its way into his hands."

"It's not in his hands now," I say, clasping the necklace. "It's in mine."

Prince Tetsu leans forward with a growl. "You'll do well to hand it over."

"Now, now, brother." The king chuckles. "I'm sure that's his plan."

"Of course," I say. "As soon as the right offer is made."

Yukiko's smile is slow and devious. "You have to admire his courage," she says.

King Kazue rises to his feet. "You want entry to our

mountain so you can find the Crystal of Keto," he says. "Then what?"

"Then I give you back your priceless necklace and, when I'm done with it, the crystal, too. This is the chance for Págos to make history as the kingdom who helped destroy the sirens once and for all. Your family will be remembered as legends."

"Legends?" The king's sharp laughter slices the air. "What's to stop me from just taking it from you now?"

"Once the Crystal of Keto is freed, the Sea Queen will know it," I tell him. "And you're a lot of things, Your Highness, but a siren killer isn't one of them. If she's going to die, it'll have to be by my hand. Let me climb the mountain and we can make history together."

"It's a perilous journey," the king says. "Even with our sacred route. What would your father say if I put his son in danger like that? Even if it was for something as noble as saving the world. Furthermore" – he nods toward his sister – "Yukiko traveled all this way, finally returning home after so many years. It seems curious to me that she would do that just because she believed in your cause."

Yukiko eyes me with amusement, taking pleasure in the idea that I might just squirm. As though I'd give any of them the satisfaction. I'm not sure if the king is goading me, or if Yukiko really hasn't told him about our engagement, but I know I won't be the first to speak of it.

"Of course I didn't," Yukiko says to her brother. "I came because I want to be the first one to see it. I want to be there when the Crystal of Keto is finally found."

My jaw tightens as I clench my teeth together. The last thing I need is a murderous princess following me up the Cloud Mountain.

"I don't think that would be particularly safe," I say. "As the king mentioned, it's a dangerous journey."

"That she has taken before," Hiroki cuts in. "That we all have."

"Not all of us," Koji amends.

Hiroki casts an endearing look at his youngest brother and then turns his pale eyes to the king. "If she goes with him, then at least we can be certain we won't be double-crossed."

I try not to look insulted.

"And that way, one of our own will be there when the crystal is finally freed from the depths of the dome," Tetsu says.

Yukiko reclines. "I'm glad you're all so eager to get rid of me after just a couple of days in my company."

King Kazue casts a sideways glance to his sister and then looks at me with a guarded expression. "If you manage to kill the Sea Queen and the Princes' Bane," he says, "you'll have to tell the world that we had a hand in it."

It isn't a request, and so I bow my head in agreement, sensing the fragility of the moment. I'm so close that I can almost feel it in the back of my throat, like a thirst.

"The crystal, the necklace, and the glory." King Kazue slides back onto his throne with hungry eyes. "I want Págos to have it all."

"I'll tell them whatever you want me to," I say. "As long as the Princes' Bane is dead, it won't matter to me."

The Págese siblings look down at me from their icicle thrones and, one by one, they smile.

WHEN I FINALLY LEAVE the grand hall, Lira is waiting, a foot kicked up against the icicle doors. Her hair is damp from the cold and she's wearing a thick knitted sweater that dwarfs her spindly wrists. When she sees me, she lets out a breath and pushes herself from the door.

"What are you doing?" I ask.

Lira shrugs. "Just making sure you weren't dead."

I shoot her an unconvinced look. "You were eavesdropping."

"And now I'm done," she says, and raises her eyebrows, as if daring me to do something about it.

Before she has a chance to walk away, I make a quick grab for her wrist and pull her back toward me. Lira whirls around so quickly that her hair splays across her face. She shakes her head to throw it from her eyes and then looks down at our locked hands, frowning.

"I want to know what you were thinking before," I say. "Threatening to kill a princess in her own kingdom like that. It's not your best attempt at humor."

Lira snatches her hand from mine. "Kye thought it was funny."

"While I'm glad the two of you are bonding, you should try to remember that Kye is an idiot."

She smirks. "And so are you if you trust the Págese."

"I don't need to trust anyone. I just need for them to trust me."

"For a pirate, you're not a very good liar," she says. "And you're not very good at bargaining. Everything you've given up seems so vast compared to the nothing you've received in return."

"It's not nothing. It's to end a war."

"You really are a child if you believe it'll be that easy."

"You think surrendering my kingdom to Princess Yukiko was easy?" I ask. "It's not just having to marry her, you know. I have to give up every dream I've ever had and stay rooted in duties I've spent my life trying to escape."

My hands clench reflexively at my sides as I watch for her reaction. I want Lira to understand that I didn't just make that

~ 277 ~

deal on a whim and that every day since I've regretted it. I know the consequences of my actions, and I'm doing everything I can to find a way out.

Lira looks at me wordlessly and I'm not sure how I expect her to react, or if I have the right to expect anything at all, but her silence is more unnerving than anything I could have anticipated.

The clock in the great hall chimes, marking the beginning of the night winds. Lira waits a moment, until all three bells have cried out, and then, finally, she swallows. The sound is too loud.

"Are you really going to marry her?" she asks, and then shakes her head like she doesn't want to know the answer. "It's a smart plan, I suppose," she says. "You get the Crystal of Keto and an alliance with a powerful kingdom. Even if you have to give up life on the *Saad*, you still come out a winner." Her forced smile falters a little at the last part, and when she speaks again, her voice is quiet and severe. "You never quite seem to lose, do you, Elian?"

I'm not sure how to respond to that, since I feel like all I've been doing lately is losing. And this deal with Yukiko is just one more strike in that column.

I sigh, and when Lira pushes her hair from her face, I feel the need to explain my plan. Everything I've orchestrated to escape my deal with Yukiko lingers on the tip of my tongue like an impulse. I know I shouldn't have to defend myself to Lira, or to anyone, but I feel the compulsion to do just that.

"It won't matter what bargain I've struck when this is over," I say. "If I survive, then I have a proposition that Yukiko won't be able to refuse."

"Don't you think you've done enough proposing?" Lira asks.

There's nothing endearing about the way she looks at me now.

"You're putting your entire kingdom in danger by letting yourself be manipulated by a power-hungry princess who—"

She breaks off and looks to the floor with an unreadable expression.

"Lira."

"Don't." She holds her hand up, keeping the distance between us. "You don't owe me anything, especially if it's an explanation. Royalty never owes anyone anything."

Her use of the word *royalty* stings more than it should. I've spent so long trying to escape that as my only marker, and for her to say it with such certainty, as though she's never once seen me as something else, pinches. Always a prince, never just a man.

I exhale carefully and shove my hands into my pockets. "I never said I owed you anything."

Lira turns. Whether she heard me or not, I can't be sure, but she walks away without looking back and I don't follow. There's part of me that wants to – a part larger than I'd like to admit – but I wouldn't know what to say if I did.

I run a hand through my hair. This night really can't end fast enough.

"I'm not blind to it."

Yukiko steps out from the shadows like a ghost. In the pale torchlight, her eyes look near-white, and when she walks closer to me, the glow of the fire smooths the harsh lines of her face until she looks kind. Gentle.

The light really does play tricks on the mind.

"It just doesn't matter to me," she says.

"I'm pretty sure that I don't know what you're talking about."

"That girl," Yukiko says. "Lira." .

"I suppose she's pretty hard to be blind to."

"Yes." Yukiko's smile burns brighter than the fire. "It's clear you believe that."

I rub my temples, not up for yet another cryptic conversation. "Say what it is you have to say, Yukiko. I'm not in the mood for games."

"A change from the usual, then," she replies. "But I'll grant the request, since you're a guest in my home."

She threads her fingers through her hair and bites down on the corner of her blue lips. The gesture looks far more foreboding than teasing. "You may care about her," Yukiko says, "but it won't change anything. Love is not for princes, and it's most certainly not for kings. You promised me that you would become a king. My king. I want to remind you of that promise."

The savage look in Lira's eyes flashes across my mind. She didn't even give me a second glance before she walked away. The last thing she seemed to want to hear were reasons or explanations. *You're letting yourself be manipulated*, she said. *Royalty never owes anyone anything.* But that isn't true. I owe a lot of people a lot of things, and Lira is no exception. Maybe I don't owe her an explanation, but I do owe her my life, and that seems like the same thing.

I shift, and when I realize that's exactly the reaction Yukiko wanted, I glare. "I didn't promise you a king," I say. "I believe the condition you were sold on was a kingdom. Do you even care which one it is?"

"That sounds an awful lot like you want to break our deal."

"Not break," I say. "Renegotiate."

Yukiko grins and leans over my shoulder, brushing a catlike hand against my chest. Her cold breath presses against my neck, and when I turn my head away, I hear the smile in her voice.

"So many tricks," she whispers. "You'll need sturdier sleeves to hold them all."

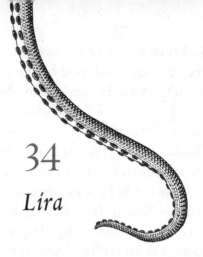

34
Lira

THE MOUNTAIN TIP IS hidden by its namesake clouds, and a never-ending snowstorm obscures most of its magnitude. Even so, I marvel. I know that long past the sky that hides half of the rock face is an endless peak. A gateway to the stars. The Cloud Mountain of Págos is the highest point in the world, farthest from the sea and so farthest from my mother's hold. From mine. If the Second Eye of Keto really is on this mountain, then it would have been the perfect hiding spot. Far from where I could follow. Until now.

My face is covered by layers of thick fabric that obscure everything but my eyes. I itch to pull the cloth and furs from my face, but the cold is more than I can bear. And I dare not let go of the snow poles clenched tightly in my grasp. I'm not even sure I could if I wanted to. My hands feel like they've been frozen into solid fists.

We follow the trail up the great mountain for days that turn to weeks, with more silence than I've ever failed to hear from the crew of the *Saad*. Even Kye, who walks so perfectly in step with Elian, glancing back to Madrid every now and again – to make sure, perhaps, that she hasn't turned into some kind of frozen sculpture or been blown from the cliff by the brutal winds – remains quiet. Elian is no different.

I'm strangely comforted by the fact that it's not just me he doesn't seem to be speaking to. He remains perfectly stoic, following the princess's lead ardently. For some reason, that part is less comforting.

I know that marriage is a side effect of royalty. So many things are. Obstacles to content, so cleverly masked as duties. Trials made out to be solutions and burdens tailored for only the least willing to bear them. All of them, nothing more than a series of consequences that stem from being heir to a kingdom. Yukiko is Elian's side effect, as the Flesh-Eater was mine. He traded the map for himself in a noble attempt to salvage his mission by sacrificing his pride. Things like this are expected. Predictable. But they're also vexing.

I don't know what I expected to achieve when I confronted Elian in the palace, but it wasn't weeks of terse silence. I'm not sure why I even asked about Yukiko; it wasn't why I waited for him while he dealt with the Págese royals. But I couldn't help myself. Lately it has seemed impossible to try. Maybe that turned out in my favor, because my original reason to talk with him – to ask, maybe, if he'd ever considered an alliance – wasn't much better. It was stupid to think I could just walk right up to him and ask if he was willing to forge a peace between our kind. *I won't kill you if you don't kill me.* It's ridiculous. It's simple for me to consider making a deal with someone who's shown me nothing but loyalty and a way to walk a path I hadn't thought possible before. Free from the shadows of my mother's reign, a new era not determined by death. A delicate peace, even. But how can I expect Elian to do the same when he doesn't even know who I am? When I murdered his friend and countless other princes? When I plotted to murder him?

I climb with Elian's back to me, but his face is clear in my mind. As the sky fades to darkness and then the sun climbs higher again, we carry on that way. The farther we get up the mountain, the more I begin to drive myself crazy with thinking. Replaying conversations and actions and opportunities. Wondering when I began to feel so utterly human.

The sky turns to so many shades of blue that I lose count. It's a quilt of color, blending perfectly through the clouds. Painting itself like a backdrop for the white glow of the moon and its guiding starlight.

"We have to move faster!" Yukiko yells. I can barely hear her voice above the ice winds. "Our next camp is two hours ahead, and we need to make it before sundown."

Elian pauses and holds out the map, and the storm batters it in his grasp. The edges are crisp with winter, and when his fingers clasp the parchment tighter, trying to keep hold as the wind gathers strength, it splinters.

"Sundown is in an hour!" Elian yells back.

Yukiko's breath clouds between them. "Hence, we need to move faster."

The wind muffles their voices, but even I can hear the sound of Elian's sigh. His shoulders slump a little and he casts a quick glance to check that we're all still behind him.

"It's doable," he calls over to us, though I'm not sure if he's telling us or trying to convince himself.

"I'm not sure I can walk without my toes," Kye says.

"Madrid will carry you."

"I don't have toes either. Or fingers, actually." Madrid holds up her gloved hands and whimpers. "I think I lost a few yesterday."

"At least they'll be well preserved then." Kye presses his

boot into the snow for emphasis. "If we pick them up on the way down, a healer should be able to stitch them right back on."

Though I can only make out Madrid's eyes, I'm sure she grimaces.

"We don't have time for this," Yukiko says. "Stop wasting your energy and move."

Madrid sticks a snow pole into the ground and pulls her fur mask down. Frost gathers on her lips. "Is that a royal command?" she asks.

Yukiko throws back her headdress and it's like the weather parts for her. She commands the cold like I once did. "You are in my kingdom."

"But not in your court," Madrid says. She wipes her tattooed cheek, where the wind has begun to blister it, and nods to Elian. "Our king is right there."

"You're forgetting something, aren't you? He's not a king yet."

If the air hadn't already been frozen, I'm sure that last comment would have done it. Kye stiffens and I see his hand twitch by his side. Quickly, Elian shoots him a sharp glance, and reluctantly, Kye lets his posture relax. Still, his hands keep twitching.

I notice that mine do too.

Torik grunts. He doesn't seem to be able to translate Elian's expressions as well as Kye can, and no sooner does Elian slump in hesitant submission does his first mate lurch violently forward. As Torik approaches Yukiko, I see the threat of his large frame for the first time. No longer is he the gentle giant who watches over the *Saad*. He advances toward the princess, kicking the snow with each heavy footstep.

"You little—"

"Enough."

Elian's voice cuts into Torik's path. He holds out an arm and Torik stops short.

"Captain," he says.

"I said that's enough," Elian repeats. As usual, his voice betrays nothing but what he wants it to. Perfect calm and indifference. But even from here, I can see his eyes blinking against the storm, like fierce gateways into his heart.

"Are we finished now?" Yukiko asks.

With every second her blue lips inch higher, mine turn to a snarl beneath my mask. I step forward and pull the cloth from my face. The air bites.

"Not yet," I say.

Yukiko turns her steel gaze to mine. Out of the corner of my eye, I see Elian go suddenly rigid. When Yukiko takes a step toward me, his hand moves slowly to his side. To the knife I know is hidden there.

"Is there something else?" Yukiko asks.

Many things, I think.

The way she looks at Elian being the worst, like she's better than him. Manipulating a prince to get her hands on his kingdom, just as my mother manipulated me to steal mine and extend her reign. Just like I fell into the Sea Queen's trap, Elian is going to fall into Yukiko's. Maybe it was different once, but now I know there's no way I can steal the eye and let my kingdom rise while Elian's crumbles beneath his debt to her. There has to be a way for us both to win this battle.

We are not naïve little heirs to be molded as they wish. We are warriors. We are rulers.

"Elian may not be a king," I tell her, "but you're not a queen, either. Not unless you kill your brothers."

"Who has time for murder these days?" Yukiko says. "Better

to just take another kingdom than wait around for this one."

The insinuation is not lost. She thinks she can goad me with the deal she and Elian made. And I suppose she can. Because I can't help but hate seeing him stand submissively by her, not giving him a choice in his own future. Using him for her devious plans, just like I intended to. It's too much of a reminder of my life before the *Saad*. Before Elian made me realize what it was like to be free. The very person who gave me a glimpse of hope is now so willing to sacrifice his own.

"You should be careful," I tell Yukiko. "The thing about taking something that's not yours is that there will always be someone out there ready to take it back."

"I suppose I'll have to watch my back, then."

"No need," I tell her. "I can see it perfectly."

Yukiko bites down on the corner of her lip, half-amused, half-curious. When she turns from me, I dare a glance at Elian. There is a dangerous corner to his smile, and I count the seconds while he looks at me. Green piercing through the new white of the world. Until, finally, Kye clasps Elian's shoulder and pushes him onward.

When night falls, we set up camp on the flattest part of the mountain. Tents stapled into the ground circle a quickfire station. We crowd around it and cook what sparse remnants of food we have left. The cold seems worse when we sit still, so we hover our hands over the fire so closely that we risk getting burnt.

The wind wails harder, and the crew warms their throats with the rum Madrid brought in place of more food. When night deepens and the crew's laughter fades to heavy breathing, I listen to the sound of the wind, knowing I won't be able to sleep. Not with the Second Eye of Keto so close. My mission to overthrow my mother and Elian's fate threaten to intertwine, and I can't close my eyes without thinking about how this war will end.

After a while, the snow begins to fall more softly against the tent, and in the dying wind I make out a pair of soft footsteps approaching. I hear them before I see the shadow, drawn on the shelter by the fading glow of my lantern.

When the door unzips, I'm not at all surprised to see Elian crouching beside it.

"Come with me," he says, and so I do.

I'VE NEVER SEEN THE stars. Not the way Elian has. There are so many things I haven't done. Experiences Elian seems to have that nobody else, especially me, could dream of. The stars are one of them. They're Elian's in a way that they're no one else's.

Elian doesn't just look at the stars, but he imagines them too. He draws pictures of them in his mind, creating stories about gods and wars and the souls of explorers. He thinks about where his soul will go when he dies and if he will become part of the night.

All of this he tells me at the height of the Cloud Mountain, with the moon and the wind and the empty space of the world before us. The crew is sleeping, along with the Págese princess. It feels like the entire world is asleep. And us – just us – we are finally awake.

"I've never shown this to anybody," Elian says.

He doesn't mean the stars, but the way he sees them. They are his secret just like the ocean is mine, and when he speaks of them, his smile is as bright as they are. I wonder if I've ever had that look. If it glittered in my eyes when I thought of home, washing over me like a wave and transforming me as I was so easily transformed before.

"I think there are a lot of things you haven't shown anybody."

We don't talk about Yukiko, or the marriage that seems as impending as our war. We don't do anything but pretend there's something other than darkness and choices woven from the nightmare ahead of us both.

Elian takes in a breath. His hand lingers beside mine. "I had this idea that when I found the crystal, I would feel something," he says.

"Victorious?"

"Peaceful. But we're so close, and I feel the complete opposite. It's like I'm dreading the moment we open that dome."

Something shifts in my chest. Hope, maybe.

"Why?"

Elian doesn't reply, and that's enough of an answer. Despite everything, he doesn't want to be responsible for destroying an entire race, no matter how evil he thinks we are. I want to tell him that I feel it too: the sense of dread mingling with the pull of duty. I want to tell him that we weren't all born monsters.

The Second Eye of Keto could destroy either one of us, and neither of us seems to want to be the one to wield it. I toy with the idea of revealing the truth to him, like maybe it will sway him over to my side as he has seemed to sway me over to his. But it seems like more of a fairy tale than the eye ever has been, because if I tell Elian who I am, he'll never accept it. I could promise I've changed. Or not changed, but changed back. To who I was and could have been if not for my mother. This humanity has transformed me in a way that is so much deeper than fins for legs and scales for skin. I'm as different on the inside now as I am on the outside. I feel the horror of what I've done and the overwhelming desire to begin again. To become the kind of queen I think Crestell always wanted me to be.

I turn to Elian, letting the snow wet my cheek.

"You once asked me to tell you something about the sirens you didn't know," I say. "There's a legend among them that warns of what can happen if a human were to take a siren's heart."

"I've never heard it."

"That's because you're not a siren."

"Neither are you," Elian says, matching my wry tone.

I give him a hollow smirk and continue on. "They say that if any human were to get ahold of a siren's heart, then they would be forever immune to the effects of the song."

Elian arches a cynical eyebrow. "Immunity from a dead siren's song?"

"From any siren's song."

I don't know why I'm telling him, save for the hope that if this war can't end, then the least he can do is survive it. Or stand some kind of a chance.

"According to the stories," I say, "the reason sirens dissolve so quickly into foam when they die is to prevent such a thing from happening."

Elian considers this. "And you think that's possible?" he asks. "If I somehow manage to cut out a siren's heart before she melts away, then I'll suddenly be able to face any siren without needing to worry about falling under their enchantments?"

"I suppose it won't matter," I tell him, "if you plan to kill them all anyway."

Elian's eyes lose a little light. "I think I understand why the original families didn't use the crystal back when it was first crafted," he says. "Genocide doesn't seem quite right, does it?

Maybe once we kill the Sea Queen, it will be enough. They might all stop. Maybe even the Princes' Bane will stop."

I turn back to the sky, and quietly, I ask, "Do you really believe killers can stop being killers?"

"I want to."

His voice sounds so far from the confident prince I met all that time ago. He's not the man who commands a ship or the boy born to command an empire. He is both and neither. He is something that exists in the in-between, where only I can see. A slip in the world where he is trapped.

The thought lights something inside of me. I steal my gaze from the stars and turn to him, my cheek damp on the snow-soaked blanket. Elian is so much like the waters he plunders. Still and peaceful on the surface, but beneath there is madness.

"What if I were to tell you a secret?" I ask.

Elian turns to me, and suddenly just looking at him hurts. A dangerous longing wells, and I dare myself to tell him over and over in my mind. Reveal the truth and see if humans are as capable of forgiveness as they are of vengeance.

"What if you were?"

"It would change how you saw me."

Elian shrugs. "Then don't tell me."

I roll my eyes. "What if you need to know?"

"People don't tell secrets because someone needs to know them. They do it because they need someone to tell."

I swallow. My heart feels loud enough to hear. "I'll ask you something instead, then."

"To keep a secret?"

"To keep a favor."

Elian nods, and I forget that we're murderers and enemies and when my identity is revealed, he might very well try to kill me. I don't think of Yukiko claiming him like a prize she doesn't know the value of. And I don't think of the Sea Queen or the notion of betrayal. I think of my human heart, suddenly beating so fast – too fast – and the crease between Elian's eyebrows as he waits for my answer.

"Are you ever going to kiss me?"

Slowly, Elian says, "That's not a favor."

His hand moves from beside mine, and I feel a sudden absence. And then it's on my cheek, cupping my face, thumb stroking my lip. It feels like the worst thing I've ever done and the best thing I could ever do and how strange that the two are suddenly the same.

How strange that instead of taking his heart, I'm hoping he takes mine.

"Do you remember when we first met?" he asks.

"You said I was more charming when I was unconscious."

Elian laughs, and he's so close that I feel his body shake against mine. I can see every scar and freckle of his skin. Every streak of color in his eyes. I lick my lips. I can almost taste him.

"Ask me again," he says.

His forehead presses against mine, breath ragged on my lips. I close my eyes and breathe him in. Licorice and ocean salt and if I move, if I breathe, then whatever fragile thing it is between us will disappear with the wind.

"Just do it already," I say.

And he does.

35

Lira

THE PATH ENDS IN water, just as it began.

With Yukiko as our guide navigating us up her sacred route, we slice our journey in half, never lost or wavering. She leads us to camps with quickfires bright enough to burn a hole through the mountain itself, and up paths that cut as much through time as they do the mountain. Quicker routes, faster courses, trails littered with cheats. Technology that sometimes even carries us part of the way. It's not a surprise that the Págese royalty are able to survive the climb with so many tricks at their disposal. It's also not a surprise that anyone not from their bloodline doesn't survive.

Though I hate to find any common ground with the likes of Yukiko, even I have to admit that her family's scam is clever. Using everything they can to perpetuate the legend of their origins, ensuring the loyalty of their people through awe alone if nothing else. It's not a bad hand to play. Like Elian and his golden blood. Or me and Keto's deadly power. Though in my case, the legend happens to be true.

I stop dead and the rest of the crew stills alongside me. Elian's gloved hand hovers dangerously close to mine, and though I feel the air spark and warm between us, I don't look at him. I can't. I can only stare ahead, my feet burying themselves farther into the snow the longer I stay still. But I can't move, either. Ahead, there are wonders. There is the palace, carved from the last breaths of my goddess Keto.

Though we're no more than five hundred feet from the peak of the mountain, we find ourselves at the base of a great canyon, surrounded by chutes of falling water that crash onto a pile of black rocks. They look like the remnants of a landslide, and when the water thrashes against them, it creates mounds of steam that hisses as it rises, before finally dissipating into the clouds. Amid the froth, the rocks float aimlessly on the edges of a great moat, like borders to keep the miraculously unfrozen water inside. In the center, surrounded by island tufts of snow, is the palace. It's an iceberg that towers to the height of the waterfalls, with windows made from solid wind and ornate steeples that curve and protrude at awkward angles. It is a body of sculpted snow, a fortress of slants and edges that eclipse the glory of the mountain itself.

A broken path of ice leads to the palace, but it is too fragmented and unstable to ensure safe passage for an army of one hundred. Instead, we find a batch of large rowboats secured on the outskirts of the moat, where it is at its calmest, farthest from the three sides of the falling water surrounding us. We split ourselves between the vessels and row toward the mouth of the palace, our boat pushed half by Torik's strength and half by the great gusts of wind that propel us forward in a crooked line.

When we dismount, the palace is leagues above us, and I have to arch my back just to get a good enough look. But there's no time to take it in, or wonder how it's possible that a palace built from snowstorms can seem somehow warmer. A degree or two above the rest of the Cloud Mountain.

Yukiko powers ahead with purpose and we follow her into the depths of the iceberg, using her torchlight to guide us when she walks too fast for us to keep pace.

The walls gleam like halls of mirrors, so that suddenly our numbers are doubled. Tripled. All I see are faces and tufts of breath that mingle among us like fog. We can't help but linger a little behind, walking slower as we try to decipher what is a reflection and what is actually Yukiko. When we fall too far behind and she rounds a corner much too far ahead, we're forced into a fleeting darkness. Elian's hand finds mine. He squeezes, just once, and everything in me quickens. Heats. My body curves toward him and I press my free hand to the glacier walls. When we find the curve to the corner, Yukiko's light illuminates our faces once more.

I don't drop Elian's hand.

Yukiko pauses at a large ice wall that shines against the heat of her flame, echoing our faces back to us. She hooks the torch onto a small brace and takes a step back.

"We're here," she says.

Elian gives me a quick glance and then unhooks the key from his neck and hands it to Yukiko. His eyes are impatient as Yukiko holds it up against a concave in the wall. The dip mirrors the patterns on the necklace perfectly, from every ornate swirl to its fanged encasing. It's the perfect lock for our key, and when Yukiko presses the necklace to the wall, it clicks securely into place.

Snow drops from the ceiling and runs from the walls like water. There's a heavy groan, and then the thick pane of ice heaves itself backward and reveals a cavern too large to be housed inside this moderate palace.

Elian enters like the thirsty explorer. I follow quickly behind him, paying no mind to the princess I brush past.

Everywhere is blue. Thick trunks of frost press against the ceiling and then drop back down in leafy tufts. They stem from the walls like branches, veins of ice paving the floor in roots. It's a forest of snow and ice.

The crew swaggers slowly in and gazes around in wide-eyed wonder. Unlike the rest of this iceberg, the cavern is truly a place of beauty. A place touched by Keto. But Elian doesn't marvel at his surroundings. He stares resolutely ahead, at the center of the dome.

A steeple of ocean water floats in a perfect mixture of emerald and sapphire, and I recognize it instantly as water from the Diávolos Sea. From my home.

In the heart of it is the Second Eye of Keto.

It's like nothing I have ever seen. Even the eye of the Sea Queen's trident doesn't quite compare, with its form so roughly slashed into shape and its color dimmed from the decades underwater. This stone is unaffected by any of that. Crafted into a perfectly geometric circle, it is tinged with the florid eyes of my mother and the gallons of blood spilled in its name.

The steeple that houses it is a solid ice sculpture, but when Elian reaches out to touch it, he doesn't recoil. It's not frozen, but suspended. In time, in place.

"We can't melt it, then," Elian says.

"We can't break it," Yukiko urges. "It might shatter the crystal."

He turns to her. "I doubt we could break it anyway. It even *feels* impenetrable."

Yukiko shakes her head furiously. "We have to open it," she says. "The ritual. What is it?"

All eyes turn to me, and I take in a breath, readying myself. This is the moment I've been working toward. The very thing I maneuvered myself back onto Elian's ship to do. I look at him and how his hair curls by his ears, sticking up in a way that shows every moment he slept in a damp tent. The frown that pulses down to his jaw. The ridiculous smell of licorice whenever he sighs.

I am too close.

I clear my throat. "Siren blood," I say.

Elian turns to me. "What?"

"Do you think just anyone can wield the Crystal of Keto?" I ask. "It has to be a warrior worthy of its magic."

"A warrior," he says.

"A siren killer."

Lies and lies, all mingling with half-truths on my tongue.

Kye throws his hands up in the air and stalks forward. "Where are we supposed to get siren blood?" he asks. "Why would you wait until now to tell us that?"

"It wouldn't make a difference when she told us," Madrid says, staring at me with an unreadable expression. "Sirens don't have blood; they have acid. We can't capture that if they turn to sea foam, and even if we did, it would eat through anything we put it in."

"Your knife." I point to Elian's belt. "The only thing on this earth that can carry the blood of a siren."

"It doesn't carry it," Elian says. "It drinks it."

"Absorbs it," I correct. "Don't tell me you haven't noticed that with every siren you kill it feels a little stronger? A little heavier?"

Elian stays silent.

"How would you know?" Yukiko tilts her face to the side. "There's something about you I can't quite settle on."

I ignore her and keep my focus on Elian. His eyebrows crease, and I know in that moment he doubts me. That even if I'm ignoring Yukiko, he isn't. He's suspicious – perhaps he always was – and though he has every right to be and part of me is proud of him for it, it hurts all the same. I cannot be trusted and it kills me that he might know that.

All the same, I can't let him be the one to free the eye.

I give him a carefree smile. "I told you that I would be useful to keep around."

Elian pulls the knife from his belt and holds it up to the cavern light. He twists the blade in his hand and takes a step toward me. I consider backing away, but stay rooted in place. Retreating now will only make me look guilty.

"Well?" I ask.

"Well, nothing," he says. "I believe in you."

He pauses a beat, as though waiting for me to contradict this and tell him that it's a mistake. Even more ridiculous is that I want to. I have the urge to tell him that he should never do something as stupid as believing in me. But I say nothing, and so Elian turns to the frozen waters of Diávolos and plunges his knife into the center.

I WAS SUPPOSED TO be happy when it failed.

The blood inside the knife is long gone. Drunk and swapped into magic that kept it invincible and allowed it to absorb the life of a siren. I knew this, but I gave Elian hope, because that's what liars do when they don't want to get caught. And I had to let them think I believed the knife would work, because why else would I have waited until now to tell them blood was the key?

I had to let Elian fail so I can succeed. I just wasn't supposed to feel so bad about it.

Hours have passed, and I'm sure it must be night. Either way, the crew is sleeping in various small chambers outside the dome. Sentries and trespassers. They're determined not to leave until they find a way of freeing the eye. If Elian's resolve wasn't enough, Yukiko's fury would have kept them all there anyway.

Try, she said. *Try leaving without the glory you promised my brother.*

I grip the lightweight sword and stare down at the Second Eye of Keto, suspended in the water of my home. Against my skin, the seashell necklace calls out. It yearns to be reunited with the powerful sea that created it. I can feel it too, the steady pull of Diávolos stretching out its arms to jerk me into its wake.

I grip my sword and slice it clean across my palm.

I'm indifferent as blood dribbles down my arm and drops onto the eye. There's no scorching pain or endless acid cold. It's warm and red and so very human. And yet.

When the blood touches the water, it dissolves. The top of the steeple folds down on itself, melting into an opening large enough for me to reach inside. I pick up the stone and sigh. It looks so tiny now, but I can feel the power coursing through me. The potential for savagery. It almost burns in my hand.

"All along, I sensed something in you."

I whirl around, clutching the eye tightly in my fist.

"I knew something was not quite right," Princess Yukiko says. She sniffs the air as though she can smell the monster in me. "You're not quite human."

I sheathe the sword and keep my voice low. "You don't know what you're saying."

"Probably not, but let's say it anyway. You're one of them, aren't you? A siren."

I don't reply and she seems to take this as an answer. She grins, her thin lips slanting to create apples in her cheeks.

"How did you achieve this disguise?" she asks. "How is it possible?"

I grind my teeth, hating the way she looks at me, like a fish on a hook. As though I'm something to be examined and studied, rather than feared. She walks toward me, circling until she is on the other side of the frozen steeple.

I cast her a withering look. "The Sea Queen seemed to think it was more of a punishment than a disguise," I say.

"And stealing the crystal is your redemption?" she asks. Still so curious, still so unafraid. "I wonder what crime you committed to inflict such a thing."

"Being born was the start," I tell her. "The Sea Queen has never been one for competition."

Just like that, the smirk leaves Yukiko's lips, and something new paints itself in place. Awe, replaced by shock. Wonder, by uncertainty. Curiosity, by fear.

"You're her," Yukiko says. "The Princes' Bane."

Her expression stays faltered for a moment longer and then, just as quickly, the hesitation leaves her face. She smiles, cunning and shrewd.

"You of all people didn't know?" she asks.

It takes me a moment too long to realize that she's not talking to me anymore.

I whip my head around to the entrance of the dome, where Elian stands. His face is slack and expressionless, eyes lingering on the eye in my hand. I blanch and my heart goes still in my chest. Suddenly nothing feels solid except for the air that lodges itself in my throat.

I believe in you.

For a moment I entertain the pitiful notion that maybe he didn't hear. But when his eyes hit mine, I know he knows. I know he has pieced together the puzzle I tried so hard to shatter. And when he reaches for his sword, I know this night will end in blood.

36

Elian

THE PRINCES' BANE.

There's nothing past those three words. The world stills and I search my memories for something – a clue, a sign, a *trace*. Instead of coming away empty, I come away with the idea that I'm a fool.

We rescued Lira from the middle of the ocean, with no other ship in sight. When she first gained consciousness, there was something inexplicably enthralling about her, broken only in the moment when she tried to attack me. She spoke *Psáriin* on the deck of my ship. And – gods – that siren. What had she said? *Parakaló*. She begged for her life and I hadn't thought to question it, even though no siren had ever done such a thing. Of course she would beg. Not to me, but to one of her own. To her princess.

"You of all people didn't know?" Yukiko asks.

I don't reply.

I knew Lira was hiding something, but I never imagined this.

My hand flies to my chest, pressing against the scars that lie under the fabric of my shirt. Scars so similar to the ones I saw on Rycroft after Lira was through with him. That day in

Midas, the Princes' Bane found me when I couldn't find her. She let a mermaid drown my strength and then scraped her claws across my heart as she readied to rip it from my chest. If the royal guards hadn't come, then she would have killed me.

Lira would have killed me.

I draw my sword the moment Lira's eyes dash to mine. At first I'm not sure what I plan to do past gripping the blade so tightly, it crushes my bones. But when Lira doesn't move, even as I advance closer and closer, it only ignites the anger inside me. The betrayal. She doesn't even have the decency to flinch.

"Elian."

She says my name in a breath and I lose all sense.

"I'm going to kill you," I say.

Even as a human, Lira is quick. Faster than most novice fighters I've encountered and far more fluid. She's sloppy, but there's something primal in it. I cut my blade toward her and she rolls her shoulder back in one swift movement. She looks shocked but recovers enough to launch a punch in my direction. I grab her wrist inches from my face and twist. Teeth bared, she kicks with brutal force. I whirl out of the way, but her foot clips my thigh and pain shoots up my leg.

I nod at her belt. "Your sword," I say.

"You care if I'm unarmed?" she asks.

"Don't mistake honor for caring," I seethe. "If I have to, I'll run you through defenseless."

I swing toward her again and she twists awkwardly out of my path. The second she's not within reach, I hear the sound of metal being drawn.

Lira lifts the sword in a perfect arc, just as I taught her, and snarls.

I see the animal in her then.

Our swords scream together. Steel on steel.

I block as Lira hacks a blow through the air, and I seize her wrist once more. When I bend it harshly to the left, her sword falls from her hand. I spin her into me, pinning her arms against her. My heart pounds furiously on her back as she writhes against my grip. She feels cold – she always does – but sweat licks between us.

"Finish her!" Yukiko screams.

I swallow and consider the sword locked between us. My hands can't move from Lira to get the right angle, and the thought of being this close – of being able to hear her gasp and feel the life leave her – is too much.

I'm sick with it.

I think of the taste of her kiss, with the stories of stars roofing us. An entire galaxy watched while her body curved into mine. As she asked me to kiss her and it was all I could do to keep myself steady.

Lira angles her cheek toward me now and lets out a low breath.

Then she brings her elbow up and cracks it across my jaw.

I drop my hold on her and she pitches forward to retrieve her sword. With a mirthless laugh, I press a hand to my mouth.

"You certainly live up to your legend," I say.

"Enough, Elian." She points her sword between us like a barrier.

I spit blood on the floor. "It'll be enough when you're dead."

When I charge again, I ignore everything but the betrayal that roars through me. I land blow after blow, striking my blade on hers. Again and again. Each attack shrieks through the air, and time seems to move all at once and yet stop dead just the same. Endless seconds and minutes, until she falls to her knees and the crystal rolls onto the floor with her.

Lira doesn't reach for it and so neither do I. I can't do anything but wonder how much longer she will keep the sword roofed above her head. Sheltering her from my onslaught.

She takes each blow with a dead look in her eyes. Then her elbows start to shake and her ankle finally collapses. The blade clatters to the cold floor. Lira sprawls on the ground, waiting, her expression indifferent. Giving me the opening I thought I wanted.

She squeezes her seashell necklace and I flinch. It's like she's teasing me with every clue I was blind to. I raise my weapon again, feeling heavy steel in my hands. I can have Cristian's revenge. The revenge of every prince who died in the ocean and every one who may die yet. I can kill her and be done with it.

I drop my sword.

Lira heaves a breath. Sweat paints across her brow and the unsettled look in her eyes slits straight through me. I wish I had killed her. I wish she had killed me. Instead we stare at each other, and then Lira shakes her head and kicks my legs out from under me.

When I slam to the floor beside her, she lets out a frustrated sigh. "Next time you want to kill someone," she says, "don't hesitate."

"Shouldn't I be saying that to you?"

"What are you doing?" Yukiko asks. I sit up as the Págese princess scowls down at me. "She's the Princes' Bane."

She says it like she thinks I might have forgotten. As though it's a possibility that I let Lira live because I really am that stupid and not because I really am that human.

I stand and brush myself off. "I'm aware," I say, and snatch both swords from the floor.

"She came for the crystal," Yukiko says. "Just as we did."

"And now she's going to leave without it."

Lira eyes the Crystal of Keto a few inches from where she sits hunched over on the floor. But she doesn't even try to reach for the very thing she came here for.

"Get up," I say.

Yukiko lurches forward. "You can't do this," she says, outraged. "If your crew wasn't sleeping like corpses on the other side of this palace, they would tell you that you can't just let her go."

I incline my head slowly toward Yukiko. "You're not a queen yet. Don't think for a second that you can tell me what to do any more than they can."

I wipe the dried blood from my mouth. I always seem to have it on me, but tonight is one of the few times it has been mine. Last time it was below the deck of Rycroft's ship. Last time it was Lira's.

On cue, Lira gets to her feet and watches for what I'll do next. I don't want to be shaken, but I am. I see her standing there, waiting for my next command like a loyal member of the crew, and the chains holding me together break like cords.

"Go back to where you came from," I tell Lira. "Right now."

I crouch down to scrape the crystal from the floor and Lira wavers. I see her shadow move uncertainly in the dim light. Time drags through the room like mud.

"I wish this could be the end," she says.

It sounds more like a warning than a threat, if there was ever a difference between the two. A divination of the inevitable battle to come. I don't answer. Instead I wait for her footsteps to disappear from the dome, and it's only when I'm sure she's gone that I stand.

"You can't let her live," Yukiko says darkly.

"She'll have plenty of time to die." I palm the crystal. "Right beside her mother."

Yukiko is disbelieving. "I warned you about this," she says. "Love is not for kings. You'll see that soon enough when we're married."

"You can stop talking about marriage now," I tell her. "It won't happen."

Yukiko matches my look with added sharpness. "A prince who goes back on his word? How novel."

"I told you that I was going to give you an alternative." Impatience seeps into my voice. "I may not want to be king of Midas, but I know I sure as hell don't want you to be queen."

"And what offer could you give me that would be any more appealing?"

I grit my teeth. Reactions are all Yukiko ever seems to want, and Lira took the last I had left in me. "I assume you know of Queen Galina's affliction."

"My brother made me privy to the information when he took the throne."

"Kardiá is gaining prominence through trade deals with other kingdoms. Their queen is proving to be popular in the north. Galina can't compete with that if she can't interact with her people for fear of infecting them. Eidýllio is suffering because she has chosen not to take another husband to help her rule."

Yukiko's disinterest is well-practiced. "Why should I care?"

"Because she said nothing about not taking a wife."

"You want me to become the queen of Eidýllio?" Yukiko cackles disbelievingly.

"*A* queen," I correct.

"And why would Galina agree to that?"

"Her power doesn't affect women. You'd be able to liaise

~ 305 ~

with the other kingdoms on her behalf, meeting dignitaries and diplomats. You'd see the people and inspire loyalty. All the things that Galina can't do."

"And the heirs?" Yukiko asks.

"She has no interest in continuing her cursed legacy."

"You've thought it all through," Yukiko practically purrs. "Even speaking to the queen?"

"Galina agreed it would be a mutually beneficial arrangement, especially if it gives her ties to Efévresi as well as Págos. And, of course, places Midas in her debt."

"And if I refuse?"

I set my jaw. "Either you marry a powerful queen and rule by her side, or you stay in Midas with a future king who will question your every move." I slip the crystal into my pocket beside my compass. "Who knows if I'll even survive today? Do you really want to be engaged to a prince with a death sentence?"

Yukiko studies me and I know that it's irrelevant whether or not this is a good deal. Right now she only cares about winning, and if she concedes so easily, then it won't matter if she gets a powerful kingdom as a prize. To her, losing face is worse than winning a kingdom.

"I have a condition," she says.

"Of course you do."

"When the time comes, I want the Princes' Bane to die by your blade."

My hands clench in my pocket, knuckles cracking against the compass. Just like the owner of the Golden Goose to be as immoral as her patrons and just like a princess to make demands with the fate of humanity on the line.

I blink back the image of Lira's wavering shadow and the look in her eyes when she realized I knew the truth of her identity. How she pushed me from the path of Rycroft's bullet and asked me to kiss her on the edge of a mountain. I force myself to remember that lying is her greatest talent.

I school my features into indifference. "I can assure you," I tell Yukiko, "the next time I face her, I won't even blink."

I feel the compass jolt against my hand and, slowly, the pointer shifts.

37

Lira

I RUN FASTER THAN I thought I could. Through the maze of the ice palace and the tunnels where Elian's crew still sleeps. I run until it doesn't even feel like running, but as though I'm floating. Flying. Swimming through the labyrinth as I did the ocean. I run until I smell water and see light peek out from the end of the path.

Elian let me live, but it was a small act of mercy that will be undone in the coming battle. Did he do it because he knew it wouldn't matter? Because he wanted me to see my mother die first? I don't want to cling to the idea of it being anything more, but I can't help myself. I toy with the possibility that the betrayal of my identity didn't undo whatever bridge had built itself between us.

When he dropped his sword, there was something so utterly depleted about it that I can't find the words to describe it in any language. The idea that he doesn't want me dead is impossible, but I hold on to it more desperately than I have ever clung to anything in my vicious life. He kissed me, after all. Brushed my cheek so delicately and pressed his lips to mine in a way that shot fire through me, melting away any pieces of the mountain that had slicked itself to my skin.

Things like that can't be forgotten any more than they can be undone.

I break free from the ice palace and grab the oars to one of the small rowboats. I reach the other side of the great moat breathless and clutching the seashell necklace in my hand. The thick grooves of it press against my palm as I debate the choice ahead of me. Elian will think he can use the eye to kill my mother and every single siren in the ocean. He'll risk his life, believing he has a weapon, when in fact that weapon is useless in his hands.

With my blood coating it, it can have no other master.

There were a lot of things the Sea Queen told me about Keto's eye, but the one I remember most clearly is this: Whoever frees the eye will become its master. I hadn't lied to Elian when I said blood was needed; it just didn't have to be siren blood. If Elian had sliced his own hand across the waters, the Second Eye of Keto would have been his to use. It would have given him the same powers my mother's trident gifted her. That was how the original families planned for the humans to take down the Sea Queen: an even battle of magic.

I thrust the seashell necklace into the moat as I did in Eidýllio, only this time I focus on my mother's image. I call to her inside my mind, loud enough to have it puncture through an entire mountain and spread across the seas. At first, I'm not sure if it will work, but then the water begins to boil and around me the ice that scatters over the moat melts.

It singes like an invisible fire and a gust of water spouts up. Black flows like shadows spilling into light. I hear a familiar humming and then, unmistakable, the sound of laughter.

From the abyss, my mother appears.

She is still beautiful, as all siren queens are, and horrifying in a way that only she has ever managed to be. Her eyes burnish mine and her long fingers stroke her trident like a pet. All the power in the world at her fingertips, ready to bend the seas and its monsters to her whim.

For some reason, she looks so strange to me now.

The Sea Queen smiles with fresh blood on her teeth. "Are you going to speak?" she asks.

I glance back to the palace, expecting Elian to come hurtling out at any moment, but the entrance stays clear and the water is steady by its feet and the Sea Queen simply waits.

"Do you know where we are?"

She casts an unconcerned look at her surroundings, resting her long, webbed fingers on the trident. There is barely a flicker in her chiseled eyes when she says, "The Cloud Mountain."

"This lake" – my breath rattles between us – "is where the Second Eye of Keto was hidden. I followed the prince whose heart you wanted me to take and he led me here. To the very thing you've been searching for. I found this place when you failed to. Couldn't you sense it with all of that power in your damn trident?"

It is not until she blinks that I realize I'm screaming.

Suddenly every deception and excuse I was so sure I could weave doesn't seem important. My mind is blank, save for one thought: how unreasonably righteous I feel. When the water parted, I thought there was something odd about her. A small change in my absence that I couldn't quite place my finger on. Now I realize it isn't that she looks strange, but that she looks like a stranger.

The Sea Queen laughs and the ground cracks by my feet. She reclines and the water bubbles up to meet her like a throne.

"You're still the stupid child," she chides. "Can I sense every cup of water a human presses to its lips? You think this is part of our world just because it flows the same way?"

The Sea Queen scrapes a fang across her lip. "All of it is a disguise," she says. "This mountain – this moat – is not ours. It's theirs. The original sires of this infestation of human kingdoms. Man-made; *magic-made*. There is nothing of our goddess in these waters. I wouldn't have been able to surface here if you hadn't used the seashell to call me. I wouldn't have known such a place could be reached."

"And now you do."

"And when you give me the eye, I can bring it all crashing down to the depths of Diávolos."

I smile faintly. "That sounds like quite the plan. If only it was what I had in mind."

The Sea Queen holds out her palm, fingers sharpened to the bone. A hand of knives. "Daughter," she commands, "give me the Second Eye of Keto while I'm still being pleasant."

"That's a little impossible, since I don't have it at the moment."

The Sea Queen's sculptured face cracks. A small twitch in her grooved brows and the tight pull of her lips too sudden to be a smile. She angles her head, studying my rigid stance. Assessing this sudden change in me. Still the insolent child, but with something far more duplicitous to my gaze.

Slowly, the Sea Queen arches forward. Her eyes gleam against the light. "Where is it?"

I summon the parts of myself best learned from Elian. The well-practiced bravado that comes from a knack for survival and the notion that luck may never end. Just this once I want to see something true from her. A reaction she hasn't measured or calculated.

"It's with the prince who came looking for it," I say. "I let him have it in exchange for my life."

I feel the impact of the ground before I register the blood. When I open my mouth to breathe, it pools from my nose and onto my tongue.

"Insolent trash!" the Sea Queen screeches.

Her tentacles thrash wildly, pounding through the air between us. I feel her boiling against my skin as she locks a tentacle around my neck and squeezes.

"Do you think your life is worth more than that eye?"

My mother lunges forward and her fingernails slice across my wrists like razor blades. I try to snatch myself free, but her grip is unbreakable. The more I struggle, the harder she presses, until I feel that with one more movement my bones will snap.

She drags me across the way, closer and closer to the ice palace. My joints crack with each violent jerk, feet dragging along the water. My throat burns in her grip, but I don't let my smile falter. I don't do anything except wait until she comes to a halt and tosses me back to the ground.

I don't even think of telling her that it was me who freed the eye and that when I'm reunited with it, its power will belong to me. Admitting that would put Elian's life at risk. Right now my mother sees him as the threat and that's exactly what I need.

Misdirection, Elian said. He'll be proud to see how well I've learned.

The Sea Queen regards me like a disease. "Do you think your life is worth anything?"

"Maybe not to you," I say. I angle my head to the side and spit. "But to him it might be."

"I knew you were weak," she says. "But I never realized the extent of it. The heir to the sea kingdom of Keto, who I had to beat into brutality. Who would sooner see a young prince drown than rip out his heart while it still beat. Who cried while she murdered my sister."

At the mention of Crestell, my chest heaves. The Sea Queen looks at me like I am a pitiful thing, no more her daughter than any other creature in her dominion. The complete opposite to the way Crestell had looked at Kahlia when she saved her life.

"I thought I clawed it out of you," the Sea Queen says. "Yet look how much survived. Like a plague, this humanity infected you long before I stole your fins."

"I'll take that as a compliment," I say. "You wanted me to learn a lesson through this punishment and I have. I know that the prince isn't my enemy. In fact, he's just a more honorable version of me." I stare into her stone-glazed eyes. "And in another life, if I ever had a choice about who to be, maybe I would have been like him."

"Enough!" she demands. "You will give me what's mine before I kill you."

"No," I say. "I think first I'll take what's mine."

A derisive sound punctures from her lips. "You want my crown?"

"It's my crown, actually."

The points of her fangs glisten in the daylight. "You think you can kill me, Lira?" she asks. "The very one who brought you into this world?"

No fear, just curiosity. Layered in as much amusement as disbelief.

"If we were in the ocean, you would have an army," I say. "But this is the Cloud Mountain, and we're the farthest we can possibly be from home. In this place, with Elian and his crew, you're practically carrion."

"*Elian?*" She says his name with bile in her mouth. "You

and your filthy human prince think I need the ocean for my army? Wherever I go, my power follows and so do they. If you truly want to end this war, then I'll oblige. As a mother, I must grant my daughter her wish."

She lowers her trident deep into the water, watching my face tick. Black weeps from the trident's spine like tears. It blots across the moat and then floats a few inches from the water, forming large, dark circles across the way. Portals to Diávolos.

A hand punctures through the first one, closest to my feet. Then another. An army's worth follow, and the water groans with this dark magic, shaking as one by one sirens rip their way into the mountain. Claws and teeth and fins and cold, cold eyes.

And then, not too far from me, a sight far worse.

I feel the power of the eye before I see Elian step out from the palace with his crew like an army lining up behind him. He surveys the rising army with a look equal parts awe and horror. I let out a breath, and even from here I can smell his angler scent on the breeze. It chips away part of me that is already raw.

As though he can sense this, Elian's eyes find mine. He looks tired but ready for war. Always prepared for what's to come, even if that thing may be death. As he watches me, something strange crosses his thunderous eyes. Uncertainty. Relief. A thing so utterly conflicted that I can only frown in response. Whatever it is, it's gone far too quickly for me to decipher.

I open my mouth to call out to him – warn him to run, or hide, though I know he'll do neither – but then he blinks and his expression sharpens. I can tell by just that one look that the Sea Queen has clawed her way into his line of vision. The moment they set their sights on each other, my heart jerks against my ribs.

The sirens grow, preparing for attack, and I know that not one of them will use their song to let Elian and his crew die peacefully. This isn't a hunt; this is war. And they will want a fair kill. A victory brutal enough to make their queen proud.

The Sea Queen curves downward, her tentacles brushing my hand, lips like broken glass on my ear. "Stupid girl," she whispers, and then – as though it's the worst thing she could utter – "stupid human girl."

38

Elian

THE WATER IS BLACK with sirens and the world follows.

They soot the mountain with their near-demonic presence, and as the sun struggles to pull itself higher, it bruises the sky. There's a string of hissing and infernal screams as the sirens claw their way to the top of the water, their smiles impious and seductive. I can't help but be mesmerized. Such beautiful creatures. Such bewitching, deadly things. Even as they sharpen their fangs on their lips and run taloned hands through their liquid hair, I can't look away.

Everything about them is awful, but nothing about them is hideous.

The moat stretches to half a mile in each direction, and the sirens seem to fill it all. There must be a couple hundred of them, outnumbering us two to one.

"Gods." Kye's voice is dazed. "They're everywhere."

"We noticed." Madrid lines the sight of her crossbow. "What are we going to do, Cap?"

"Be on your best behavior," I say.

She lowers her crossbow and frowns. "What?"

I nod to the center of the chaos. "We're in the presence of royalty."

The Sea Queen is a vision in front of us, with sweeping midnight tentacles and her daughter poised allegiant by her side. A formidable dyad. Regardless of Lira's new cloak of humanity, when she stands beside her mother, they look like they can char through daylight.

The Sea Queen floats through the water, Lira following the unsteady path by her side. When she reaches me, I notice that her eyes are the same color as her lips.

"Siren killer," the Sea Queen says, by way of greeting.

When she speaks, even just those few words, and even in my language, it's like nothing I have ever heard. Foul and hateful, alluring and repulsive. The melody of it leaves me with a fiendish kind of melancholy. It's like she speaks in funeral songs.

"Your Majesty." I bow just low enough that my eyes never leave her.

"Lira." Madrid shakes her head, betrayal soaking her voice. "It can't be true, right? You're one of us."

The Sea Queen's laughter bubbles like water. "You'll soon learn that my daughter has no allegiance." She twists her eyes to Lira's. "She's nothing but a traitor."

"I knew it," Kye says, though there's no satisfaction in his voice. "I knew we shouldn't trust you and I did anyway. You were playing us this whole time?"

It's a question, like he can't quite believe it. Like he won't, despite all of his suspicions, until Lira confirms it for herself. But she doesn't answer. Whether it's because she doesn't care enough to or because there's just too much to say, I'm not sure. But she doesn't look at him, at any of us, at me. Her eyes are fixated on her mother. Roaming over her. Whenever the Sea Queen moves, Lira's shoulders twitch toward us.

"You have something of mine," the Sea Queen says.

The crystal thrums in my pocket. "Don't worry. I plan on returning it."

The Sea Queen inclines her head downward, arms out in a goading gesture. "Then by all means," she says, "let us begin."

I surge forward.

The Sea Queen slides out of my line in one sleek movement, and once she's out of the way, her horde ascends. Sirens spill from the water, leaping onto my crew and screaming as their nails and teeth dig into whatever flesh they can find.

Lira dives to the side, and a tally of my crew rushes after her. I try to keep her in my focus, but there're too many swords and bodies, and it's only seconds before I lose sight of her.

I can see the queen, though. She hovers in the center of the moat on a line of frost that breaches the water like a small island. With the Crystal of Keto in my possession, she'll let her sirens do the dirty work. Watch as they sacrifice themselves for her treasure, never once risking her own neck for it.

If I can just get close enough to her, then I can use the crystal to send her back to the hell she came from.

I dart in and out of leaping sirens, my crew hot on my tail. We slice our swords into them, careful to avoid the sprays of acid blood. Kye yells something, and I turn just in time to see him crash to the floor, a siren skewed on top of him. Madrid kicks her off before the blood has time to do damage, and hauls Kye back to his feet.

"Keep going!" Yukiko yells, gesturing to the queen with her sword. "We'll hold them off."

She is the epitome of a Págese princess in that moment, above the holds of jealousy and bids for power. A pure, raw warrior, like each of her brothers and the kings and queens before them. She swoops her sword over her head, circling it through the air with enough force to create a storm. She's ready to kill.

"Come on!" Kye roars.

He thrusts me onward, Madrid shooting cover fire behind us. The sound of gunfire and screaming rattles the mountain. With every step we take, another member of my crew branches off to wage war on an attacking siren. They are everywhere, springing from the water and slithering along the ground like snakes. I run past so many bodies, my boots slick with ice and death, until a legion of devilish shrieks stops me dead.

A group of six sirens leap from the water, their nails shining like daggers. They land like cats, fins bent in the middle and hands arched to claws.

"Watch out!" Kye yells, and Madrid grunts from beside him.

"I know," she says, peppering the deadly creatures with arrows. "I'm not blind."

The sirens pounce out of the way, deceptively agile even on land. Their gills expand against their bare ribs, revealing the raw flesh beneath.

"You sure about that?" Kye asks, and Madrid elbows him in the side before thrusting the crossbow to the ground and unsheathing her sword.

We attack with more brutality than ever.

I go for the throat before any one of them can open their mouths to sing. Around us lullabies crash and echo alongside the cries for mercy, but there's too much noise for it to have any effect past dizziness. Too much death for their songs to take shape. Still, I won't risk it. One note and they could send us into a frenzy.

I lash out with my sword, slicing across a jugular. And then another. They come thick and fast and like the heads of the Hydra. Whenever I leave one siren severed on the floor, another leaps out in her place.

One of them stabs Kye, her nails sliding into his knee. Her finger goes so far through, I half-expect the rest of her hand to follow, but he presses a pistol to her temple and when she falls lifelessly to the ground, he pulls his leg out from her grip without so much as a wince.

"Go ahead!" Madrid yells, slinging Kye's arm over her shoulder. She plunges her sword into the mouth of a siren. "Get the queen!"

I sprint, rolling to the floor in a duck as another siren leaps toward me. I can feel my skin sizzling underneath my shirtsleeve when I stab her. Siren blood, eating its way through. I rip the fabric away and heap snow onto the charred skin before continuing on.

Bullets cascade around me, shooting through the air like fireworks. The water is riddled with them, alongside the floating bodies of sirens. I hear the battle cries and death cries. My crew is dying, the sirens are dying, and I can't seem to tell which screams belong to who.

I gasp a breath when I finally reach the fork of land in the water. My feet pound across it, but I barely have the chance to get close enough to the Sea Queen before something slams into me, lifting me off the ground. My cheek cracks on the ground.

It's not a siren. It's a merman.

The creature flips back into the water and roars with the splintered teeth of a shark. I choke a little, but when it attacks again, I'm ready. I'm a tornado of steel and fury, slicing clean into its rubber flesh, across its branded chest and deep grooved stomach. But the merman doesn't relent no matter how much it bleeds.

It grabs me by the throat with a webbed hand and roars loud enough to split my ears. I drop my sword. The edges of its spiked fingers puncture my neck and it lifts me off the floor with one muscular arm. I scramble, fumbling blindly as I gag for breath. When my hands latch around the screaming blade, I don't waste time.

I slam my knife through the base of its chin, driving the blade up until the handle slams against bone. The power surges back through the steel, like no kill before. It is pure animal and instinct and as my knife drinks it up, I do too.

The creature falls to the floor by my feet and the Sea Queen's nostrils flare.

"*Tha pethánete*," she barks.

"Sorry, I rub a hand over my throat. "I don't speak bitch."

The water boils in fury around her. "When you die," she says, "do you think my daughter will weep?"

I lift my knife. "Kill me and find out."

39

Elian

I KICK MY SWORD up off the floor and catch it, holding both blades before the Sea Queen.

She hisses. "Just like a human, to rely on weapons to make a kill."

With a raised hand, the Sea Queen hoists a body of water up and sends it thrusting toward me. I dive out of the way, but the edge of the great wave clips my ankle and sends me spinning through the air. I land with a skid, ice burning through the fabric of my leg.

She regards me with an impish look of satisfaction and then raises her hand once more. I ready myself for the impact, but the hit never comes. Instead she sends a hammer of water toward a line of half a dozen of my men. It envelops them instantly and then drags them into the clawing pit of sirens.

I snarl and throw my sword in her direction, but it bounces from her glass skin.

"Fool," she spits. "*Ilthia anóitos.*"

"You've lost already," I tell her, heaving myself to my feet. "I have the Crystal of Keto. Lira couldn't take it from me."

But even as I say the words, I'm unsure. The crystal may

have been humming before, but if anything, it feels like dead weight in my pocket now.

The Sea Queen recoils at the sight of the crystal in my hand.

"I'll make sure Lira is punished for that when this is over," she says, sliding backward. "In fact, I think she already is."

I follow her line of vision and freeze.

Across the way, Lira is fighting Yukiko. The princess shoves her roughly against a pillar of ice, and Lira lurches forward to slash her sword against her chest. I don't have to hear them to know Yukiko is laughing. Lira may be a killer in the ocean, but Yukiko is a Págese warrior, and on land and on snow and especially on this mountain, that means so much more. The Págese are trained to be merciless, and to Yukiko, Lira is just another siren. Only now she's easy prey.

A few members of my crew surround her, their blades eager to take a stab at the traitor. I've lost sight of Kye and Madrid, but even if they were near, I don't know what they would do. If they would help Lira or Yukiko.

Yukiko raises a hand to keep my crew back. Signaling that she wants Lira for herself.

Lira twists her arm up to punch, but Yukiko dodges and then backhands her hard across the cheek. I can almost feel the impact. Lira spits, and in the next moment, Yukiko grabs her roughly, ripping the material across her shoulder. Lira kicks out, but when Yukiko hits her this time, she slams to the ground.

The Págese princess removes a pistol from her holster and the Sea Queen makes an admonishing sound. "See," she purrs. "Just like a human."

The lack of concern in her voice shocks me more than it should. It's a game to her. Everything from this war to her daughter's death. She would let Lira be killed so I could carry the guilt of it. She would refuse to save her so I could be disgraced when I did.

I'm hurtling toward them before I think of a solid plan, and the Sea Queen lets me abandon her in the watery depths. I don't need to glance back to know she's watching me with a satisfied smile. Grinning as I do her dirty work, like another one of her subjects.

I arrive too late.

Something crashes into Yukiko, sending her skidding ten feet across the snow. The siren growls, yellow hair curling in front of her eyes. She arches her shoulders, licks her lips, and then springs once more. Shots fire out, but the beast is too fast for bullets to keep up.

Ribbons cut across Yukiko's body, and I choke back a gag as the siren snarls and presses her hand against the princess's chest, poised to take her still-beating heart as a trophy. I fist my sword, breathe in a low rumble, and ready for the killing blow.

"Kahlia!" Lira screams.

The siren slashes around to face me, red droplets on her face and hair.

Lira jumps between us like a lightning bolt. I'm barely able to stop the blade before it slices across her neck. I widen my eyes, arm shaking as I keep the sword hovering unsteadily by her throat. Daring myself to let her live again.

Lira swallows – the movement knocking against the steel – but she doesn't back down. Her cheek is hashed pink and I struggle to look away from the mark.

"Not her," she says, angling herself between me and the siren.

Furious, I advance until my shadow looms over her face.

"You think I won't kill any of these things because you tell me not to?" I ask. "It just tried to kill the princess of Págos."

Lira casts a backward glance at Yukiko. "She looks alive enough," she says, and spreads her arms out from her sides, shielding the siren. "The princess was the one with a gun to my head."

"I don't care."

I make to move past her, but Lira presses her hands to my chest. It's almost a shove, but when I stumble back a few steps, she follows, her palms still flat against my shirt. The connection sets off a storm in me.

It's not skin on skin, but it might as well be. I feel the cold echoing from her and the confused warmth it brings. I want to reach out and pull her closer, save her just like we saved each other on Rycroft's ship. But that instinct is the problem, and the fact that she would try to use it against me – the very weakness she created – makes me seethe.

I look down at Lira's hand, pressed flat against my heart.

"Are you insane," I say. Not a question.

"Elian," she whispers. "You can't."

I throw her hands from my chest and glare. "Wrong."

I go to shove past her again, but she grabs me in desperation, fingers slipping into mine like it's the most natural thing in the world. I seize.

"Elian," she says again. Her pulse strums against mine. "She's my cousin."

I recoil.

When I look at the siren again, I see she can't be more than fifteen, with one eye the same milky yellow as her hair, and the other a perfect match for Lira's. *Cousins*. She looks up at us questioningly, but it's not my sword, or the stone clenched in the same fist, that seems to hold her interest. But my other hand, threaded wildly into Lira's. Her thin brows dimple over wide eyes and suddenly she looks far more girl than demon.

I back away, my hand falling from Lira's.

Lira reaches out for me again, but I square my jaw and open my palm to reveal the Crystal of Keto. A warning, I think, though I'm not sure if it's for me or her.

Lira shakes her head, undeterred, and takes a determined step forward.

The crystal sears against my palm as she nears. Pounding as furiously as my heart.

"Stop," I demand, and my voice cracks.

To not end this war now would put humanity at risk. The sirens have shown they can't be trusted or bargained with. To let their murderous race continue would be an affront to everything I believe in. And to let the Princes' Bane live . . . of all the things I've done, that would be the worst. To put so many people in danger would be monstrous. And yet, one look at Lira's pleading eyes, and I know that's exactly what I'm going to do.

I drop my hand and look to the ground, disgraced.

By falling for a monster, I have become one for her.

"*Anóitos.*"

The Sea Queen's voice is clinical as she descends into my line of sight. Beautifully grotesque. Rage simmers through me, and just seeing her leaves me overcome with the need to plunge my knife into her cold black heart.

"Lira." The Sea Queen's head cracks toward her daughter. "*Párte to apó ton.*"

Lira watches me carefully, her eyes like magnets on mine. When she shakes her head, it's slow and barely noticeable. She doesn't look at her mother.

"I won't," she says in crisp Midasan, letting me know that

she's not just talking to her mother. She's talking to me. To the crew she became a part of. To the army of her kin that stare onward from the water. Disobeying whatever order she has been given so everyone can hear.

The Sea Queen arches a high brow. "You love this tongue more than your own?" she asks. "Perhaps I should cut yours out, then?"

A tentacle strikes out at Lira's back, flinging her forward. The sound of fin against skin cuts through the air like a whipping, and I lurch toward Lira. I grab her before she hits the ground, skidding to the floor in her place. My leg burns against the snow, ankle twisting as my arms catch her waist.

Lira's hand curls around my neck and she slumps on the hilt of my knee. "You've got good reflexes," she says, and smiles in a way that detonates through me.

I tighten my grip on her. "You don't."

The Sea Queen snarls and whips around in a flourish to address the rest of her subjects. Everything she does is a show, every threat disguised as a spectacle. She is a performer as much as she is a queen.

Around us, the war comes to a pause.

"See how these humans can turn even my most loyal against me," the Sea Queen says in Midasan, so even my crew can understand. "My daughter has fallen prey to lies and charm. So much so that I have to sully myself with this language to even get her to listen to me. You see now how the humans can kill us with more than just spears and knives? This prince" – she points a finger at me like a loaded pistol – "must die at the hands of the siren he has bewitched. And so I will restore her to her former glory." She turns to Lira with a serpentine smile and raises her trident in a toast. "Long live the Princes' Bane."

It happens in seconds.

The Sea Queen pushes her trident toward the sky, and when her arms can't stretch any farther, it ascends without her. Hovering over her head, then spinning so rapidly that the glare from the ruby becomes a perpetual ray of sunlight, blinding us all. And then just as suddenly it stops.

Lira rips my arms from her and pushes me away. I fall back just in time for the light to shoot like a spear from the trident into her chest. And then explode.

Lira is on her knees and her arms burst like wings from her sides.

An inhuman scream rips free from her throat and suddenly Kye is beside me, hand clamping brutally around my wrist. It's only then that I realize I've pitched forward. That I was about to run to her again. That even now, with his hand gripping me so tightly that my bones crunch, I can't take my eyes off her. I can't let her out of my sight.

The light comes in a blast, but once there's no more scream left in her, it curls down her body. Lira convulses, stiff and shaking all at once. Her eyes roll back and then close, and I can practically hear her teeth grinding together.

Everyone stops. My crew pauses in horror. The sirens watch fervently.

Some let out songlike breaths in anticipation, jaws hanging hungrily open. Others watch on in uncertainty, their eyes narrowed to slits and their fangs clamped across the edges of their lips. The siren from earlier – Kahlia – watches Lira's every shudder. When her cousin's neck snaps back, she blanches.

All the while, the Sea Queen salivates.

Against the crushed ice, Lira's legs sew together. The skin melts and mingles until scales erupt from her feet and medley up to her waist. It's a color I've never seen before, flecked with so many shades of orange, it's like caught sunlight. It blends flawlessly into her hips, just below the curve of her belly button.

Above that, her skin begins to brighten.

It starts along the curve of her ribs and then curls out like a tide. It's not that she becomes paler – I don't think that's possible – but her skin starts to glisten. Liquid light dancing down her arms and across her chest. Rolling over the newly delicate arc of her collarbone. Her hair streams over her shoulders like pomegranate beads, and when she throws herself back, arms spread wide, the snow flurries into an angel around her.

Lira arches, relishing the cold on her body, opening the gills that run across her ribs with every shift. She curls onto her side, half-facing the water and half-facing me. There's a moment where she lies like that – eyes still closed, nestled in snow that mirrors her skin, never looking less human – where I feel strangely at peace.

Then Lira opens her eyes, and I see that only one is the blue I remember. And the other is pure hellfire.

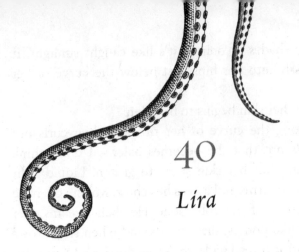

40

Lira

I HAD ALMOST FORGOTTEN my strength – my speed – but when I dart into the water, it surges back through me. I roar a hunter's howl beneath the surface, and the cold gurgles down my throat and slashes through my gills. It may not be the ocean, but it's enough. Water as wild as I am.

Elian is watching when I emerge. There's so much written on his face and so much rushing through me that I can't seem to decipher one emotion from the next or decide which belong to him and which to me. Seeing him now is like seeing him with new eyes.

He's brighter, more vivid. Eyes reflecting every glint of the sun and skin no less than the burnished gold of his land. Every inch of him is a contrast, light and dark mixing and rolling into one until I can barely think of looking away.

I lay my arms against the snow and watch him like a hunter.

"Bring me his heart," the Sea Queen says.

Her order hisses through the wind, and when I tear my gaze from Elian, I see her fingers tighten over the trident, where her share of Keto's eyes waits to be reunited with its sister. I can hear it now. The call of the two halves as they hover so close to each other. It's too steady to be a song and too wild to be a drumbeat. A heartbeat, then. Thumping mercilessly in my ears, as the stains of my blood coat one and the stains of my mother's magic coat the other.

"Take it from him," the Sea Queen hisses in our murderous tongue.

There is a note of desperation in her voice, birthed from the fact that she thinks Elian freed the eye from its hiding place. She fears what will happen if he tries to use the eye against her and if its magic will overpower that of the trident she has used to enslave our kind into slaughter.

Elian may not know it, but right now the Sea Queen thinks he is her match.

I crane my neck to the side and hold out a hand to beckon Elian forward. His eyes twitch, but he doesn't come, and I would smile if I didn't think the gesture would crack my newly stone-etched face. Instead I lean my head back and breathe in the wind, letting my hair drift onto the water.

Behind me, the sirens begin to chorus.

Their melodies reach out and take ahold of the humans. Delicate refrains that cause the crew to sway where they stand, losing all sense of danger. Threats become dreams and fears a fading memory, until their hearts begin to thrum in time to the deadly aria.

"It's beautiful," Madrid says, her body slack.

Elian watches his enchanted crew linger on the melody of the Sea Queen's army, bewildered at their sudden change. When he turns back to face me, his jaw pulses, and just that look nearly turns this impossibly unfrozen body of water into a glacier.

I smile, part my lips, and let the music follow.

At the sound of my voice, Elian walks forward, and when I turn my humming to singing, he drops to his knees in front of me. He still has a plan for every letter that follows in the alphabet and though he plays the part well enough, I can sense his heart racing through each beat. His movements are slightly too rigid. Too prepared. And I can see the wildfire blazing in his eyes.

He is unaffected by the song.

Elian clutches the Crystal of Keto as though it's his lifeline. As far as he's concerned, this newfound immunity is down to the tiny piece of my goddess that nooks in his palm. I smile at that, because Elian of all people should know better. He should know to have more faith in myth and fairy tale.

When Maeve dissolved to sea foam on the deck of the *Saad*, the small part of me that believed in stories was glad the prince didn't have a chance to take her heart and glean immunity from the siren's song. But when I told Elian about the legend of our deaths, I knew it wasn't a story anymore. I felt the truth of it. And now that truth is kneeling before me with savage eyes cut from land and ocean. Leaves and seaweed flooding together.

Any human who takes a siren's heart will be immune to the power of their song.

Only Elian didn't need to take my heart; I gave it to him.

I reach out a hand to touch his face, and his eyes flit briefly closed. He inhales as though the very act of breathing is marking the memory in his mind. My fingers graze his arched cheekbones. He's still warm, and unlike before, when the sun made my siren body crack and throb, Elian's warmth makes me ache in an entirely new way.

I slide my hand around his neck and tug his head toward me, using his weight to inch my waist from the water. The longing is more than I can bear.

"Do you know what I want from you?" I whisper.

Elian swallows. "I'm not going to give you the crystal."

When I reply, my voice is throaty. "I'm not talking about that."

"Then what?"

I grin, feeling more wicked than I have in so long. "Your heart," I say, and I kiss him.

It's nothing like the soft and tentative tryst we shared under the stars. It's wild and burning, something newly territorial in it. His lips crash fiercely onto mine, hot and soft, and when I feel his tongue slip against mine, every animal part of me comes alive. It's inside of him, too. The predatory impulse. We claim each other, right here on the edge of war.

Elian drags his hands through my hair and I clutch him, pushing and pulling him closer against me. Even no distance feels like too much. His hand tightens on my jaw and we're a tangle of fingers and teeth and the world obliterates around us. It's all stardust.

I bite his lip and he moans into me. We devour each other, gasping desperate breaths until we exhaust the air.

Elian breaks away, as savage and brutal as the kiss itself. He doesn't pull back, so much as he severs himself from me. Tearing his lips from mine. When he looks at me, his eyes are a feral mirror of my own. Dazed and furious and so, so hungry.

I run my tongue across my bottom lip, where his angler taste still lingers.

My mother watches us to the side, gleaming. She doesn't realize that Elian isn't enthralled, any more than she realizes that his army is about to gain another soldier.

"Elian," I whisper, low enough that the Sea Queen can't hear. I keep my fingers pressed to the base of his neck, inclining him toward me. "You have to trust in it."

"In what?" he asks, hoarse and disbelieving. "In you?"

"In your dream," I say. "That killers can stop being killers."

Elian's eyes search mine. "How can I believe anything you say?"

"Because you're immune to our song."

He frowns and it takes a moment, his gaze narrowing, before my words dawn on him. I can practically see the memory run through his mind and the new kind of uncertainty it brings. It kills me, but there's nothing I can do but have faith that he'll remember more than just the story and less than just my betrayal. I need him to linger on the taste of me and think about how we saved each other. How we could do that so easily again now, and take the world along with us.

"Elian," I say, and he wets his lips.

"I heard you." His face gives nothing away.

"And?"

"And nothing." Slowly, Elian pulls my hand from his neck, eyes fixed like a target on my own. He shakes his head like he can't quite comprehend what he's about to do. And then: "I believe in you," he says, and slips the eye into my palm.

The moment it touches my skin, I am infinite.

What I felt inside the ice palace is a mere fraction of it, and now I am a forest fire, burning, burning. A tidal wave rising and crushing and sweeping across the world. I don't just have power; I am power. It flows through me, replacing the acid blood with thick, dark magic.

The Second Eye of Keto speaks to me in a hundred different languages, whispering all the ways I can use it to kill the humans. A picture paints itself so vividly in my mind, of the eye merging with my mother's trident and creating a Sea Queen with all the might of Keto. A goddess in her own right, molding a world where sirens walk and hunt with grass and gravel between their toes. Impenetrable skin and enchanted voices and so much death that will follow.

And beside that, a dream.

The ocean glitters as though crystallized, and a human ship stops halfway through its journey, no land in sight for miles. The tired and bedraggled crew leaps off the edge of their vessel, feeling the soft wind butterfly on their skin before they hit the water. Sirens hover nearby but don't attack. They aren't hunting or assessing, but watching in a haphazard kind of harmony.

Peace.

"Give me the eye," the Sea Queen demands, breaking me from my trance.

I close my hand around it. "I'd rather kill you instead."

Elian lets out a breath, amusement and surprise and something far too close to pride. I shoot him a look and then turn back to the Sea Queen, as resolute as this new strength allows.

"You don't have that kind of power," she says.

"Oh, but you're wrong." I give her a smile to start wars. Or maybe to end them. "You see, it wasn't the prince who freed the eye from its chamber, Mother. It was me."

When she screams, the mountain shakes.

I'm her worst nightmare come true. The daughter she was always so reluctant to let take her crown, primed to usurp her. It hits me now that she has no power over me. For the first time, we're on even footing. Each with the eye of a goddess, and each with the somewhat wavering loyalty of our kin. There's an army in these waters, but their allegiance could pass between us so easily. They could choose my side as readily as hers.

The Sea Queen snarls a glance to her left and lets out a vicious roar of *Psáriin*. Her throat strains and throbs, and in moments a slice of gray swipes across my vision.

It takes me a moment to realize that Elian is gone.

I whip my head to face the vast body of water behind me, scanning with my hunter's eyes. There's a blinding flash of movements, so swift and barbaric that even I have to pause to narrow in on the sight.

Elian is in the center of the moat, surrounded by sirens who foam at the mouth when his scent salts the water. They drift toward him, but when they get too close, he's jerked violently to the side. Pulled farther into the distance by the scruff of his shirt.

My breath shudders through me as I stare at his attacker.

The Flesh-Eater.

His shark tail is thick, gray, ribbed and spotted like a virus slowly devouring him. Every bit the demon I remember, with the face of a true killer. His features lie flat, eyes like gaping holes in his head and lips a mere slice across his face. They are marked by crusted orange, from whoever he has eaten in battle.

The Flesh-Eater grins, saliva clinging between the lines of his shark teeth, cutlass tail primed by my prince's heart.

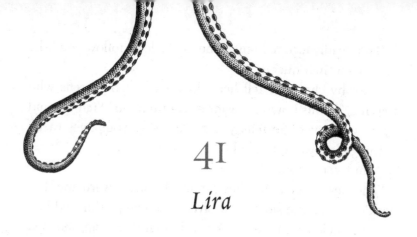

41

Lira

I'm pinned in place by half a dozen arms. The sirens flank me, nails braced on my skin. The Flesh-Eater is deadly enough in the wilderness of the ocean with the mermen who live in brutal solitude, but he's most dangerous here. Under the Sea Queen's command.

I pant, fighting the sirens, but it's no use against so many, and with Elian's crew meandering hypnotically to the side, he'll be torn apart by the Flesh-Eater in minutes.

The eye sparks in my palm. The dark magic calls, begging for me to surrender to it. Obliterate every enemy in my way. It sings with the same vengeful lust that my mother has. But to give into it would mean following my mother's path, and I can't allow that. It'd only prove to the others that I'm just like her and every queen who came before. If they're going to swear their allegiance to me, then it has to be because of something other than fear.

"Let me save him," I say.

I half-turn to see the Sea Queen slither closer to me, tentacles weaving through her soldiers. "You really think I would allow you to rescue him?"

"I'm not talking to you," I hiss.

Her deadly face tightens. "The sirens don't follow you," she says. "I am their queen."

"Not by choice," I tell her. I look back at the sirens who trap me. "Is this how you want to continue on? Fighting and dying whenever she tells you to, knowing your lives mean nothing if they don't help her in some way?"

"Shut your mouth!"

The Sea Queen thrashes a tentacle out toward me. My neck cracks to the side as she strikes, drawing a thin red line on my cheekbone. I feel the sirens loosen their grip, shocked by her outburst.

"This is your chance," I continue on, more fearless than I have the right to be. "If you follow me, I'll put an end to this once and for all. You can be free."

The Sea Queen raises another tentacle. "You little bitch," she says.

And then—

"Free?"

One of the sirens drops my wrist and combs a heap of deep blue hair from her face. "How would we be free?"

"Be quiet!" the Sea Queen barks.

"What would change?" another asks, her hold on me faltering.

"The world," I answer honestly. "There could be peace."

"Peace?" the Sea Queen arches an eyebrow. "With those filthy humans?"

The eye burns in my hand with every word she speaks. Just one movement and I could send a wave strong enough to knock her back half a mile. I could make her bleed right here, in front of them all.

"What does the Princes' Bane care about peace?" a siren asks.

"Because I've seen the truth of the queen's lies." I look directly into my mother's eyes. "I've spent enough time with the humans to know they don't want war. They just want to live. The sooner this is over, the sooner we can all stop dying in the name of a feud none of us were alive to see created."

There is a sudden discord among them. Murmurs spilling into clear, angry shouts. The sirens hiss their disapproval alongside their temptation, and I blink, trying to figure out which direction the scales are likely to tip and if I can still save Elian either way.

As time passes, I grow more and more impatient. Every second longer they take to decide is another second Elian is in the Flesh-Eater's hold, his teeth ready to puncture Elian's neck.

"I'm with you."

A voice erupts from the chaos, and I turn to see my cousin. Kahlia is surrounded by a group of young sirens, unsullied youth fresh in their saltwater smiles. Children ripe for rebellion.

"Lira has always been the strongest," Kahlia says. "And now she has the Second Eye of Keto under her command. Are there any of you here who really doubt she'll be a worthy ruler?" The authority in her voice takes me aback. It's clear-cut and assured, as though the very idea of not siding with me is ludicrous.

"You mutinous eel," the Sea Queen seethes.

"It's not mutiny if we're following our queen," she says. "It's loyalty. For my sovereign and for my family."

I know she's thinking of Crestell in that moment, because I am too.

"Lira was ready to take your place in just a few hearts," Kahlia says, her voice growing louder, bolder, with every word.

"This only means that when she does, her first act as queen will be to end a war that has killed so many of us. And when she takes the trident" – Kahlia's yellow eye twitches under her defiance – "she'll have twice the power you ever did."

"I could be using the eye right now to force you all to bow before me," I say. "I could strike each of you who holds me with all the power of Keto." The sirens stir, lengthening their distance. "And yet I'm reasoning with you instead. Asking for your allegiance when I have every right to just take it."

I lift my head and survey them each in turn, fire flickering in my right eye. At first the silence gives me pause, and I begin to wonder if my mother's hold is just too tight. Then, slowly, I see a new kind of understanding descend on each of their faces.

One by one, they incline their heads in a bow, and the sirens who surrounded me move back, their hands dropping from my body and rising to their chests in a show of fealty. Then, as though my eyes cut right through them, the army begins to part and a line draws neatly down the moat.

A clear path to the Flesh-Eater.

The monstrous soldier takes one look at the treasonous sirens before him and drags Elian below the surface.

I follow with maddening speed, like an arrow shooting toward him, arms out and coated more in rage than water. It's seconds before I reach them and too many for me to be grateful. The Flesh-Eater pins Elian to the shingle, hand braced on his throat and ready to snap in either direction.

He sees me when I'm only inches from them both, and lifts Elian up with oil-slick talons as though he's a prize to be beheld. I grind my teeth together, a snarl gurgling in my throat. The Flesh-Eater is a monster and a warrior and a ravenous killer. And he doesn't stand a chance.

I don't need the eye for this. I'm going to tear him apart.

I lunge, and the Flesh-Eater throws Elian away like garbage. I pause just long enough to see the prince swim back to the surface for breath before I rush forward.

The Flesh-Eater's fist explodes against my face. There's a pop and the odd feeling of everything bursting and shattering before the pain hits. Pure fury and power resonate from his knuckles, and when he hits me again, the world goes dark for a moment.

I grab his fist and shake the dizziness from my bones. He's strong, but it's an empty strength, dwelling in the idea of duty and violence for violence's sake. For the first time, I'm fighting for something. Elian's face runs on a loop in my mind, and the moment I remember it's his life, the life of my kingdom, the pain seeps away.

I twist the Flesh-Eater's arm, and a crack splinters through the water. He thunders, jaw stretching wide to show every one of his predator teeth. He rolls back toward me, ready to slam his elbow into my chest. But I'm lithe and quick, and when I twist out of the way, he growls.

I tackle him from behind, pounding my body into his as hard as my bones allow. He crashes against the water bed, face burying into the sand. There is blood. So much that I taste it.

He throws himself upright and strikes an arm out to me. For a moment I'm surprised that he grabs me instead of pummeling me, and he uses that to his advantage. Pulling me forward, I realize a second too late what he is about to do. He bites into my shoulder, and I feel flesh being torn from my bones.

I scream and slam my head into his, again and again, until my pain mixes with his. But he is relentless, gnawing and ripping and chewing through me. Tasting me in a way he was never able to before. It's not until I feel a sharp stab, like a hot poker sliding into my palm, that I remember the eye clutched in my fist.

The power calling to be harnessed.

In one clean move, I slam my closed hand into the Flesh-Eater's stomach, and when it comes out the other side, he stills. I push him from me, not daring to glance at the wound on my shoulder. He blinks slowly, surprised that suddenly there is a hole through him. That something could puncture that stone-forged body so easily.

Behind him, Elian drifts down.

He stares past the Flesh-Eater and locks his eyes on to my shoulder, which no doubt looks as bad as it feels. I do the same, taking in the hashed red on his cheek and the cracks in his lips and the way his left arm doesn't quite move right as he hovers in the water.

I'm about to swim toward him when the Flesh-Eater wraps a callous claw around my neck. It's one final act of brutality, and I feel the instability of his strength. With each passing moment, his grip ricochets between insufferable and barely there.

Slowly, I curve a hand around his thick wrist and squeeze.

Around us, the sirens descend. They watch the barbarian soldier cling desperately to their princess. They see me wait fearlessly for death to claim him. And when Elian plunges his knife into the back of the Flesh-Eater's skull, they do nothing but smile.

WHEN WE RISE TO the surface, a piece of the Flesh-Eater comes with us.

Elian wipes the flay of skin from his blade and curls his lips. For some reason, this strikes me as funny. The Sea Queen's most loyal and unstoppable warrior, destroyed by a human prince who is nauseated at the sight of dead flesh. I snort, and Elian turns to shoot me an incredulous look.

"That was funny to you?"

"Your face is always funny to me," I tell him.

He narrows his eyes, but under the water his fingers slip into mine.

I squeeze his hand and face the Sea Queen, who watches us with broiling hatred. Her tentacles are spread out in every direction, creating a parachute that inches her over the water as though she's floating.

"You both die today," she growls.

The water begins to churn around us, a whirlwind spewing scalding black bubbles. Elian flinches as it spits against his skin, and when I see the raw flesh it leaves behind, I pull him toward me and clutch tighter on to Keto's eye. I summon the magic inside to protect us, answering its desperate calls with one of my own. My skin radiates and my body loosens as the power pours out from me, parting the water like a tide.

The black disperses from around us, leaving an untouched circle of cool water where Elian and I linger safely.

The sirens leap out of the scalding water, hissing as their skin begins to blister and dissolve. They throw themselves onto the snow and Elian's crew jumps back, no longer under the spell of the song.

Not all of them make it.

Sirens in the center of the water torch like kindling before I'm able to think of saving them. It takes no time at all for their screams to turn to wind and their bodies to foam, and the cauldron of water claims them as though they never existed at all.

The remaining sirens cower against the snow and let out a legion of grievous screams.

"Let's see your treacherous army help you now," the Sea Queen says.

"Elian, duck!" Kye's call punctures across the ravine.

We turn in unison to see Madrid aim her gun at the Sea Queen. The shot fires, and true to Madrid's skill, it hits the queen square in the back. If it was any other beast, it would have pierced straight through to its heart. But my mother is forged in something from below the depths of hell, and when the bullet ricochets off her, she cackles.

In one swift movement, the Sea Queen swirls and aims her trident at them. An inferno shoots from each pitchfork point, embers discharging through the air until a line of fire blazes across the snow, cutting our armies off. I can barely see them over the flames.

The Sea Queen screams a laugh. "Nobody can save you," she says.

I seethe, squeezing Elian's hand just that bit tighter. "I can kill you just fine on my own."

"But you're not on your own," she says. "Yet."

My eyes widen and the moment she turns to Elian, I use all the power I have to shove him to the side. He arcs through the air, the eye's protection still holding like an orb around him. I hear the crash of his body hit the water just in time for my mother's tentacle to smash into my chest. My ribs crack.

My mother wastes no time. Small tornadoes burst from the air, circling around her like loyal subjects. They move like they have minds, and when my mother points a finger in my direction, they lurch toward me. Without thinking, I thrust my arms into the air and drag the water up like a shield. It leaps at my command and then curls into a wave, swallowing the swirling thunderclouds.

My mother may have tricks, but now I have just as many. As soon as the wave demolishes her magic, I feel quenched. As though each time I use the eye, a small piece of my hunger chips away. Feeding the power inside.

The Sea Queen shrieks, and a crack of thunder shoots beside me. Above, the clouds begin to rumble and turn black. Thunder moans, and I smell the electricity of the incoming storm.

"You have a lot to learn," my mother says.

She raises her trident in the air, swirling it around and around. With every circle, the sky seems to twist, clouds lurching and swarming until the entire sky is made of nothing but gray.

Then lightning rains down around me.

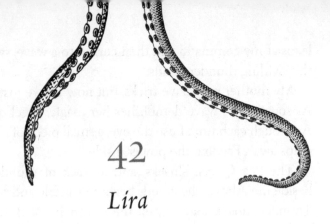

42

Lira

A BURST STRIKES THE water inches from my waist. The charge vibrates through me like hot pokers, and more lightning bolts spit in a circle, trapping me in a cage of light and fire.

Elian calls my name and I grit my teeth. At the sound of his voice, the Sea Queen turns a lazy gaze to him. As though he's a fly she has just been reminded of. I'm not sure how much more protection the eye can offer him while still managing to keep me alive, but the only clear thought I have is that I can't let her hurt him. I can't let her kill him in the depths of these black waters.

Another surge of lightning drops from the air, and I spring out of the water to catch it. My skin feels like liquid against the ray of cracking light, and I know I can't hold on for long. But I don't need to. Just a few seconds – long enough to aim with precision that would rival Madrid's – and I throw it through the air.

It blows clean through the Sea Queen's side.

She lets out a monstrous cry. Skin and bone and blood and magic. They burst from her and scatter like stardust. The wound is gaping, but even if pain is the only thing the Sea Queen can feel, she barely lets it give her pause. She lashes out with a curl of water that sends me hurtling through the air.

I sink deep into the water with the force of the impact before I feel Elian's hand on mine, dragging me back up to the surface.

"Get away," I tell him, sending a blast of wind toward my mother.

She continues to approach with frightening speed, and I search desperately for something – *anything* – that might slow her down. My eyes catch the structure of the ice palace, and I don't stop to think it through before I raise spouts of water and turn them into a blockade of icebergs. They climb higher and higher, looming pillars of frost that guard us like the spikes of a fence.

"I have to get you to safety," I tell Elian. "We can swim under. If I put out the fire, you can take cover behind your crew."

Elian eyes me savagely. "I'm not *hiding*," he says.

A resounding boom rattles through the line of icebergs as my mother smashes into them. With her fists or her magic, I'm not sure. But the force of it is enough to make the water tremble, and I know the new wall won't last long.

"Fine," I snap. "Don't hide; run instead. I don't care just as long as you get out of here."

Elian laughs an offbeat, exhausted sound. "You're not understanding me," he says, grabbing my hand. "I'm not leaving you."

"Elian, I—"

"Don't say something heroic and self-sacrificing," he tells me. "Because then I might start thinking you've actually got some humanity in you."

I smirk. "That would be boring."

He nods, pressing against me. The icebergs I've conjured rattle, and large blocks of ice tumble around us in monstrous hailstones. It's as though the world is crumbling.

"I don't like you because you're nice," Elian says. His forehead touches mine, his lips hovering a breath away.

"That says a lot about your psyche."

He kisses me then. Just once. Delicate in a way I've only known with him. And then the icebergs fall and the impact creates a wave high enough to swallow us whole. I throw my arms around Elian and let my magic coat us. Shielding us from the bursts of snow that threaten to crush us to the water bed.

When it's over, I lift my head from the comfort of his shoulder and let out a breath. Beyond the decimated wall of crushed ice, my mother beckons.

"It would be a discredit for your legend to die in such an embrace," she says. "I could make it so they still sing songs about the mighty Princes' Bane. I could have them forget your cross-contamination and remember only the glory of your past."

I push Elian behind me, keeping my hand tangled in his.

"That's funny," I tell her, "because I plan to make them forget everything about you. Except your death. I'll make sure they remember that."

The wind picks up speed, my mother's fury swirling and tossing the air, further igniting the flames that keep my army from me. Elian's crew. The very people who would lay down their lives for us. But I don't need people to die for me anymore. And I don't need them to die because of me either. The killing and the sacrifice end here, and I want each of them to see it so they can trust in the changes I've preached. A new world, with a new queen at its helm.

Smoke effuses from the air, only this time it's my magic that drives it. I wrap the wind in on itself until it grows into a cyclone that spills to the height of the sun. And then another. A third and a fourth, and all the while the water rages and my mother watches with a cold, empty expression.

The fire blots out and the smoke clears, and in the abyss of charred snow and melted gravel, two armies stare back at us. Human and siren, side by side. Waiting for their prince and their princess to deliver the promised end.

"I'm sorry it has to be this way," I tell my mother.

Even if I hate her, there's something woeful pressing onto my chest, alleviated only by the gentle tug of Elian's hand as he remains by my side. Tethering me to this precious residue of humanity.

The Sea Queen's expression remains vacant. "You're weak, then," she says, no hint of regret. "For both of us to survive would show true ineptitude." She runs a forked tongue over her lips, an unrelenting darkness in her eyes. "I could never let you live."

"I know," I tell her. The wind gathers faster. "I can't let you live either."

I throw my hands forward and the cyclones explode against her. She thrashes and snarls, wild tentacles whipping against the unstoppable gusts. Her trident is alight, but she doesn't use it. Even when she's carried from the water and thrown through the air like a rag.

I realize then that she can't. My body pulses with power, but it takes every ounce of focus I have to keep the cyclones going. Such things require as much concentration as ferocity. One slip of my mind and my mother could drop back into the ocean and take that split second to regain her ground.

I syphon more magic from my fingertips, ignoring the Sea Queen's nefarious howls. The cyclones gather like spun sugar, merging as they devour her.

Something splinters. A heavy rumble that shakes the mountain. And then there is the distinct feeling of the world turning on its hilt.

Elian calls my name and I drop my hands, letting the cyclones falter. I don't see where my mother's body lands, but there's a crack like no other and the trident hurtles to the ground by Kahlia's fin.

"Lira!" she screams.

A shadow descends.

I glance up and see a summit hurtle toward us.

Slabs of rock roll from the waterfalls with frightening speed, molding with the blizzard air to form giant bursts of white smoke. Quickly, I clinch my arms around Elian's waist and use all of my might to throw a blanket of energy over us.

The glacier rubble pounds against the magical shield. I don't look, my eyes closed as I cling desperately to Elian, praying the defense holds. Grateful that the others are safe on the far side of the water.

Snow chokes the air and I cough against Elian's chest as the ice crystals slip into my gills. He squeezes me closer to him, so tight, it should hurt. But my bones feel like dust already, and with every rock that hammers away at our shield, my skull bursts.

A lifetime spins around us before the crumbling finally stops and a weight lifts from my battered body. I search to make sure the others are unscathed, but the air is an expanse of white. Elian runs his hands over my shoulders and then down my arms. For a moment I'm not sure why, and then I realize that he's checking for injuries. Making sure I'm okay until he can see it for himself.

His hand slides into my hair, and I want nothing more than for this feeling of total contentment to stay like a shelter over my heart. But as with all things, it seizes, wiped clean as soon as the world comes back into focus.

When the fog clears, my mother's body lies broken on the snow.

I swim to her, Elian following behind. His crew heaves us both up from the water. Madrid stares at my fin, but her hand firmly grips mine. I want to explain things to her – to them all – but the words don't come to mind.

Elian settles beside me, gathering me in his arms. When he lifts me, my hands curl around his neck as though it's the most natural thing in the world. I don't think about how it feels to have him hold me – to truly see every inch of me. I can't focus on how much my heart knocks against my chest, because whenever I catch sight of the crippled tentacle before us, it stops dead once more.

The sirens gather around my mother, slithering away as Elian approaches with me in his arms. He places me onto the ground beside her and takes a step back to give me the space I need but don't want.

The Sea Queen is a dent in the snow.

Her great piceous tentacles cross together like the silk of a spiderweb, creating a pattern of broken limbs. There's no blood, and for a moment I think she can't possibly be dead. It doesn't seem right that she can look so pristine, like the sharply carved statue of a slain beast.

I stare in stunned silence, fin gleaming against the sleet, the weight of two armies on my back. I wait like the dutiful daughter, for the sea foam to froth from her bones and melt her like the ice she lies on. Seconds pass with nothing but her oddly jarred body and the red, shimmering light of her eyes.

Nobody speaks. Time becomes something outside of the mountain, in the world below. Here there is only silence and the infinity that comes with waiting. It takes a lifetime before I finally hear a small shuffle of movement and smell the fresh scent of black sweets on the wind.

Elian crouches beside me, his arm wrapping around my shoulders, enveloping me in his warmth. We sit like that for an eternity until, finally, the Sea Queen fades away.

43

Elian

THE RAIN COMES IN torrents, slicking my hair to my neck. The sun is still high, like a crescent half-hidden behind the clouds, creating a warp of colors in the air. My sister's kingdom glistens somewhere behind me, though with our destination so near, it may as well be a world away.

In a sense, I suppose it is a world away.

"Not long now," Kye says, clapping a hand on Madrid's back. "Soon you'll be able to enjoy me in my full glory."

She arches an eyebrow at him, a smile well past coy on her lips. "Drowning, you mean?"

"No," he says, with mock injury. "Soaking wet."

Madrid eases his hand off with a frown. "I'd prefer the drowning."

I grin at them and pull the compass from my pocket. The point spins madly in all directions, letting me know that Kye's right. We're near. Close to a place where truth and deceit mingle alongside each other like old friends. Where every word spoken is soaked in both and neither.

The *Saad* sprints through the water, and I walk to the edge of the ship as Torik steers a little to the left. Below, our guides keep the pace as easily as if we were trawling along in a rowboat. Their fins rainbow through the beaten water like prismatic arrows. Blurs and blends and hues creating a shield of color around my ship.

They swim with no effort at all, and I almost want to be insulted that the *Saad*'s pace is so easily matched. Instead I take it as a compliment. That the *Saad* can keep step with them is proof of her glory.

A few of the sirens break apart from the throng and head to the front of the ship, leading the way. As if I don't already have it memorized. It's a little funny to see them settle into these precariously carved roles so easily. Guiding sailors, rather than stalking their ships for signs of weakness. Helping, instead of hunting.

The Sea Queen has forged a new world, as much on land as in sea.

Once the eyes of Keto were reunited, creating a trident without limit, there were as many choices to be made as there were promises to be broken. Though one thing remained clear throughout it all: The ocean needed a queen. I spent a lifetime trying to evade becoming king, knowing that Amara would make a far better ruler – her heart staying grounded for every beat mine wandered – but even I understood that some things were more important than whim. Dreams could not always triumph over duty, and compromise was the foundation to any good peace treaty.

Lira knew it too. And so instead of exploring the world, she created a new one.

As Diávolos opened its waters and the sea kingdom of Keto threw wide its gates, the human kingdoms returned the gesture. At least, most of them. Peace doesn't come easy, but over half the world has accepted the new order, and with the backing of the new Midasan queen and her roaming brother, hesitancy is becoming a thing of the past. New treaties are being struck, and after the initial dozen returned from the sea kingdom of Keto with their lives intact, others have made the journey to seek an audience with the Sea Queen. To offer trade alongside treaties and bask in the wonders of this newly unlocked dynasty.

Kingdom one hundred and one.

"Captain!" Torik bellows from above, signaling our arrival.

I don't need his call, because I know the moment we cross from human waters into the seas of Diávolos. The water becomes an endless stream of sapphires, blending into the sky and catching every ray the sun scatters down. There's no more rain, or darkness. It's brighter than anything has a right to be, but not warm. Never warm. The sapphires are crisp and glacial, soaking into the tips of my fingers. Arctic blue glazes over us all.

Below, the sirens chorus.

We continue on until we reach the arch. Blue merges into dusty orange, and the rock formation towers to the height of a hundred ships. A marker for the world, to signal the kingdom of Keto below.

Stretching to the width of a mile, the arch is as much a gateway as any door. Ships tether to the large spikes that slice from its curve, empty, save for a few humans left to watch the decks in case of pirates. Though pirates seem to have become some of the most regular divers here and the sirens delight in their company as much as their queen does.

There are five ships in total, and I recognize at least one as royal. The Eidýllion flag waves a windy greeting. Yukiko didn't mention she was coming, but then, she doesn't like to mention much to me if she can help it. If she weren't already adept in the art of secrecy, I'd say that Galina has schooled her well. Their marriage is one of constant collaboration and trade-offs; teaching each other every trick they've kept hidden until now. A formidable dyad, slowly overshadowing the Kardiáns that threatened Galina's reign.

Not that I expect them to thank me, but since my father has already sent more gold than is befitting – as compensation for both my sly marriage evasion and Yukiko's new scars – I thought that would make us even. Or at least, on solid enough ground to give notice of a visit to the Sea Queen. So the other party could avoid the region entirely.

Apparently, Yukiko still likes surprises.

We dock the farthest from them we can, and my crew readies their diving gear. They slip into wetsuits like a second skin, which I suppose they have become. I hover back, watching as they prep the heavy Efévresic apparatus. Something I've never needed – not with magic on my side.

I smile when the sirens begin to croon, knowing better than anyone what that song means. The water froths and parts, turning to a glorious silver around the small whirlpool that forms. When their song reaches its peak, the Sea Queen appears.

She ascends from the ocean in a way that is nothing short of celestial. The water follows her in a throne, elevating her to the height of my ship. Ocean-soaked hair runs down the length of her body, and she retains the otherworldly glow that always seems to illuminate her moony skin. Only now she is something more than just a siren, or a girl masquerading as a pirate.

She is a goddess.

Eight broad onyx strokes stream from Lira's curved body, more like wings than tentacles. Glorious violet spheres halo underneath, and when she rises high enough that her eyes connect with mine, I grin. Her eyes are still the same, like sharp buds of night-blooming roses that only grow wider, blossoming as I step closer.

She can't see the world with me, so we settle for me bringing the world to her. No longer hunting, but always searching. For experiences, for adventure, and for the stories to save and bring back. For days like this, that never come soon enough.

"Your Majesty," I say.

"You're here already."

Her voice is like music, and even now I find it hard to adjust. Every word a refrain, spoken with regal command.

"If you want, I can leave and come back."

Lira's lips skim to a smile, and time becomes a thing of the past. "Would you?" she asks, matching my teasing tone. "It would give me more time to prepare for your arrival. I planned on erecting a statue."

I hold out my hand for her. "Thoughtful of you."

The change is as remarkable as ever.

One moment, she's the Sea Queen, as much a fairy tale as any I've read, and the next she's something even more miraculous. Her tentacles flood into each other and take the shape of legs; their plum hues fade to give way to furiously pale skin. Her waist clinches and curves, and the burnished clovers that covered her breasts transform into a ruffle-collared shirt with heavy fringe sleeves. Her hair remains the color of wine, far from the mottled red brown I was used to, and her eyes still flicker in two distinct colors. A combination of Sea Queen and pirate, of a past lived and a future yet to be written.

Lira descends gracefully onto the *Saad* and takes a firm hold of my outstretched hand. I bring it to my lips with a provoking smile and then press a hand to her cheek. It's soft and sharp and as full of as many contradictions as she is.

"Are you ready?" she asks.

I kiss her by way of reply, surprising myself that I waited a full minute. It's an unusual show of patience on my part.

Lira grins, her teeth skimming my lips, and lets her tongue run across mine. She clutches on to the collar of my shirt and I wrap my arms around her waist. It's like holding a story rather than a person; she feels wild and infinite in my arms.

She loops my hand in hers and pulls me up onto the side of the ship. The intertwined eyes of Keto are draped over her collarbone in an ornamental lavaliere. On the Sea Queen that greeted me moments ago, it looked like a grandiose choker, befitting an ocean ruler. On Lira, in her deceptively delicate humanity, it looks heavy enough to sink her to the bottom of the ocean.

Lira catches my eye and arches her brow. "Are you staring at my chest or my necklace?"

I give her a shameless smile. "Which one won't earn me a slap in the face?"

"I'm just trying to gauge whether or not you're planning on stealing it." She runs a slender finger over the stone. "You are a pirate, after all."

"True," I say. "But then, so are you."

Lira looks down at her outfit. The navy pants that puff out at the thighs and the knee-high brown boots with enough gold on the buckles to buy a kingdom. She laughs, and the ruby glows against her bust. Salt and magic.

She pulls me closer to her, her fingers held tight over mine, and together we dive.

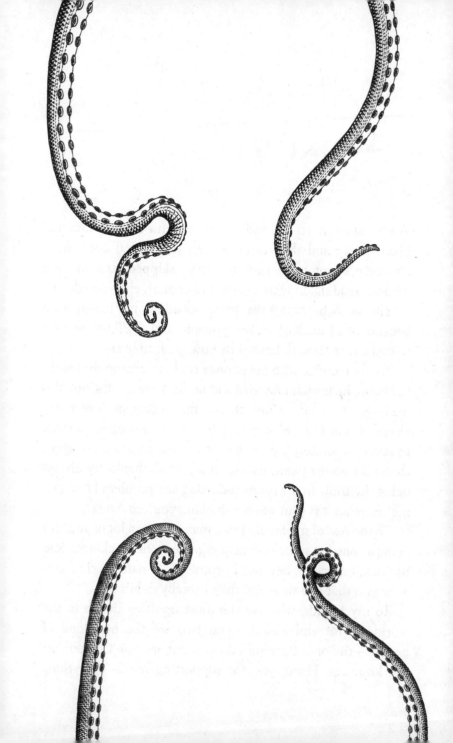

ACKNOWLEDGMENTS

You've made it to the end! Thank you for reading Lira and Elian's story and then turning the page to find out a little bit more about mine (unless you've skipped straight here without reading. In which case, spoiler alert: everyone dies).

This book became a real thing outside of my imagination because of a bunch of amazing people, and so I'll try my best to make sure they all know just how great they are.

To my parents, who never once told me to stop dreaming. For being hilarious and weird and not just great folks, but also really great friends. Mum, thanks for ringing me every day to check that I'm still alive and for being someone I can talk to about absolutely anything (but not for always picking out the exact wrong paint. Every. Time.). Dad, thanks for always being the smile in the room and fixing any problem I have, no matter what it is (but not for thinking you can Artex).

To the rest of my family (and, man, there's a lot of you) for being a constant source of encouragement and wackiness. And to Nick, especially, because I promised I'd name a character after you that one time and then I totally didn't.

To my friends, who are the most uplifting bunch in the world. Jasprit and Rashika, you two are the best kind of people – the ones I couldn't do without and can't remember not knowing. Thank you for supporting me in everything

I do, being endlessly on my wavelength, and making me laugh more than I ever have. And to Siiri, for being a burst of positivity and one of the first true friends I made in the blogging world (and for being someone I can gush to about K-dramas whenever I'm procrastinating. Which is always).

To Charles and Alan, two of the most bizarre and talented creative writing professors. You guys made me forget everything I thought I knew about writing and learn all the fun stuff instead.

To the folks at Feiwel & Friends for being the dream team and giving me the most amazing cover! And to Anna, for helping me to iron out the kinks and tell the story that needed to be told, and for making me feel right at home in this whole process.

To the team at Hot Key Books, for being such an awesome, passionate crew to work with and for helping this book find its way to the UK. Now everyone at home can believe me when I tell them I really do have a book out!

To my agent, Emmanuelle, whose love and excitement for this book kept mine from ever wavering. Thank you for championing Lira and Elian so much and for seeing potential in their story. And in me. And to Whitney, for making sure that Lira and Elian truly got to travel the world!

Lastly, to the readers, all of you, for continuing to inspire and throw yourselves into new stories each day. For believing in magic and wonder, both in the real world and the not-so-real worlds.

'This is Rapunzel glistening
with dark magic galore.'

CHLOE GONG,

New York Times bestselling author of
These Violent Delights

'Christo has cast a spell with this
decadently dark tale of witches,
fate, and defying death.'

CIANNON SMART,

author of *Witches Steeped in Gold*

'Princess of Souls sucked me in
from the very first sentence.'

TRICIA LEVENSELLER,

author of *The Shadows Between Us*

Coming from
Alexandra Christo

PRINCESS
OF
SOULS

@HotKeyBooksYA
@alliechristo

Read on for an extract . . .

1

SELESTRA

I can tell someone when they're going to die. All I need is a lock of hair and their soul.

Just in case.

That's the job of a Somniatis witch, tied to the king with magic steeped in death. It's all I was ever raised to be: a servant to the kingdom, an heir to my family's power.

A witch bound to the Six Isles.

And because of it, I've never glimpsed the world beyond the Floating Mountain this castle stands on.

Not that I'm a prisoner.

I'm King Seryth's ward and one day I'll be his most trusted adviser. The right hand to royalty, free to go wherever I want and do whatever I want, without having to ask for permission first.

Just as soon as my mother dies.

I stride through the stone halls, ivory gloves snaking to my shoulders where the shimmer of my dress begins. They're meant to be a safeguard for my visions, but sometimes they feel more like a leash to stop me from going wild.

To keep my magic at bay until the time is right.

But I'm not a prisoner, I tell myself.

I'm just not supposed to touch anyone.

Outside the Grand Hall, a line of people gathers in a stretch of soon-to-be corpses. Most are dressed in rags and dirt that cakes them like a second skin, but a few are smothered in jewels. A mix of the poor, the wealthy, and those who fall in between.

All of them are desperate to cheat death.

The Festival of Predictions happens once a year, during the month of the Red Moon, where anyone from across the Six Isles can wait for a prediction from the king's witch.

The line rounds the corner opposite me, so I can't see how far it stretches, but I know how many people there are. It's the same each year: two hundred souls ready to be bargained.

I try to move past them as quickly as I can, like a shadow sweeping across the corner of their eyes. But they always see me.

Once they do, they look quickly away.

They can't stand the sight of my green hair and snake eyes. All the things that make me different from them. They stare at the floor, like the tiles are suddenly too interesting to miss.

Like I'm nothing but a witch to be feared.

I'm not sure why. It's not like I have that much magic in me yet. At sixteen, I'm still just an heir to my true power, waiting for the day I inherit my family's magic.

"Would you hang on for a second?" Irenya says.

The apprentice dressmaker—and the only friend I have in this castle—heaves in a series of quick breaths, running to catch up with me as I finally come to a stop outside the Grand Hall.

She smooths down my dress, making sure there are no wrinkles in sight. Irenya is a perfectionist when it comes to her gowns.

"Quit squirming, Selestra," she scolds.

"I'm not squirming," I say. "I'm *breathing*."

"Well, stop that too, then."

I poke out my tongue and start to fiddle with my gloves. Pulling the fingertips up and then pushing them back down so the fabric rubs against my skin.

The repetition is soothing.

It stops me from overthinking everything that's about to happen.

I should be used to all of this by now. Grateful that I've been allowed to stand by King Seryth's side for two years, gathering hair and watching as people from across the islands filter in to seal their fates.

I should be excited for the Festival and all the souls we'll reap. To watch my mother tell death's secrets, as though it's an old friend.

I should not be thinking about all the people who are going to die.

"We don't want you coming loose during the first prediction," Irenya says. She pulls the strings tighter on my dress and I just *know* that she's smiling. "Imagine, you bend down to take a lock of hair and your chest falls out."

"Trust me." I gasp out a breath. "I'm not bending anywhere in this thing."

Irenya rolls her eyes. "Oh, be quiet," she says. "You look like a princess."

I almost laugh at that.

When I was young—before my mother became a stranger— she'd read me stories of princesses. Fairy tales of demure women, powerless, locked up in towers and waiting to be rescued by a handsome prince, who would whisk them away for love and adventure.

"I'm not a princess," I say to Irenya.

I'm something far more deadly than that. And nobody is rescuing me from my tower.

I push open the heavy iron doors of the Grand Hall. The room has been emptied.

Gone are the wooden tables that cluttered the center, rich with wine and merciless laughter. The band has been dismissed and the room is drained to a hollow cavity.

To an outsider, it's impossible to tell that just a few hours ago, the wealthiest people in the kingdom celebrated the start of the Festival. I could hear the swells of music from my tower. Smell the brandy cakes and honey drifting in through the cracks of my window.

It still smells now. Cake and candle fire, charred wicks and sweet, smoky air.

I spy the king at the far end of the room on a large black throne carved from bones. A gift of love from my great-great-grandmother.

His gaze quickly meets mine, like he can sense me, and he beckons me over with a single finger.

I take in a breath and head toward him.

The cloak of my dress billows behind me.

It's a hideously sparkling thing that glitters under the candlelight like a river of plucked stars. It's a deep black blue, dark as the Endless Sea, that curls around my neck and drips down my pale skin like water. The back, tied by intricate ribbons, is covered in a long cape that flows to the floor.

It might be Irenya's creation, but it's the king's color.

When I wear it, I'm his trophy.

"My king," I say once I reach him.

"Selestra," he all but purrs. "Good of you to finally join us."

He leans back into his throne.

King Seryth is a warrior as much as a ruler, with long black hair and earrings of snake fangs. The tattooed serpents of his crest hiss across his face, and he's dressed in animal furs that break apart to reveal the ridged muscles of his chest.

All of it is meant to make him look menacing, but I've always thought his eternally youthful face was far more beautiful than frightening.

The real danger is in his eyes, darker than night, which hold only death.

"You look glorious," he says.

"Thank you."

I tuck a lock of dark green hair behind my ears.

I've never been allowed to cut it, so like my mother's it hangs well past my waist. Only unlike my mother's it curls up at the ends, where hers is as straight as a cliff edge.

Everything about her is edges and points, designed to wound.

"Good evening, Mother," I say, turning to bow to her.

Theola Somniatis, ever beautiful, sits beside the king on a throne that glitters with painted Chrim coins. A black lace gown clings to her body in a mix of swirls and skin.

She looks sharp and foreboding.

A knife the king keeps by his side.

And unlike me, she doesn't need gloves to keep her in check.

She purses her lips. "You were nearly late."

I frown. "I walked as fast as I could in these shoes," I say, lifting the hem of my dress to show the perilous heels hidden under its length.

They're already rubbing against my feet.

The king smirks at this. "Now you are here we can get started."

He raises his hand, a signal to the guards by the door.

"Let the first one in."

I take an unsteady breath.

And so it begins.

I wonder what curses death will show us today.

2
SELESTRA

The guards open the doors to the Grand Hall and I see the first woman emerge.

She approaches the throne hesitantly, two guards flanking her closely on either side as she takes slow, shuffled footsteps toward us. She's dressed in a dark red skirt that's damp with mud at the ankles.

My skin pricks on the back of my neck the closer she gets.

There's death in the air.

I can practically taste it.

Smell it on the woman's bones.

As she steps forward, skirt the color of dried blood and decaying rose petals, I know somehow that she won't last the week.

I can *feel* it.

Then my mother will snatch up her soul and King Seryth will gobble it down, like he's done for over a century. Feeding his immortality.

"Your Highnesses," the woman says, once she reaches the steps that elevate the thrones.

She curtsies, low enough that her knees touch the floor and her ankles shake with the weight.

She glances at my mother and I see the flicker of panic in her eyes before she bows her head.

They fear us. They hate us.

And they're right to.

I lift my chin up, reminding myself that I should be pleased.

This is the one time a year when I'm surrounded by magic. When I can feel the thrum of it coating the castle, as the power of my ancestors drifts through the air like sweet wine.

When I don't have to stay locked in my tower.

I grab the scissors from the table and descend the stairs.

"With these scissors, I'll take a lock of your hair and seal your place in the Festival of Predictions," I tell the woman. "Death will mark you on its list for this month of the Red Moon. It will come for you once this first week, then twice the second, and the prediction we give you today will be your only help to survive."

I recite the lines easily, as I've done since I was fourteen.

"If you die, your soul becomes forfeit to the king. But if you live through the first half of this month, you'll be rewarded with a wish of your choice and be released from your bargain."

The woman nods eagerly.

The promise of a wish makes the Festival a celebration in the realm. I've heard that the townsfolk even make bets, gambling Chrim on who might make it, throwing parties and drinking into the early hours.

People only ever enter into this bargain for the wish.

For the poor and the desperate, it's a chance to ask for gold Chrim or healing elixirs. For the rich and the arrogant, it's a chance to curse their enemies and amass more fortune.

And all of them think it's worth risking their souls for.

It's only three deaths, they probably tell themselves. *I can live through that.* And some do. Each year a handful of people get to resume their lives with a wish granted, inspiring others to try it for themselves next year.

But each year at least one hundred people don't.

It's funny how they're less remembered.

"If you choose to continue beyond this halfway point, be warned," I say, voice foreboding. "As in place of death, the king himself will have earned the right to hunt you until the month's end. For if you survive past the Red Moon, his immortality will be yours."

I feel Seryth's smile on the back of my neck.

He's not afraid.

He doesn't worry that he could ever lose his throne to any of these people.

"This bargain may kill you or bring you unrivaled glory," I say.

It will be the former. It always is.

Death has a funny habit of getting its way, and so does the king. I've seen that firsthand.

Besides, nobody who survives ever even *tries* to go past the halfway mark. Having death hunt you is one thing, but the king himself? Even before he amassed the deadliest army to ever live, the king was the most skilled warrior in all of the Six Isles. He has survived centuries, blessed by cursed magic.

It would be madness to even try to kill him.

Best to just take your wish and run home to safety.

"Do you accept this bargain?" I ask.

The woman gulps loudly.

"Yes," she says, voice trembling. "Please just take it."

With hands as unsteady as her voice, she gestures toward her hair.

I reach out with my scissors and cut a piece. The woman sucks in a breath, eyes sharpening.

I wonder if she feels something. A fragment of her taken to be stored away, so her soul is tethered to this world when she dies.

Ready for my mother to collect in her ritual.

Ready to be bound to the king.

"It's done," I say.

I turn away from her and place the hair into one of two hundred glass jars that line the steps to the thrones.

"Step forward," Theola says. "And keep your arm out."

I hear the woman's breath stutter as she ascends the first two steps. She takes a knee.

Theola extends her hand and daintily strokes the woman's palm.

She closes her eyes, smile slow and damning.

Somniatis witches are like siphons. We draw in energy and let it pass through us. Energy like death that we call into our veins and let wet our lips. It's what gives us our visions and allows us to take the souls of the doomed and pour them into the king.

It's cursed magic, but it's the only magic left in the Six Isles.

My family saw to that.

Theola bites her lip as she looks into the woman's future.

There's a part of me that wants desperately to see what she sees. I want to feel the power that comes from knowing the future, from telling fate's secrets and letting my magic free from its shackles.

From *touching* someone, for the first time in years.

But then I remember Asden, my old mentor. I remember what happened the last time I touched someone.

I remember how he screamed.

The mere thought of it knocks into me as hard as a fist. I quickly right myself, swallowing the memory before the king notices the slip in my smile.

My mother withdraws her hand and looks down at the kneeling woman, whose palm is newly branded by King Seryth's crest: a blackened serpent eating its tail.

It appears on all death seekers, marking them and the deal they've made.

"In the next week, your youngest daughter will succumb to ill-ness," Theola says.

Her voice is like ice, cold and smooth, like she's talking about the weather instead of death.

It wasn't always like that.

Once it was warm.

"She will die," Theola says. "And days later when you go to pick her favorite flowers, you will be attacked by a creature of the woods. Left to rot among the trees."

The woman gasps and even her hands stop shaking, as though terror has frozen her in place.

"No, my daughter cannot die." She shakes her head, no regard for her own life and the death my mother foresaw for her. "There must be a way. If I survive until the halfway point, then I can wish for a healing elixir and—"

"She will not last long enough for that."

With a tight jaw, my mother closes her fist and then opens it to reveal a single gold coin of Chrim that wasn't there seconds before.

She drops it into the sobbing woman's hand.

"For your troubles," she says. "Spend time with your child while you can. If you live, perhaps we'll see you again for a new wish. If you die, remember what you owe us."

The woman blinks and opens her mouth, as if to scream or cry or try to fight her future. But all that comes out is a whimper, before her eyes shift to mine.

I can see the accusation in them as the guards pull her up and drag her from the hall. The notion that I should be ashamed of my monstrous family and the evil we let seep into the world.

But she doesn't know.

She doesn't understand what it means to be a Somniatis witch, bound to the king by an ancient blood oath. Given the choice between prisoner or queen of magic, I doubt this woman would choose differently from me. She doesn't understand what could happen if I tried.

Still, once she's out of sight, I turn to my mother.

"Do you think she'll avoid the forest and forgo her daughter's flowers?" I ask.

It's a stupid question, and the moment I speak it, I wish I could take it back.

"What does it matter?" Theola's voice is scolding. "So long as we get the amount of souls we need, it's irrelevant which ones they are."

I know that she's right.

What's important is that we have at least one hundred souls by the end of the month. Enough so that the king can sustain his immortality and continue his rule forever.

"Don't you agree, Selestra?" my mother asks when I fall silent.

She looks at me with warning, telling me to nod, quickly.

"Of course," I say.

A practiced lie.

"My witches don't concern themselves with such questions."

The king stares at me tersely.

His eyes are black, black, black.

"You'll remember that, Selestra," he says. "If you ever manage to become one, rather than remain a simple heir."

I bow my head, but beneath the gesture my teeth grind together.

He calls me an heir like it's an insult, because it's all I'll be to him, to everyone, until I become the Somniatis witch.

Heirs to magic are useless until they reach their eighteenth birthday and are bound to the king by the blood oath, ready to be taught the true essence of magic and trained to take over once the old witch dies. Until then, I am irrelevant.

Sometimes I feel like a weed, pushing out from the roots of a strange garden, never quite able to blend in.

The rest of the evening goes the same way.

People are escorted in and out by the guards, kneeling as Theola recounts their new fates with little more than boredom. Betrayals from trusted friends, drowning in the local river, or stabbed in an alley outside the tavern they visit every night.

Each of them has the same horrified look as their deaths are revealed. They act as though it's a curse thrust upon them rather than something they sought out.

All the while I remain silent, only speaking to recite the rules of the Festival. I gather the hair dozens of times over, descending the stairs and watching as the king looks hungrily at each person who enters into his bargain.

Each potential new soul he'll use my family's magic to devour.

Only a handful of them will survive until the halfway point and be granted their wish.

And not a one of them could ever survive beyond that, even if they were reckless enough to try.

Enter a world of Gods and monsters . . .

A dark fantasy romance from ALEXANDRA CHRISTO,
author of TikTok sensation *TO KILL A KINGDOM*.

HOT KEY BOOKS

Thank you for choosing a Hot Key book!

For all the latest bookish news, freebies and exclusive content, sign up to the Hot Key newsletter – scan the QR code or visit lnk.to/HotKeyBooks

Follow us on social media:

bonnierbooks.co.uk/HotKeyBooks